THE CREEPER

MARK L'ESTRANGE

For Tabitha, Tonka, and Melody.

Your daddy misses you all so much.
Sleep well my babies.

PROLOGUE

The woman screamed out in agony!

Around her were gathered several men and women in white uniforms with face masks and rubber gloves. Some of them had blood splatters randomly speckling their gowns as they moved swiftly around the large tent gathering instruments and replacement bandages upon the orders of those obviously in charge.

At the opening in the canvas enclosure there stood a young man.

His face was as white as the sheets on the operating table had once been.

He was sweating profusely; his shirt and shorts virtually sodden with damp patches.

The expression on his face was a combination of terror and panic.

He felt completely helpless.

The men and women surrounding the patient spoke quickly to each other in their own tongue. The man had not been in the country long enough to be able to pick up more than a few words here and there, so he was completely oblivious as to what was being said.

But he knew from the overall speed with which the nurses moved that they were short of time.

From outside the sound of drums grew louder and the rhythm more fevered.

The young man desperately wanted to lend his assistance, even if it was only by holding the young woman's hand in sympathy at her plight. But he had already been warned off with gestures and incoherent ranting by those outside who had been left to guard the tent.

He was amazed that they had actually allowed him in this far, but they could probably tell by his desperate pleadings that he meant no harm and would not interfere with the proceedings taking place inside.

The woman screamed out again and began bucking and shuffling on the bench. Her naked body, bathed in perspiration, began to slide closer to the edge of the bench.

One of the men shouted something and two of the female nurses quickly ran to the woman and held her down, manoeuvring her back into place. Meanwhile one of their colleagues brought over some thick ropes and together they began to bind the poor woman by her wrists and ankles to prevent her from falling off if she continued to struggle.

The woman being bound looked to be about twenty years old, with long blonde hair tied back in a ponytail and beads of perspiration streaking down her contorted features.

With her arms and legs bound tight in a star formation the doctors huddled round and began to poke and prod her between her legs.

The woman's swollen belly stretched her skin so tightly that it appeared to the young man as if it was about to burst.

From behind him another native rushed in with two large

metal buckets filled with boiling water. He held them out to his sides at arm's length to avoid being scorched should any of the liquid splash as he transported it.

He placed the two buckets down on the ground.

One of the nurses shouted something to him and nodding he turned and tried to usher the white man outside.

But the man was having none of it.

The native tried once more before giving up and rushing back outside into the night.

The nurses who had finished binding the woman to the bench started to soak towels and torn sheets in the boiled water, carefully laying them out on a nearby table close enough for the doctors to grab should they need to.

One of the doctors suddenly opened his eyes wide, making it look as if they were about to pop out of his skull.

He pointed frantically between the bound woman's legs and shouted something at one of his colleagues.

One of the other doctors immediately ran over and plunged his gloved hands into the hot water and then rubbed them together before making his way back to the bench.

He looked at his colleague and waited for him to nod his head before he leaned forward and placed his hands between the woman's legs.

As he delved in deeper the woman on the bench yanked hard against her restraints and let out a scream which was so loud that it almost pierced the eardrums of all those in attendance.

The nurses recoiled and turned their heads away.

The young man, the only person in the room who was not wearing gloves, shoved his hands up against his ears to try and block out the blood-curdling sound.

The doctor administering to the woman turned his head to one side but kept his hands in place.

Once the scream had died down, he continued to focus his attention on his patient, gently trying to ease himself forward to allow his greater access.

But with each movement the woman on the bench reacted more violently, kicking and pulling against her restraints until the ropes cut in so deeply that they began to draw blood.

Once again, her terrible screams pierced the night.

Outside the drums grew louder, their rhythm faster.

The young man could hear the chants and incantations being muttered aloud outside by the elders as they sat around the open fire while young men and women in various states of undress danced and swayed around the outskirts of the camp.

One of the nurses pried open the young woman's mouth while another of her colleagues tried to pour something from a clay urn into it.

The woman choked and spluttered as she coughed most of the liquid back up.

The woman with the urn spoke to her other colleague who brought over a large wooden stick which she proceeded to wedge inside the woman's mouth in an effort to keep it open.

Once in place, the other nurse began to slowly pour the rest of the contents of the urn down the patient's throat.

The young woman gurgled as the liquid bypassed her tongue and travelled directly down her oesophagus. But as she instinctively attempted to draw breath, her trachea opened, and the liquid quickly rushed down causing her to choke and splutter again more violently until finally she cleared the last of it away.

Once the urn was empty the nurses removed the stick from between the girl's teeth and stood back as one of them mopped the patient's brow with a damp cloth.

The liquid began to take effect and the girl seemed to relax visibly for a moment, inciting the doctor the move his hands further inside her.

For a moment she did not react as he manoeuvred his hands within her, and then suddenly he stopped.

With his face turned towards him, even with his mask covering half of it, the young man could tell from the doctor's eyes that something was definitely wrong.

The doctor turned to his colleagues and muttered something which made the nurses start to cross themselves several times over as they slowly backed away.

Finally, the young man could take no more.

"What is it?" he pleaded, taking a few cautionary steps forward. "Please, tell me, I have to know."

Immediately the three nurses pounced on him and tried to usher him backwards and out of the tent.

The man pushed them away and broke free, but he did not try and move any closer to the patient.

Instead he stayed where he was and glanced down at the young girl on the bench before looking back up at the doctors with a beseeching look on his tortured face.

The doctors all looked at each other before one of them turned back to the man and slowly shook his head.

The young man leapt forward and grabbed the doctor by the shoulders, shaking him violently, and begging him to do something.

The other doctors came to their colleague's aid and together they prised the man off him.

The young man was frantic with rage.

He fought back against those restraining him, shaking his body from side to side in a desperate effort to break free.

Finally, two more natives entered from outside and relieved the doctors of their burden.

The young man kicked and cried out as he was physically manhandled out of the tent.

Once outside, the man was held down by his captors and forced to watch the ceremony which unfolded before him.

The chanting grew louder and the dancing more frenzied, the participants looked to all intents and purposes as if they were there in body but not in mind or spirit.

One of the nurses emerged from the tent carrying a huge carving knife.

The man watched as she approached the elders and holding out the knife allowing it to rest on both hands, she spoke to them.

One by one they nodded their response.

The nurse took the knife over to the fire and gripping the handle tightly she held out the blade letting the flames lick at both sides.

After a while, the nurse carried the knife back into the tent.

The man struggled in vain against his guards as he watched the nurse disappear back behind the canvas screen.

Seconds later a scream emerged from behind the canvas which tore through the night and made the man feel as if his heart had been severed.

His captives felt his resolve diminish and they released him.

He slumped to the floor, unconscious.

CHAPTER ONE

G ina Steele staggered down the deserted street, her six-inch heels *clacking* her presence on the pavement.

This had not turned out to be the night she had hoped for.

Rob had promised her a candlelight dinner in one of those posh restaurants up in town, before whisking her away to the Crofton hotel for the night, with their sumptuous four-poster beds and champagne on ice.

All paid for on his company credit card, naturally.

Rob was way too tight to put his hand in his own pocket.

He may be a company director with a brand-new Mercedes and no less than three personal secretaries and two holiday apartments, one in Paris and the other in Dubai if you please, but when it came to getting him to part with his cash it was like drawing blood from a stone.

Tonight, was supposed to be a celebration for their anniversary.

They had been together for a full year now, and in all that time he had never taken her away on holiday, not even to one of his apartments, or so much as treated her to a night in a posh hotel, like she had been promised tonight.

No, such luxuries were reserved solely for his wife, the bitch!

In truth, Gina did not mind being the 'other woman'; there were after all several perks that went with the title. Not having to attend any of his boring work functions for one. Not having to play nursemaid to the three spoilt brats he lovingly called his brood.

She had had the misfortune of meeting them once. It was during their summer break from private school and Rob had brought them in to lunch at the restaurant where she was wait-ressing.

A little down at heel, she thought, especially for someone of his means, but then of course where she worked offered discounted lunches for groups of four or more, so in effect it made perfect sense for him to be there.

Naturally, Gina had to pretend that she did not know him and treat him like any other patron.

Which she did, using her most professional manner.

Not that it was good enough for his snotty little brats, with their complaints about everything ranging from the quality of the food, to the temperature of the cola. They even whinged about the colour of the tablecloths the restaurant used.

She was certainly glad to see the back of them.

Under the circumstances she at least expected a decent tip from Rob. But then she should have remembered with whom she was dealing.

He left two quid which was not even ten percent of the overall bill.

That was one of the reasons tonight was so important for Gina.

When Rob first suggested it, she had nearly fallen off her

chair in shock. They had been having a drink in one of the out of the way places Rob always took her so that no one from his set could possibly see them.

With his brats at school and his wife allegedly staying with her mother to help whilst she recovered from her latest hip operation, it seemed like the perfect opportunity for Rob to finally show her some appreciation.

After all those 'quickies' on the back seat of his car, crammed between a couple of drinks and him dropping her off at the bus stop, Gina felt that she fully deserved a little pampering.

She had even had her hair done especially for the occasion.

What a waste!

Before they had even seen the menu Rob's wife suddenly appeared at the door of the restaurant glaring daggers at the pair of them through the glass.

Gina made good her escape out through the back door and left Rob to deal with his missus. She did not even bother to hang around for Rob to retrieve her overnight bag from the boot of his car.

Somehow it did not seem a viable option at the time.

After all, there was no point in her trying to stay and make up an explanation for why the two of them were there, never mind the hotel room.

No, that was Rob's problem!

Someone had obviously tipped his wife off, so that probably signalled the end of this particular relationship.

And if Rob did get back in touch with her once things had cooled down, then Gina was going to lay down some ground rules of her own if he wanted to keep getting his end away with her.

No more back seat of the car action, for a start!

Gina stopped by a bench opposite the bus stop and sat down to remove her shoes.

She lifted each foot in turn and placed it on her opposing knee so that she could massage her aching soles. Typically, for once she had broken her cardinal rule of always carrying a pair of flats in her handbag, because she thought that tonight, of all nights, she would not need them.

Bugger Rob and his stupid wife!

The least he could have done was slip her the money for a cab. But then she was forgetting how attached he was to every penny in his wallet.

Gina gazed down the lane, hoping for the welcome sight of a bus to peer over the horizon.

No such luck!

This was one of the downsides of moving out to the sticks. It was true that you had the beautiful scenery, the wide-open spaces, fresh clean country air, and of course the people were a lot friendlier, but the public transport did leave a little to be desired.

Buses were few and far between, and unlike when she lived in London, the bus stops out here did not have indicators informing you when you could expect the next one to arrive.

She considered calling one of her roommates to pick her up, but then she realised they would be at least halfway through their second bottle by now, so there was no point.

In the distance she could hear the pealing of St Luke's bells as they echoed across the fields.

It reminded her that she had not been to mass in over two months.

Fortunately, Father Grace was a forgiving soul who, unlike the vast majority of priests she had known being raised a catholic, had a genuine capacity for understanding the ways of the modern world and did not condemn you for living your life however you chose to do so.

Even in the confessional he was never shocked or appalled at anything you revealed, no matter how embarrassing you found it personally.

Gina looked up at the sky. The autumn evenings were starting to close in. It would soon be dark although at least there was no rain forecast.

Gina let out a long weary sigh.

Sitting here was no longer an option.

She picked up her shoes, letting them dangle from her fingers by the straps and began to walk up the hill in her stockinged feet towards home.

The pavement felt cool through the flimsy nylon fabric. She kept an eye out for stones and anything sharp which might be in her path. The last thing she needed was to snag the most expensive pair of stockings she had ever bought.

Another waste for bloody Rob!

As she reached the end of the turning, she looked back once more for any signs of a bus. From this distance she could still wave it down and run back to the stop in time to catch it.

But there was not one in sight.

Again, she heard the bells from the church.

It suddenly occurred to her that if she were to cut across the field and use the lane which ran by the side of the church, she could save herself a good twenty minutes off her journey.

The sky was beginning to grow darker, but she had crossed the field before, and it only took five minutes. Then once she was in the lane, she would not feel so exposed, and besides what was she afraid of, this was the country after all?

Bad things did not happen out here!

Then she remembered that report in the local paper a couple of months ago.

A girl hitchhiking on her way home from a music festival, who was last seen climbing out of a car at the edge of town, mysteriously vanished.

Her body was found a week later, mutilated beyond recognition.

At least, that's what the papers said.

But she had not heard anything about the incident since.

It was probably just the papers trying to drum up some business embellishing the simple facts to catch the headlines.

Her mind made up, Gina slipped her shoes back on and crossed the road towards the field.

Fortunately for her, it had not rained in over a week, so at least the ground should be firm and not too slushy.

She opened the gate in the fence which ringed the field and locked it behind her before starting across.

The going was quite firm although a couple of times Gina had to prise her heels out of the soft earth.

The church bells serenaded her as she made her way across.

At the other end of the field Gina could not be bothered to trek to the far side to use the gate, so she hitched up her skirt and climbed over the fence, making sure first that no one was coming down the lane who might see her flashing her knickers.

Once she was safely over, Gina took a moment to admire the church.

She had always been enamoured by medieval architecture, and St Luke's was one of the finest examples she had ever seen.

What made it even more fascinating was that as dusk began to settle the outside spots would come on, illuminating the front entrance, and casting a mysterious eerie shadow behind the main structure overlooking the graveyard at the back.

It often reminded Gina of those mysterious gothic mansions they used to use for black and white horror films where all the relatives were called over at midnight for the reading of a will.

The mere thought of it gave her goose bumps even now.

She took one last look before turning to head down the lane which would eventually lead her back towards home and a stiff drink, or three!

Gina continued down the lane, leaving the church and its melodious bells behind her.

A couple of hundred yards up ahead the lane narrowed, barely allowing two people to pass without touching.

The trees on either side of the path were overgrown and the branches hung down far enough so that she could touch them just by raising her arm above her head without having to stretch. The floor was littered with fallen leaves and most of the remaining ones had already begun to turn brown in keeping with the season.

Gina shivered as the wind picked up momentarily, and she pulled her cardigan a little tighter around her shoulders.

In the crisp autumn breeze with the faint lull of the church bells drifting on the wind behind her, Gina felt completely at ease and the frustration at her disappointing evening began to slowly melt away as she looked forward to surprising her flat-mates and sharing their wine.

The hand that grabbed her around the throat was huge, with long whip-like fingers and raggedy nails encrusted with dirt.

Before Gina could draw breath to let out a scream the grip tightened cutting off her windpipe.

Gina gasped and choked, trying desperately to make some sort of noise that might bring help, but her efforts were all in vain.

She felt herself being lifted off the ground and started kicking her legs wildly. She could feel her heels making contact with the shins of whatever was holding her, but their impact seemed to have no substantial effect on her assailant.

Gina clawed at the arm which suspended her, raking her freshly manicured nails across the skin, praying for the grip around her neck to loosen just long enough for her to draw breathe, but once again her actions were to no avail.

She gripped at the arm that held her and tried to pull it away.

The skin was bare and covered with what felt like thick course matted hair. So dense was the mane that the arm almost seemed to be covered in fur rather than hair.

Gina grabbed great clumps of the locks, but her tiny fingers would not allow her to gain purchase on them long enough to be of any useful purpose.

The thing holding her let forth a low guttural growl.

Gina could feel its hot fetid breath on her neck.

The pungent odour the thing emitted permeated her nostrils making her want to gag.

The faint sound of the bells started to drift away.

Gina felt the creature grab her around the waist with its other arm before her senses faded into darkness.

CHAPTER TWO

The earthy sound of organ music combined with the joyful singing of the faithful parishioners echoed through the cavernous arches of the stone structure of St Luke's church, and filled the rafters with melodious harmony.

The autumn morning air was cold and crisp and even with the main doors closed could still be heard whistling through the gaps in the oak.

The eerie shadows cast by the bright sunlight shafting through the stained-glass windows, help to create an atmosphere of solemn reflection and purpose which all those in attendance found completely conducive to their weekly devotion.

The church itself had always had a foreboding countenance which contrasted the warm and inviting atmosphere the resident priest Ambrose Grace tried to create for his flock.

The original structure, according to parish records, dated back as far as the 7th century AD and was originally enclosed within a much larger structure commissioned by the church as a place of respite for travelling friars, monks and those undertaking a pilgrimage to the holy land.

Like so many ecclesiastical establishments the main building was suppressed on the orders of King Henry VIII in the 16th century, and most of the medieval monuments and treasures were looted, and the main structure was all but demolished.

Having lain in semi-ruins for the best part of three hundred years it was decided by Rome during the 19th century, that due to the solid foundation and catacombs underneath the structure, that major restoration work would be financed in order to rebuild the church to serve the growing local community.

The new building was given an external perpendicular-style appearance with a flint clerestoried nave and aisles with battlements at both levels. The west tower was also battlemented and was prepared with squared rag stone blocks and a south-east circular stair-turret.

Fortunately, several of the interior arches and square columns in the nave had survived and were fortified by the architects to recapture the spirit of the original structure.

While excavating the catacombs, the builders came across an almost perfect Norman font, with a deep circular stone bowl with twelve arches on shafts with some very decorative ornamentation of the period above and below.

Naturally, all the stained glass had to be replaced, but due to the survival of the parish records and the descriptions detailed within, the glaziers were able to reconstruct replacements to match the original pieces.

As the singing ended and the final note was left hanging in the air, Father Grace blessed his congregation one final time and invited them all to go in peace with love in their hearts, to serve the lord.

As always, those in attendance waited patiently whilst the old priest ambled down the main aisle, flanked by his two altar boys as they made their way towards the large oak door which acted as the main entrance.

Regulars knew that Father Grace liked to say goodbye to his flock as they left each service. It was a task which in itself could take almost as long as some of his sermons.

But the loyal community had too much respect for the priest to deny him his little caprice.

During his many years at St Luke's, Father Grace had presided over most of his congregation's most important ceremonies. In some cases, from their baptism right up to their weddings, or on sadder occasions, their funerals, and then in some cases, starting the process anew with their offspring.

He was renowned for his understanding and sympathetic nature, especially in the confessional.

Although he was a man of the cloth and pious in his own beliefs, his view on the world, and his flock in particular, was that times were forever changing and actions which might once have been considered almost heretical by his predecessors now needed to be dealt with using kindness and acceptance, but still without indulgence.

Father Grace's views were often at odds with the church's hierarchy, but he managed to maintain a reasonable balance which allowed him to stay where he was, attending to the needs of his flock, without drawing too much criticism from those above him.

The sunlight poured in as the two altar boys pulled open the mighty oak doors. They both took their place on either side of the stone steps like sentries guarding their charge, as Father Grace took up his usual position just inside the door to bestow his blessing on those leaving.

At seventy-two he still had a mind as sharp as a razor, and he prided himself on being able to remember the Christian names of everyone who attended his services.

To some, a wave and a fond farewell until next time was more than enough. But others, however, could be more demanding and thus required a longer consultation. So, the good Father did what he could to ensure that no one individual monopolised all his time at the expense of someone wanting a quiet word before they left.

Not always an easy task!

Through the crowd, Father Grace could see young Kelly Soames making her way furtively towards him. Her head was bowed as it had been during much of the service, even when she came forward to receive Holy Communion the Father noticed that she kept her head down while she held out her hand for the host.

The priest could guess the reason behind her reluctance to show her face.

And, sure enough, when she drew closer and he made a point of speaking to her directly, much to the annoyance of one of his usual fogies who was wittering on about nothing in particular, and when she lifted her head to answer he saw the bruise below her right eye.

Kelly's husband was a thug and a bully. And those were two of his nicest qualities, as far as Father Grace was concerned.

As much as he strived to see the good in everyone, Jack Soames had few redeeming qualities that he had ever noticed.

Why such a lovely girl like Kelly had married him in the first place he could only wonder at.

To his knowledge their relationship had always been volatile, right from the start. He could remember Kelly's mother, whilst she had still been alive, breaking down in tears in front of him while she related the latest tale of heart breaking distress her future son-in-law was putting her beloved daughter through.

She had lost Kelly's father in a freak accident in the glass factory where he had worked when Kelly was still a babe in arms. And she blamed herself for never remarrying as the reason behind Kelly's horrendous taste in men.

As far as she was concerned it was male guidance that Kelly needed, someone in a position of authority whom she could look up to and go to for advice where men were concerned.

That was the main reason Kelly's mother had come to him.

But as the priest so often had to explain to her, his advice was only on offer to those who sought it.

But Kelly, despite her mother's pleadings, never did.

When her mother collapsed at home as a result of a fatal heart attack at only forty-eight, she left Kelly alone in the world and with no one else to turn to she naturally craved the love of her boyfriend.

They were married at a registry office in town, against Kelly's wishes the priest knew. But her husband was not devout, and he could never remember seeing him so much as once in church.

But Kelly was still loyal to god, and never missed a Sunday service.

Even on days like this, when she was afraid to show her face in public.

"Good morning, young Kelly," he beamed, making sure that neither his voice nor his expression conveyed his horror at the state of her face. "And how are you this fine morning?"

The young girl managed a smile although it was not convincing enough to reach her eyes.

"Oh, fine thank you, Father," she replied, courteously. "And, how are you?"

"A little more achy than last week, but doubtless not as achy as I'll be next week," he chuckled.

"Oh Father, you'll outlive us all and that's a fact."

The old priest laughed. "Heaven forbid." As he spoke, he looked up towards the sky and pulled a face.

This made Kelly laugh.

He liked to hear her laugh and secretly he suspected that she did not do so on too many occasions because of that husband of hers.

The moment passed, and Kelly felt it was time to move on and let someone else speak to the Father.

"See you next week, Father," she announced as she moved away.

"God willing," The priest called after her.

He watched her from the corner of his eye as she made her way towards the graveyard on the far side of the church.

She often visited her parents' graves, and always on a Sunday after service.

Kelly stopped at the flower stall by the main gate and bought two small bunches of mixed flowers.

She placed one in front of each of her parents' gravestones and collected those from last week which had withered and died for disposal on her way out.

She stayed there for a few moments of silent prayer before moving off.

"Hey, Kelly."

Still lost in thought, Kelly did not immediately hear her name being called.

"Wait a second," the voice urged.

Kelly turned to see Desmond Radcliffe running up the path towards her.

She smiled and wiped away a tear. She was pleased to see Des. They had known each other since primary school and had always been the best of friends.

Even when he had moved away to attend university they still kept in touch via e-mail and Facebook. But since she started seeing Jack, he made her delete her account. In his eyes social media was a slippery slope towards unfaithfulness and adultery, and no wife of his was going to be tempted to stray.

Regardless of how many times Kelly had tried to convince him that she would remain faithful, the constant nagging and demanding finally wore her down, so she deleted her account for a quiet life.

Kelly attempted to cover her black eye with her hand, then realised how ridiculous she would look, trying to speak to Des like that, so she lowered it and left the bruise to show.

When Des caught up to Kelly, he noticed the bruise straightaway.

He was aware of how badly Jack treated her, but like most of her other friends he chose to ignore the signs so as not to embarrass her.

He gently placed his hand on her shoulder.

Instinctively, Kelly reacted by shrugging him off, but no sooner had she done so than she wished that she had not. Des was the last person she wanted to alienate.

"Sorry," she said quickly, I didn't mean to do that." Kelly had had Jack's 'no touching' rule drummed into her so many times that now it was an automatic reaction to push anyone who tried to touch her away, regardless of how welcome the attention might have been.

Des held up his hands and laughed. "No worries, I didn't mean to scare you. I did call out first, but you seemed miles away."

Kelly indicated behind her. "I was just thinking about my mum and dad, that's all."

"I understand," Des smiled, "I didn't mean to break your reverie."

Kelly burst out laughing. "Reverie, you and your big posh university words, I'm sure you make up half of them just to fool idiots like me."

Des was glad that he had made Kelly laugh.

Her face could brighten the darkest of rooms when she was happy which, unfortunately, was not too often these days.

"It's a genuine word," Des protested, holding his hand against his heart. "And besides, you are nobody's idiot."

For a moment, their eyes locked.

Des would have given anything to move in and steal a kiss, but he knew all too well what would happen if word ever reached Jack, and the last thing he wanted was to cause trouble for Kelly.

Though they had always been close, they had never been a romantic couple as such, although they had gone out together several times over the years as friends, usually as part of a bigger group.

Des blamed himself for not having the courage to ask Kelly out officially on a date. He did not usually have any trouble chatting up girls, but Kelly had always been different.

Special, in fact.

At least as far as he was concerned.

When Des finally decided to make his move, Kelly started seeing Jack.

Although everyone said how poorly suited they were, Des felt that he had to respect Kelly's decision, so he kept his feelings to himself.

Then when he was accepted at Exeter University, he had

to leave the area and although they kept in touch, Des never felt that the time was right to broach the subject.

When Des came home for Kelly's mother's funeral, he too could see how wrong Jack was for her, but once again the timing was not right.

Then Kelly announced that she and Jack were to be married.

Des still remembered where he was and what he was doing when he heard the news. It hit him far harder than he would ever have expected, and then more than ever he wanted to rush home and blurt out his feelings for her, but once again the gentleman in him decided that that would not be fair on her, so he left things as they were.

Des, on Jack's orders, was not invited to the ceremony. But as it turned out neither were most of Kelly's friends, so that was no real surprise.

Those who did attend said after that considering it was meant to be the happiest day of her life, the bride did not appear overly excited. Especially when her new husband got plastered at the reception and started trying it on with every female in the place, including those accompanied by their partners.

Since returning from university, Des had found it increasingly hard to see Kelly without the old feelings flooding back.

Even now he could feel his heart skip a beat just being in her presence.

A group of passing churchgoers broke the moment for both of them.

Kelly could feel her cheeks flush slightly as if she had been caught in the act of doing something naughty.

"Can I walk you to the bus stop?" Des asked, hopefully.

Kelly bit her bottom lip and caught herself looking around in case Jack might suddenly appear out of nowhere.

But, of course, in Jack's world, Sunday morning was for getting over Saturday night, not wasting time in church. So, the coast was clear.

"Lovely," Kelly replied, and they set off down the lane.

CHAPTER THREE

Kelly made her way slowly up the stone steps which led to her flat on the fourth floor of the tower block. As usual the lift was out of action and if the council's previous track record was anything to go by it would remain that way for weeks, if not months, to come.

When her mother had passed away, she had hoped that the council might allow her to continue living in the spacious three-bedroom ground-floor apartment they had moved to when Kelly was born. But apparently the council waiting list would not allow for such a luxury, so Kelly had to settle for what she was offered.

The one aspect of her abode that she did like was that at night being higher up she was able to see all the other blocks with their intermittent lights sparkling in the blackness. She could happily sit at their bedroom window for hours on end at night and just look out over them and imagine that she was somewhere far more exciting like Paris or Los Angeles.

Gazing at the town by night always reminded her of the scenes in spy films when one of the characters would look through a pair of binoculars and the camera would switch to the view the actor was allegedly looking at.

Watching planes fly overhead at night also had the same effect on her.

At school she was often chastised for drifting off into her own little world during class. Her mother used to refer to her as a dreamer. Jack was convinced that she suffered from ADHD because one of his nephews had the condition and he was unable to focus on anything at school for more than five minutes without growing bored.

Kelly much preferred her mother's diagnosis.

Just as she reached her front door Kelly heard the door at the far end of the corridor open. She watched as Carol Ledbetter emerged from her flat. She was immaculately dressed as usual in a matching trouser suit and heels and a very expensive-looking leather jacket resting over her shoulders. Clutched under her arm was one of her many designer handbags.

When she saw Kelly, she waved and smiled.

Kelly returned the gesture and waited for Carol to pass her before putting her key in the lock.

"Hi, kiddo, how's tricks?" Carol asked, in her usual bubbly tone.

The minute Carol saw the state of Kelly's eye, her expression changed.

Kelly subconsciously tried to cover up her bruises, but she knew that it was already too late. Her friend had seen them.

Carol was in her late forties, but she certainly looked younger, even without make-up. She was the first friend Kelly had made when she moved into the block, and they had enjoyed many a happy hour in each other's company with a couple of bottles of wine as an accompaniment.

Carol worked up in town as a PA for a company director,

and she was probably the most positive person Kelly had ever met.

Deep down Kelly had always wished that she and Carol had met before Jack came on the scene. Somehow, she knew that with Carol's positive influence she would have been strong enough to resist Jack's attentions and the two of them would never have been an item, let alone married.

Now of course, it was too late!

"I see Dickhead has been using you as his personal punch bag again?" Carol remarked, not attempting to disguise the sarcasm in her tone.

Before Kelly had a chance to answer she felt the hot sting of tears welling up in her eyes.

Carol flung her arm around her friend's shoulder and pulled her towards her.

For a moment Kelly allowed herself to be comforted, unashamedly.

The reassurance she received from the warmth of her friend's embrace reminded her of the feeling of protection she always experienced whenever her mother would hold her as a child to console and reassure her if she was sad.

Carol held on until Kelly was ready to pull away.

Once she had, Carol produced a clean tissue from her jacket pocket and gave it to her friend to dry her eyes with.

Having dabbed her eyes, Kelly used the tissue to blow her nose, loudly.

"That better?" Carol enquired. Kelly still had her head slightly bowed so Carol had to bend down and look up at her, to see if she was alright.

Feeling foolish for allowing herself to become so overemotional Kelly raised her head and sniffed the air to staunch any chance of her nose starting to run.

She forced out a smile which did not fool Carol.

"I'm sorry about that," Kelly apologised. "I don't know what came over me."

Carol shook her head, sadly. "You don't need to apologise to me, kiddo," she replied, reassuringly, "what you need to do is to get rid of that useless fat lump you call a husband before he really hurts you!"

Kelly pinched her eyes between her thumb and forefinger in an attempt to stop a fresh batch of tears from brewing.

She knew that every word Carol spoke was the truth, but to her marriage was an honourable institution and even though she and Jack had not been married in a catholic church before a priest as she had wanted, the fact remained that when she had spoken her vows she had meant every single word, and registry office or not, they were still in the presence of god so she could not simply abandon their holy union upon a whim.

A marriage needed work. That was what her mother had always told her, and she was determined not to give in without giving it her very best effort.

Kelly attempted a half-hearted smile. "I'll be OK," she mumbled, unconvincingly. "You don't need to worry about me."

Carol placed her hand on Kelly's shoulder and squeezed it, tenderly.

Kelly met her friend's gaze and held it for a moment.

When Carol leaned in to place a kiss on the end of her friend's nose, Kelly almost caught herself lifting her head just enough so that it would be their lips that met instead.

Kelly flushed at the thought of what she had almost done.

She had never had any of those kinds of feelings for Carol, or any other woman for that matter, so she was as confused about her intentions as she was curious as to why she had almost acted on them.

Whether or not Carol noticed the gesture she did not acknowledge it.

After a moment, Carol said. "Listen, kiddo, I'm off out to meet some of the girls for lunch, why don't you come along. It'd do you good to get glammed up and hit the town, what about it?"

Carol already knew the obvious answer, but she waited patiently to hear it, just in case.

"I can't," replied Kelly, starting to lower her head once more. "I have to get Jack's lunch ready; you know what he's like?"

"Only too well, I'm afraid to say," Carol responded with an unashamed look of disappointment.

"But thanks for the thought," Kelly smiled, trying painstakingly to make herself sound as if she had actually considered Carol's offer.

Carol bit her bottom lip while she thought. "Tell you what," she announced, "why don't you come over tonight and we'll have a girl's night in. I've got some wine in the fridge and we can go through my collection of weepy DVDs together, how about it?"

This time, Kelly really did give the idea some thought. "Well..."

"Well?" Carol asked encouraged by the fact that her friend had not automatically refused.

"I'll have to see what Jack's got planned for tonight first."

Carol sighed, loudly. "Oh, let's see now, it's Sunday so after lunch he'll have his usual forty winks on the sofa, then he'll be down the pub for the rest of the evening until he finally staggers home so that you can make him a late-night snack before he collapses into bed. That about right?"

Kelly blushed and shrugged her shoulders as if she did not know what else to say to her friend.

29

Carol knew that she was laying on the sarcasm good and thick and she did feel bad for her friend, but she needed to ensure that the message made it all the way through.

One day she hoped that Kelly would realise that she deserved far more than Jack was ever willing to give. But until that day the best that Carol could offer was the occasional shoulder to cry on and the odd bottle of wine round at her place.

Kelly waited for her friend to begin her descent of the stairs before she slipped her key in the lock.

"I'm back," she called out as she entered the flat.

She could hear Jack in the living room playing on his X-box, but he was either too engrossed in his game or he just did not hear her because he did not reply.

Kelly took off her coat and hung it on a peg in the hall before she entered the kitchen to start preparing their lunch.

The sight of the pile of dirty dishes still lying in the sink from the previous night made her stop dead in her tracks. Jack had promised her he would wash up while she was out at church.

He had not even bothered to fill the sink to let them soak.

Then she also noticed that he had used one of her mother's best china plates for breakfast, doubtless because he could not be bothered to rinse even one single plate for himself.

Kelly sighed, deeply.

She considered confronting him, but then she thought better of it.

What would be the point?

He rarely apologised for anything, and even when he did, there was no sincerity in his voice. It was more like he was just going through the motion of saying what he felt she wanted to hear in order to get her off his back.

This was not the life she had envisaged for herself as a married woman.

For a moment, Kelly could almost imagine her mother looking down on her from heaven with sorrow in her eyes at the state of her daughter's relationship.

Why had she ignored her mother's advice?

Kelly felt a single tear trickling down her cheek so she brushed it away with the back of her hand and started to remove the dishes from the sink so that she could fill it with water.

As she worked, she began to think about Desmond.

Sweet, kind, thoughtful Desmond.

It had been a lovely surprise meeting him after church that morning and he had seemed genuinely pleased to see her too.

Kelly could not help but imagine how different her life might be if she was married to him instead of Jack.

For a start she knew that she would not be coming home to a sink full of dishes and a husband who could not even be bothered to stop playing his stupid video games long enough to welcome her home.

With Desmond, things would be so very different.

She could not see him leaving her alone night after night while he went drinking with his mates.

Nor could she believe that Desmond would ever raise so much as a finger to her, let alone beat her the way that Jack did.

In fact, she could not even remember a time when she had seen Desmond lose his temper with anyone.

If she were his wife, he would appreciate her and treat her with dignity, respect and above all, love.

She imagined them going for long walks in the park on sunny days, holding hands as they watched the ducks on the pond.

Jack refused to hold her hand in public. In fact, he refused point blank to offer any gesture of affection in front of others. Even at her mother's funeral he kept shrugging her off whenever she tried to rest her head on his shoulder during the service. His idea of comforting her while she was grieving was handing her a tissue while she was crying.

She imagined how Desmond would comfort her if she was sad.

How he would wrap his arms around her and assure her that everything was going to be alright.

How he would kiss her tenderly and whisper in her ear how much he loved her and how he would always be there to look after her.

"Will dinner be long?"

The sudden appearance of Jack behind her caught Kelly completely off guard, making her jump and lose her grip on the plate she was holding.

Before she could regain her composure, the china hit the linoleum floor and shattered into a myriad tiny pieces.

Kelly held her head in her hands as she gazed down at the smashed china.

The plate had been part of a dinner set which had been given to her parents as a wedding present. Kelly had been so proud when as a little girl her mum had trusted her to lay the table for Sunday lunch using their best china.

She always made sure that she was especially careful because she knew how much the service meant to her parents, and now here was a treasured piece of it lying on the floor at her feet, way beyond repair to even the most painstaking of restorers.

As much as she wanted to and felt that she needed to, Kelly could not cry!

She was all dried out of tears. She just kept staring fixedly at the mess on the floor.

It was the harshness in Jack's words which brought her out of her trance.

"Stupid bitch," he sneered, turning to leave the kitchen. "I hope you don't expect me to pick that lot up?"

His words struck Kelly with far more force than any slap or punch he had delivered to her in the past.

She could not believe the sheer lack of empathy her husband was demonstrating, especially when he knew only too well how precious some of her mother's possessions were to her.

Kelly felt herself starting to sway; the sudden head rush made her feel dizzy. She reached out to the draining board to steady herself.

As she did, her fingers fell upon the handle of their largest carving knife.

Without realising what she was doing, Kelly picked up the knife and held it tightly in her hand as her eyes became fixed upon the open doorway where her husband had stood moments before.

She could feel the blood pumping in her veins, her pulse quickening.

For a while she remained poised, ready to strike, like a coiled spring awaiting release.

If Jack reappeared in the doorway Kelly knew that she would pounce at him and plunge the knife deep into his wicked heart, burying the blade right up to the hilt.

As she stood there, waiting in anticipation, she could feel her anger beginning to assuage. The thundering sound of blood rushing in her ears began to die down and she could feel herself relaxing her hold on the knife.

Without being aware, Kelly had been holding her breath ever since she grabbed the knife.

Now she relaxed and let it out, slowly.

She could feel her pulse slowing down and as her breathing stabilised, she could sense her head starting to clear as the momentary anger abated.

Kelly stood there for a moment, and then as if she was only now aware of its presence, she looked at the knife in her hand.

The thought of what she felt herself capable of doing only moments before filled her with dread and horror.

Kelly released her hold on the knife and it too clattered on the floor amongst the broken china.

"Now what?" the sound of Jack's voice coming from the next room filled her with anger once more, and this time she was powerless to act upon it.

Kelly raced into the living room and flung herself at her suitably astonished husband and began beating him with her fists all over his upper body and head.

With each blow she could feel the pent-up anger and frustration oozing out of her. She was only a little thing compared to her hulking great lummox of a husband, but he was still cowering with his hands over his face during her onslaught.

"Get off me yer stupid cow!" Jack demanded, as Kelly rained down another shower of blows on his head. The effort was making her grunt and groan with each new blow and Jack could feel her strikes starting to lose their impact.

Either way, he was not about to stand for his wife beating up on him, regardless of whatever the reason was or even how little damage she was able to inflict.

A man could not be pushed around in his own house and a woman needed to know her place and show the correct amount of deference and respect to her husband.

Jack waited until Kelly had almost completely exhausted her arsenal, and then he threw a punch which landed straight on Kelly's jaw.

The force of the blow sent her flying backwards over the couch and she landed shoulder first on the floor.

The jolt from the landing sent a shuddering spasm of pain through her entire body. It was then that she could feel the tears, which earlier she could not cry, start to resurface.

Kelly lay there in a crumpled heap, holding her head and sobbing.

Jack walked around the sofa and stared down at his prostrate wife.

As he watched her lying there, helpless and vulnerable, Jack could feel his own anger still raging within him.

How dare she raise a finger to him!

Just who the hell did she think she was?

Kelly tried to lift herself off the ground; the throbbing in her shoulder from where she had hit the ground so hard was already starting to pound with ferocity far worse than the ache in her jaw from where Jack had struck her.

As she moved slightly, turning her body to one side, her jumper rode up exposing her bare back to her husband.

Not one to let such an opportunity pass, Jack lifted back his leg and drove the toe of his boot straight into Kelly's tailbone with all the force he could muster.

Kelly let out a shriek of fear and pain as the kick landed.

Being on her side and facing away from her husband she had not been prepared for the attack, and the shock of the powerful blow took her completely unaware.

As she writhed around in agony on the floor Jack stood over her with his hands planted firmly on his hips.

A slow grin crept across his lips as he watched his wife suffering.

Eventually he grew bored with her performance, so he walked out into the hallway and grabbed his jacket from the peg.

"I'm going down the pub," he shouted, "I'll be back in two hours so make sure my lunch is ready and waiting!"

With that, he walked out through the front door and slammed it behind him.

Kelly lay in a crumpled, sobbing heap on the living room floor, silently cursing her husband, her marriage, and her life.

It was almost a full half-hour before she found the strength to lift herself up to a standing position.

CHAPTER FOUR

B en Green sat slumped in one of the three matching armchairs which, along with the three-seater and two-seater settees, formed part of the new living room suite belonging to his girlfriend Natasha's parents.

Natasha's parents were both solicitors and their four-bedroom house, which was situated in one of the more affluent streets in the village, was where Ben was *forced* to spend every Sunday lunchtime for the last four weeks.

Ben knew full well that Natasha's parents did not think that he was good enough for their daughter. Not so much because of what they actually said to his face, but more by virtue of the way that they spoke to him. Not to mention the sideways glances he often caught sight of when they thought that his attention was elsewhere.

Natasha was their only child and as a result had been spoilt rotten from a very young age.

Deep down, Ben was under no illusion that they were a couple for any reason other than as a way of Natasha rebelling against her parents and holding up a metaphorical two fingers at them for their demanding and domineering attitude.

But the prospect of being used by Natasha as some kind of yardstick to beat her parents with suited him perfectly.

At nineteen, one year older than his girlfriend, Ben was in no rush to settle down or even bother with finding a soul mate as his partner.

In truth, he relished the freedom their so-called relationship offered him as it allowed him plenty of time to spend with his mates whether it was downing pints at their local or cheering on their local team to victory.

In fact, if it had not been for his dad's constant nagging and jeering as to why he never had a girlfriend, Ben would probably have still been single.

It was not that Ben did not like girls, quite the opposite in fact. It was just that he preferred his own company most of the time, and when he did not want to be alone, he had his mates.

There did not seem to him to be enough time left after that for anything akin to a proper relationship, which was another reason why when Natasha *chose* him as her boyfriend it seemed to suit everyone.

Except of course, her parents!

The only real benefit of any positive kind that he gained from his association with Natasha was the sex she allowed him to have on occasion, when she was in the mood, naturally.

Ben suspected that given the right circumstance and with the right person, Natasha could be quite an enthusiastic lover.

He just accepted that he was not *that* person.

Even so, she allowed him the occasional grope, and when she was really up for it, he was allowed to go all the way.

They had even done it on her parents' super-king size bed, which was another example of Natasha showing contempt for her parents.

The thought of committing the deed in her parents' room had certainly not appealed to Ben, but he managed to do the business none the less, so Natasha was at least happy at the time.

Natasha had taken a gap-year before starting university which had not gone down at all well with her parents.

They naturally wanted her to follow both of them into a legal career, but Natasha had other ideas.

Natasha had an artistic streak which neither of her parents possessed; therefore, they could not understand her wish to become an artist.

Ben had seen some of her work and even though he was no expert he could tell that she had a talent. Her eye for detail and the way she managed to flesh-out characters in her paintings was truly something magical.

She had studied art at 'A' level along with law *naturally* and history, and although Natasha had achieved extremely high grades in all three subjects, it was her art which she was most passionate about.

Several of her paintings had sold at the annual end of year exhibit the art department put on, and they were not bought by friends and family members only. There was even a double spread in the local paper which featured three of her landscapes, and the reporter covering the event had spent more time interviewing her than any of the other entrants.

Though to be fair, Ben did suspect that the reporter probably fancied Natasha as he caught him eyeing up his girlfriend's legs more than once during the evening.

Still, he decided not to share his concern with her. After all, he did not want her to think that he was in any way diminishing the overall reaction to her talent.

The fact that Ben openly supported his girlfriend's artistic pursuits was just another reason why her parents did not like him. But along with the fact that he was born and still lived on a council estate, had left school with minimal qualifications and, as far as they were concerned, did not act or speak in a manner worthy of courting their little girl, Ben knew that there was very little he could do to ever be on the receiving end of the graciousness.

He resigned himself to the fact that it was just a cross he would have to learn to bear.

Ben was convinced that the only reason that Natasha's parents kept inviting him round for Sunday lunch was so that they could keep an eye on him and their daughter.

They had been in the routine of going out for lunch at their local and then taking a stroll through the wood, occasionally followed by afters, if Ben was lucky.

He could usually tell if Natasha was in the mood when they went out.

If she decided to wear trousers, he knew that there was no chance of any fun that evening. But if she greeted him at the door wearing a dress or a skirt, then he knew that he was in with a chance.

It humoured him that whenever Natasha was feeling frisky it usually followed an argument with either one or both of her parents. Not that he was complaining.

Today, typically, everything in the home was lovely and Natasha was wearing a pair of tight black trousers that really accentuated her pert behind, which somehow made the torture worse.

The three of them had been laughing and joking with each other over lunch, hardly even including Ben in their private conversations. And then afterwards it was the usual, retiring to their enormous living room decked out with their brand-new suite, so that the parents could scroll through one of the umpteen colour supplements which came with their Sunday paper, while Natasha amused herself in a corner with her latest artistic endeavour, and Ben was left to sit there and glance through what was left of the newspaper whilst listening to the awful dirge that they classed as music.

He was not even allowed to watch the television as it interfered with their enjoyment of the peaceful afternoon.

Peaceful? Boring was more like it!

Ben gazed up at the clock on the mantelpiece. He could not believe that it was only ten minutes since he last checked the time.

The day was really dragging.

He could think of any number of things he would rather be doing right now, and none of them involved the present company.

Unless of course Natasha was up for it!

Finally, after what seemed to Ben like an eternity, Natasha put down her brush and stood back from her easel.

"There now," she announced to no one in particular. "That should do for one day."

Ben felt his heart skip a beat.

Regardless of whether she threw him out or decided to go for a drink with him, either way he was out of there.

Natasha studied her hands, turning them over to look for splashes of paint. As usual her hands were spotless, but nonetheless she stated. "Right then, I'm just going to wash my hands and get this mucky paint off, and then you," she turned to look at Ben, "can take me for a well-deserved drink."

Ben nodded in agreement and shifted uncomfortably in his chair as he watched her parents exchange glances.

"Oh, really, darling, must you go out tonight?" Her mother began. "I told you on Friday that the Henderson's might be calling round this evening; you know how much they look forward to seeing you."

Natasha pulled a face as she walked past Ben.

He had to make a supreme effort not to laugh.

When she reached the door, Natasha turned back. "I haven't forgotten, Mother, but I did say that I couldn't promise."

"Oh, but really, darling," it was her father's turn to lay on the guilt. "They're our oldest and dearest friends and they expressly said how much they were looking forward to seeing you this evening."

Natasha raised her eyes to heaven. "Don't fuss, Daddy, I'm sure that they'll survive a visit without seeing me."

Ben had noticed that whenever Natasha wanted something, whether it was money, a lift or even just to win an argument, she always called her father 'daddy' and that seemed to do the trick.

Even now, Ben could see the affect that his girlfriend's words were having on him. His entire expression softened the moment she uttered the magical word.

Natasha's mother immediately picked up on her husband's surrender.

"That's not the point, Natasha, we promised them that you would be here, would you make us out to be liars?"

"Well, why did you assure them without speaking to me first, surely that would have been the proper thing to do?" Natasha now had her hands planted firmly on her hips. It was obvious to Ben that she had no intention of backing down.

The problem was, neither did her mother.

Hilary Spencer shot up from her chair so fast that she almost knocked over the drinks table next to her with her knee.

For a moment, both women looked directly at each other across the floor, each glaring at the other with a contempt born out of stubbornness.

The CD which had been playing ended abruptly,

plunging the room into silence. For a second Ben would have sworn that he could hear the sound of his girlfriend breathing heavily through her nostrils like a wild animal making ready to charge.

It was obvious that neither woman was about to back down.

Ben was starting to feel extremely uncomfortable in the oppressive atmosphere. He did not care which of them spoke next, he just prayed that it would not be too long before one of them broke the uncomfortable silence.

Finally, much to Ben's delight, Natasha's father decided to try and lighten the mood. "Now come on, girls, there's really no need for all this," he began, keeping his tone as light and non-confrontational as possible. "I'm sure that we can entertain the Henderson's until you get home, darling."

He was looking at his daughter when he spoke, but it was his wife who retaliated. Turning to face him she screamed. "Oh, for goodness sake, Gerald, you are completely useless!" Hilary Spencer redirected her anger away from her daughter and straight at her husband instead.

The expression which spread across Gerald's face when he realised that he was the new target for his wife's venom was a combination of shock and terror.

Ben always thought that it was a little odd that his girl-friend's father was taken so easily by surprise when his wife started yelling at him. After all, it appeared to be a semi-regular occurrence, so in Ben's mind Gerald should be used to it by now.

Gerald's mouth opened and closed several times without any words managing to escape his lips.

Hilary Spencer was evidently not in a patient mood and thus she was not prepared to wait for her husband to find his reply.

"Why in god's name you let this child get away with things

over and over again never ceases to amaze me," there was certainly no let-up in the woman's ferocity.

Ben was now feeling uncomfortable for a different reason altogether.

It was one thing to hear his girlfriend argue with one of her parents, but to hear them at it was quite another kettle of fish.

"I'm not a child, thank you, Mother!" Natasha's face was starting to flush red and Ben knew that it was only a matter of time, if things continued to escalate, before there would be all-out war in the Spencer household.

"You are a child as long as you're living under my roof, young lady!"

Ben could almost see the steam emanating from his girl-friend's ears.

Her mother's words hit their target with maximum impact, just as they were expected to.

Natasha was by now on the verge of tears.

Ben could feel himself shrinking further down into the armchair, wishing that he could somehow make himself invisible.

This was a family argument and although he was not actively part of it, he knew full well that most, if not all, of it was aimed at him.

He was to blame for taking their precious daughter away for the evening, and if it was not for him then Natasha would have no qualms about staying in and entertaining the Henderson's.

Eventually, Gerald found his voice. He looked up at his wife, almost pleadingly "But, my dear—" he began. And that was as far as he was allowed to get.

"Never mind *BUT*," Hilary retorted, cutting her husband off in mid-sentence. "How am I expected to instil some modicum of discipline in our daughter when you keep letting her have her own way over everything?"

Before poor Gerald had a chance to reply, Natasha cut in. "I am here in the room, Mother, you might have the courtesy of acknowledging me instead of speaking as if I am invisible!"

The tears were starting to brim over and trickle-down Natasha's cheeks.

Ben was afraid to move, even to offer her a tissue.

Fortunately, he did not have to.

Gerald pushed himself up out of his chair and ignoring his wife, strode across the room and threw his arms around his daughter's shoulders, holding her tightly whilst he whispered words of comfort in his most apologetic tone of voice.

He removed a hanky from his pocket and passed it to Natasha. After dabbing her eyes, she took a huge breath and trumpeted into the square. It was more for effect than necessity in Ben's opinion.

The action signalled victory for Natasha, defeat for her mother.

Hilary Spencer released a pent-up shriek of frustration and anger as she stormed out of the room.

Gerald raised his head to watch her leave.

Ben could tell from the weary look of resignation etched on his face that he understood that he would suffer for his actions later.

Ben actually felt sorry for the man.

After Natasha had settled down and finally stopped snivelling, her father took out his wallet and removed a crisp £20 note which he placed into her hand, closing her fingers around it.

Natasha offered a token resistance before accepting the gift, graciously.

She planted a large kiss on her father's cheek and ran from the room and up the stairs.

Gerald turned to Ben and shrugged his shoulders as if he had the world balancing on them, before he too left the room in search of his wife.

Ben waited patiently.

Finally, he heard his girlfriend skipping down the stairs, so he stood up and made his way out into the hall to meet her.

Ben's heart skipped a beat when he saw what she was wearing.

Natasha had obviously washed her face and reapplied her make-up, expertly as always.

She was wearing a tight-fitting black polo-neck jumper which afforded her ample bosoms maximum exposure.

In place of the trousers she had on a dark green plaid skirt which barely made it halfway down her thighs so that even from this distance Ben could see that she was wearing sheer stockings.

When she reached the bottom of the stairs, Natasha slipped her legs into a pair of low-heeled black leather boots which she grabbed from the foot stand in the hallway.

Once she was satisfied with her ensemble, she held out the ends of her skirt and twirled from side to side as if to gain Ben's approval.

The look on his face was all the reassurance that Natasha needed.

She grabbed her coat from the stand by the door and called back a hasty 'goodbye' as she pulled Ben out after her, barely giving him the chance to retrieve his own jacket.

CHAPTER FIVE

B en and Natasha walked down the road hand-in-hand. Neither of them spoke about the confrontation back at Natasha's parents' house, but Ben could tell from his girl-friend's overall demeanour that she was secretly pleased with herself over the final outcome.

He also knew that the £20 note her father had surrepti-tiously placed in her hand would not see the light of day when they arrived at the pub.

Not that a free drink was Ben's main focus at the moment.

The fact that Natasha had changed into a short skirt was not lost on him.

During their relationship Ben could count on very few certainties, but one of them was that Natasha only wore revealing outfits when she was horny, regardless of what had caused the sensation.

In this case, Ben surmised that it was most definitely the argument with her mother. Allowing Ben to have his way tonight would be Natasha's way of saying 'screw you' to her mother.

And that was all good with him.

The main question on Ben's mind right now was would she want it before or after their visit to the pub.

In the past Natasha had never shown an actual preference, and on either occasion her performance had been virtually the same, so Ben had no inkling as to which scenario his girlfriend was considering, so as usual he decided that he would play it by ear.

They continued their walk-in silence. Natasha was, as usual, lost in her own little world, conjuring up ideas which she would later express on canvas.

The autumn sun was already setting behind the town and Natasha had mentioned on several occasions that autumn sunsets were one of her favourite endeavours.

Although Ben never claimed to boast any artistic ability, he too loved the early sunsets at this time of year. Not because of the glorious change of colours as the leaves lost their youthful glow or the fresh crispness of the early evening air, but more because he knew that when the sun went down Natasha would come out to play.

As they crossed the road and headed toward the field which was their usual short-cut into town, Ben could feel his erection starting to push against the crotch of his denim jeans in anticipation of their eventual union.

The warmth he felt emanating from Natasha's soft silky-smooth skin as her perfectly manicured fingers wrapped around his, only served to increase his ardour.

He imagined those same luxuriously smooth fingers sliding gracefully up and down his rigid shaft as Natasha whispered words of promise and encouragement in his ear.

Ben secretly blessed Natasha's mother for causing such a fuss about them going out tonight.

As they reached the gate which was attached to the fence

surrounding the field Ben stepped forward and unhitched the clamp to afford Natasha entry. She smiled at him as she went through still keeping hold of his other hand.

As Ben followed her inside the compound, he swung the gate shut with his free hand leaving the clamp to fall back into place when the two ends collided.

They walked on through the field. The sky to the west was fast losing the last of its orange tinge as the blanket of night crept across the sky.

In the distance they could hear the chimes from St Luke's tolling the prelude to evening service.

Ben knew that if he wanted some play time before they reached the pub that he would have to make his move soon.

Another five hundred yards and they would be in sight of the congregation. Once they passed the church there were no more secluded areas between them and the edge of town, so if he missed his chance now, he would definitely have to wait until after they left the pub.

And anything could happen between now and then!

It certainly would not be the first time that Natasha had given him signals of encouragement during the evening only to have a change of heart when it finally came time to do the dirty deed.

At least if she was in the mood now it was worth Ben's while to make his play and then he could really enjoy the rest of the evening.

Ben chose his moment and pulled Natasha gently towards him.

The smile playing around her lips told him that she knew what he was in the mood for.

They held each other tightly as they kissed, their tongues darting in and out of each other's mouths as they moaned together softly.

Natasha could feel Ben's excitement growing as he thrust his hips towards her. She slid her arms around his waist and lowered her hands so that she could slip them into the back pockets of his jeans allowing her to gently squeeze and massage his buttocks as she pulled him tightly against her.

Ben responded, gratefully. He moaned even louder as his hips gyrated in response to her touch.

Ben pulled his mouth away from Natasha's and lowered his head so that he could start to kiss her from her under her jaw down to her neckline. Natasha shivered and squirmed as he planted soft kisses against her lightly scented skin. Ben could feel the voluptuous mounds of her ample bosoms as he crushed her against him in an effort to gain deeper access to her slender neck.

In response to her movement Ben slid his hands around Natasha's pert bottom and then let them slide down her thighs before lifting them back up, bringing her short skirt up with them.

Bingo!

No panties.

Ben allowed his hands to roam freely over the peachy smoothness of his girlfriend's pert bottom. He clutched her cheeks firmly, squeezing and fondling them whilst ensuring that he did not *twang* her suspender strap and destroy the moment.

By the way Natasha was thrusting her hips against his groin; Ben knew that she was passing the point of no return.

He slipped one hand around his girlfriend's thigh until he had it strategically placed between her legs. As he slid his hand forward his fingers could feel her moist slippery entrance.

Testing the accessibility with his middle finger elicited a groan of pleasure from Natasha, and as she pulled him towards her even tighter, he moved his finger back and forth across her opening until he felt her lips parting sufficiently to allow him to plunge his finger all the way in and tenderly begin to caress her sensuous cavern.

Natasha's breaths came in shuddering jolts as Ben expertly massaged her inside, thrusting his finger in as far as he dared and then exploring her on all sides. After a while, Ben manoeuvred two more of his fingers inside his girlfriend and manipulated them with as much dexterity as he could conjure until Natasha grabbed his hand tightly and started to use it as if it were a makeshift vibrator. She shifted Ben's hand fervently from left to right and back and forth, propelling her hips forward to meet his eager fingers until finally she felt herself orgasm.

As Natasha's shudders began to subside, she opened her eyes and looked dreamily into Ben's.

Without speaking, she led him towards a clump of bushes off to one side of the field.

Once they passed through a convenient gap in the shrubbery, they found themselves in the centre of a clearing which afforded them sufficient protection from any passers-by.

The area had a comforting familiarity about it, and Ben could not help thinking that they had used this particular space before.

Ben removed his coat and laid it out on the floor for Natasha. She made herself comfortable while Ben fumbled with his belt buckle. Once he had managed to release the button on his jeans and slide the zipper down Natasha leaned forward to assist him with his boxers.

Ben was already fully erect, so Natasha expertly lifted the waist band of his shorts over the head of his penis, freeing it from its confinement.

She guided Ben down towards her, gently massaging his throbbing member with her slender fingers.

Once he was in position, Natasha guided Ben inside her and waited for him to thrust forward to secure his position.

As Ben began to propel himself back and forth on top of her, Natasha lay back on his coat and closed her eyes. She splayed her arms out on the floor to give Ben ample access to her breasts. Ben did not need further prompting. He let his hands glide up under Natasha's jumper until he felt the supple ripeness of her naked breasts.

Kneading them gently with both hands Ben could feel her nipples hardening between his eager fingers.

Lowering his head, Ben pressed Natasha's breasts closer together and buried his face between them. He massaged them tenderly with his face before slipping one of her nipples into his mouth and gently sucking on it.

Natasha moaned softly as he continued to roll her nipple between his tongue and the roof of his mouth.

She could feel his pace quickening as he thrust ever deeper inside her.

Natasha raised her knees on either side of Ben's body and crossed them behind his back. The sudden cold caress of her leather boots against his bare skin caused Ben to arch his back and cry out with pleasure.

He could feel himself building to a final crescendo and he tried to hold back to prolong the ecstasy.

Natasha gripped the grass beneath her hands as she anticipated his eruption.

Then suddenly, Ben was gone!

It took a moment for Natasha to realise that Ben was no longer inside her as she was still lost in the moment.

She felt his loss deeply, her loins still aching for release.

In confusion and frustration, she opened her eyes to see what he was playing at.

The hideous monstrosity which had taken Ben's place stared down at her with malevolent eyes and drooling jaws.

Before she had a chance to scream the thing slammed a huge hairy hand over her mouth and nose with such force that Natasha felt cartilage pop.

A sharp pain seared through her nose and she could feel blood pouring out of her nostrils from beneath the creature's grip.

Trying to forget the sheer insanity of her predicament and focus her mind on escape, Natasha decided that attack was the only resource she had at her disposal, so she started to try and wrench herself free from her assailant.

Although she twisted and turned with all her might her efforts were in vain, the creature had her pinned to the ground with no chance of escape.

In terror Natasha clenched her hands into fists and started beating at the beast as it lowered its face closer to hers, but her meagre efforts did not appear to have any impact.

The spittle from the thing's slavering jaws dripped down onto Natasha's chin as it appeared to be studying her. Even though the creature's hand virtually covered the lower half of her face, Natasha could still smell the fetid stench of its breath and she gagged twice only just managing to keep her lunch down for fear that she might choke on her own bile.

Her tiny fists continued to beat pathetically against the beast until she could feel her strength starting to ebb.

In desperation she opened her hands and tried to dig her nails into the thing's flesh. But as she raked them down its arms, she barely managed to contact its skin through the shaggy pile which covered them.

Natasha tried to force out a scream from behind her assailant's hand as it leaned in and began to lick her cheek with its enormous, scaly tongue and once again she had to fight to keep down her food.

With renewed vigour Natasha dug her nails in even harder against the thing's bare flesh and although on this occasion she felt as if she had made at least some progress through the clumps of its matted coat, when she scraped her fingers down-ward instead of having the affect she had hoped for all she could feel were her own nails starting to give way against the thing's unyielding skin.

Natasha could not vent her anger and frustration any more than she was capable of screaming for help.

She could not understand where Ben had gone.

Why was he not trying to help her?

And where had this monstrosity come from?

Through the anguish and fear that was wracking her brain she could hear her mother's voice scolding her for going out that evening when she had specifically asked her not to.

For once Natasha wished that she had done as she was told.

Too late now of course!

Natasha could feel the panic rising inside her as her breathing became more laboured. The effort of trying to suck in oxygen through the creature's hand was becoming more diffi-cult by the second.

What made it even worse was that Natasha could now taste blood in her mouth and she knew that it had to be as a result of the snap she heard when the beast slammed its hand against her nose.

She coughed and spluttered as the first drops made their way down her throat.

The tears in her eyes blurred her vision until the monster on top of her became no more than a dark shape.

Natasha felt herself starting to pass out. Whether it was from shock, fear, or lack of oxygen she did not know, but in many ways, she was grateful that she would not be conscious for whatever this thing intended to do to her.

Suddenly, she felt the creature swivel its grotesque body until she could feel something hard and rigid pressing against her pelvic bone.

Before she had a chance to react the creature was inside her.

It did not so much enter her as impale her, and unlike the warm, loving, passionate feeling she experienced when Ben made love to her, this penetration felt more like she was being stabbed with a large blunt instrument.

Mercifully, Natasha passed out before the onslaught continued any further.

CHAPTER SIX

The piercing ring tone from his mobile phone brought Detective Inspector Malcolm Hardy out of his deep slumber.

As usual, he found himself curled up on his armchair still fully dressed from when he arrived home for work. Falling asleep in front of the television after a couple of drinks had become something of a regular occurrence with him recently, and although he had promised himself that he would make more of an effort to sort himself out in the evenings his plan had so far not come to fruition.

As he sat up abruptly, he managed to dislodge the glass that had been nestled in his lap, and before he could make a grab for it, it fell to the ground and shattered on the hard-wooden floor.

Hardy surveyed the scattered splinters of glass splayed around his shoeless feet and heaved a sigh of resignation.

He reached over and grabbed his phone.

The illuminated screen showed that the call was from his station.

Before he pressed the button to answer he noticed the time at the top of the display, it was 1:30 a.m.

"Hardy," he barked loudly.

The female voice which answered was shaky and slightly timid. "Sorry to bother you, sir, it's Constable Grant here."

Hardy knew the PC in question. He had seen her around the station on numerous occasions and thus far he was very impressed by what he had seen.

Although Grant was only six months out of training school, Hardy had heard around the station that she had proved herself as being both brave and resourceful when out on the job.

There had been one particular incident where Grant had been called in at the last moment to cover for another PC in a sting to uncover an underage prostitution racket. Grant had leapt at the chance and during the operation she gave chase and single-handedly apprehended one of the more unsavoury members of the gang.

Witnesses stated that the assailant had turned on Grant and produced a large switch-knife, but she still managed to disarm him and handcuff him on her own before backup had arrived.

There had also been the incident in the staff canteen when one of the male PC's had decided to try his luck and grabbed her behind in the queue.

Without saying a word, Grant had the PC on the floor in seconds begging her to let go of his finger which Grant was holding in a very precarious position while she stared him out.

When word reached her sergeant's ears, he insisted that she put in a formal complaint about the PC, but Grant declined, stating that she did not wish to bring the force into disrepute because of the juvenile behaviour of one of the other officers. Besides which, she had already taught him a lesson he would not forget in a hurry.

Grant had gained a lot of respect for her actions from her peers as well as her superiors, and the offending PC was made to feel extremely unwelcome until he put in a request to transfer.

Hardy cleared his throat. "I trust that you have an extremely essential reason for disrupting my beauty sleep, Constable?" he asked, rubbing the sleep from his eyes.

"Yes, sir," Grant assured him, "the sarge asked me to call you, sir, as it appears that we have a missing girl on our hands."

Hardy leaned forward in his seat. "Another one, oh Christ, what are the details?"

"Well..." He could hear PC Grant swallowing hard on the other end of the line as if she were reluctant to answer.

Hardy could feel his patience ebbing away. "Well, what?" he demanded.

PC Grant coughed lightly before answering. "Well it appears that the lady in question, a Natasha Spencer, eighteen, went out with her boyfriend last evening, and she was due home no later than 10 p.m. But when she hadn't arrived home by 11 p.m. her parents became concerned and called us."

"Hang on a minute," Hardy cut in, "do you mean to tell me that this girl has only been missing, what," he glanced at his phone display for a second before bringing it back into position, "two and a half hours, and you're calling me?"

"I'm sorry, sir," Grant sounded as if she meant it, too. "It appears that the girl's father is a friend of the superintendent, and he called him directly."

The young PC waited patiently for the information to set in.

Hardy rubbed his head briskly with the flat of his free hand.

Without realising what he was doing, Hardy made to stand

up and in doing so trod on a sharp piece of glass from his broken tumbler.

"Fuck!" Hardy fell back on the chair, dropping the phone while he attempted to extricate the shard from his foot.

PC Grant winced and pulled back slightly from the receiver. She knew full well that the inspector was not going to be pleased with the order when she delivered it, which she suspected was probably the reason that her sergeant suddenly had to use the toilet and so left her in charge of making the call.

She could still hear the inspector shouting and cursing, but he somehow seemed further away now.

Finally, the constable started to grow concerned that Hardy was not speaking to her.

"Sir, are you OK?" she called, raising her voice whilst still being careful not to shout.

There was a loud clattering on the other end as Hardy retrieved his phone.

"Yes, I'm still here!" He sounded more abrupt than he had intended to. His foot was stinging from where he had pulled out the broken glass fragment, and he knew that he had not had nearly enough sleep to compensate for the amount of single malt that he had demolished before falling asleep.

That and the fact that he was now expected to set off on what would doubtless be a wild goose chase, looking for a grown woman who was probably fast asleep in the back of her boyfriend's car having worn herself out giving him a blowjob.

But he reminded himself that none of that was the constable's fault, so he tried to moderate his tone. After all, he had once been in her position and he remembered what it was like having to take the brunt of the abuse from every senior officer he had ever had to wake up in the middle of the night.

He had sworn to himself then that he would never be like

them, and to give him his due, he had—for the most part—kept to his own promise.

"Right then, Constable, text me the address, I'm on my way."

"Thank you, sir," Grant could not hide the relief in her voice. "Detective Sergeant Russell will meet you there."

"OK, thanks." Hardy ended the conversation.

He reached over and switched on the table lamp beside him.

He waited a moment for his eyes to adjust to the light.

The amount left in the bottle of Glenfiddich next to the lamp reminded him of how much he had consumed before drifting off.

He was not pleased with himself, but it was too late to do anything about it now.

Hardy picked up his shoes and shook them to make sure that none of the glass had found its way in, before he slipped his feet into them.

Disregarding the broken glass until later, he took himself into the downstairs toilet and checked his reflection in the mirror.

One of the reasons he kept his hair cropped so short was so that on such occasions as this he would not need to concern himself with how well it was groomed. It never ceased to make him laugh when he would meet up with other officers who had been called from their warm beds to a crime scene and their hair was sticking up in all directions making them look like a character from a children's television programme.

Speaking of grooming, he knew that he could do with a shave but there was no time.

He took a gulp of mouthwash and swirled it around his mouth to try and clear the lingering smell of the Glenfiddich.

After that, Hardy straightened his tie in the mirror and grabbed his raincoat on the way out.

The drive to the address which PC Grant had sent him took less than fifteen minutes. At this hour of the morning there was not much traffic on the road and he also seemed to make every green light on route. Not that he believed that the occasion warranted his blue light, superintendent's friend or not.

As he pulled into the kerb, Hardy spotted DS Sam Russell waiting patiently outside the premises.

As Hardy stepped out of his vehicle, he called over to his colleague.

"Hello, Sam," he said, cheerily. "You weren't doing anything important when they called you, were you?"

Sam laughed. "Just trying to fall off to sleep, the baby had only gone down ten minutes earlier."

DS Russell's wife had given birth to their second child three months earlier and the constant look of sleep-depravation etched on Russell's face had long since stopped being a cause for concern for Hardy. He knew that Russell could take it in his stride and that he was always up to the task at hand no matter how little sleep he had managed to steal the previous night.

"Have you been in yet?" asked Hardy, indicating towards the front door. He could see through a gap in the curtains that the lights were on inside, much as he had expected them to be.

Russell nodded. "Yeah, I thought I had better let them know that I was here, not that it did any good."

"How do you mean?" Hardy asked, quizzically.

Russell glanced over to the house to make sure that the Spencer's still had their front door shut before answering. "Well," he began, keeping his voice down. "When I arrived, I thought it best to let them know how quickly we were responding, you know guv, because of the super an' all. Anyway, the minute the bloke opens the door and I introduce myself he starts ranting on about why has such a junior officer been sent to deal with his missing daughter, and did I know that he was a close personal friend of the super, and he was going to contact his member of parliament right this minute if I didn't get someone senior to respond."

"Sounds like a real charmer," Hardy cut in, opening the gate which led up to the Spencer's abode.

"Yea," replied Russell, "just you wait until you get a load of the missus, she's on another planet altogether."

They walked up the path towards the door in silence.

There were certain aspects of his job which he loved, but this was not one of them. Meeting parents of a missing child was never easy, although the younger the infant the harder the task.

Hardy had had his share of such meetings when he had been a DCI in London.

No amount of training could prepare you for the reaction of parents when you were trying to ascertain where their child might be at the moment. You always had to cover the basics first: friends, other relatives, parks, playgrounds etc, but every parent always believed that their child had been abducted.

And unfortunately, sometimes they were right.

And when a missing child became a murder victim, the subsequent conversation of having to inform the parents that the worst-case scenario had in fact occurred, that was by far Hardy's least favourite conversation.

It did not matter how many times he had to relay such details, he could never get used to it.

Some DCI's of his acquaintance used to send in their DI's to break the news, but Hardy was old-school, and he firmly believed that the buck stopped with him.

Most parents' response was the same.

It was a combination of feelings: grief, sorrow, frustration, anger, bitterness, failure, anguish, all mixed together and jumbled about.

During his twenty-odd years in service Hardy had been on the receiving end of their tether more times than he could count as they lashed out and screamed obscenities at him and his entire force, before finally crumbling to shivering, sobbing wrecks on the floor.

His only comfort came in finally ensuring that the scumbag responsible spent the rest of their natural life behind bars.

It was a small comfort, especially for the parents, but comfort, nonetheless.

This present case, however, was somewhat different.

An adult missing less than twelve hours did not warrant the same response as a missing child or even a vulnerable adult.

But the fact that this Spencer character knew the superintendent changed the rules. Suddenly the dictum of ensuring that resources were being properly maximised went straight out of the window.

Of course, Hardy had been on the force long enough to appreciate that obviously adults were abducted, kidnapped and murdered too. But if the force had to respond to every call such as this one in such a tiny time-frame the detective division alone for every station would probably have to triple the size of its force.

Before Hardy had a chance to press the bell, the front door swung open.

Gerald Spencer walked forward and stood in the doorway, almost obliterating the sight of his wife standing behind him. For a moment it seemed to Hardy as if the man was not prepared to let them enter his house.

Hardy opened his wallet and flashed his badge. "Mr. and Mrs. Spencer?" he asked, replacing his wallet before the husband a chance to inspect it. "Detective Inspector Hardy, sir, I believe you have already met my sergeant?"

Russell gave a slight nod of his head in acknowledgment.

Spencer opened his mouth as if he was about to make an announcement, and then promptly closed it again as his wife barged him out of the way and from her vantage point at the top of the step glanced out over the officer's heads and out towards the street.

"Where are all your other officers?" she demanded, still looking towards the road and not at either of them directly.

"What other officers, madam?" Hardy enquired, obviously confused.

Hilary Spencer shifted her gaze down to the inspector.

She regarded him through narrowed eyes as if she were looking at something which she had stepped on while walking in a field.

"The search party of course!" the woman almost screamed out the words. "The ones you are supposed to have organised to help search for my daughter!"

Gerald Spencer moved forward and placed his hands gently on his wife's shoulders.

Before giving him a chance to speak, Hilary Spencer spoke again.

"Gerald, why aren't they out looking for Natasha, why are they wasting so much time?"

Spencer guided his wife back inside the hallway.

He handed her a tissue which he produced from his pocket and she started to dab her eyes.

Once he was sure that his wife had her temper back under control, Spencer turned back and surveyed the two officers who were still standing outside below the front step for a moment, before finally saying. "Please, gentlemen, come in."

The officers followed Mrs. Spencer into the living room with her husband bringing up the rear.

"I apologise if we were a trifle curt with you before, officer," Gerald Spencer was obviously aiming his comment at Russell. "You must understand that we're at our wits end at the moment, but it was rude nonetheless."

Russell smiled and reassured them both that no apology was necessary.

Once they were all seated Russell took out his notebook and prepared to take down anything which might seem pertinent, during their conversation.

Hardy started the ball rolling with what he had already been told by Constable Grant. "So just to confirm Mr. and Mrs. Spencer, your daughter Natasha went out last evening with her boyfriend at about seven o'clock, and you were expecting her to return home by no later than ten or eleven?"

"That's right," replied Spencer, "whenever they go to the pub Natasha always ensures that she returns home at a reasonable hour."

"Plus," his wife added, "we had some friends round for the evening and Natasha knew that they wanted to see her before they went home," Hilary Spencer spoke clearly, but Hardy detected a slight tremor in her voice which conveyed to him the fact that she was seriously worried for her daughter's safety.

Hardy gave her a reassuring smile. "I take it that your daughter is not in the habit of staying out later than expected without contacting you first?"

Spencer opened his mouth, but his wife beat him to it.

"Never, officer!" she snapped. And then as if suddenly realising the harshness of her tone she took a deep breath to settle herself before she continued with her statement. "Natasha knows how much we worry; you hear about so many attacks these days, it's really quite disconcerting."

Hardy noticed that Hilary Spencer was twisting her hands together tightly as she spoke, another indication of her concern.

"Sorry to have to state the obvious," Hardy said, "but I take it you have tried to contact your daughter yourselves?"

This time Spencer jumped in. "Yes, of course, we've been phoning her mobile constantly since about 10.30 p.m."

"It just keeps going to voicemail," Hilary added.

"And her boyfriend?" offered Hardy.

"Ben Green," answered Spencer. From behind he heard his wife *tut* at the mere mention of his name.

Hardy turned to Russell; they had both picked up on the wife's reaction.

The DI looked back at Hilary Spencer. When he caught her eye he smiled warmly, but still managed to convey the message that he was waiting for an explanation for her response.

Hilary flushed.

Spencer immediately picked up on his wife's discomfort, so he decided to come to her aid. "I am afraid to say, Inspector," he began, "that my wife and I have never really approved of our daughter's latest choice of boyfriend."

"I see," replied Hardy, "and can you tell me why that is, exactly?"

"Is that really pertinent with regards to finding our daughter, Inspector?" Hilary shot back. She was obviously losing patience with Hardy's questions and was not concerned with hiding the fact.

"That would depend on your answer, Mrs. Spencer," Hardy responded, keeping his tone even and professional. The couple, but especially the wife, it appeared, clearly did not want to divulge the reason behind her gesture.

Gerald Spencer once again stepped forward to save his wife any further embarrassment. "To be honest, Inspector," he began somewhat hesitantly as he was trying to be careful in his choice of words so as not to appear like a snob, "with Natasha's educational qualifications and promising future both her mother and I were hoping that she would meet someone a little closer to our circle."

Even as the words left his lips, Spencer could hear himself sound exactly the way he had intended to avoid coming across.

By way of elucidating his point, he added, "By that I mean someone who would inspire her to continue with her education."

Hardy nodded as if he fully appreciated the point being made.

After all, he did not need to agree with the man, his job was to find his daughter, not to make moral judgements of his own.

"We'll need all the information you can give us about your daughter's boyfriend," Hardy continued, "name, address, mobile number, etc."

"As my husband mentioned just now his name is Ben Green, Inspector," Hilary chimed in, "we don't know exactly where he lives but it is somewhere on that Hazelwood Estate at the other end of town." Though she was trying valiantly, Hilary could not keep the contempt out of her voice at the mere mention of the Hazelwood.

The estate was well known to the local police.

It was one of those places where the council seemed to offload their biggest problems.

Hardy had been called out there more times than he could remember over the years and it was always too soon before he had to go back again.

"I have his mobile number," said Spencer, taking his handset off the arm off the chair and thumbing through his address book.

Russell took down the number and reread it back to make sure.

"We have been trying his number too, naturally" continued Spencer, "but alas that is also going straight to voicemail."

Suddenly, Hilary Spencer stood up from her seat.

Feeling obliged to follow suit, the man all rose to their feet in unison.

"You have to find her, Inspector!" Hilary announced, as if her words should be treated as a revelation. "You have to find her, now!"

This time her tears came out in floods.

Gerald Spencer turned to comfort his wife.

Hardy felt a familiar pang of empathy that was all too common whenever he found himself in this situation.

Suddenly, it did not matter that their daughter had only been missing a few hours.

Neither did the fact that she was an adult, not a child.

She was still their precious daughter, and he had to do everything in his power to reunite them.

Hardy cleared his throat. "Well I think we have enough information for now," he offered, in his most assuring tone of voice. "If I could just ask if you have a recent picture of Natasha that I could take with me. It will be returned, I'll see to that."

Once they were outside the Harpers' home and the front door had been closed, Hardy and Russell conversed in the street about what to do next.

It was now almost 3 a.m. and the sky was still pitch-black.

"Are you thinking what I'm thinking?" asked Russell before cupping his hands and blowing into them for warmth.

"What?" replied Hardy, with a quizzical look in his eyes.

"Caroline Seymour," replied Russell. "Do you think there's a connection?"

Caroline Seymour was a twenty-four-year-old bank employee who had vanished without trace having been dropped off at the end of town after visiting a music festival.

Her badly mutilated body was discovered a week later by a young couple out jogging.

The forensic examination revealed that she had been brutally raped both vaginally and anally before being quite literally torn apart. Some of her internal organs had been removed, but not by any surgeon's scalpel, whilst others had been chewed on and torn at, leaving behind only remnants of their former state.

It was by far the most depraved result of a violent assault that Hardy had ever witnessed.

Hardy shook his head in reply to Russell's theory. "She was on her own walking back from town in the small hours; this Natasha was with her boyfriend in the early evening and..." Hardy trailed off his sentence.

In his mind he believed that the differences between the two cases were both obvious and numerous, but the more he thought about it now, the more he feared that the perpetrator might be the same man.

Hardy looked back at his sergeant. "Oh god, I hope not!"

CHAPTER SEVEN

The Creeper carried the lifeless corpse of Ben and the unconscious form of Natasha on its broad shoulders, as it meandered its way through the labyrinthine tunnels which led to its lair.

Ben outweighed his girlfriend by a good forty pounds but to the Creeper the uneven weight made no difference, such was the creature's awesome strength and power.

The extra weight of its load did not compel the beast to breathe any harder than it did when it was merely sitting or standing still. In truth, it could carry several hundred pounds of weight hoisted above its massive frame for miles, without even breaking a sweat.

The Creeper acted purely on instinct.

It had only two cravings, both of which it felt compelled to satisfy whenever the occasion arose, each one as important as the other, although one was decidedly more pleasurable, but both were vital for its survival.

One was the need to feed; the other was the necessity to fulfil its more carnal desires.

The Creeper's meat of choice was human flesh!

Over the years whenever it was served with cooked or processed meat the Creeper had always tried to comply, but its internal organs often rejected the offering leaving it feeling nauseous and in pain until it eventually purged itself of the cause.

Afterwards, once the heaving had ceased, it was left with the overwhelming sensation of being ravenous and in desperate need of a fresher more unsullied supply.

It had finally found fulfilment by attacking animals whilst scouring the surrounding area of its previous abode at night.

It had always known that it was a creature best served by the darkness. Bright, or even moderate, sunlight brought on immense pain thundering through the Creeper's brain, like a hammer constantly smashing down against an unyielding anvil. This would often last for hours with the only cure being for it to lie alone in the darkness and wait until the pain finally subsided, and sleep replaced it.

Being a creature of the night suited the Creeper enormously.

Not only did the darkness serve to keep the pain away, it was also a perfect camouflage for its nightly ventures.

The night offered excellent protection against the Creeper being discovered as it prowled the darkened countryside in search of fresh meat.

As enormous as it was, the Creeper had learned the art of blending in with its surroundings whilst on the hunt.

Over time, the Creeper progressed from the smaller, more vulnerable animals which shared its night-time ventures to larger, more fulfilling specimens.

Sheep, lambs, cows, anything available and accessible became the Creeper's meat of choice. Even horses were no match for its incredible speed and agility when homing in for the kill.

But it always knew not to return to the same field or paddock more than once during every full moon cycle.

Fortunately, the area it had resided in was vast and plentiful and the Creeper was able to cover great distances and return home before the sun began to rise on a new day.

Its first taste of human flesh had come about quite by accident.

That had been on its first night out, having escaped from the confines of its prison-like shelter.

The next time it chanced upon such bounty, it was on a rainy night in the middle of winter. The Creeper stumbled upon a man-made refuge consisting of several small wooden structures covered by discarded bits of tarpaulin and plastic.

The men within were huddled together taking shelter from the inclement weather, passing round a half-empty bottle of spirits.

But it was the barking dog protecting its master's territory that first drew the Creeper's attention to the gathering.

The dog was brave, fearlessly raising the alarm while standing its ground to ward off the intruder.

But the poor dog was no match for the Creeper who despatched it with one wave of its mighty arm which sent the hapless animal careering against the nearest tree before falling to the ground in a crumpled heap.

The commotion brought the men from within the makeshift tent outside to investigate.

In their alcohol-induced state none of them could believe their eyes when they saw the Creeper devouring their sentinel.

As the Creeper grew aware of their presence it stopped its feasting and turned to face them. This action ignited the men's survival instincts and they all made a dash for a different part of the forest, leaving behind the bottle, the contents of which up to a moment before, was all that they could think about.

With practised ease the Creeper caught up with each victim in turn and severed each man's carotid artery with a single strike across their throat.

Once it was satisfied that the last man was dead it began to feast on its meat animal, savouring each tasty morsel until it was finally satiated.

As always, the Creeper gathered up the remains of its prey and carried them back to its lair, eradicating any evidence of its feeding frenzy.

It had been instructed to do this and had soon learnt that it was a vital part of its survival to help it remain undetected.

Back at home and sheltered from the outside world the Creeper could rest undisturbed and protected from the daylight. The remains of its latest kill permitted it the luxury of not having to scavenge for several nights until the meat eventually became too old and dry to satisfy the Creepers appetite.

And so, it was from that day on that the Creeper knew that it could not be satiated by mere animal flesh alone, it craved the spicier more flavoursome taste of the man-animal.

Although, it had to accept that such a commodity would not always be available to it, the Creeper had quickly learned how to make any such kill last for longer by mixing the meat with that of the smaller less substantial farm and wild animals it slaughtered.

The first time the Creeper had come upon a female victim, it knew instinctively that this meat-game had more to offer than its male counterparts.

As it held the suitably astonished woman in its mighty grasp it detected an aroma from the body unlike any it had sensed before. The smell was pungent and completely overpowering.

Instead of merely killing and consuming its victim, the Creeper used just enough force to render the woman unconscious before carrying her back to its lair for investigation.

There was something about this victim which intrigued it far more than any previous meat-animal.

Once cocooned in the safety of its den, the Creeper studied the female more closely. The scent from this creature was really quite alluring, and although the Creeper was ravenous and eager to devour its kill, there was another underlying craving which it had felt often during its life which it had never fully managed to explore.

Until now!

Through trial and experimentation, the Creeper quickly managed to discover how best its prey could satisfy its craving.

Even though it did not fully understand the concept of mating in order to reproduce, the Creeper had always known that there was something missing, which if discovered, could potentially bring it ultimate satisfaction. It was akin to an urge it could not relinquish, a thirst it had not yet learned how to quench.

Once it was spent, the Creeper was filled with an exhilaration that it had never experienced before.

Now that it knew the secret of fulfilment on every level it would never stop searching to experience it again.

The female of the species had much more to offer than mere satiation of the Creeper's primal need. It was also the resolution to the other craving it had felt so often before and had fought against for fear that the yearning would ultimately lead to its destruction.

But not anymore!

Tonight, had been an exceptional kill.

Once the Creeper had satisfied its lust it set about using its victim to fulfil its other need.

Since then the routine had always been the same, the male-meat was purely for feeding, the female-meat had another, equally important, role to perform before the Creeper was ready to devour it.

With both Ben and Natasha as victims the Creeper had enough game meat and sport to keep it entertained for several days.

That was, as long as it was not disturbed!

The Creeper hated it when the keeper intervened to remove its game before it was finished with it.

It had no way of communicating its displeasure other than by screeching and roaring its disproval. But the keeper always did his best to calm it down before leaving it alone once again.

Although the Creeper could not understand the words the keeper spoke, it could tell by the kindness and compassion in the keeper's voice that he meant him no harm.

The Creeper had learned to accept that it would only have the time with its victims that the keeper allowed it to have. As a result, it always ensured that it took full advantage of the situation and dealt with the female kills first.

The Creeper lifted Ben's limp corpse off its shoulder and let it slump on one of the stone benches scattered around the room.

It then carried Natasha's body across the room and placed it with care and even a modicum of tenderness onto a mattress of straw in one of the corners which it had prepared in advance for such an occasion.

The Creeper lifted its head and strained to listen for the echoes coming from above its lair. It needed to make sure that the keeper was not already on his way down to ruin its sport.

After a moment it was satisfied that it would be left in peace for at least some time.

Time to enjoy its treasures!

CHAPTER EIGHT

Hardy reversed his car into the only available parking space adjacent to the Hazelwood estate.

He glanced at the clock on the dashboard, it was now 3:45 a.m.

His sergeant had volunteered to return to the station to start preparing the incident board for the morning's briefing, but Hardy had insisted that he go home to his wife and try to catch a few hours' sleep, before the morning shift.

Hardy could see no benefit in both of them ruining their night. In his mind this case was still most probably going to turn out to be of the 'wild goose' variety, but he at least had to show some enthusiasm as the superintendent would expect a full report by the morning.

On his way over Hardy had contacted the station and asked for an address for Natasha's boyfriend on the estate.

Their initial finding was a listing for a Roger Green who, judging by his age, might possibly be Ben's father. Roger Green was on the system because of a fracas he had been involved in a year earlier outside a local pub. It was not an ideal scenario to go knocking on someone's door in the middle of the night only to find out that they were not in fact the person you were looking for. But for now, this was Hardy's best lead.

Hardy locked his car door and studied the numbers on the downstairs flats.

Typically, Roger Green lived at number 33 which was on the third floor, and as Hardy did not fancy the prospect of being stuck in a council-operated lift in the early hours, he elected to take the stairs.

Walking past the communal refuge area Hardy jumped when a huge rat ran out from behind the bins and fled across the courtyard.

The DI checked himself for being so jumpy. Back when he was a young boy, he had lived on a council estate much like the Hazelwood and in those days the sight of a rat was as commonplace as the sun rising in the morning.

The combined stench of urine and vomit assailed his nostrils as he made his ascent to the third floor and served as yet another reminder from his childhood.

As Hardy walked along the corridor towards number thirty-three he could see a light on in one of the flats. He hoped that it might be the one he was looking for because then at least there was already someone awake.

Unfortunately for him, the light was coming from the neighbouring apartment. As Hardy grew closer, he could hear music blaring out from behind the door, someone was evidently enjoying themselves.

Hardy placed his ear against number 33, but it was impossible to ascertain if anyone was moving around because of the music emanating from the next-door flat.

Hardy made a fist and pummelled the door.

He waited a few moments and then as there appeared to be no response he repeated the action.

This time a light came on behind the glass.

After a moment, a gruff, sleepy voice shouted, "'oo the bloody 'ell is it?"

"Police, Mr. Green, would you open up please?"

Another few seconds passed before the voice behind the door shouted back again. "Are you 'avin' a laugh, do you know what fuckin' time it is?"

Hardy sighed. He had not intended to raise his voice because he did not want to attract too much attention. No one was thrilled by the prospect of the police turning up at your door in the middle of the night, and most residents would like to keep the fact as low-key as possible.

Not in this case, however.

"I am fully aware of the time Mr. Green; now, will you please open the door?" Hardy managed to convey the immediacy in his tone without actually having

to shout, which surprised even him. It appeared that after so many years on the job certain skills and tactics automatically took over, even when you were least expecting them to.

Hardy could hear the man grumbling as he fumbled with the key to unlock the door.

After much cursing and frustrated mumblings Hardy finally heard the lock snap open.

Roger Green appeared in the doorway dressed in a torn vest, shorts, and a pair of black socks. He was shorter than Hardy with a bald head and two bushes of black hair behind each ear. He appeared to Hardy as if he had not shaved for several days. The dressing gown he had wrapped around him was no longer able to meet in the middle—Hardy presumed that at some time in the past it must have—due to the circumference of the man's rotund belly, but Green continually kept trying to hold it together while they talked.

Hardy flashed his photo ID. "Mr. Roger Green?"

The man squinted at the badge whilst nodding.

"Detective Inspector Mal Hardy of County CID, may I come inside?"

Green hesitated for a moment before nodding and moving out of Hardy's way to allow him access.

The inside of the flat was very messy and very cluttered.

As he passed the kitchen, Hardy noticed the dirty dishes overflowing from the sink and several others sitting on the counter awaiting their turn in the water.

Green ushered Hardy into the living room. It was sparsely furnished with two sofas, a single armchair, a television unit, and a sideboard.

There were two chocolate-box style pictures hanging on the walls, and on the sideboard, there sat a couple of framed photographs of a young boy, one with him playing on a swing, laughing, and the other on what looked to Hardy to be a merry-go-round horse.

"So, what's all this about?" started Green, not giving Hardy a chance to speak. "I've got to be up for work in a couple of hours an' you need yer wits about yer when yer driving one of 'em big cranes."

Hardy nodded an acknowledgement and then he indicated to the frames on display. "Is that your son, Ben, Mr. Green?" he asked, casually.

Green glanced at the photos as if he had not noticed them there before.

He turned back to Hardy with a quizzical expression on his face. "Yeah, why?" he answered, defensively. "What's the stupid bugger gone an' done now?"

Hardy ignored the question. He was hoping for a quick result without having to go into any long explanations.

"Do you happen to know where your son is now?" asked Hardy, optimistically.

Green scratched his head. "'e's probably in bed, I dunno, 'e's a grown man now. I don't monitor all 'is comings and goings, hang on."

With that, Green left the room and walked down the corridor.

Hardy could hear the man knock on his son's door and call out his name twice before he heard the door open.

A few seconds later Roger Green returned to the living room.

Hardy noticed that the man's expression now showed signs of genuine concern. "Do you know where 'e is?" he demanded. "What's all this about?"

Hardy took a deep breath before he began. "We had a call just after midnight from the parents of a Miss Natasha Spencer, do you know them?"

Green rubbed his chin thoughtfully for a moment before shaking his head.

This was going to be more complicated than Hardy had anticipated. If Green did not even know that his son and Natasha were together then there was little to no chance that he would know where they might be.

Hardy continued. "They are the parents of Natasha Spencer," while he spoke, he watched for any hint of recognition in the man's eyes.

There was none.

"She is the young lady who's apparently going out with your son, Ben."

Now the penny dropped.

Roger Green's eyes suddenly lit up. "Oh, you mean that posh sort 'e's been shaggin'?"

Hardy smiled in spite of himself. "That's her," he confirmed.

"So, what about 'er?" asked Green. "Don't tell me the stupid berk 'as got 'er up the duff?"

Hardy sighed. "If he had, it would hardly be a matter for the police, now would it?"

Green considered the officer's observation and nodded in agreement.

Before he could say anything further, Hardy continued. "Apparently your son and his girlfriend went to the pub last evening and they haven't been seen since."

He waited for his last sentence to take hold before continuing.

"Now as this is the first time that their daughter has not returned home when expected, her parents are understandably concerned."

Green nodded his understanding once more.

"Natasha's parents have been trying to contact both their daughter and your son since eleven o'clock last night without success, which is why they called us in."

"Well they 'ain't 'ere," Green responded, shrugging his shoulders. "You just saw me check."

"And you have no idea where else they might be?" Hardy asked, already expecting a negative response.

"None whatsoever," Green replied, nonchalantly. "I told you, 'e's a grown man now an' 'e does what he wants, so long as 'e pays me 'is rent on time, I leave 'im to it..." Green stopped himself, abruptly.

His face suddenly drained of colour and Hardy was sure that the man had remembered something pertinent which would assist with his investigation.

He waited for Green to continue.

When, after a few moments, he was still silent, Hardy urged him on.

"Mr. Green, were you about to say something?"

Green looked flustered. "Er, what, no, nothing really, it's just..."

Again, he trailed off leaving the conversation hanging.

Hardy was beginning to lose his patience with the man.

He could understand if Green was shaken or traumatized as a result of finding out that his son might be missing, but this was clearly not the case.

Hardy knew that he was trying to hide something, and he needed to find out what it was!

"Mr. Green!" Hardy almost shouted the man's name. "Is there something you wish to tell me?"

Green flushed beetroot.

He made an effort to clear his throat before continuing. "Listen, officer," he began. Hardy knew instinctively that whatever was coming next it would not be good. No civilian ever addressed the police as 'officer' unless they were trying to hide something or fob them off with an excuse.

There was another pause.

"Yes, Mr. Green!" Hardy demanded.

The man flushed again. "It's just that, when I mentioned about Ben paying me rent, 'e doesn't actually pay me rent as such you understand, 'e doesn't earn much where 'e works so it's just a bit of pin-money, I pay the rent on this place meself."

So that was it!

All Green was afraid of was Hardy reporting him to the council. Doubtless he was up to something untoward and had actually let slip to the officer that he was receiving money from his son for staying there.

But Hardy had much bigger fish to fry for now, so Green's little scam could wait.

Hardy stared back at Green who was barely able to hold the inspector's gaze.

Eventually, Hardy asked. "So, in answer to my original

question you have no idea where your son and Miss Spencer might be at this moment?"

Roger Green shook his head whilst still avoiding the officer's eyes.

Hardy took a business card from his wallet and handed it to Green.

"When you hear from your son, please give me a call straightaway, all my contact numbers are on this card."

Green held out his hand and took the card willingly. "Thank you, officer, I will be sure an' do that." Then, almost as an afterthought, he added, "And if you find 'im first, be sure an' give me a call, won't yer?"

Hardy nodded, unconvinced of the man's sudden sincerity.

As they walked towards the front door, the music from the flat next door was still playing. The heavy base reverberated through the walls.

Green indicated with his thumb towards his neighbour's flat. "As yer 'ere," he began, "yer couldn't 'ave a word with them next door about that racket, could yer?"

Hardy turned at the door. "Have you made a complaint to the council, or is this the first incident?"

Green harrumphed. "First, more like a hundred an' first yer mean. Bloody council don't do nothin'. But miss payin' yer rent by a day an' all 'ell breaks loose!"

Hardy nodded his understanding.

As much as he could not reconcile the man's lack of concern at the disappearance of his son, he still believed in the importance of neighbours showing consideration for each other.

"I'll see if there's a uniform patrol in the area," he assured him, "in situations like this a uniform seems to have the desired effect."

They shook hands at the door and Hardy returned to his car.

True to his word, he radioed for the nearest uniform patrol to stop by the estate and have a quiet word with the occupants of number thirty-five.

Hardy checked the time, it was now 4:30 a.m.

He considered driving home for a nap, but then decided that there was little point, as by the time he dropped off it would be time to wake up again.

A shower would help wake him up, and a change of clothes might also be a good idea.

In Hardy's position, especially when in the middle of a murder investigation, there was no guaranteeing when you might get home, so even if you had to grab a few hours' kip at your desk sometimes; it was a good policy to shower whenever the possibility arose.

Once he had showered and changed, Hardy made his way to the station.

Upon entering, he saw that PC Grant was still operating the front desk.

When she saw him arrive, Grant smiled weakly, and Hardy noticed her starting to blush.

He walked over to her. "You still manning the front?" he asked, curiously. "Where's the desk sergeant, then?"

The young PC cleared her throat before replying. "He's just gone down the corridor to speak to one of the uniform officers, Inspector."

Hardy noticed that she could not keep his gaze.

He wondered if the desk sergeant was up to something and had asked Grant to cover for him.

It would not be the first time, if that were the case.

Desk sergeants were notorious for persuading newbies to

cover for them whilst they slipped off for a crafty smoke, or forty winks in one of the cells.

Hardy smiled at the PC. "You make sure that he doesn't take advantage of your good nature," he said, using his most encouraging tone.

As he was about to zap himself into the main office, Grant called him back.

"Sorry again about having to wake you up so early, guv," she offered, apologetically.

Hardy wondered if that was the reason for her reddening face.

It was probably the first time she had had to contact a senior officer in the middle of the night.

"That's all right, Constable," he reassured her, glancing back over his shoulder. "It's all part of the service."

It was too early for the canteen to be open, so Hardy had to make do with a vending machine coffee.

He took his drink back to his desk to begin his report.

CHAPTER NINE

Hardy had just finished the morning briefing when word reached him via a junior officer that Superintendent Carlisle wanted to see him.

He passed his papers over to a very groggy-looking Sergeant Russell and made his way along the corridor to the superintendent's office.

Hardy knocked and waited.

Carlisle had a habit of making his junior officers wait outside his office for at least five seconds before he would answer to their knock. Hardy had heard a rumour from one of his colleagues, that the superintendent had let slip once at a Christmas party, that he purposely kept his officers waiting outside his door, as a way of unnerving them.

Hardy believed the story, but as to whether the reason behind it was to be believed, that was still up for consideration.

As far as Hardy was concerned, Carlisle was just a dickhead!

Finally, Carlisle called out. "Come in."

Hardy waited, on purpose.

He counted, slowly, in his head.

By the time he reached five, Carlisle called out again.

He was louder, this time. "Come in."

Hardy opened the door and stepped inside. "Morning, sir," he announced, cheerfully. Closing the door behind him, he sat down opposite his superior officer.

Carlisle's office was immaculate, right down to the books on his shelf all being in order of height.

There was never more than one file or stack of papers on his desk, at any given time. Hardy often wondered if perhaps that was the real reason he kept junior officers waiting, outside his door. So that he had time to clear his desk, before allowing them entry, by way of demonstrating how an orderly desk should look.

Carlisle had spent ten years in the army, before joining the police force, and his military training had become ingrained in his very being.

No one knew why he had left the armed forces, for a life behind a desk. But the man still exuded all the characteristics of a solider, even after fifteen years on the job.

Speculation was still rife around the station, as to why Carlisle had left the army to begin with. It was obvious to anyone who worked with him that he still considered himself to be a military man, even more so than he did a copper.

But Hardy for one, had never been able to find out the full story, not that he ever lost any sleep over it.

The file on the superintendent's desk today, was one that Hardy recognised immediately, even when he was looking at it from an upside-down position.

The investigation into the murder of Caroline Seymour, had reached a dead end. Every possible enquiry that could be undertaken had been made, and still they were no closer to catching the perpetrator.

The wretched remains of the poor girl's body had been found a week after she disappeared, mutilated beyond recognition. They had only been able to verify that it was in fact her remains, by her dental records.

The post mortem revealed that Caroline Seymour had not left the world without first suffering immense torment and suffering.

The forensic examiner concluded that she had been brutally raped, both vaginally and anally, before being literally torn apart by what appeared to be, a pair of razor-sharp claws, or teeth.

Or even, a combination of both!

In the course of his career, Hardy had often been in the unenviable position of accompanying family members to view the remains of murder victims, or those who died as a result of an accident.

But he knew that as long as he lived, he would never forget the reaction of the Seymour girl's parents, when he escorted them into the police mortuary, to view the dismembered remains of their daughter.

"Caroline Seymour!" Carlisle's sudden announcement shattered through Hardy's train of thought.

He lifted himself up in his chair to correct his posture; by way of showing the superintendent that he had his undivided attention.

"Any progress in that direction, at all?" Carlisle continued, sifting through the file on his desk.

"Nothing new, sir," Hardy responded, keeping his voice steady. "We've followed every lead to date, tracked down all those who saw the young lady leaving the festival. We've taken a statement from the driver who gave her a lift into town."

Carlisle looked up from the file. "Anything there?" he asked, his eyebrows rising, in curiosity.

Hardy shook his head. "No, I'm afraid not," he replied, dejectedly. "The driver was our initial suspect, but once we had interviewed him...." Hardy trailed off.

"What, man?" barked Carlisle, impatiently.

Hardy shrugged his shoulders. "There was no way a man like him, could have done...that, to the poor girl."

Carlisle slammed the file down on his desk, before continuing.

"What the hell is that supposed to mean, Inspector?" he bellowed, obviously not caring whether or not, anyone outside his office could hear him.

If his manner was intended to unsettle Hardy, then it did not have the desired effect.

Hardy stared at his senior officer for a moment, without speaking. His expression formed a combination of curiosity and disbelief.

After a while, the silence seemed to unnerve Carlisle and he found that he could no longer hold Hardy's gaze.

The superintendent began opening and slamming shut the drawers of his desk. It was obvious to Hardy that the man was not actually looking for anything inside them, and that he just needed to do something, for effect.

Finally, Hardy decided to put his superior out of his misery, a situation which he himself had created, and continue with his report.

"We interviewed the driver and his family, they verified that he returned home at 11:30 p.m. exactly ten minutes after he was seen dropping Caroline Seymour off at the end of town."

Carlisle had by now retained his composure. His elbows were planted firmly on his desk with his hands joined together to form a triangle, and he was now looking up at Hardy over the top of his linked fingers.

"Did you have his car checked for forensics?" Carlisle enquired his voice calm and in control, once again.

Hardy shook his head. "There was no need to, sir." He noticed Carlisle's expression harden, immediately.

The senior office opened his mouth to speak, and then he closed it again without making a comment.

Hardy continued, before Carlisle had a chance to revaluate his decision.

"The driver was a retired librarian in his late sixties. Caroline Seymour was a fit, young, athletic female who, according to her friends, was more than capable of taking care of herself. If anything, she would have probably knocked him for six if he tried anything on."

Carlisle spread his hands before him. "But he could have managed to overcome her, somehow, perhaps he used chloroform, did you consider that?" The superintendent appeared very satisfied with his new theory.

Hardy kept his cool, although he could feel his temperature rising. "And how and where would he then have managed to hide her body? He certainly didn't have it with him when he arrived home ten minutes later."

Carlisle bristled, evidently unwilling to relinquish what he believed to be a crucial line of investigation. "He may have dumped her in the boot of his car, once he had drugged her."

The DI had to fight the urge to lean across the desk and slap the smug expression off his superior's face.

Instead, he took a deep breath, and continued as if the look had escaped his notice. "There is no way on god's green earth that the old boy could have so much as dragged her across the ground, let alone lifted her and carried her to the boot of his car."

Carlisle opened his mouth again, but before he managed to let any words escape, Hardy jumped straight back in.

"And besides, our witness saw Caroline get out of his car, and then watched him drive off."

This seemed to do the trick.

The superintendent was lost in thought again for a moment.

After a moment, he asked. "Is there nothing from forensics?"

Hardy paused, briefly, before replying. "There was nothing conclusive, at least nothing that we can use."

Carlisle immediately picked up on the uncertainty in Hardy's voice.

"What do you mean, exactly?" he asked, his curiosity pricked.

Hardy sighed. "Well, the pathologist picked up several different samples of DNA from the victim. Bearing in mind that she had just come from a music festival, where she must have come into contact with hundreds, if not thousands of people."

"And so, what?" ventured Carlisle.

"Well," continued Hardy, trying not to sound too unsure of himself. "One of the samples which she removed from the corpse, she is having trouble identifying."

"How do you mean?"

"She suspects that it might be animal DNA, but she has not been able so far to distinguish the sub-species."

"How's that?" asked Carlisle, suspiciously. "Surely whatever left the specimen must be somewhere on the database?"

"Apparently not." Hardy shrugged. "She has sent it away to a lab in London to see if they can distinguish where, or what, it came from."

The senior officer scratched his chin, aimlessly, as he digested this new information.

Hardy waited a moment before continuing. "Mind you, the

poor girl's body was left out in the open, so any number of animals might have come along to explore her remains, before she was found."

Just at that moment the phone on Carlisle's desk came to life.

The senior officer snatched up the receiver before the second ring.

"Carlisle!" he snapped, into the mouthpiece.

Hardy sat back and waited whilst his superintendent took his call. He knew better than to excuse himself before he was dismissed. Other colleagues had made that mistake, much to their own chagrin once Carlisle had chewed them out for it afterwards.

Even from this distance Hardy could just make out that the caller was shouting, from the other end of the line.

He could not make out any actual words, but the overall mannerism seemed to border on the aggressive.

Carlisle, for his part, acted extremely graciously, offering murmurs of comfort and sympathy, using tones which Hardy had never heard escape the man's lips before today.

When the call finally finished, Carlisle replaced the receiver and glared across the desk at his subordinate.

After several deep breaths, he spoke. "Do you know who that was?" he asked, almost through gritted teeth.

Hardy shook his head, innocently.

From his senior officer's mannerism, he somehow suspected that the venom aimed at him from whoever was on the other end of the phone, was about to be deflected in his direction.

"That was Gerald Spencer," continued Carlisle, pointing at the handset. "He wanted to know why he hasn't received an update yet on the whereabouts of his missing daughter."

Before Hardy could open his mouth to speak, Carlisle stood up, abruptly. As he rose, the backs of his knees smacked the edge of his seat with such force; that it propelled his chair backwards on its castors, until it struck the wooden plinth beneath the window, at the back of his office.

The senior officer, ignoring the noise of the chair's collision, clasped his hands behind his back and proceeded to walk around the office, purposely avoiding Hardy's gaze.

Hardy sat still, refusing to turn in his seat to follow his superior's progress.

Once Carlisle reached the far end of the room, he studied the plaques and framed certificates on the wall for a moment before speaking again.

Hardy heard Carlisle turn on his heels, behind him, but he still refused to pander to the man's ego by shuffling around to face him.

Instead, he allowed his superior to speak to the back of his head.

"Did I mention to you that Gerald Spencer is a friend of mine?" he began. His voice appeared much calmer than Hardy had anticipated.

Hardy cleared his throat. "I believe someone mentioned that you and he played golf together," he replied, very matter-of-factly.

From behind, Hardy could hear Carlisle breathing deeply. It sounded as if the man was forcing the air out through his nose, instead of his mouth.

"Did they, indeed?" Carlisle finally responded. "And did that person also mention that Mr. Spencer is also a Queens Counsel? And that he sits on several boards, including the police standards and behavioural one?"

"No, I don't believe that they did," Hardy's response came out far more nonplussed than he had intended. But by now he was getting a little tired of Carlisle's bullying tactics.

Hardy was tired and hungry, and he had far better things to

be doing right now than sitting in the superintendent's office, listening to twaddle.

Carlisle was clearly trying to unnerve Hardy as part of some kind of power struggle he felt that he needed to win. But the DI was not someone who could be easily intimidated. His job was hard enough at the best of times, and he had little respect for senior officers who had never been on the beat.

At least those who had, had some idea of what it was like on the front line.

They were the ones who viewed situations like this through experienced eyes.

They also tended to be the ones who earned the respect of their junior officers. Those, like Carlisle, who seemed to demand it merely because of their rank,

were always the ones who tended to be a little less well thought of by everyone else in their team.

Carlisle circled back around his desk without speaking.

In his mind he wanted his last statement to hang in the air, long enough for the weight of it to take hold in Hardy's mind.

Hardy, on the other hand, just wanted his superior officer to hurry up and let him get back to his job. He still had a million things he needed to, not least of all was to get something to eat from the canteen before they finished serving breakfast.

Carlisle retrieved his chair from near the window, where it had stayed since his abrupt ascension.

Once he was seated, the superintendent placed his head in his hands and rubbed his eyes, vigorously, as if he were trying to erase an unpleasant image which refused to go.

Eventually, he looked up at Hardy. "Don't you realise that Mr. Spencer could make life very difficult for me, and in turn you, if we do not find his daughter pronto?"

Hardy could feel his exasperation starting to get the better of him.

Even so, he did his best to keep the sarcasm out of his tone.

"She's only been missing since last night, since which time we have completed our initial interviews, scanned her photograph throughout the country, put out a missing person's report on both of them, and tried to triangulate the whereabouts of both of their mobile phones." Hardy looked Carlisle directly in the eyes and leaned forward in his chair. "Now, please tell me what else we can possibly do, that we are not already doing?"

Carlisle's face was growing increasingly redder whilst Hardy was speaking.

He reminded Hardy of a pressure cooker about to explode.

It was obvious that the senior officer was struggling to find an answer that warranted being put forward.

But there was also no way that he was going to allow his junior officer to have the last word.

Finally, a look of euphoria spread across Carlisle's face. "You could start a search for them!" he announced, unable to keep the exhilaration out of his tone.

Hardy seriously considered leaving the conversation right there.

His senior officer looked so pleased with himself that he actually felt bad for having to burst his enthusiastic bubble.

But in the end, Hardy decided that it would be worth it.

"I've already instigated a search; I've just come from the briefing." He announced, somewhat smugly. "As soon as I leave here, I'm going to join them."

Hardy leaned back in his chair, smiling to himself whilst managing to maintain a stone-faced expression.

He knew that whatever the super had to say now would just be for the sake of him saving face.

CHAPTER TEN

When Natasha first opened her eyes, it took a while to adjust to the dimness of her surroundings.

Her memory of what had happened to her prior to this moment was temporarily screened off in her psyche, in the same way that a childhood torment might be banished for the purpose of self-preservation.

As she blinked and attempted to focus on the unfamiliar environment, her mind was unable to fathom why it was that she was not in her own bed, surrounded by her countless possessions, and embraced by the morning sun, which on bright mornings shone in directly through her bedroom window.

This place was not only dank and poorly lit, but there was a strange sour-sweet odour which was starting to assail her nostrils that reminded her of a combination of bad body odour, urine, and excrement.

Without realising it, Natasha took in a large lungful of the foul-smelling air. She immediately felt as if she were about to gag, and so she thrust her hand to her mouth in an attempt to staunch any potential flow.

She found it hard to swallow and the effort made her feel even worse.

The acrid taste of bile was already sitting at the back of her throat, and at first, she genuinely believed that she would not be able to stop herself from vomiting.

Since her sixth birthday party when she had been violently ill as a result of overindulging in too much cake and ice cream, Natasha had always had an irrational fear of repeating the experience.

That was the main reason why she was always very careful about what she ate, and why she refused to consume more alcohol than she was comfortable with, or ever experimented with any kind of recreational drugs.

Natasha kept her hand planted firmly across her mouth as she waited for the feeling to pass.

When eventually it did, she tried to breathe slowly through her nose so as not to trigger another attack of nausea.

She waited until the sensation had passed before she tried to move.

Natasha could feel the roughness of hessian fabric beneath her. She reached down and rubbed the surface with her hands. She surmised that she was sitting on some old sacking, and with further investigation she realised that the thin fabric was covering a large clump of straw which had been loosely strewn on the concrete floor below.

As she pushed herself up to a kneeling position, Natasha could feel the stiffness in her joints impeding her movement. She had obviously fallen asleep at an awkward angle, and she must have stayed like that throughout her slumber.

Added to that fact, her bedding, such as it was, provided virtually no lumber support, and there was dampness in the air which, she decided, had doubtless permeated her joints as she slept.

Then it occurred to her that she had no way of knowing how long she had been asleep.

Still on her knees, Natasha felt around herself trying to locate her mobile phone. She doubted that she would have a signal as she was obviously somewhere underground. But she hoped that at least the phone would provide some light, as well as being able to tell her the time.

It was whilst she was searching that it suddenly dawned on her that her clothes were in disarray.

As she attempted to settle herself, she realised that her dress was in tatters, and that large clumps of the fabric seemed to be missing from it, altogether.

Confused, and more than a little concerned, Natasha rose to her feet.

As she pushed herself up from the floor to reach her full height, the top of her head smacked against the corner of the stone arch above her.

Natasha screamed out in shock and pain.

She could hear her cry reverberate and echo all around her.

She wrapped her hands around her head and held it tightly, waiting for the pain to subside.

The initial shock had scared her more than the actual contact with the stone frame, and after rubbing her head vigorously for a moment she could feel the pain starting to ebb away.

She moved forward keeping one hand above her so that she could feel when she was no longer directly below the arch.

Once she could no longer feel the stone, Natasha stood up, slowly.

She tried once more to focus on her surroundings, but the area was still too dark for her to discern where she might be.

She wanted desperately to call out for help. But self-preservation prevented her from raising the alarm too soon. First, she decided, she needed to try and ascertain where she might be.

She stood there for a moment trying to concentrate on any sound which might give her an indication of her location.

But there was only silence.

Natasha strained once more to see through the gloom, but beyond the shadows there was nothing but darkness.

Desperate though she was to try and find her way out of her predicament, Natasha was still wary of moving around in case she crashed into another wall or low ceiling. Or worse still, she was afraid that she might plunge down an open well or pit.

She bent down and stared at the floor, but even at such a short distance she could not properly make out how safe the path before her was.

Frustrated by her lack of viable options, Natasha decided to focus once more on trying to locate her phone.

Upon investigation, she quickly realised the full extent of the damage which had been inflicted on her clothing.

Her boots still seemed intact, but the stockings she wore beneath them had been ripped to pieces, especially at the top around the thigh area, and even her knickers now barely consisted of two shreds of material dangling from the waistband.

Instinctively, Natasha closed her legs together.

She examined the top half of her dress and discovered that it too had been torn asunder, so that it now resembled nothing more than a few meagre strands of fabric held together by a few loose threads.

The clasp on one of her bra straps had also come away, and the limp band was now dangling in front of her.

Natasha tried in vain to reattach some of the shredded fabric together, but she soon realised that it was a fruitless task.

The air around her was cold and dank, and she could feel the dampness seeping into her bones.

Her mind raced as she tried desperately to think how she

could have possibly ended up where she was, and in such a compromising condition.

Through her hazy memory Natasha remembered being at home for Sunday lunch, and then leaving with Ben to go for a drink.

In her mind's eye she pictured them walking hand in hand through the park, and then the two of them diving into the bushes for a quickie.

But after that, it was all a blank.

A sudden horrendous thought crashed through her mind.

Did Ben rape her?

Was that why her clothes were all tattered and torn?

But that did not make any sense!

Why would Ben need to force her when she was giving herself over to him willingly?

Not to mention the fact that it was not in his nature to be vicious in the first place. In fact, Natasha could not even think of an occasion when she had seen Ben lose his temper.

The thought of him attacking her was just plain ludicrous!

But why then did she feel as if she had been violated?

Why were her clothes in tatters?

And now that she came to think of it, why was there a sore-ness throbbing from between her legs?

The more that she thought about it, the worse she felt, but she had to convince herself first that it was not just psychological, a knock-on effect from thinking that she might have been attacked.

Natasha stood there for a moment and tried to concentrate on the pain.

There was definitely something there, and it reminded her of the time when she lost her virginity to Dave Gordon, her childhood sweetheart.

What a mistake that had been!

She had only been sixteen at the time, and although he had tried to be as tender and caring as he could, it was Dave's first time as well and his priority, once they started, seemed to be a simple matter of getting inside her at any cost.

She could still remember screaming at him because it was hurting so much, but he was intent on ejaculating, and kept begging her to let him finish as he thrust deeper and deeper inside her.

That was the first and last time with him!

But Natasha could still remember the raw ache the union left her with for the next couple of days, and even after the worst of it had healed, she was still sore down there for what seemed, at the time, to be an eternity.

And that was exactly how she felt now!

Gingerly, Natasha slipped her hand down between her legs.

The moment her fingers made contact with her soft, moist cleft she recoiled in agony. It was worse than she had feared. The merest touch from her gentle fingers made her feel as if she was using sandpaper to wipe herself with.

Natasha tried desperately not to scream out in pain but was helpless to prevent a high-pitched whine from escaping her mouth.

She held herself upright, her legs clasped firmly together. But even the modest friction caused by her thighs rubbing together, brought with it a burning sensation which spread rapidly up through her vagina.

Natasha held her hands out against the cold stone arch to support herself.

She waited patiently for the pain within her to start to subside.

Eventually, it did. But it was quickly replaced by a dull

throbbing ache which seemed to linger without any intention of eradicating itself in the near future.

Natasha began to sob, quietly. Not merely as a result of the pain she had just experienced, but also due to the circumstance she was in.

Where on earth was she?

And how did she get here?

In the cavernous surroundings, the sound of her sobs echoed around her.

She tried desperately to control them. Regardless of where she was at the moment, Natasha felt it prudent not to let on that she was awake.

She stuffed her fist into the entrance of her mouth to try and stifle her cries.

From somewhere inside her subconscious, the events from before started to seep through her psychological defence shield.

She remembered being with Ben in the bushes. They were making love. She could feel him inside her. His arms around her, holding her shoulders for purchase as he thrust deeply within her. His hands slid down over her arms, cupped her breasts and began to massage and fondle them, through her blouse.

Natasha imagined herself starting to raise her knees, crossing her ankles behind Ben's lower back as she could feel the explosion inside her start to erupt.

Then all of a sudden, Ben was gone!

At first, Natasha could not understand what was going on. She still had her eyes closed in anticipation of the ecstasy which she was about to unleash.

Ben had withdrawn himself abruptly, almost violently.

Why?

She was sure that Ben too, was about to reach orgasm. So why would he suddenly withdraw himself in such a fashion.

Through the haziness of her memory, Natasha opened her eyes.

The creature she saw descend upon her in Ben's place had caused her capacity for reason to rebel.

It was at that moment that her subconscious had shut down, completely.

Mercifully!

Natasha shuddered at the memory.

Her protective barrier was now well and truly shattered. The pieces were too small and countless to ever be fitted back together.

Here in this immense cavern, where the only sound that she could hear was that of her own heartbeat. Where the darkness was so profound that it was impossible to see her hand when it was held at arm's length, Natasha felt as if she was trapped in some sort of deprivation tank.

Alone with her fears!

Alone with the vague memory of what had befallen her!

Natasha could feel her grip on sanity slipping away, until it was firmly, and finally, out of reach!

CHAPTER ELEVEN

K elly had stayed indoors for the whole day, refusing to go outside and show the world what her husband had done to her the previous afternoon.

She phoned her work that morning and made an excuse about feeling poorly, which she suspected that, her boss only part-believed.

Other than being beaten to a pulp, the rest of her Sunday panned out exactly as her friend Carol had surmised. Jack returned from the pub half-cut, demanding his lunch, which Kelly had prepared for him in spite of what he had done to her earlier.

Once he had eaten, Jack fell asleep on the couch watching football, whilst Kelly cleaned up the flat. When he woke up at about 5pm, it was off back down the pub for the rest of the night, leaving Kelly at home, alone.

For once, Kelly did not mind being abandoned.

There was no way that she was going to show her face down the pub, although she knew that Jack would not care one jot, if she did. Kelly sometimes thought that the bruises he gave her were like some twisted badge of honour to him.

It was almost as if he took pride in showing her off to the world, after he had given her a good battering.

But Kelly had decided after the last occasion Jack paraded her bruises in front of his mates that she was not going to give him the satisfaction, ever again.

Once Jack had left for work, Kelly spent the first half of the day curled up under the duvet, watching television.

Eventually, she grew bored with talk-shows and decided to spend the rest of the day in a more industrious mode. So, she cleaned the entire flat from top to bottom. She completed two full loads of washing and ironed all the clothes they had left out since the last wash, before putting them neatly away in the wardrobes and chest of drawers.

By 6 p.m. Kelly was completely shattered.

Being a Monday, she knew that Jack would not return home until closing time, as it was his weekly darts night. At least it meant that she did not have to make dinner for him, as he would eat at the pub.

Kelly considered the options for her own dinner. There was nothing specific in the freezer which took her fancy, so for now, she just grabbed a bag of crisps and collapsed back in front of the television.

Halfway through her salty snack, Kelly developed a sudden hankering for a glass of wine.

After her days labour, she felt that she deserved something to lift her spirits.

Other than the eight cans of strong bitter in the sideboard, which Jack made a point of insisting that Kelly replenished whenever he decided to stay in for the night instead of going down the pub, there was usually an array of spirits and even the odd liqueur.

But alas, there was no wine.

Kelly went back into the kitchen and rummaged through the fridge, just in case there was any of the Chardonnay left that her friend Mel had brought over, when they had a girls' night in.

But it was gone!

Kelly presumed that Jack must have polished it off at some point, because she was sure that there was at least half a bottle left over.

Kelly sighed as she let the fridge door swing shut.

She gazed up at the kitchen window. Although it was still early, but it was already dark outside, and she wondered what the chances were of her making it to the local off-licence and back home again, without being seen by anyone she knew.

Kelly's need for a drink was fast becoming more of a craving, so she decided that there was no possibility of her foregoing her treat and leaving it for another night.

She took herself into the bedroom and switched on the side lamp by the dressing table.

Her bruises raged back at her from the mirror.

She had not bothered to check her appearance since first thing that morning, and as most of the initial pain had by now toned down to a dull ache, Kelly was not prepared for the horror of her reflection.

She stared at herself for a while as she contemplated her next move.

The rim under one of her eyes had turned a dark purple, almost black, and there was a matching bruise on her opposite cheek, as well as a sizeable lump on the left-hand side of her bottom lip, where Jack had caught her with his ring the previous day.

Kelly let out a deep sigh.

Part of her wanted to curl up in a ball and cry. But from

somewhere within her reserve, Kelly could feel anger welling, and it overtook her need for tears and self-pity, and left her feeling stronger, and more capable of dealing with her present situation.

With a stubbornness born of rage, Kelly began applying make-up to cover up the worst of her battle scars.

Once she was ready to face the outside world, Kelly slipped a scarf around her neck and lifted the fabric so that it also part-covered her mouth and chin.

Her long brunette hair, which she had kept tied back in a ponytail all day, was left to flow around her face and shoulders, affording her another shield behind which she could hide her embarrassment.

The early evening air was cold and crisp, but at least it had stayed dry, so there was no moisture in the atmosphere.

Kelly walked across the courtyard which led to the small parade of shops on the other side of the estate.

She managed to reach the off-licence without encountering anyone she knew. Some of those whom she passed in the street were familiar to her, but no one she knew well enough to engage with, so for that she was grateful.

Once she reached her destination, Kelly stood outside for a moment and glanced through the window to see if there might be anyone inside she recognised. But the coast was clear.

As she entered the shop, Kelly glanced over at the Asian man behind the counter, but he appeared to be too engrossed in his newspaper to acknowledge her presence.

Kelly made her way to the shelves of wine at the far end of the shop.

As she scanned the cardboard signs displaying the latest deals and bargains on offer, she was unaware of the main door to the shop opening and closing, behind her.

Lost in thought, it was not until a familiar voice behind her announced, "I'd go for the three for a tenner on the Merlot, if I were you," that she realised that someone had crept up behind her.

Taken by surprise, Kelly spun around, only to see Carol standing behind her trying to control her laughter.

Once the initial shock had passed, Kelly too began to laugh at the sight of her friend.

She slapped Carol playfully on the arm. "You scared the shit out of me, you bitch!" she scolded, smiling broadly.

Carol laughed even louder at Kelly's statement. "Bitch, well that's charming, I must say."

Without saying another word, Kelly stepped forward and threw her arms around her friend, and hugged her, tightly.

Although somewhat taken aback, Carol reciprocated.

The two held onto each other for a full minute before Kelly finally pulled away.

Once they were apart, Carol noticed the state of her friend's battered features.

Realising that she had momentarily dropped her guard, Kelly tried to look down so that her friend could not see the worst of her injuries.

But Carol was having none of it. She reached out and gently placed her hand beneath Kelly's chin, and although there was a token resistance, she managed to lift her friend's face up towards the light so that she could view the full extent of her latest beating.

Carol held her other hand to her mouth to stop a gasp from escaping.

Their eyes met for a moment, before Kelly looked away.

"It's not as bad as it looks," she stammered, unconvincingly.

"It's every bit as bad as it looks!" Carol assured her. "You looked bad enough yesterday lunchtime when I saw you, but that was nothing compared to this."

Although she did not mean to sound angry, Carol could not keep the livid undertone out of her voice.

But she was not cross with Kelly, even though there were occasions, such as this, when she could cheerfully grab her by the shoulders and try to shake some sense into her.

No, Carol's rage was firmly aimed at Jack.

Even so, she quickly realised that her manner must have made it seem to Kelly as if she was indeed mad at her, because no sooner had she spoken than her friend started to cry.

Carol pulled Kelly towards her and held her closely.

She looked over her friend's shoulder to make sure that no one else had come into the shop. The last thing she wanted was to cause Kelly any more embarrassment, although at this moment, it did not seem as if her friend cared about any witnesses.

The assistant behind the till was still reading his newspaper, and he did not even glance up when Kelly released a huge pitiful sob.

Carol held her friend in a comforting embrace until her weeping subsided.

Taking a clean handful of tissues from her bag, she handed them to Kelly for her to wipe her eyes and blow her nose.

Kelly could not help feeling embarrassed by the fact that she had broken down in front of her friend. She could feel the warm rush of embarrassment flooding to her cheeks, but the time for hiding her face was long past. Carol had already witnessed her breakdown, and seen her bruises in all their glory, so by comparison the redness of her cheeks hardly mattered.

Kelly's pitiful state only served to further enrage Carol, and her contempt for Kelly's husband was starting to reach a new height.

She had bitten her tongue for long enough, now the time for action had well and truly arrived.

Carol held her friend's face between her hands and looked into her tear-stained eyes. "Right then, my girl," she announced, "I think it's high time I had a word with that useless lump you call a husband!"

Carol's voice was firm, but she still managed to convey some much-needed empathy for her friend, as she was conscious of how fragile Kelly appeared to be at the moment.

Nevertheless, as she spoke, she noticed that Kelly's eyes took on a look of sheer horror and trepidation.

Kelly did not speak. She was still afraid that another bout of tears might be unleashed if she tried.

Instead, she just shook her head slowly from side to side.

"Now look," insisted Carol, raising her index finger, and pointing it at her friend for emphasis, "you cannot let him keep treating you like this, you're supposed to be his wife, not his bleedin' punch bag."

"No, please," Kelly stammered, "it'll only make things worse, it was my own fault really, I made him angry."

"Stop right there!" Carol raised her voice louder than she had intended, but she found herself caught up in the moment.

The assistant behind the counter looked up from his paper, finally aware that something was going on in his shop.

Carol caught his eye and smiled back, reassuringly.

It was enough to convince the man that everything was alright, and he quickly returned his attention to his paper.

Carol turned back to her friend.

This time she made a point of keeping her voice low, so that only Kelly could hear her. "I don't ever want to hear you say that again, understand?" She waited for Kelly to nod, before continuing. "None of this is your fault, and you must never think otherwise, no one has the right to do this to you, especially not the man who is supposed to love you."

Carol's words made perfect sense to Kelly, so she nodded her understanding. But, deep down, she wondered if her acquiescence was merely a ruse to keep the peace, as opposed to a promise to stop allowing Jack to take out his temper on her whenever he felt like it.

Either way, it had the desired effect, in that Carol seemed to calm down, quite noticeably.

Kelly instinctively felt relieved that she had managed to take some of the wind out of her friend's sails. The last thing she needed was for Carol to have a set-to with Jack, by storming into their flat with both guns blazing.

It was then that she remembered that Jack would not be home until much later.

That would at least give her some time to calm her friend down.

She appreciated the fact that Carol was only standing up for her, and, deep down, she loved her for it, but Kelly knew that such a confrontation could only end badly, most of all, for her!

Even if Carol unloaded on Jack, and by some miracle he pretended to change, Kelly knew that the moment Carol walked out the door that she would be on the receiving end of Jack's wrath.

And what then?

Would Jack keep her a prisoner in the flat whenever she had a new bruise in order to prevent Carol from seeing her?

Would the frequency and the ferocity of the beatings increase?

Whatever the outcome, Kelly knew that she would be on the receiving end one way or the other, and regardless of what happened, it would not be a pleasant experience, for her.

"Tell you what," Carol burst through Kelly's train of thought. Reaching out, Carol grabbed three bottles of wine from the special offer shelf and placed two of them in Kelly's hands, the third she held onto herself. "You're coming with me back to my place, and we're going to have a girl's night in, no arguments!"

Kelly mulled over the idea for a moment, and then she nodded, gratefully.

"That-a-girl," replied Carol, seeming much calmer and more relaxed since her momentary outburst.

They both carried their bottles over to the counter.

As Kelly pulled out her purse, Carol grabbed her hand. "No, this is on me, kiddo," she explained. Her tone was soft, but still with enough authority to convey to her friend that she would not accept no for an answer.

Having paid for their drinks, the two women left the shop and headed back towards their estate.

As they reached the bottom of the staircase, Carol placed her hand gently on Kelly's forearm. "Now, let's agree," she began, looking Kelly directly in the eyes, "if that no good old man of yours sticks his head out and asks what's going on, I do all the talking."

Kelly bit her bottom lip.

She felt guilty for not telling Carol that Jack was out for the evening, but decided that under the circumstances, ignorance was bliss, so she just nodded her acceptance and smiled.

CHAPTER TWELVE

The Creeper lurched through the winding tunnels and
archways of its darkened labyrinthine enclave.

It had feasted well on the carcass of one of his earlier
victims, and afterwards it had slept for several hours.

The visions and ghoulish nightmares which invaded the
Creeper's dreams would be horrific to most people, but to the
Creeper, they were merely what it expected, and it had grown
used to them over the years.

In fact, because it had nothing else to compare them to, it
was no longer disturbed or traumatised by them, as it had been
during its early years.

From as far back as the Creeper could remember its world
had been a dark and sinister place. A combination of shadows
and gloomy surroundings, from which it was never allowed to
venture out to explore the wonders the rest of the world took
for granted.

As an infant, the Creeper was kept under lock and key in a
dungeon-like room, much smaller than the one it was now
allowed to exist in.

The room had no windows, not even a couple of cracks in the structure through which the slightest shaft of sunlight could penetrate. Nothing in fact, that could act as a portal to the outside world, and therefore, nothing which would assist to dispel the dismal encasement of its prison.

When frustration and yearning for another to comfort it would lead to tears and wailing, no one would come to offer kind words of comfort, or to hold it close and soothe its heartache.

Its first keeper in those early years had been an old woman, who ventured down once a day to leave it a dish of raw meat, which it would devour ravenously while the old woman went about the task of clearing up after it.

But she would not stay.

Never once did she linger in its cell for longer than it took her to clear away his mess and replace his water.

The Creeper often heard the old woman speak to herself as she set about her task, but it could not emulate the sounds she made, try as it might.

The only noise which would leave his mouth would at best be described as a combination of soft moans and gurgles. So instead, the Creeper tried to communicate with its hands and body language. But the old woman refused to take notice of its pleadings, or just chose to ignore them.

Either way, the end result was the same. The Creeper would be left alone again with only itself for company, until it was time for its next feed.

That was how it spent the early years of its life.

Alone, unwanted, unloved, and above all else, afraid.

But the fear it suffered from was not that of ordinary mortal human beings.

It did not have any concept of death to be afraid of. Nor did it comprehend the idea of physical pain and suffering.

Its fear grew from within. It possessed a deep yearning for the chance to interact with others of its kind. To feel the touch of a kindred spirit and to hear the comforting vibration of another's heartbeat close to its ear.

But as time passed, the Creeper came to accept that such things were never going to be available to it.

Instead it continued to dwell in darkness, with no sense of hope or rescue.

On one particularly cold winter's night, the Creeper was more restless than usual.

When its keeper brought down its food, it waited until she was busy dealing with his business and had her back to him, it looked up and noticed a small crack of light seeping in under the door from which she had entered his cell.

This in itself was unusual, because generally the woman took great pains to ensure that the door was locked behind her before she made her way down the stairs to his level.

On this occasion however, she must have forgotten to slide the bolt all the way home when she turned the key.

The Creeper grew transfixed by the slant of light slicing through the darkness.

It called out to him like a siren from the rocks, urging him to drop everything and run to it.

Before the old woman had a chance to react, the Creeper took the stairs three at a time and flung open the door at the top.

The full impact of the light dazzled the Creeper, and it staggered back from the initial shock, almost losing its balance and falling back down the stairs into its pit.

But, fortunately for him, he managed to regain his balance just in time, and he ran through the door shielding his eyes behind his arm as he crashed into tables and chairs, and any other furniture which blocked his path.

From behind, the Creeper could hear the old woman

shouting and cursing, demanding that it stop in its tracks and return to its den.

But the Creeper knew instinctively that this might be the only chance it would ever have of discovering what else lay beyond its prison walls.

Before the old woman had even managed to climb to the top of the basement stairs, the Creeper had found the door which led to the courtyard, outside the house.

Once outside and away from the harsh glare of the light, the Creeper managed to uncover its eyes and take in the wonder and beauty of its surroundings.

A full moon hung lazily in the night sky, surrounded by clusters of bright, twinkling stars.

The Creeper stood there in awe for a moment, desperately trying to drink in all the new sights and sounds which emanated from the forest around it.

After a few moments it could hear the cursing and shouting coming from the old woman as she made her way up out of the cellar. It knew then that it had to make a choice, either to run or to return to the misery and solitude of its lonely existence.

Deciding that this might be its only chance of ever escaping, the Creeper lurched forward into the darkened countryside. It never once looked back, even when it could hear the wretched screams from the old woman filling the night air.

Filled with a new exuberance born of liberty and wonder, it ploughed on through the night, relishing each new sight, sound and smell that filled its senses, until the caterwauling cries of the crone could no longer be heard.

Surrounded by dense foliage, the Creeper instinctively knew how to camouflage itself and lie in wait for some unwitting prey to pass.

It dined on several creatures of the forest, virtually spoilt for choice by all the wondrous variety and diversity of meat-animal which nature had to offer.

Although not completely satiated, once it had eaten enough to stave off the hunger pangs, the Creeper meandered through the night in search of adventure, relishing the clean scented air which filled its lungs with a gentle sweetness which could not compare to the dank fetid air it had grown accustomed to during its incarceration.

On through the forest it roamed until finally it came upon a clearing and beyond that, a lake.

The Creeper was eager to investigate this new-found source, but just as it was about to venture out from the relative safety of the cover the surrounding trees afforded it, it heard the sound of laughter and shouting coming from somewhere over to its right.

On impulse, the Creeper stopped in its tracks and hunched down to blend in among the shadows.

The moon above was full and cast a long shadow across the lake and the open land leading up to it.

It waited patiently, keeping its breathing steady and low as it tried to focus through the branches to see where the raucous laughter and merriment was coming from.

Through the noise it could just about distinguish the sound of wood snapping and popping as yellow and blue flames licked against them, hungrily.

As its eyes focused on the area where the campfire was burning, the Creeper was just about able to make out the forms of the three men sitting around it.

One of them was mixing something in a large metal pan which was hanging from a horizontal pole suspended between two long spikes secured in the ground.

The Creeper sniffed at the air. The aroma of whatever was

being cooked immediately permeated its nostrils, and it could feel its belly start to grumble in anticipation.

Cautiously, the Creeper edged forward, testing the support of the loose branches and twigs beneath its feet, mindful of not announcing its presence to the three men.

As it drew closer it could see that the men were all drinking from individual bottles containing some sort of brown liquid. They were all totally oblivious to the Creeper's approach, but still it tried to keep itself hidden from their sight, not sure of how its arrival would be received.

Close enough now so that it could see everything illuminated by the fire's glow, the Creeper sunk down on its haunches to keep itself hidden whilst it observed the men's behaviour before deciding how best to proceed.

When the scent of whatever was cooking in the pot reached its nostrils, the Creeper could not prevent its belly from growling, loudly.

One of the men stopped drinking and looked up. "'ere, what was that?" he asked, turning around in his seat, and scanning the darkness.

"What's what?" replied one of his companions, rising to his feet in order to obtain a better view of whatever it was his friend was alluding to.

"I didn't 'ear nothing," said the third man, as he continued to stir the pot over the fire.

The first man turned around a hundred and eighty degrees in his seat and stared straight ahead in the direction of the Creeper.

Although the Creeper was able to focus on all three of the friends in the darkness, close enough that it could actually see the expressions on their faces, the men were unable to discern anything as far away as it was in the dim glow offered by their fire.

The three men stayed motionless for a moment.

None of them spoke as they all concentrated on listening.

Eventually, the man stirring the pot broke the silence. "It must've been a fox or summink runnin' through the woods." He surmised, taking another swig from his bottle.

Obviously in agreement with his companion, the second man patted his friend on the back and slumped back down on his seat, his attention now firmly placed back on his drinking.

The man who had heard the Creeper's belly rumble continued to stare ahead at it for a few seconds more, before he too shrugged and turned back towards the fire.

The Creeper waited, unsure of what its next move should be.

It considered skulking away, back into the night, far from the three men and the delicious odour of their food.

But somehow it felt compelled to stay.

Not just because it was still hungry, although that reason was fast becoming a priority. But also, because these were the first human beings it had ever seen besides the old woman.

Now that it had escaped, the possibility of finding kindred spirits had become a reality.

Was it possible that the old woman had kept it locked away merely because it was different to her?

Perhaps these men might recognise a fellow outcast and allow it to stay and take refuge with them.

It had never known the warmth of companionship, but somehow listening to the three men laughing and joking together, the Creeper felt drawn to their company.

The warmth of their fire and the heady bouquet of their food convinced it that it had arrived at the right place, and at just the right moment.

Overcome by a new-found sense of belonging, the Creeper

moved forward through the trees, snapping branches in its path as if they were no more than dry twigs.

At the sound of the Creeper's approach, the three men all rose as one and stared in its direction.

As it emerged from the shelter of the woods and ventured into the surrounding glow of the firelight, the Creeper instinctively held out its arms in friendship towards the three friends.

It tried to make a welcoming sound of warmth and friendship conducive to the occasion, as it drew closer, but due to its malformed vocal chords the noise which emanated from its mouth was more aggressive-sounding than it intended.

As soon as they saw it approach, the three men screamed in terror and automatically backed away.

The second man tripped and fell backwards, dropping his bottle and splashing his whiskey into the fire. The flames leapt up and enveloped his arm, catching onto the flammable material of his shirt and quickly spreading up his arm.

He screamed in agony as the fire caught his skin.

The man who had been stirring the soup ran forward and grabbed his friend, but in his haste, he too slipped and fell face-forward, cracking his head against a jagged rock. For a second or two he lost consciousness, but the commotion taking place around him helped to bring him around.

The first man—the one who had initially heard the Creeper approach—lifted back his arm and, holding his half-empty bottle by the neck, launched it at the Creeper's face.

The solid rim at the base of the bottle hit the Creeper square in the face.

Although shocked by the initial impact, the Creeper barely felt any pain as the bottle glanced off it and fell to the ground, spilling what was left of its contents onto the dirt floor.

However, it knew instinctively that the action by the man

was not friendly, and it could feel its anger rising in its chest, forcing it to seek retaliation.

The man with his sleeve on fire was now rolling around in the mud, trying to douse the flames as best he could. Without meaning to, he rolled against his friend who had just thrown the bottle and took his legs out from underneath him.

The man came crashing down onto his half-conscious companion, knocking the wind out of both of them with the impact.

Having finally managed to put out the fire on his shirt, the second man rolled himself up into a sitting position and stared up as the Creeper approached.

Careful not to set himself alight once more, he leaned over his two companions and grabbed hold of the unlit end of one of the branches in the fire.

He stood up, holding the burning piece of wood at arm's length towards the Creeper, swinging it back and forth so that the flames made patterns in the night air.

The Creeper could feel the heat given off by the wooden torch, and although it had never felt the burning sensation of a naked flame, it somehow knew that to get too close would be harmful to it.

Why it was on receiving end of such unprovoked hostility the Creeper could not imagine. But as it stood its ground watching the three men who, seconds before, it had hoped might welcome it into the warmth of their circle, it realised that it had completely misjudged the situation, and now it had to take steps to defend itself against its foe.

The Creeper bent down and grasped hold of the first rock which came to hand. Still in a crouched position, it threw the missile at the man holding the flaming log.

In the dark, even with the burning torch, the man was not

prepared for the speed or accuracy of the oncoming projectile, until it was too late.

The rock caught him square in the forehead, killing him instantly.

As the man's body crumpled to the floor in a heap, his blazing log came to rest on his prone body. The fabric of his jacket immediately caught light and within seconds searing flames were licking hungrily across his back.

His two friends, still groggy from their collision, fumbled across each other to try and smother the flames, neither realising that their friend was already beyond help.

In their haste, both men seemed to have temporarily forgotten about the Creeper's presence.

As they shook and shouted at their fallen comrade to get up, the Creeper closed in from behind and grabbed each man by the nape of the neck.

With a strength and power which, even acting together, neither man had the strength to oppose, the Creeper lifted them both off the ground and slammed their heads together, caving in both their craniums simultaneously.

The Creeper held the two limp bodies out at arm's length for a few seconds, before finally dropping them on top of their burning friend.

Within minutes the flames from its first victim began to spread to the other two, and as the Creeper looked on at the human pyre, the acrid stench of burning flesh permeated the night air, filling its nostrils and causing its belly to rumble even louder than before.

Remembering the soup, the Creeper walked around the burning corpses and leaning in over the bonfire, inhaling deeply at the bubbling contents of the pot.

Encouraged by the savoury aroma, the Creeper grabbed hold of the vessel with both hands. It could feel the warming sensation from the metal container as soon as it made contact with it. But unlike human hands, the skin which covered the Creeper's palms was thick and callused and designed to withstand much higher temperatures than those of its human counterparts.

The Creeper sniffed the boiling liquid, and then proceeded to tip the scorching contents of the pot straight down its throat.

It could feel the searing heat of the soup as it made its way past its tongue and down its oesophagus, but it did not flinch or stop for breath until the pan was completely empty.

Casting the empty pot to one side, the Creeper wiped its mouth with the back of its hand and raised its mighty head before letting forth a shriek of joy and contentment.

This was the first time in its living memory that it had ever felt so satiated. The meagre portions that the old woman brought it of a night were barely enough to keep its hunger at bay for a few hours, the rest of the time the Creeper had learned to do without.

But now there was a veritable feast roasting right in front of it, and the Creeper fully intended to take advantage of its bounty.

The flames had burnt through the men's clothes leaving fragments of cloth hanging from their scorched skin.

The Creeper leaned down and sniffed the scent of their burnt flesh. It was far more pungent than the aroma of the soup.

With salivating jaws, the Creeper lifted the first man off of his friends and held his limp body in front of its face before sinking its fangs deep into the warm flesh. Tearing out a huge chunk of meat and it chewed it slowly once or twice, before swallowing it almost whole.

Immediately, it took another bite, then another, and

continued to feast on the corpse until all that remained was the skeletal frame.

Casting the bones to one side, the Creeper picked up the second of the men and immediately began to feed on its next course, barely pausing long enough to let the first meal start to settle.

By the time the second victim was no more than a bunch of bones, the Creeper finally felt satiated. But it had no intention of allowing its last victim to go to waste. It considered burying the feast deep under the ground until such time as it felt hungry enough to reclaim the body.

First though, the Creeper decided to venture down to the edge of the lake.

It had never seen a body of water like it before, so it decided to investigate.

The surface of the water was still and flat, almost like glass. On that hot summer night there was barely a breath of air, so consequently hardly a single ripple broke the water's exterior facade.

The Creeper lurched along to the edge of the bank, listening out for any sound of movement which might indicate another watcher in its midst.

But it was alone, as it always had been; only now for the first time in its entire existence it had a real sense of freedom. It had escaped the confines of its solitary prison and was now finally able to experience things which other beings merely took for granted.

The Creeper stood at the water's edge and stared up at the huge moon hanging above it in the night sky.

It stared in admiration and wonder at the myriad stars which twinkled brilliantly, before finally lowering its head and gazing down at the water.

It was then, for the first time ever, that the Creeper saw its own reflection.

The monstrosity that stared back up at it from the calm surface of the lake caused the Creeper to cry out involuntarily, from a combination of fear, revulsion, and horror.

Although the Creeper had no real concept of physical beauty or proportion, its brain could not comprehend that the hideous freak that was reflected in the water, was indeed its own mirror image.

Mad with a rage born of insanity, the Creeper entered the water and smashed its massive fists down at the surface, obliterating the cruel reflection the lake had offered up to it.

Over and over again it flayed its arms, determined to destroy the image, but the futility of its task soon left it feeling overwhelmed with frustration.

Eventually, the Creeper backed away from its nemesis, and turned and ran back to the relative safety of the camp.

Bending down, it grabbed hold of its last victim and pulled it up so that the two of them stood face to face. Even though the lifeless corpse had singed and burnt features, the Creeper still wished that there was some way that they could change identities

It gazed into the vacant face of its prey, and soon its vision began to blur with tears of self-pity and loathing.

Now it knew why the old woman had kept it hidden away for all these years.

The men it had attacked had not reacted in the way they had out of hostility or anger, but from fear and repulsion.

The Creeper realised that its new-found freedom meant nothing if it could not go out in the world and experience the wonders of the unknown. If it had to spend all its time hiding in the shadows, afraid to show itself because of the animosity the terror of its ugliness would reveal in the eyes of the suitably astonished strangers it encountered.

Casting its last victim to one side, the Creeper fell to its knees and wept.

It was used to tears.

But whereas before it had cried as a result of loneliness and abandonment, at least then there had always been the hope of escape.

Now it realised that escape merely meant a torment of a different hue, one that left no hope, no anticipation and above all no sense of belonging.

Once its sobs had subsided, the Creeper retrieved its trophy, and slinging the corpse over its shoulder it slowly began to make its way back to the only place it had ever known as home.

Dawn was beginning to break by the time the Creeper reached its destination, and although the sky was only just beginning to lighten in the east, because the Creeper had only ever known darkness throughout its life its eyes were already starting to hurt from the brightness.

Although the welcome it received was not exactly warm, at least the old woman did not try and stop the Creeper from re-entering her home.

When she saw the dead body draped over its shoulder, the Creeper could tell from all her shouting and gesticulation that she was not best pleased with his trophy.

Nevertheless, she allowed the Creeper to carry its bounty down to his cellar, and she returned the following day to clear away the debris, as usual.

From that day the two of them had an unspoken under-standing, of sorts.

The old woman would allow the Creeper to venture out at

night whenever it wanted to. Fortunately for her, it learned to dispose of its kills before returning at daybreak.

This situation continued until one day, the keeper arrived and brought the Creeper to its new domain.

Here it was content.

Here it had space to roam and the freedom to venture out whenever the mood took it.

The keeper had shown it a way that it could leave its lair without the risk of being seen, so that it could come and go at will. Now it had plenty of space to store its victims and feast or play with them as it saw fit, and it had learned to dispose of the remains from its kills where they would not be found easily.

The keeper made no real demands on the Creeper, and he always spoke to it with a kindness, in soothing tones.

Over time, the Creeper had explored the furthest depths of its dwelling, until it was now familiar with every nook and cranny.

Compared to its previous existence, the Creeper was as happy now with its new way of life, as it was possible for such a creature to be.

CHAPTER THIRTEEN

Hardy crashed down on his sofa, exhausted. It had been a very long, hard day, with very little to show for it at the end.

The search of the area between Natasha Spencer's house and the edge of town where she and Ben Green were apparently heading to had not produced a single clue as to their whereabouts.

They knew from the report that they had received back from their telecommunications branch that the couple's mobiles had last received a signal close to Natasha's home, so that in itself was of no significant use.

Naturally, there were no eyewitnesses to anything untoward taking place, or at least, the house-to-house investigation had not unearthed anything. Not that that was unusual. It never ceased to amaze Hardy how suddenly everyone became deaf and blind whenever the police needed help.

Just as he was leaving the station for the day, Hardy was called back in by the superintendent who demanded a blow-by-blow account of the investigation so far.

Hardy ran through the events of the day, but he had nothing substantial to show for all their hard work, and they both knew that.

Carlisle seemed more concerned at having to go back to Natasha's parents and explain why they were no further forward in the investigation, than anything else.

Hardy offered once more to act as liaison, but as he suspected, the superintendent would have none of it.

As Hardy was leaving his office, Carlisle made a snide remark about bringing in a DCI to take over the case, if there a breakthrough was not imminent. Hardy could feel his temper rising as he stopped halfway through the door, but miraculously he managed to keep his temper under control and did not rise to the bait.

He knew that his lack of response would annoy his superior, so in that respect he was pleased with himself for keeping a lid on his anger.

His silence would have far more impact than any retort.

Besides which, he was sure that Carlisle was only doing it to antagonise him.

Before Hardy left London, he had been an acting DCI for nine months, and during that time he had brought to fruition four separate murder investigations, including one that had been side-lined as unsolved, for over two years.

Everyone who worked on his team knew that Hardy deserved the promotion.

Then suddenly, out of the blue another DCI was brought in from another region to take over Hardy's squad.

It subsequently transpired that this new DCI had in fact been working in vice and people trafficking but was caught taking backhanders from a well-known gang of eastern European people smugglers who were responsible for operating the largest group of brothels in the London area.

Instead of being disciplined and sacked, or at least demoted, the DCI was transferred without any loss of pay or privileges, and word soon reached Hardy's ear that the reason behind this miraculous act of forgiveness lay in the fact that the DCI was a member of the same Masonic lodge as the Chief Constable.

As if to add insult to injury, the new DCI took an instant dislike to Hardy, due mainly to the fact that Hardy's team had come to trust and respect him, and the new replacement believed that such admiration should be reserved for him due to his rank.

He and Hardy clashed swords on several occasions, and it was obvious to anyone within earshot that Hardy had his new superior outgunned on all borders.

Alas, that did not sit well with his then superintendent who, after several complaints from the new DCI, felt compelled to step in and resolve the situation as best he could.

This resulted in Hardy being given two options, resign, or transfer.

By this point in time, Hardy had grown tired of working in London. The constant non-stop battle against both the villains and their legal briefs had, over time, worn him out. He began to see the job as a futile waste of time and energy, and although he did consider throwing the towel in, he soon realised that he was not trained for anything else and that being a copper was all he knew.

Therefore, he accepted the first transfer that came his way, which was as far away from the crowded, dirty, noisy streets of London as he could go.

His then girlfriend worked for the Crown Prosecution Service, and although she fully understood Hardy's decision to leave, her career was far more important to her than their relationship. To her, there was nowhere else to work other than in the centre of the city if you ever wanted to make a big splash, and she certainly intended to do that!

They had only been seeing each other for just over a year and as they each had their own flats at least there was no major upheaval with them arguing over how to split the proceeds and quibbling about the furniture and other household items.

Their parting was amicable, and they each wished the other well.

Hardy believed that he would miss her far more than she would him, but he understood her conviction to stay put, and he did not blame her for it.

As it was, his move to the country had several benefits.

First of all, with the cheaper property prices he was able to afford a house with the proceeds from the sale of his flat in London.

In reality, the property was far too big for his simple needs, but he decided that it was too good an opportunity to miss, and since then he had grown accustomed to having the extra space around him.

The station he worked from was much smaller than any he had operated from back home, but Hardy immediately warmed to the cosier, more intimate atmosphere where, after a short while, he knew the names—or at least the faces—of all the officers working there.

Plus, it was the little things which he had begun to notice that helped enhance the overall impression of peace and tranquillity that a life in the country lent itself to.

Things like the lack of traffic on the morning drive to the station, the charming sound of the dawn chorus and the freshness in the air that encouraged you to take a deep breath whenever you were outside. Even the surrounding woodland took on an altogether mystical quality at dusk, which Hardy had never experienced in London.

But above all else, Hardy appreciated the gentle pace of life out here, and the fact that he was not constantly bombarded with evidence from several cases being thrust upon him at all hours of the day and night.

For a while, Hardy had become to believe that he would never have to plunge his hands into the murky waters of murder again. Although there had been several fatalities in the vicinity since Hardy's arrival, thus far, none of them had been as the result of homicide.

That was, until the mutilated remains of poor Caroline Seymour were discovered.

Even with all his experience and training on the front line, Hardy had never seen anything quite so horrific as the slaughtered remains of that poor girl.

At the time, it reminded Hardy of the description he had read of the condition of Jack the Ripper's final known victim Mary Jane Kelly, when her landlord unlocked her rented room and discovered her mutilated corpse scattered around the room.

In poor Caroline's case there was no room, just a remote area of scrubland where her dismembered remains had been dumped unceremoniously.

The first officers on the scene were a couple of uniformed constables, both fresh out of training. Neither of them had returned to active duty yet.

Although Hardy liked to think of himself as case-hardened, even he felt his stomach turn as he surveyed the scene.

Later, once a positive identification had been made, Hardy had to break the tragic news to Caroline's parents. Standing in their front room whilst the two of them crumbled in each other's arms, it was hard for him to believe that those scattered remains he had witnessed had once been the sweet-faced, smiling, angelic girl in the pictures which adorned the room.

As Hardy stood there listening to the wracking sobs and howls of disbelief from the couple, he swore to himself that he would bring the perpetrator to justice.

Since then, however, they had not received a single worthwhile lead.

Regardless of what Carlisle thought, Hardy knew that the last man to have seen Caroline alive before she disappeared was not responsible for her death.

Even if the man had not had a cast-iron alibi, after all his years on the force Hardy could tell instinctively when someone was lying, and that retired librarian was definitely not.

At first, Hardy had hoped that as the murder of Caroline Seymour was so out of character for the area that the assailant might actually stick out, like the proverbial sore thumb.

But as the days and weeks rolled by with no real progress to speak of, Hardy and his team were becoming more and more convinced that the individual that they were looking for may have just been passing through, and by now had already left the area.

Hardy had instigated all the usual checks and reports of the incident had been circulated throughout the country, but as yet to no avail.

Now with the disappearance of Natasha and her boyfriend Ben having passed the twenty-four-hour stage, Hardy was beginning to grow concerned that he might have a maniac on his patch.

So much for a quiet life in the country!

Hardy hoisted himself of his sofa and made his way upstairs to take a shower.

The hot water felt so good after the sort of day he'd had. He stayed under the hot stream long after all the shower gel had been washed away, until reluctantly he turned off the tap before he started to prune.

Back downstairs, Hardy fixed himself a large scotch and carried it into the kitchen to decide which frozen meal to throw into the microwave.

He downed a second scotch before his meal was ready.

He ate in front of the television, as usual. His dining table still groaned under the weight of several unopened letters and handbills which he had been promising himself for ages that he would sort through. He knew that amongst them would be some overdue bills, so he decided if he was still awake half an hour after he finished eating that he would make a start to try and unearth the important ones.

Hardy watched the news.

He was very encouraged by the fact that so far, they had managed to keep all the details pertaining to the discovery of Caroline Seymour's remains out of the public eye.

As close as he was to his team back in London, somehow the press always managed to get wind of information which only his unit was privy to.

He hated the idea that one of his own was selling information to the papers, but in such a large station it was virtually impossible to keep anything a secret for long.

At least out here loyalty seemed to matter.

The murder itself had been reported, the public needed to know in case there was a witness somewhere who could come forward. But the grisly details had been kept under wraps. Vital details concerning where the girl's dismembered remains were found, and the state they were in when discovered, could prove vital to securing a conviction once the perpetrator was caught.

Hardy finished his meal and poured himself another large tumbler of scotch.

As he eased back in his seat to savour it, the television

suddenly switched to a picture of Gerald and Hilary Spencer standing outside their house.

Hardy spluttered as his drink caught in his throat in mid-swallow. Trying to catch his breath, he replaced the glass on the table in front of him and reached for the control to turn up the volume.

He listened intently as Gerald Spencer relayed the fact to the viewing public that his only daughter had been missing for over twenty-four hours now, and that he was personally offering a reward of £20,000 for any information which would lead to her safe return.

Hardy sat with his mouth open, gasping in air to clear his throat.

In truth, he could not blame Spencer for his concern. But the fact that he had offered a sizeable reward for information meant that by tomorrow the station would be awash with every money-grabbing crank in the country claiming that they had vital information concerning the lost girl.

Every lead they received would need to be followed up, which in turn would mean that his entire team would waste countless hours investigating worthless clues and inaccurate accounts, none of which would leave them any further forward than they were right now.

Hardy looked at his mobile. He was surprised when he saw that he had not missed a call from Carlisle. Doubtless his superior must have known about Spencer's intention to inform the media. After all, they were friends, and Hardy knew that Carlisle was intending to speak to Spencer earlier that evening to give him an update, such as it was.

Perhaps Spencer decided to bring in the big guns after Carlisle had informed him of their lack of progress. Or maybe he intended to do so all along if there was no sign of Natasha by this evening.

Either way, Hardy knew that he was going to feel the full weight of the fallout from this situation first thing in the morning, and he was already dreading the prospect.

Hardy decided to ignore the stack of mail on his table.

Instead, he poured himself another tumbler of scotch and knocked it back in one go, before he headed upstairs to bed.

CHAPTER FOURTEEN

K elly and Carol managed to polish off their first bottle of wine within half an hour of opening it. Before Kelly could stop her, or at least ask her to slow down, Carol had plucked the cork from the second one and was splashing into Kelly's glass.

The velvety smoothness of the Merlot slid down Kelly's throat, immediately warming her from the inside. She was not used to drinking red wine so quickly, but the pleasurable effect it was having on her as both a relaxant as well as a painkiller, made Kelly realise just how much she needed this to escape the realities of her life, even if it were only for a few precious hours.

The music which Carol had chosen for background was purely instrumental and the inspired combination of pan pipes, percussion, and timpani set the mood perfectly.

While they drank, they talked, mainly about the way Kelly allowed her husband to treat her. Carol was a very sympathetic listener, and when she offered advice it was not designed to sound in any way condescending or patronising, which Kelly fully appreciated.

By the end of the second bottle, both women were beginning to feel ravenous.

Much to Kelly's surprise, Carol managed to order a pizza to be delivered. With the reputation that their estate had in the area, it was well known that no takeaway was prepared to deliver to anyone above the ground floor, as none of the local restaurants could risk leaving their vehicles unattended, even for the short time it would take the driver to ride the lift or take the stairs, to the upper floors.

Even so, as Carol made the call she had to smile at the look of astonishment on Kelly's face when she heard her friend making the order.

When Carol finished the call, Kelly stared at her with an open mouth.

"How on earth did you manage that?" she asked, unable to keep the surprise and admiration out of her tone.

Carol winked at her as she climbed off the sofa. "You get the plates and the napkins, and I'll show you."

Kelly made her way into the kitchen and retrieved a couple of large dinner plates from the cupboard and grabbed a roll of paper towels from off the draining board. She presumed that that was what Carol meant when she mentioned napkins.

While she was setting the plates out on the table in front of the sofa, Carol came back into the room wearing a black silk negligee and a matching dressing gown.

Kelly could not help but utter the word "Wow!" as her friend eased herself back onto the sofa.

"Now you know my secret," Carol purred, leaning back against the upright and carefully crossing one leg over the other to reveal as much thigh as she could.

Kelly laughed out loud, slapping her hand over her mouth to try and quell the noise.

Just then, the doorbell rang.

Carol reached down for her handbag which was sitting on the floor where she had left it earlier. Before she had a chance to reach it, Kelly leaned over and put out her own hand, placing it gently over Carol's perfectly manicured fingers and squeezing. "No, please let me get this," she said, almost pleadingly, "you paid for the wine."

Carol placed her free hand over Kelly's. "I told you, kiddo, tonight is on me, no arguments."

Their eyes locked for a brief moment, before Kelly looked away, embarrassed.

Carol collected her purse from her handbag and removed a £20 note. She looked back up at Kelly, who was still blushing, although she was not completely sure why. Perhaps, she considered, it was a natural reaction whenever she remembered her husband's 'no touching' rule.

From the look on Carol's face, she seemed to find her friend's shyness amusing.

The moment was broken by the impatient knocking from the delivery driver outside.

Carol slipped the note between her breasts. "It's amazing what a good tip and a hint of cleavage will get you around here" she whispered, sensuously, as she slipped off the sofa and sashayed out into the hall.

Kelly waited as if frozen to the spot for her friend to return.

"Ta-dah," Carol announced, as she walked back in with the large pizza box balanced on one hand.

They both ate, voraciously, neither one fully appreciating until now just how hungry they were. Although she tried to stay focused on the matter at hand, Kelly found her gaze drifting magnetically towards her friends exposed thighs and cleavage.

The belt on Carol's dressing gown had slipped open while she ate, and she did not bother to tie the two ends back together. Instead she seemed relaxed enough to allow the soft fabric to fall asunder, revealing her perfectly proportioned torso beneath her negligee.

At one-point Carol caught her friend sneaking a crafty peek at her body, and she waited with a knowing smile on her face for Kelly to catch her eye. When she did, Kelly's blush turned her cheeks bright red, and she quickly averted her gaze, which caused Carol to laugh and almost choke on her next mouthful of pizza.

After a moment, Kelly looked back at her friend.

Carol still wore her smile and her eyes appeared to sparkle with mischief.

"I'm sorry" Kelly offered, sheepishly. "I didn't mean to stare."

Carol took a sip of wine before answering. "No problem," she assured her friend. "I take it as a compliment."

Carol's remark only served to make Kelly blush once more.

Without speaking, Carol placed her glass on the table and moved towards Kelly.

Kelly caught herself involuntarily shifting in her seat just as Carol went to pass by her, which in turn caused Carol to swerve and jolt Kelly's arm.

The wine glass which Kelly had been holding fell from her grasp and the contents splashed down the front of her blouse and spilled onto her lap.

Reacting as quickly as she could so as to save her friend's sofa and carpet from ruin, Kelly stood up and just managed to catch the fallen glass before losing her balance and falling back on her rump.

She quickly tried to regain her composure and holding the now empty glass upright, Kelly stood up holding the bottom of her soaking blouse balled up in her hand to try and prevent any leakage.

"Oh lord, I'm so sorry," cried Kelly, apologetically. She replaced her glass on the table out of harm's way and began to scour the area around her to see if she had indeed made a mess.

Carol on the other hand, appeared totally unconcerned. "Don't worry about it, kiddo," she laughed, "no harm done."

Still holding the ends of her blouse, Kelly walked around her friend and headed towards the bathroom. "I'd better try and sponge this off before it stains," she called back, as she left the room.

While Kelly attended to her clothes, Carol cleared away their plates and opened the last bottle of wine.

Once she had poured them both a glass, she went back out in the hallway to see how Kelly was getting on.

"Is it coming out?" she asked, standing in the bathroom's open doorway.

Kelly looked up from scrubbing her clothes. "I think so," she offered, half-heartedly, "I think I'd better go home and change."

Carol looked shocked. "And ruin our perfect evening in, tish." She waved her hand as if to dismiss the idea. "You take yourself into my bedroom and get out of those wet things, put on one of my dressing gowns; they're a couple hanging up behind the door."

Carol did not wait for answer. Instead she turned and walked back into the sitting room.

Kelly stood there for a moment longer.

Even though she was feeling very indecisive about what to do, she had the distinct impression that Carol would not take no for an answer.

Deep down, she was not ready to go home yet. If Jack was back already, he would doubtless be drunk and demanding, as usual.

The truth was, Kelly was enjoying herself this evening,

more so than she had in a very long time, and she was not keen for it to end, at least, not just yet.

As she stood there dithering about what to do, Carol's voice called out from the other room.

"Come on, kiddo, your wine's getting cold."

Kelly took her cue. She strode into Carol's bedroom to get changed.

While she undressed, Kelly could feel a weird sensation starting to build in her stomach. It was a combination of nervous excitement tinged with mischievousness.

The reason behind the feeling escaped her. After all, this was not the first time she had undressed in a girlfriend's bedroom, although it was her first time in Carol's.

Checking first to make sure that the curtains were drawn shut; Kelly switched on the light and was immediately captivated by the décor of the room. The beautiful hand-crafted matching furniture reminded her of something out of 'House and Homes', as did the enormous bed which dominated the room.

As she removed her wet jeans and socks, the carpet beneath her feet felt luxuriously soft and plush, and the pile made her feel as if her feet were being caressed in a fluffy towel.

After undressing and placing her damp clothes on the radiator at the far end of the room, Kelly stopped for a moment to stare at her reflection in the full-length mirror which adorned the larger of the room's two wardrobes.

The slouching figure staring back at her from the mirrored glass did nothing to enhance her overall demeanour.

Hearing one of her teacher's voices in her head telling her to stand straight, Kelly lifted out her chest and sucked in her stomach. The simple change of stance caused a marked improvement in her reflection.

Kelly had never been overly proud of her body, but she was by no means ashamed of it either.

True, she had always dreamt of having larger breasts and a smaller bottom, but overall, she was very happy with what god and nature had given her.

Kelly turned from one side to the other to survey her posture.

The only part which looked out of place was the distinct bruising around her face.

Kelly leaned in closer for a better look.

"If you break that glass, you pay for it!" Carol's voice from behind her took Kelly completely off guard, and she almost toppled over as she spun around on the spot.

Instinctively, Kelly covered her naked breasts with one arm and placed her other hand between the legs.

She stood there for a moment, not sure if she was feeling foolish for being caught out for her vanity, admiring herself in the mirror, or because of her naked vulnerability.

Either way, she immediately wished that she had not reacted to Carol's presence in the way she had, but it was too late now, and Kelly was not sure what to do next.

Fortunately, Carol made the decision for her.

As she approached her friend, Kelly noticed that Carol had something in her hand. As she grew nearer, Carol raised her hand and Kelly saw that it was a chocolate cup cake.

When she was close enough so that Kelly could smell her friend's expensive perfume, Carol held out her hand towards Kelly's mouth.

Without hesitation, Kelly parted her lips and took a bite of the offering.

As she bit into the lush sponge Kelly felt the hidden gooey filling starting to trickle its way down her chin.

Without thinking, she lifted the arm which had been

covering her breasts and just managed to catch the chocolaty filling with her index finger, before it dripped off the end of her chin and fell to the floor.

Kelly licked the creamy treat off her finger, savouring the luxurious depth of the flavoursome dessert.

Once she had finished, Kelly did not see any point in covering up her breasts again. Instead she allowed her arm to fall by her side, casually removing her other hand from between her legs, and letting that hang beside her, also.

Whether she noticed, or indeed appreciated the view or not, Carol did not give any obvious indication. She merely offered up another bite of the cake to Kelly, once she had noticed her swallow her first mouthful.

Kelly eagerly took another helping.

Carol watched her friend slowly chew her offering. The sight of her perfectly formed jaw line moving up and down brought a wry smile to Carol's lips. She had always considered Kelly to have perfect facial features, and her skin was always so smooth and silky, almost like porcelain.

She reminded Carol of a Botticelli angel.

Although, seeing her friend's flawless features tarnished by the bruises left behind by that ignorant twat of a husband of hers, did spoil her overall appreciation of her friend.

Carol placed the last piece of cake inside her friend's eager mouth.

As she continued to watch her chew, Carol took a step back and gave her friend's naked form an admiring once-over.

Before she had a chance to look back up at her face, she noticed Kelly lifting her hands to rest on her hips.

"See something you like?" Kelly asked, cheekily, swallowing the last of the sponge, and licking away the last remnants of the filling.

"Mmmnn," Carol nodded, licking her own lips, provocatively.

Kelly laughed. She tried to cover the nervousness in her expression, but in doing so her laugh turned into a snort, and she quickly slapped her hand over her mouth in embarrassment.

Carol glided towards her friend, and before Kelly could stop her, she placed a firm hand behind Kelly's neck and pulled her towards her.

Their lips met, and though Carol instigated the union, Kelly was quick to respond. She was not sure if it was as a result of the copious quantity of wine which she had consumed or the fact that she was feeling generally unloved and insecure after Jack's attack on her, but Kelly needed this more than she had been willing to admit, until this moment.

Carol let her gown fall back off her shoulders and flutter to the ground as she wrapped her arms around Kelly and pulled her towards her.

Their tongues danced inside each other's mouths as their hands began to explore their bodies.

After a while, Carol guided Kelly back onto the bed, stopping just long enough to release the shoulder straps from her negligee and slide the garment down towards her feet.

She kicked it off to one side before joining her friend on the bed.

Immediately taking charge, Carol slid forward and lay on top of Kelly, almost pinning her to the duvet.

Although Carol's frame was much broader than Kelly's, it was all muscle, so she was able to control her movements and ensure that she was not crushing her friend.

Their naked flesh meshed together as they resumed their passionate kissing session.

After a while, Carol began to ease her way down Kelly's

torso, covering her skin with gentle but firm kisses, nibbles, and bites.

Kelly squealed with excitement whenever Carol's teeth nipped her.

Kelly lay back and spread out her arms as Carol continued her journey downward, towards Kelly's pelvis.

When she reached the tight curls, which spread out from Kelly's soft mound, Carol used the tip of her tongue to cut swirls through the bristles. She slowly traced a figure of eight over and over while Kelly moaned and sighed in anticipation.

As Carol's tongue began to trace a moist line towards Kelly's labia, Kelly lifted her hips off the mattress to meet her friend's mouth.

Just then, Carol withdrew herself and shuffled across the bed towards the night stand.

Kelly looked up in shock, her expression a combination of surprise and disappointment.

Under different circumstances, thought Kelly, this might be the part when a man makes a grab for a condom. But clearly, that would not be required on this occasion.

Before she could speak, Carol removed a tiny silver box from her top drawer.

Kelly watched as her friend opened the box, it appeared to be half-full of white powder. Kelly continued to look on in silence as Carol scooped out a small heap of the powder with her fingernail and gently placed it on the tip of her tongue, before closing the box and replacing it in the drawer.

She winked at Kelly as she slid back down the bed towards Kelly's parted legs.

Excited and bemused by her friend's actions, Kelly lay back down and awaited Carol's next move. Whatever was in the silver box, Kelly trusted her friend not to cause her any harm, and she was determined to enjoy whatever it was she was about to experience.

She was actually surprised with herself for being so adventurous and open to such a new experience.

Deep down she suspected that later on she would feel the full weight of the guilt, but for now she was happy to just go with the flow.

The minute Carol's tongue made its way past her lips and in through the more delicate and sensitive area leading to her clitoris, Kelly felt an immediate rush of ecstasy which caused her to cry out, involuntarily.

She reached down and grabbed hold of Carol's hair and began to caress and massage it, sensuously gliding her fingers through her curls as she thrust her hips forward against Carol's searching tongue.

Kelly lifted her legs and wrapped them around Carol's back as their two bodies rocked back and forth in perfect rhythm with each other.

After Kelly had reached orgasm for the third time, they switched places, exploring each other's nooks and crevices as they changed position.

Kelly had never given oral sex to a woman before, but the experience felt totally natural to her, and from Carol's reaction to her efforts she felt confident that she was doing it right.

Afterwards, once they were both completely spent, they lay together in each other's arms without speaking, and eventually they both drifted off to sleep.

CHAPTER FIFTEEN

The Creeper used Natasha once more to satisfy its carnal lust, until it was finally spent. Exhausted, it rolled off her and lay beside her motionless form sharing her mattress of hay covered with some old sack cloth.

As a result of its exertion, the Creeper's chest expanded and retracted with each huge lungful of air. Natasha on the other hand, merely lay still, hardly showing any outward signs that she was still alive.

Even her eyes, once so vibrant and full of life, were now no more than dull orbs staring straight ahead of her focused on the ceiling of the alcove in which they lay, never blinking, even in the shadowy darkness of her surroundings.

The Creeper, although not accustomed to willing recipients, had still noticed the lack of response on Natasha's part when it had entered her. Although it did detect a few subtle moans and whimpers from its comatose victim the further it forced itself inside her, there was no actual movement, no struggling, no fighting, and none of the usual combination of screaming and kicking that it had grown used to.

Instead, it was almost as if Natasha had relinquished herself completely to her captive and was no longer willing to partake in any way shape or form with whatever the Creeper had in store for her.

Uncharacteristically, this annoyed the Creeper!

Usually, it did not care what its concubines said or did, so long as it could satisfy its own wants and needs. Besides which, it would generally despatch them once it had quenched its sexual thirst.

But there was something special about Natasha. The Creeper had no understanding of what it was about her that compelled it to keep her alive, it only knew that it needed to, and not just to satisfy its lust.

Natasha possessed a quality the Creeper had hitherto been unaware existed. Even though the exact constitution of the said quality was something it could never fathom.

Deep down the Creeper knew that its time with Natasha would be short-lived, as its keeper would soon venture down to its lair wanting to dispose of whatever remains were left of the carcases the Creeper had already dealt with.

It was true that over time the Creeper had come to trust its keeper, and therefore had never remonstrated against his decisions concerning when to dispose of its victim's remains.

But this time it would be different!

The Creeper needed to communicate to its keeper that Natasha was special, and that it needed more time with her before it was willing to relinquish its prey.

It even considered the possibility of covering her body with straw and rags and anything else it could find in order to trick its keeper from discovering her until it was ready to release her. But it knew, deep down, somehow that its keeper was too wise for such a subterfuge to work.

At that precise moment, the Creeper could hear the sound

of a faraway door creaking open on rusty hinges. It was the sound which always announced the approach of its keeper.

The Creeper listened to the familiar echo of the door being slammed shut, followed by the grinding of the lock as it reluctantly surrendered to the forcefulness of the key, as it turned in its chamber.

It waited in the darkness, listening.

After a moment it could hear the footfalls of the keeper as they echoed throughout the cavernous lair. The louder they grew, the more the Creeper could feel itself tensing in anticipation at the confrontation that was bound to ensue when the keeper tried to remove plaything.

From around the corner, the Creeper could see the shadowy circle of light which emanated from the keeper's torch.

Torn between its urge to keep hold of Natasha for just a little while longer, and its subservience to its protector, the Creeper could feel its insides starting to churn and knot with anxiety.

As the keeper came into view the Creeper automatically sprang up to a crouching position with its arms flared out by its sides with its talon-like claws at the ready, as if it were preparing to pounce on its unsuspecting prey.

The Creeper's aggressive stance was not lost on its keeper as he turned the corner and came face-to-face with it.

For a moment neither of them moved.

The Creeper looked up with its dull grey eyes and it sensed from the unfamiliar expression of concern on its protector's face, that its actions were not welcome.

Unable to make more than just a pitiful whine of desperation, the Creeper tried gesturing with its open hands to convey to its keeper its overwhelming need to be allowed to keep hold of Natasha for the time being.

Certainly, this was a reaction that its keeper was unprepared for; therefore, it took a little while for him to understand what was being asked of him.

Ordinarily with the Creeper, once its lust and hunger were satiated, it was content to just sit back and watch as its protector removed whatever remains were left of its poor unfortunate victims, for disposal. So, in effect, this was a definite first in their relationship.

Even so, once the keeper comprehended the situation he smiled down at his charge and spoke to him using his usual kindly placating tone.

"It's alright, Eric," he smiled, affectionately. "There's no need for you to get excited, if you want to keep hold of her for a little while longer than that is fine."

Although the Creeper could not understand the actual words spoken, it knew from the reassuring tone that its keeper affected that its treasure was not about to be taken away from it.

The Creeper visibly relaxed its stance.

Its protector smiled warmly and reached down to gently pat the Creeper on the shoulder. At the same time, the keeper glanced down at the comatose form of Natasha and watched for a moment until he was sure that she was still breathing.

Once he was certain that he could still see the girl's chest rise and fall, the keeper looked back at his charge once more and nodded his compliance, before he turned away to make a search amongst the hidden crevices and alcoves of the cavernous warren, for whatever remained of the Creeper's earlier discarded victims.

* * *

KELLY NESTLED her face against the soft supple side of one of Carol's ample breasts.

Their feverish lovemaking at an end, both women had fallen asleep in each other's embrace, completely exhausted.

Still half-asleep, Kelly snuggled up closer to her lover, burying her face in her cleavage and inhaling deeply to appreciate the sweet subtle fragrance of her delicately perfumed skin.

Until this moment, Kelly had never realised that the act lovemaking could be so intense, so pleasurable, so intoxicating.

Being with Carol, even for so short a time, convinced Kelly that there was a whole world of excitement and contentment outside the confines of her married life with Jack, one which hitherto she had never even contemplated existed.

This was Kelly's awakening!

Her moment of serendipity when suddenly for the first time she could see past her own miserable existence, and imagine a life free from drudgery and pain, and above all else, free from Jack.

Jack!

It was in that instant that the realisation of her present predicament suddenly shattered through her fantasy and brought Kelly back down to earth with an almighty bump.

Gripped by a sudden flash of panic, Kelly leaped off the bed and stood up to gather her thoughts, as well as her bearings. But the act of standing so quickly caused her to lose her balance and before she had a chance to sit back down, Kelly missed the end of the bed and landed firmly on her rump on the carpeted floor, before rolling to one side and falling flat on her face.

Kelly released a cry of pain at the sudden jolt from her landing. This, combined with the sound of her hitting the floor, brought Carol out of her doze.

Rubbing the sleep from her eyes Carol leaned over the edge of the bed and gazed down at Kelly's prostrate form.

"Are you OK, hon?" asked Carol, sleepily.

"No!" Kelly moaned, trying once more to push herself upright, but only managing to reach a sitting position with the bed for support.

Carol laughed out loud. It was not a spiteful laugh, nor was it aimed at Kelly's expense. It was just the comical way that her friend was trying to take control of her situation and failing, dismally.

Even so, Kelly looked up at her friend with a hurt expression on her face, obviously feeling a little sorry for herself.

Carol swung her legs around off the bed and reached down to help Kelly up. Unfortunately, she had not anticipated just how little control Kelly had over her own body at that moment.

As Kelly took hold of her friend's offered hands and tried to hoist herself back up, her feet slipped on the carpet, and she dragged Carol off the bed and brought her crashing down on top of her.

Now the pair of them started a fresh fit of laughter which neither of them could control.

Once their mirth had finally waned, Carol took the lead and forced herself into a standing position.

This time she placed her bare feet on top of Kelly's to stop her from sliding out from under her, and then she grabbed her friend firmly by the wrists before helping her up.

The manoeuvre succeeded and both women stood face to face for a moment before Carol gently slipped her hand behind Kelly's neck and pulled her forward for a kiss.

Although Kelly had a vague memory of the alarm which she had experienced a moment earlier at the realisation of her predicament and the fact that she needed to get back to her husband before he started to suspect that something was going on, she still did not offer any resistance against Carol's offering.

The two of them remained locked in an intimate embrace as their tongues re-explored the inside of each other's mouths.

Once they had finished, Carol realised that she was still balancing on her friend's feet.

"If I get off now, are you sure that you won't fall back over?" she asked, mockingly.

Kelly smiled. "I think I'll be OK now."

Carol carefully stood back, releasing her friend's feet from underneath her own, but she still kept hold of her hands, until she was sure that Kelly was not about to fall back.

Still feeling a little woozy, Kelly eased herself down gently on the end of the bed and started to rub her head.

"Would you like me to get you some water, or maybe an aspirin?" asked Carol, genuinely concerned. "That stuff was a bit stronger than my usual brew."

Kelly, suddenly realising what her friend had said, looked up, frowning.

"What stuff?" she asked, perplexed.

Carol shrugged. "The hash," she replied, matter-of-factly.

Through her hazy state, Kelly was still having trouble focusing on what Carol was saying.

She rubbed her eyes once more to try and clear away the grogginess.

"What hash?" she asked, sounding a tad more demanding than she had intended to. "What are you talking about; did you slip me something in my drink?"

Carol looked shocked. "No," she responded, defensively, "what kind of a pervert do you think I am?"

Kelly was growing more confused by the second.

"So what *hash* are you talking about then, I take it you do mean pot, marijuana?"

Carol stifled a laugh by slapping her hand over her mouth.

"What's so funny?" Kelly demanded, starting to feel her temper rise.

"The way you said marijuana," Carol replied, unable to

keep a broad grin from crossing her face. "You make it sound like some kind of illegal contraband."

Kelly looked shocked. "Well, it is, isn't it?"

Carol slid down to sit beside her friend and placed her arm around her narrow shoulders, giving them a gentle squeeze.

She looked Kelly straight in the eye. "No, silly, when it's for personal consumption it's OK, has been for a while now."

Kelly raised her eyebrows in disbelief. "Are you sure?" she asked, timidly.

Carol leaned over and kissed her on the nose. "Positive," she reassured her. Then after a moment she continued. "However, the coke I used, that's a different matter!"

Kelly jolted upright, her eyes wide. "What coke?" she exploded, her voice uncontrollably rising in pitch.

Carol quickly realised that her friend was genuinely concerned and not just joking with her.

She placed a tender hand on Kelly's arm to calm her down.

Holding her gaze once more, she said, "Look, there was a small amount of hash in the cake I gave you, just a little to get you in the mood and help you to relax, perhaps I should have told you first, but you seemed eager enough to take it."

As Carol's words registered, Kelly began to feel a little foolish for reacting the way she had. The fact was that she had never tried, nor indeed even considered, taking drugs other than those prescribed. So, in a way she did feel as if she had been tricked by Carol, but at the same time she also realised that her friend probably had not given it a second thought and like her, had just got caught up in the moment.

But then she remembered what else Carol had said.

"What about the coke?" she asked, anxiously. "Was there coke in that cake as well; am I high, is that why I cannot keep my balance and the room is spinning?"

Carol held out her hand to calm Kelly down. "No, don't

worry; I wouldn't slip you any coke unless I knew that you could handle it." She assured her. "The coke was the white powder I slipped on the end of my tongue before I went down on you, it was meant to give you a special tingle while I worked my magic, and I think it succeeded." Carol purred, giving Kelly a sly wink.

Kelly could feel her cheeks reddening. She was not completely sure why, after all, she had thoroughly enjoyed their time together and a few minutes earlier she was still caught up in the moment and not embarrassed in the slightest by what they had done.

Kelly wondered if perhaps it was the potency of the hash wearing off.

A sudden chill left her covered in goose bumps.

Kelly instinctively brought up her hands to cover herself. It was as if she was suddenly aware of her nakedness and with it came a familiar feeling of shame.

Sensing her friend's discomfort, Carol reached down and retrieved some of her discarded clothes from the floor and handed them to her.

Kelly accepted the gesture with a nervous smile and immediately began to get dressed.

Carol pulled on her dressing gown as she walked over to the bedroom door. She decided to leave Kelly to sort herself out while she fixed herself another drink from the lounge.

After a couple of minutes Kelly joined her in the next room, still looking a little sheepish.

"Fancy a nightcap before you go?" Carol asked, holding out a bottle of brandy.

Kelly shook her head. "No, thanks, I think I had better get going, it's late, and Jack'll be home soon."

Carol poured herself another drink and replaced the bottle on the cabinet. She gazed at Kelly over the rim of her glass as she drank. It was obvious to her that her friend was now starting to regret their time together, but Carol put that down to a combination of it being her first time with another woman, as well as her guilty conscience which pricked whenever she caught herself enjoying anything without her husband.

Carol felt a sudden overwhelming surge of warmth and a closeness to Kelly, which made her want to wrap her arms around her and hold her close to reassure her that everything was going to be OK.

She knew that it was not just as a result of them making love together. Carol had slept with several partners of both sexes without having such feelings for them.

In Kelly's case it was something more than that. Her friend brought out the protector in Carol, and whereas as it had always been her rule never to get involved in other people's business, with Kelly she felt justified in intervening and doing whatever she could for her.

"I really should go," Kelly stammered, smiling weakly. "It's been lovely though," she offered, as an afterthought.

Carol put down her glass. "Listen, kiddo," she began as she moved a step closer. She was taken aback when Kelly flinched involuntarily, as if she feared being struck.

Carol stayed where she was, not wishing to make her friend feel any less comfortable than she obviously did at this moment.

"Promise me," she continued, in her most soothing voice, "that you won't start beating yourself up about what we did; the last thing I want is to be the cause of you feeling more guilt than you already do about everything?"

Kelly bit her bottom lip. She could not deny the guilt that she was already feeling, but by the same token she did not want Carol blaming herself.

She wanted to say something strong and worldly to reassure

her friend, but for the moment she could not think of anything that would suffice.

Instead she caught herself dropping her head and staring down at her shoes.

This time Carol moved in close enough to be able to place her hand under Kelly's chin so that she could lift it up and look her in the eyes.

Kelly immediately dropped her gaze, and then within a few seconds looked back up again.

She was feeling foolish without really knowing why, and that made her angry with herself and more determined to get a grip.

Carol waited for Kelly to speak first, but when it became obvious to her that it was not going to happen any time soon, she decided to make one more try to set her friend's mind at ease before she went home.

"Look, kiddo, what we did tonight was just a bit of fun between us girls, there's nothing to feel remotely guilty about, and after all we both enjoyed it, didn't we?"

She looked into Kelly's eyes for some sign of a positive reaction.

Kelly managed a half-hearted smile, which was better than nothing.

Carol leaned forward and placed both her hands on Kelly's shoulders, gripping her firmly but gently like a teacher on the last day of term trying to reassure a bullied pupil that things were going to get better next year.

"Now, please don't go taking this the wrong way," Carol continued, "I'm not a lesbian per se and I'm not promising you a wonderful life with me by your side. Lord knows, I still enjoy a fat cock between my legs as much as the next girl."

Kelly guffawed out with laughter at her friend's words. It

felt good to laugh, and it shattered any remaining anxiety she was feeling about the situation.

"There now," beamed Carol, feeling relieved that she had managed to break the awkwardness of the mood. "That's a bit more like it." She kept her eyes fixed on Kelly, relishing the warmth that radiated from the girl as she laughed.

Pulling her closer, Carol softened her tone even more, determined to hammer her message home without sounding too heavy. "Like I said, I am not trying to say that we are going to become love's young dream or anything quite so dramatic, but I will always be here for you if you need me, whether it's just to have a drink and a laugh, or to get away from that monster you're married to for a couple of hours, or even if you fancy a quick shag and another hash cake, whatever, I'm only a couple of doors down, so don't you forget it."

Without speaking, Kelly threw her arms around Carol and held her tightly for the best part of a minute.

When they pulled away, Carol could see a thin sheen of moisture in Kelly's eyes, but the smile on her face told her that everything was better.

CHAPTER SIXTEEN

Katy Staples crunched through the fallen leaves in Monk's Wood on her early morning two-hour constitutional with her two rescued Alsatians Zeus and Apollo. Though they were actually brothers, rather than father and son, she had chosen the names because of her love of Greek mythology, and they both seemed to respond when called, so the names stuck.

The early morning sun had just started to filter through the mostly-bare branches of the trees which surrounded this area of the wood and brought with it a warmth which was worthy of a summer's day.

Katy loved this time of day. Even as a child she had always felt inspired by witnessing the morning sunrise, even in the middle of winter, and she felt then, as now, that if she managed to see the sun come up, then the day would be filled with endless possibilities.

Her job as manager of the local branch of Pet Rescue Services meant that she had the freedom of working flexible hours as well as the luxury of a company vehicle which, being a van, gave her ample room for her beloved dogs to sit in the back.

In her line of work, even though she was the boss, Katy was not averse to taking to the road when they were stretched so that she could assist in a rescue, or to transport animals between centres as and when the necessity arose.

Katy took great pride in her work, and she could not imagine ever doing anything else.

Up ahead, she could see Zeus and Apollo foraging amongst the undergrowth off to one side of the lane. The pair of them seemed intent on digging something up, and both of them were frantically pawing away at the ground as if endeavouring to unearth some form of buried treasure.

As Katy drew closer, she called to her boys to leave whatever it was alone and move on. Whatever it was that had sparked their interest Katy decided that it would no doubt turn out to be the lifeless form of some poor creature, half-eaten and left covered over by a fox for later.

Unusually for her two dogs they seemed reluctant to obey her command.

Instead the two of them started walking around in circles whining loudly whilst still pawing at the ground and sniffing the area intently.

Katy called to them once more, ordering them to come to her.

This time they both obeyed, but Katy could tell that they were not best pleased with having to leave their quarry.

The two dogs stood before their mistress and started barking loudly. Not in an aggressive way, but more as if they were trying to bring something to her attention.

Katy looked down at the two of them, perplexed.

"What is it you silly woofers?" she asked, as if half expecting them to answer her.

Instead, Apollo began to stand up on his hind legs and whimper, just like he did whenever he was begging for something. Katy reached out to take his paws in her hands and spoke soothingly to him while he danced back on forth keeping his balance on his back legs.

Zeus, seeing his mistress in conversation with his brother, turned back to where the two of them had been scratching the ground and immediately began to paw the soil with one paw, just as he always did when he was leaving something half-finished with the intention of returning to it later.

When Katy released Apollo, he too joined his brother, but instead of pawing the ground he just stared at the spot in question and continued whining as if he were desperate for his mistress to join them.

Katy sighed in resignation. It was obvious to her that her two boys were determined to bring something to her attention, and nothing was going to distract either of them from the task.

Although the sun was trying to break through the wooded area, it was still too dark for Katy to make out what her dogs were getting so excited about. So, she took out the torch from her jacket pocket and pointed the bright beam towards where they were indicating.

At first, she could see nothing save for leaves and fallen branches. As she moved in closer, the two dogs backed away giving her ample room to survey their find.

In the shadowy glow of the torchlight's beam Katy squinted as she bent down to have a closer look.

When her eyesight finally focused on the human hand her dogs had uncovered, Katy let out a scream which pierced the surrounding woodland and sent her two dogs into a fit of barking as they ran around where she was standing in opposing circles.

* * *

ONCE MORE IT was the shrill shrieking of his phone which brought Hardy back into the world from his slumber.

Without waiting for his eyes to focus on who was calling, he pressed the answer button and held it to his ear.

"Hardy," he barked.

"Good morning, sir, sorry to bother you, it's Constable Grant again."

Hardy could detect the familiar nervousness in the young PC's voice. He decided that she was probably the most talked-down to officer in the entire station, especially as it was often left to her to make phone calls such as these.

He decided that he would try and lighten the mood for her, despite that fact that his head was splitting.

"Now, I know that you are only calling me to tell me that the super has decided to give me a well-earned day off, Constable."

Hardy heard laughter on the other end of the line and waited until Grant managed to recover.

"Sorry, sir," Grant apologised. He heard the young officer clearing her throat, still trying to regain her composure. For some reason Hardy was glad that the PC seemed to have a sense of humour. He knew that she would doubtless need that as a coping method during the course of her career.

PC Grant finally managed to quell her laughter, before continuing in her most professional voice. "There have been some human remains discovered over by Monk's Wood, sir, uniform is down there now, and forensics are on their way."

Hardy sighed and rubbed his forehead with the palm of his hand.

This was not going to be a good day to start with a hangover.

In his gut, Hardy knew that the remains had to be those of Natasha and Ben, and in his mind, he could already hear his superintendent screaming at him about how bad this discovery was going to reflect on the force in light of Gerald Spencer's position and contacts.

"Sir, are you still there?" asked Grant, cautiously.

"Yes, Constable, still here, but wishing I wasn't." Hardy threw back the covers and hoisted himself up to a sitting position. As he moved, he made an audible groaning sound.

"Are you OK, Inspector?" enquired Grant, with genuine concern in her voice.

"Nothing that a few weeks in the Bahamas wouldn't cure." replied Hardy, stifling a yawn. "Have you contacted Sergeant Russell yet?"

"No sir, I was told to inform you first."

"OK, tell the sergeant to meet me there," then as an afterthought he added, "and you'd better let the super know, god help us!"

Hardy heard Grant giggle again. She had a sweet voice which he had not really noticed before, so it was good to hear her laugh.

After the call ended, Hardy went into the bathroom and quickly shaved managing to cut himself twice in his haste, and then he brushed his teeth.

Once dressed, he went down to the kitchen and boiled the kettle to make a cup of strong coffee. He found a sachet of Alka-Seltzer which he emptied into a glass of water and threw it down his throat as soon as the contents started to fizzle out.

By the time Hardy arrived at the scene of the discovery, a full road block and cordon of the surrounding area had been set up. The officer operating the cordon recognised Hardy without him having to flash his badge, so he waved him on.

A light drizzle had started while Hardy was en route to the

site, so by the time he arrived the forensics team had already set their tents up to preserve the remains and protect them from the elements.

Hardy parked up and walked to the back of his vehicle to retrieve his wellingtons and rain jacket from the boot.

As he dressed, he looked around the ringed-off area and caught sight of Russell talking to a middle-aged woman who was sitting at the far end of the road with a blanket around her shoulders. Next to her were two large dogs on leads which Hardy could tell she was desperately trying to keep under control whilst she was speaking to his colleague.

Once he was dressed, Hardy threw his shoes into the boot and slammed it shut.

He made his way over to where Russell was speaking to the lady. Halfway there, Russell looked up from his notebook and signalled his acknowledgement to his superior.

Russell left the woman just as a uniformed PC brought her a hot drink. He started walking towards Hardy.

"Morning guv," announced Russell as the two of them drew closer. He turned back to indicate to the woman with the dogs. "The lady's name is Miss Katy Staples; she was walking her two dogs as she does every morning, when they both started pawing at the ground. When she went over to investigate, she saw a human hand sticking up from the dirt, that's when she called us."

Hardy nodded. "There are two bodies I understand, any indication that it might be Natasha and Ben?"

Russell glanced over towards the forensic team's tents. "Well, it's too early to say for definite, from what I saw of them unearthing them, both bodies had been ravaged and torn to shreds but judging from the description of what Ben Green was last seen wearing I'd hazard a guess that one of them is him."

Hardy sighed deeply and swatted a dribble of rain off his forehead.

He glanced over towards the tents, and then back to Russell.

"And Natasha?" he asked, already confident of the answer, although he was dreading hearing the actual words.

Russell paused as he looked back through his notes.

After a quick reread, he replied. "Well, like I said the remains are pretty mangled but judging from the description we were given by Natasha's parents concerning what she was wearing the last time they saw her, these remains were definitely dressed differently."

Hardy swung back. "How do you mean?" he asked, puzzled.

Russell flicked back and forth through his notebook once more before answering. "Natasha apparently had on a dark top and skirt and boots when she left with Ben, from what we can tell the female victim here had on a light-coloured dress and shoes." He looked back up at his boss. "As I say, it's too early to know for sure, but from the initial identification my guess would be that it is someone else."

Hardy was not sure if the news he had just heard was good or bad.

True, he would be happier if Natasha was still alive, but then if this was someone else, then it meant that he had another unidentified victim to deal with.

Either way, he decided, the news was not good.

Hardy watched as Katy Staples blew on the surface of her piping hot tea. The PC who had brought it for her was now sitting next to her, playing with dogs, doubtless trying to attract their attention so that the woman could drink her tea in peace.

Hardy had a sudden thought.

He turned back to face Russell. "Did you say that she walked her dogs here at the same time every morning?"

"Yep, that's right. She said that she always comes out at sunrise and that this is her usual route, apparently her dogs love it."

"So, she would have been here yesterday, presumably?" surmised Hardy.

"I imagine so," considered Russell, trying to get up to speed with his senior officer's line of thought.

Hardy pointed in the direction of the human remains. "So, then it follows that if those bodies had been dumped here before yesterday, her dogs would have sniffed them out on their morning walk, right?"

Russell considered the question before answering. "Well, I suppose so."

"Which also means," Hardy continued, trying not to lose his train of thought. "That if they were buried here sometime between yesterday morning and this morning, then we have a definite scope of time to concentrate on when appealing for witnesses?"

"Gotcha," Russell replied, suddenly realising the importance of Hardy's reasoning. "Right, I'll get onto the station right now and start the ball rolling."

With that, Russell turned around to make his way back to his own car. He had only taken a few paces before Hardy called back to him.

"Tell them to keep quiet about what we've found, at the moment we are just looking for anyone who saw anything suspicious, we'll go from there."

Russell nodded and continued back to his vehicle.

At that moment, Hardy noticed a police van entering the cordon. It pulled up behind his car and several uniformed officers dressed in waterproof ponchos poured out of the back doors.

The uniformed sergeant who climbed out of the front passenger seat noticed Hardy, and after barking some orders to his officers, he strode over to him.

"Morning, Inspector," he announced, as he drew nearer, "lovely weather for it."

"You can say that again," replied Hardy, offering his hand for the junior officer to shake.

Although the uniformed officer was junior to him in rank, PS Guthrie was only a year away from retirement. He was very much of the old school where the duty of a police officer was all about serving the public and protecting the rights of law-abiding citizens. He was certainly not one for sitting behind a desk staring at a computer all day and calculating resources by using spreadsheets, which was why he was often the senior officer in charge of the uniform brigade on occasions such as this.

Hardy had worked with him before and liked him.

"I've mustered as many as I could at short notice," the sergeant informed him, "what would you like us to do?"

Hardy indicated towards where the two tents were set up. There were several forensic officers in white hooded overalls milling around the area securing it the best they could before arranging to remove the bodies.

"If you can get your team to spread out and search the surrounding area for anything that might be of use," explained Hardy, waving his arm across the area surrounding the tents. "Right now, I need all the help I can get, so make sure that they are as thorough as possible."

The sergeant saluted him. "Right, Inspector, leave it with me."

With that, the sergeant turned and shouted to his constables instructing them on which protocol to follow, emphasising the need for accuracy and efficiency.

Hardy was glad that Guthrie was on the job.

There would definitely be no slacking with him at the helm.

Just then, Hardy noticed a member of the forensics team emerging from one of the tents. As the woman moved into the daylight, she removed her cap and mask. Hardy did not know her name, but he had seen her before and remembered that she was quite affable and easy to talk to.

Hardy walked over to her. The female officer was bent over with her hands on her knees, breathing deeply.

When Hardy was beside her, he asked, "Are you OK, can I get you anything?"

The officer looked up, recognised Hardy, and shook her head.

She took in another few deep gasps before speaking. "I'll be alright, thanks, you'd think that I would be used to this by now, but sometimes it just gets the better of you."

Hardy nodded. "Well I take my hat off to you; I couldn't do what you do."

"Snap!" replied the forensic officer, smiling.

Hardy moved in a step closer. "I know that you haven't been here long but is there anything you can tell me?" he asked, emphasising with his tone and mannerism the fact that he was not expecting miracles, but would be grateful for anything offered.

The officer took in another deep breath before responding. "Well, as I think my colleague told your sergeant earlier, it's definitely the remains of a man and a woman. It's too early to tell exact ages, but due to the massive amount of tissue loss and the extensive lacerations to the viscera, I'd say that whatever did this to them is some kind of wild animal, perhaps a large cat."

"Seriously?" Hardy asked, without meaning to sound in any way condescending, but he knew as soon as he spoke that the surprise in his voice may well have been misinterpreted.

The forensic officer looked up at the inspector and held his gaze for a moment.

Hardy could tell from the officer's demeanour that she was being totally serious in her estimation, but before he had a chance to apologise, she continued speaking.

"Well, we'll know more once we begin the post-mortem examinations, but in the meantime, you might want to check if any zoo or wildlife reserve in the area has a panther or a leopard missing from one of its cages."

This time Hardy merely nodded in response.

He glanced over to the tents and for a moment he considered suiting up to take a look for himself, but immediately dismissed the thought from his mind.

He had witnessed quite a few bloody remains in his time in London and the experience always left him feeling nauseous.

Hardy turned back just as the officer was replacing her mask and cap.

"Will you let me know as soon as you have something, please?" he asked, politely.

"Of course," she replied from behind her cloth mask.

Hardy smiled, broadly. "Thank you, I'll look forward to your call."

Although it was hard to tell with the starched cloth covering the bottom of her face, Hardy fancied that he saw the officer smile at him before she turned and made her way back into the tent.

At least, he hoped that she did.

CHAPTER SEVENTEEN

Father Ambrose Grace genuflected in front of the altar and made the sign of the cross before rising. With the onset of arthritis, he could feel as a result of his advancing years the aches and pains in his joints grew evermore evident whenever he had to bend or kneel down, but he treated them as the minor ailments they were, with god's grace.

During his time in the priesthood, Father Grace had visited several hundred parishioners on their deathbeds in order to administer some much-needed comfort and solace along with the final rites. He had seen at first hand the agony and suffering some of his flock had had to suffer before god called them to his mercy, so he was forever grateful that to date, his greatest affliction was merely in the form of a relatively mild case of the bone disease.

As he turned and walked down the main aisle of his church, he glanced over at the assorted bowed heads scattered amongst the pews. Most of them he recognised instantly as belonging to some of the most fervent members of his flock who stayed back after morning mass to continue their devotions.

Father Grace knew that in some areas his fellow priests insisted on closing and locking the doors of their church once the last parishioner had been ushered out after mass. But Father Grace firmly believed that the church should be a place of welcome respite where anyone, not necessarily just those belonging to his congregation, could saunter in for a moment's quiet prayer, whenever the fancy struck them.

To that end, he always left the main doors unlocked, and in the warmer months actually kept them wedged open so that passers-by could see that they were more than welcome to enter.

Father Grace was extremely proud of his church. Not just for what it stood for spiritually as a beacon of hope for the forlorn, but the structure and architecture of actual building itself. The stain glass windows were truly magnificent, and the carvings and statues which stood gazing down on the faithful were, in themselves, worthy of attention and praise for their craftsmanship and attention to the most minute of details.

The priest had often come across tourists visiting the town on one of their excursions, wandering into the church and being struck by the beauty and awe of the place. He would chuckle to himself at the startled looks he received when he welcomed them in and offered to answer any questions they might have on the history of the building, as well as allowing them to take as many pictures of the inside as they wished, and all without asking for even the smallest of contributions towards the upkeep and maintenance of the building.

As far as he was concerned, the church was rich enough to look after itself.

In the matter of his church, pride was a sin the priest allowed himself to indulge in, without recourse.

As he passed silently down the rows of highly polished dark

oak, Father Grace noticed a lone figure loitering in the vestibule.

As he drew closer, he immediately recognised the tiny form of Kelly Soames. She was standing in the shadows, with her head bowed, shuffling from one foot to the other as if she was nervous or worried about something.

Father Grace had been concerned for the girl for some time now. As much as he believed in the good in all men, he sometimes struggled to see any redeeming quality in Kelly's good-for-nothing husband Jack.

He had been especially anxious lately with the appearance of those nasty-looking bruises on her face. It was clearly evident to the old priest that Kelly's husband was beating her, and the thought of that made his blood boil.

Even so, he could only offer help and guidance when it was asked of him. It was not his place to interfere in the relationship between and man and wife. Such worldly matters were far beyond his purview as a man of god. However, Father Grace also understood that the good lord gave individuals the power to make their own decisions, and sometimes, as far as he was concerned when those decisions affected others in a detrimental way, god might just look the other way when mere men stepped in to correct the oversight.

As he drew nearer, Kelly suddenly looked up and saw him approaching. Instead of the usual sunny smile she always gave him, there was a look of deep concern, almost panic on her face, and before the priest could call to her she turned on her heel and started walking quickly towards the main doors.

Not wishing to disturb the other parishioners whilst they were at their devotion, Father Grace waited until he was in the vestibule before he called to Kelly.

"Kelly, wait a moment, please?" he called beseechingly.

He only managed to catch her in the split second before she

crossed the threshold of the outside doors and disappeared out of sight.

Deep down he knew that she would not be able to go once she had heard him call to her. Even then, she did not turn back to come inside, but instead stood framed in the outer doorway with her back still to him.

Father Grace approached Kelly as quietly and as stealthily as he could, for fear that if she realised how close he was getting she might become spooked and make a dash for it.

He had never seen her react in this, and he could not hide the concern in his voice once he was directly behind her.

"Now then, Kelly, what is all this about? Have I done something to upset you that you don't have time to stop and talk to an old friend?"

When Kelly turned around, he could see immediately that she had been crying.

The minute she saw his face, a fresh stream of tears began to slide down her red cheeks.

The priest reached out and placed a comforting arm around her shoulders and guided her gently towards the side door which led to his private quarters.

"Now, you come with me," he suggested, tenderly, "I think you need a nice strong cup of tea inside you, and then you can tell me what's troubling you."

As they walked, Kelly kept her head buried in her hands, her narrow shoulders shaking from the heaving sobs she was trying so desperately, but unsuccessfully, to staunch.

As Father Grace opened the side door to allow Kelly access to his quarters, she suddenly spun around on the spot and looked him squarely in the eyes.

"Oh, Father," she blurted, "I know that it's too early, but I really need you to hear my confession."

There was a desperate longing in her tone which the old

priest picked up on immediately. Although she was a regular at confession, this was the first time in all the years that he had known her that she could not wait until one of the advertised slots to make her confession.

That fact alone gave the Father Grace cause for concern, and though he hated to admit it, even to himself, he was somewhat intrigued to hear what this was all about.

He looked down at Kelly's tear-streaked face and offered her a smile of reassurance.

Taking a clean tissue from a pack in his robe, he handed one to her and watched as she wiped her face.

After a moment he replied. "OK, if it is really that terrible that you cannot wait until this evening, then of course I will hear your confession, my child."

Although obviously relieved by his words, Kelly did not smile or show any outer signs of appreciation. Instead she merely bowed her head once more and allowed the old priest to lead her to the confessional.

Once inside, they both made the sign of the cross and Kelly repeated her well-rehearsed introduction to her confession.

Father Grace encouraged her to make a good confession and sat back to await her monumental declaration.

"Father," Kelly began, hesitantly. "I have broken my vows of marriage and been unfaithful to my husband."

There was a moment's pause during which Kelly held her breath, almost as if in anticipation of the priest spewing forth a tirade of recriminations at her which would draw the attention of all those inside the church.

For a second, Kelly could almost imagine each of them ceasing their prayers and moving together in unison, converging on her in the confessional and grabbing at her clothing before dragging her out of the church and throwing her into the street, before stoning her for being an adulteress.

But naturally, there were no screams or cries of anguish from Father Grace.

Instead the old priest sat there for a moment, breathing deeply as he considered what to say for the best.

He was no hypocrite.

On the one hand it was true that Kelly was admitting to breaking one of the Ten Commandments, and yes, she had taken her vows before god, even if they were not spoken inside a church.

But on the other hand, Father Grace could not close his eyes to the fact that Kelly's husband was a brute, who mistreated her terribly, so, who could blame her for such a temporary, and in this day and age, relatively minor, lapse in judgement.

Through the wooden grate of the confessional, the priest could sense that Kelly was truly worried about what he was going to say.

The usual lecture he was supposed to present under these circumstances, a ritual berating which he had learnt by heart when he first entered the priesthood, did not seem appropriate under the circumstances.

In his mind he mentally skipped the introduction and the long-winded instruction about the sanctity of marriage, and instead he decided to simply cut to the chase.

"Kelly, my child," he began, "I cannot abide by what you have done, however, as long as you are willing to make a good confession here and now for what you know in your heart was a sin, then I know that the Lord will forgive you, as he does all the trespasses of those who are repentant."

On the other side of the panel he heard Kelly inhale deeply before she spoke.

"Father," she offered, meekly, "I am afraid that isn't the very worst part of it. I am not sorry for what I did, and what's more, I feel sure that if the opportunity presents itself, I will not be able to resist."

Her words shocked the priest, but he soon recovered.

"But, my child, you must understand that if you are not truly sorry for what you have done, how can I give you absolution?"

Kelly leaned in closer to the grid which separated them. It was almost as if by doing so she could draw closer to god and his mercy, for she knew that what she was saying went against everything she had been brought up to believe in.

"Father, I cannot lie, not to you and certainly not before god. I know that what I have done is a sin, a grave sin which might even put my very soul in peril." She bowed her head in shame, "but what would you have me say?"

The old priest sighed deeply before answering. "I would have you tell me the truth before god, naturally," he offered, trying to keep the sympathy in his voice whilst at the same time ensuring that he emphasised what was expected of Kelly as a servant of god.

"That is what I'm doing, Father," pleaded Kelly, her voice shaking as another flood of tears started to fall. "But what can I do?"

The question was almost a redundant one.

The priest could not think of anything he could say that would help to resolve the situation.

It was almost as if he were caught in the middle of a titanic struggle between the man inside him who understood and even sympathised with Kelly's predicament, and the priest who had pledged his service to god and in doing so swore an oath to uphold the teachings of the church without question.

After a long pause, Father Grace rubbed his forehead with the palm of his hand and looked up. Kelly could tell even through the wooden grate, that the priest was not at all pleased with the predicament she had put him in.

Kelly bit her bottom lip in anticipation of what she was about to hear.

In truth, she had not deluded herself that Father Grace would simply smile sweetly and send her on her way with a couple of Hail Mary's and an act of contrition as penance. But now she was starting to feel truly guilty for the position she had put the old priest in. The fact that he had known her for so long probably made the situation worse for him, too.

The silence between them was interminable, and Kelly was just about to apologise and make her excuses before leaving the confessional, when the old priest spoke up.

"Kelly, my child," he began, earnestly, "you have put me in a no-win situation here. You know as a good catholic that you must live your life according to god's teachings, but the decision as to how you live your life is still up to you."

"Yes, Father," Kelly responded, dejectedly.

"It's only human to err," the priest continued, "and god realises and forgives those who do, but they must be contrite in order to be forgiven, otherwise it is as if the sinner is refusing to acknowledge that they have acted against god in the first place."

Kelly tried to force back her tears.

Before today, she would have never believed that she would find herself in this position.

There was no point in lying to the priest and claiming to be repentant, because not only would she by lying to him, but to god as well, and what was more she knew then that any absolution she received under those circumstances would be worthless.

Kelly took a deep breath to try and keep her voice from shaking.

"I'm sorry, Father, I should never have come here, not

unless I was ready to be repentant and promise not to sin again."

She heard the priest sigh from the other side of the box. "You do understand then why it is above my power to give you absolution, don't you?"

"Yes, Father."

"I can only hope then that someday soon you are willing to make a good confession to me, so that I can lift this burden which I can tell weighs heavily on your shoulders, Kelly."

"I understand, Father," Kelly whispered, bowing her head once more. She paused for a moment, not sure under the circumstances how the session was going to end as there was no penance forthcoming.

It appeared that the old priest also was unsure as how best to end their session. She surmised that there was a good chance that he had never been confronted by a confessor who was not willing to repent.

Finally, Kelly decided to end the torture herself.

"Father?" she asked, meekly.

"Yes Kelly," the priest replied, his tone gentle and tinged by sympathy.

"Will you pray for me?"

"Of course I will, my child, I always do," he sighed.

With that, Kelly apologised once more and then excused herself from the confessional.

As she left the church, she could feel the burning stares of those on their knees behind her, praying for a forgiveness which she had just refused.

As she reached the vestibule, Kelly stopped just long enough to dip her hands in the holy font and make the sign of the cross, before she ran down the stone steps and out into the daylight.

Father Grace stayed where he was long after Kelly had gone.

He had always had a soft spot for Kelly, and the fact that he had not been able to offer her absolution this morning was already weighing heavily on his conscience.

It was not enough for him to simply hide behind his duty to god and tell himself that she gave him no option. He had always taken his responsibility far more seriously than that.

Kelly was obviously desperately unhappy and in dire need of help and spiritual guidance. She deserved to have some fun in her life having suffered so much heartache, and from such a very young age.

Father Grace knew that he had a responsibility to do all that he could for the young girl.

Regardless of what price he might have to ultimately pay, he had an obligation to look after those who never did anyone any harm whenever he had the opportunity, and that was far more important to him right now than his own welfare.

The old priest began the first of many prayers he would say that day on Kelly's behalf.

CHAPTER EIGHTEEN

As soon as Hardy entered the first set of swing doors back at the station, his attention was drawn to the waving arms of PC Grant as she signalled for him to come over to her. She was behind the main desk dealing with a member of the public, so Hardy hung back and waited patiently for his turn.

The young man that the PC was dealing with could not have been older than twenty-three or twenty-five, but he sounded like an old man the way he was carrying on about the illegally parked vehicles in his street and how he was unable to park his car when he arrived home from work.

After PC Grant politely informed him for the second time that he needed to contact his local council office to make his complaint, the young man finally took the hint and stormed out of the foyer grumbling to himself about the police being a waste of his tax money.

"Sorry about that, sir," offered Grant, as the door swung shut behind the complainant.

"That's alright, Constable, it's always nice to receive praise from a grateful member of the public," Hardy joked, whilst managing to keep a straight face.

The young female officer appreciated the joke and could not help but crack a smile.

"Well my little alarm clock, what can I do for you?" asked Hardy, this time forcing Grant to laugh out loud at his comment.

She slapped her hand across her mouth and looked about her, obviously embarrassed that someone might have heard her.

When PC Grant finally managed to control her laughter, she cleared her throat before speaking. "Superintendent Carlisle has asked to see you in his office as soon as you arrived, sir." She made the statement almost as if it were an apology and seeing the expression on Hardy's face when she spoke, made her feel all the guiltier for having to be the messenger.

Just like everyone else in the station, PC Grant knew that the super was a man of little patience who seemed to care more about targets and what those with influence and power thought about his operation, then the men and women who worked tirelessly under him trying to keep the area safe, and the criminal elements off the streets.

In truth, PC Grant sympathised with Hardy. She knew from what she had gleaned since being at the station that he was a well-respected officer, and highly thought of by his team. She imagined that all Carlisle wanted was a chance to bellow at the inspector by way of justifying his position.

Hardy gave Grant a sly wink. "Well the brown stuff is hitting the fan early today, it seems." The inspector's familiarity had caught the young PC off guard for a moment, but by the time she could feel her cheeks flush, he had already turned to leave, for which she was grateful.

She watched Hardy's retreating form as he made his way

out into the corridor and wondered to herself why it was that whenever she saw him, she felt a slight twinge in her tummy, which made her feel like a schoolgirl with a crush on the headmaster.

Constable Grant cleared the thought from her mind as she saw an elderly couple approach the desk, looking for assistance.

As Hardy made his way along the corridor towards Carlisle's office, he saw Sergeant Russell coming towards him, shuffling through a stack of loose papers in his hand.

As they met, Russell suddenly looked up. "Hello, guv," he said, cheerfully. "Are you aware that the super wants a word?"

"He can have two if he's lucky," replied Hardy, checking that no one else was listening. "And the second one is off!"

Russell laughed good-heartedly at his superior's joke, but then his face grew darker as he held up his stack of papers. "We've just had a report in about another missing woman."

Hardy felt his stomach drop. "Oh, wonderful, is that what Carlisle wants me for?"

Russell shrugged. "I'm not sure guv; we only received the complaint about ten minutes ago. I'm just reading over the details now."

Hardy sighed. "Alright, let me see what ol' cheerful wants, then I'll come and find you, if I've still got a job," he added as an afterthought.

Hardy was not expecting a warm welcome from his superintendent, and he was not disappointed.

After ushering him into his office, Carlisle signalled to the chair in front of his desk without saying a word.

Hardy took his seat and waited for his superior to speak.

Carlisle propped his elbows on his desk and made a tent out of his fingers upon which he rested his forehead and stared down at his desk.

Hardy waited in silence.

Carlisle's animated behaviour was really starting to get on his nerves; the man was turning into a caricature of the worst type of senior officer. The type that screamed and shouted for the sake of it, demanding results without bothering to listen to their junior officers when they were trying to explain the progress of the case to them.

But Hardy accepted that fact that as DI he was the buffer between Carlisle and his team, so he took it on the chin without complaint.

Not that there had not been times—several in fact—when he found himself on the point of exploding and telling his superintendent what he really thought of him.

Eventually, after several deep breaths which Hardy took to be more for affect than anything else, Carlisle lifted his head and dropped his hands back down on top of his desk.

Hardy steeled himself in anticipation of the onslaught to come, but he had not anticipated Carlisle's years of experience at lulling his subordinates before striking the death blow. It was a skill which his superior was well adept at springing on his junior officers whenever the need arose.

He just had to plan his moment for maximum effect.

"So, any news on those two bodies found this morning?" he asked, inquiringly.

"Well it's too early to say for definite, but after a preliminary examination we are almost positive that the male must be Ben Green, but for now we are working on the assumption that the female is not Natasha Spencer."

Carlisle's interest was obviously peeked by this news. "Really!" he exclaimed, unable to hide the shock from his voice. "Based on what?"

"Well, as I say it's still too early to tell for sure but judging by the remains of the clothes the victim was wearing and the colour of her hair, we have to presume that she's not our girl."

Carlisle mulled this over for a moment, before adding. "Well that's something at least," he said, almost gleefully.

"Of course," Hardy interjected, "this does mean that we potentially have another victim of the same killer, who we now have to identify and start to investigate."

Carlisle nodded. "Yes of course, I understand. I only meant that..." he paused for a moment lost in thought, before saying. "Well, never mind. So, do we have anything on this potential new victim to go on?"

Hardy shifted in his seat. "Possibly, Sergeant Russell has just received a report about another missing woman, so when I leave here, we can start looking into that."

Carlisle turned his gaze as if studying some of the paintings which adorned his office walls. "And we're still no further with the Caroline Seymour investigation I take it?"

Hardy shook his head. "No, I'm afraid not, we're still checking leads and banging on doors, hopefully something will turn up soon. Of course, now with the possibility that Caroline might not be an isolated incident, we may have to widen our investigation which will also mean that our resources are stretched even further."

Carlisle brooded on Hardy's words for a moment before he turned his full attention back to the inspector.

The time was right!

"I've been on the phone to the Assistant Chief Constable this morning," Carlisle began. His expression was blank but the fact that he subconsciously started to drum his fingers on his desk was a familiar give-a-way to Hardy that he was about to receive some unwanted news.

"Oh, really, sir," Hardy responded, feeling that he needed to contribute something to break the silence.

"Yes," Carlisle responded, evidently thrown off his track by Hardy's interruption. After a second or two to regroup his thoughts, the senior officer continued. "I take it that you are aware that Gerald Spencer made a public appeal on the television last night?"

Hardy nodded.

"Well the ACC, and for what it's worth, I concur, has instructed me to arrange a press conference for this afternoon, we need to get in there now before the rumour and speculation mill starts rolling."

Hardy nodded. "Well you're the perfect man for the job sir."

"Ah, well, that's the other thing I wanted to speak to you about." Carlisle's eyes darted around the room and up to the ceiling, looking anywhere other than directly at Hardy.

Hardy felt a sudden heaviness in the pit of his stomach which he only experienced in anticipation of something he did not want to do. He knew from Carlisle's expression, as well as his obvious avoidance of his gaze, that he was going to make Hardy take the press conference, and he knew full well that that was one of Hardy's least favourite tasks of all.

Hardy sighed, loudly.

Carlisle held up his hands as if to staunch any verbal attack which might be forthcoming. "Now, I know how reluctant you are to host one of these, therefore, and this is another one of the ACC's recommendations," he explained, hastily, almost as if to justify his next statement, "you are going to be receiving some more help, starting this afternoon."

Hardy looked up. His defences suddenly lowered by the prospect of not having to conduct the press conference after all.

But if he was not going to have to brave the onslaught of the press and Carlisle was not stepping up to the plate, then who exactly was going to do the honours in their place?

Then Hardy remembered Carlisle's offer of some more help.

"What help, sir?" he asked, his brow furrowed. "Do you mean I'm getting more manpower to help with the investigation, because I could certainly use it?"

Carlisle pulled a face. "Well, of a kind." He stood up from his chair and rearranged his clothing as if he were just about to go into an interview.

Inhaling deeply, he continued. "Look, the fact of the matter is that the ACC and I both believe that this investigation would benefit by being led by a more senior officer."

He waited for any response from Hardy, but the inspector merely sat in his chair and listened.

Somewhat relieved, Carlisle decided to press on. "There's a new DCI arriving this afternoon from Surrey who's on the ACC's radar at the moment, and this seems to him a perfect opportunity to allow them to test their mettle."

Hardy continued to stare ahead without reacting.

"So, I thought that it might be a good idea for you to bring the new DCI up to speed and let them deal with the press this afternoon," Carlisle smiled, hoping that he had worded his announcement to make Hardy believe that he was actually doing him a favour.

Hardy thought for a moment, before responding.

"Right you are, sir," he replied as he stood up from his chair.

The abruptness of his movement caused Carlisle to take an involuntary step backwards, which in turn caused him to trip over the castor on one of the chair legs leaving him no option but to fall back into his chair.

Carlisle reached out and grabbed the end of his desk to steady himself, before the force of his descent caused his chair to swivel around.

Hardy managed to stifle a smile. "Will that be all for now, sir?" he asked, matter-of-factly.

"Yes, indeed," replied Carlisle, gathering his composure. "The new DCI should be with us at about 3 p.m. so please ensure that you are here to give them a full report on the situation before the press conference."

"Will do, sir," Hardy responded, before turning to go.

Once his office door was shut, Carlisle let out a deep breath. He had anticipated telling Hardy that a DCI was being brought in over his head would have resulted in a much more confrontational response from the DI. But as it was, Hardy took the news in an extremely calm and sedate manner.

Perhaps, the superintendent mulled, Hardy was actually grateful not to be the first in the firing line now the press was about to get hold of the story.

Either way, Carlisle felt very pleased with himself that he managed to deliver the news without having to suffer a backlash.

Back out in the corridor, Hardy took a deep breath as he analysed in his mind everything that Carlisle had told him.

He wondered to himself just how much the suggestion to bring in a senior officer at this stage had come from Carlisle himself. After all, he had made that snide remark the day before just as Hardy was leaving his office.

Not that it really mattered; Hardy was enough of a professional to let the insult slide off his back. His priority was still to find the killer of Caroline Seymour, as well as the one of Ben Green and their latest victim, whether it was the same individual or not.

And there was still Natasha Spencer to find. He was still hopeful that she was alive and would remain so until they found her.

Hardy grabbed a couple of coffees from one of the

machines in the corridor and took it into the main office to find Sergeant Russell.

He found him updating the incident board at the back of the office.

The whiteboard was almost full of photos of Caroline, Natasha, and Ben, along with the descriptions of when and where they were last seen, and the details of the witnesses they had interviewed thus far.

"How's it coming along?" Hardy asked, as he approached Russell from behind. The sergeant turned and gratefully accepted the plastic cup the inspector offered.

He took a sip of the hot liquid before replying. "Well, as far as this morning's victims are concerned, we're still waiting for the pathologist to come back to us, not that they have a lot left to work with judging by what I saw this morning."

Hardy nodded. "It might be worth getting hold of the dental records for Natasha and Ben; it might speed up the identification."

Russell held up the file in his hand. "Great minds think alike, I was going to start the ball rolling by contacting Ben's dad, but I wasn't sure whether or not the super wanted to liaise between us and Natasha's parents, seeing as he knows them already."

"Good thinking," agreed Hardy.

Just then PC Grant appeared at the main door carrying a pile of paperwork in her arms. Hardy watched as she located the recipient and placed them on his already crowded desk, ensuring that they were not too precariously balanced.

"PC Grant," Hardy called out, causing several of the officers in the room to look up from their work.

Hardy signalled with a wave of his hand to the young constable to join him and Russell.

When Grant sidled up to him, Hardy retrieved the file

from Russell and held it out to her. "I need you to go to Super-intendent Carlisle and ask him if he is happy for us to contact Natasha Spencer's parents in order to get permission to see her dental records." Hardy watched as Grant's eyes never left the folder as if she was holding on to every word he uttered as if her life depended on it. "Also," he continued, "when you've done that, try contacting Ben Green's father and ask the same thing of him, alright?"

The constable nodded her acceptance as she reached out for the file.

"Yes sir," she confirmed, as she took the cardboard folder and tucked it under her arm.

"You did say that you were staying back to help out, didn't you?" asked Hardy.

Grant looked embarrassed. "Well, yes sir, but as a matter of fact I've just been relieved."

Hardy looked at the junior officer, keeping his expression as stern as he could, though for his own amusement. "So, you're off home then, I'll have to find someone else to help me out."

Hardy reached out for the file, but the young PC took a step back and kept it wedged under her arm. "No, that's OK, sir, I'll be happy to help."

She looked at him, and for a moment it looked to the inspector as if she were about to burst into tears if he prevented her from completing the task she had just accepted.

Hardy decided that he could not be that cruel.

He remembered what it was like to be young and eager and how important it was to be trusted to do something by a senior officer.

"Too bleedin' right an' all," he replied, off the cuff. "That'll teach you to go waking me up at the crack of dawn."

PC Grant had to stifle another laugh as she excused herself and went about her new duty.

Russell smiled at his boss when he turned back to face him. "You nasty bugger," he joked.

"Well," replied Hardy, with a wink "it'll do her good to get her hands a little dirty, all that standing behind the main desk all the time is not good for the circulation."

They both returned their attention to the whiteboard.

Russell had cleared some space at the far-right corner onto which he now put up a picture of three women all of whom were smiling and holding up drinks.

"Who're they?" asked Hardy, frowning.

Russell pointed to the girl in the middle of the picture. "This is Gina Steele; she's the one I was telling you about earlier. Her two flatmates on either side of her in this picture say that she's been missing since Saturday evening, they just reported her disappearance this morning."

"What's the story?" Hardy enquired, moving closer for a better look.

Russell picked up a report sheet from the desk at his side and began to read from it. "Apparently, she went out with her boyfriend on Saturday night, and they did not expect to see her until Sunday afternoon at the earliest. But when she did not come home, they just presumed that she was with the boyfriend, that is until one of them called him this morning and he claimed that he hadn't seen her since Saturday night."

"How come they left it so long before contacting him?"

Russell shrugged. "From what I gathered, the boyfriend is married, and their relationship depends on how much time he can manage away from his missus, and apparently on this occasion their friend told them that he was paying for them to stay in a posh hotel in town and not to expect her back anytime soon."

Hardy nodded. "Have we got the boyfriend's details?"

Russell flicked over the first page. "Yes, he's a Robert Drayton, the girls didn't know his home address, but they've given his workplace details.

Hardy looked at his watch. "Well I think we should pay Mr. Drayton a visit, don't you?"

CHAPTER NINETEEN

K elly sat slumped on a park bench, sobbing uncontrollably. She had already used up all the tissues that she had on her and was now reduced to using the sleeve of her jumper to dab her eyes and wipe her nose.

Her life seemed to be over, as far as she was concerned.

Ever since she was old enough to understand, the church had always been her rock, her saviour. Regardless of what she did or said, she always knew that once she made a good confession, her sins would be absolved, and she could start again.

Now, even the church could not save her from her sin.

The fact that Father Grace was unable to absolve her was the final nail in her coffin. She was destined to spend eternity in hell, and there was no way out for her. Her life of honesty, kindness and compassion had all been for nothing if at the end of it the gates of heaven were barred to her.

It was so unfair. Murderers, child molesters, rapists, all manner of despicable individuals in the world would still have their sins forgiven so long as they pretended to be contrite so that they could have their sins absolved.

Kelly supposed that she could always lie! Maybe look down in the confessional so that the priest could not see the deceit on her face as she confessed her sin and pleaded for absolution, promising never to commit such a heinous act again.

Once she had completed her penance that would be that, all over, her sins forgiven and her pathway to heaven reinstated.

Except, she knew, deep down, that god would not be deceived. He could see inside her soul, and he would know that she was lying when she said that she was truly sorry and that she would never commit such an act ever again.

He would know that, deep down, she knew that if the occasion ever arose again, that she would be too weak to refuse.

The sexual pleasure that she should have experienced with her husband she was giving over to another to whom she was not joined under god.

But why should she be cast out, when all she had done was spend some time in the arms of someone who treated her with kindness and respect?

And for that she was supposed to feel remorse!

How could she, when those few precious moments were the nearest thing to tenderness that she had received from another human being in so very long.

Kelly could see no way out of her present dilemma.

For a brief moment she wondered if this was what suicides felt like the moment before they decided to take their own lives.

She knew full well that that would be the ultimate sin of all, from which there would be no going back.

To throw away the precious life that god had granted her would certainly dissolve all the good deeds she had strived so hard to accomplish throughout her life into nothingness.

They would all pale in comparison to her ultimate sin if she ended her own life.

Kelly had never felt so low.

She gazed up to look at the heavens through her watery eyes and watched the silvery-grey clouds as they scudded across the sky. In the past, looking up at the magnificence of the firmament had always given her hope, a sense of something mighty and powerful looking down on her and keeping her safe.

Now however, in her mind's eye, all Kelly could see was the angry glare of her lord, reinforcing the priest's affirmation that if she did not repent, she would never receive forgiveness.

As Kelly stared at the unforgiving clouds above, she whispered a silent prayer, begging for guidance, for some sign that she could still lead a good and useful life without having to stay faithful to that monster she was married to.

Suddenly, she felt a tap on her right shoulder.

Kelly spun around and wiped her eyes simultaneously, not wanting whoever it was to see that she had been crying.

But there was no one there!

Bewildered, Kelly sat upright and scanned the area before her, but the nearest person to her was over by the path and too far away to have touched her and moved back so quickly.

Just then, she felt a gentle thud as someone landed on the seat beside her.

Kelly turned back to see Desmond's smiling face right in front of hers.

"Made yer jump," he grinned, locking eyes with her. Kelly noticed the expression on his face changing as he realised that she had been crying.

She held his gaze for a moment longer.

She desperately wanted to tell him everything.

How she had made a big mistake by marrying Jack, and how much she wished that she had told him in the beginning how she felt about him and even about what she and Carol had done the previous night, and why she was finding it so hard to make a good confession, and why she hated herself for it.

Instead, Kelly just leaned in and pressed her lips against Desmond's.

At first, she was afraid that he was not going to reciprocate.

Had she imagined the signs?

Had she actually fooled herself into believing that he liked her in that way?

But after a moment, her fears vanished as Desmond took her in his arms and pulled her close to him.

They stayed together, locked in a passionate embrace, oblivious to the fact that they were out in the open in full view of anyone passing.

All of a sudden, Jack's 'no touching rule' had lost all its power. She was no longer afraid of what he might say or do if he saw the two of them together.

They carried on kissing like two teenagers on their first date, until in the distance Kelly heard whistling and laughing.

She opened her eyes and saw a group of schoolboys across the other end of the park, pointing at them.

From behind Desmond she lifted her middle finger, which only caused the youngsters to whoop and hollow even more as they made their way out through the gate.

When they finally pulled apart, the look on Desmond's face was one of shock and surprise more than anything else.

They kept their arms around each other as they stared deeply into each other's eyes, until Desmond broke the silence.

"Thanks," he blushed, "I certainly wasn't expecting that."

Kelly smiled back. "You're welcome."

Her face was still red from crying and her cheeks still bore the streaks from her trail of tears.

Keeping one arm around her, Desmond reached over with his other hand and gently rubbed away the tear stains from Kelly's cheeks.

After a moment, he asked, "Why were you crying, has something happened?"

Desmond could tell just by looking at her face that Kelly had suffered another beating since he last saw her on Sunday afternoon, so he presumed that that was probably what she had been crying about. But he wanted to be sure. He needed to know exactly why she was so upset, because he hoped that whatever the reason was that he could do something to help make it better, and right now he did not care what he would have to do, so long as it had the desired effect.

Kelly looked away, blushing.

Desmond could tell that she was obviously embarrassed by his question, but he had asked it now so there was no point in pretending that he had not.

He leaned over and turned Kelly's face back towards his.

For a second, she could not meet his gaze, so he kissed her on the forehead and told her that she could tell him anything without fear of being judged.

He could not imagine Kelly ever doing anything to be ashamed of, but he could see that whatever it was, it clearly bothered her.

Kelly lifted her head with her eyes closed.

She heaved a big sigh before opening them. "I had sex with another woman." She blurted out without giving herself a chance to reconsider the option.

By the look of astonishment on his face, Kelly could tell that her revelation clearly knocked Desmond for six.

She waited, holding her breath, to hear his response.

After what seemed to her like an eternity, Desmond spoke.

"Wow, er, I mean," he spluttered, desperately trying to find something tangible to say.

Without realising what he was doing, Desmond removed his arm from around Kelly's shoulders and sat forward on the bench, resting his elbows on his knees.

Kelly felt the sudden loss of his embrace very deeply, and at first, she was tempted to grab him and try to kiss him again so that they could be back together, but she was afraid that the moment had passed.

Desmond took a deep breath and let it out slowly through his teeth in a whistle.

Kelly edged away from him. She suddenly felt as if she did not belong in such close proximity to a lovely, sweet-natured man such as him.

She could not blame him for reacting the way he had, after all, it was probably the last thing he expected to come out of her mouth. In fact, if anyone had told her this time yesterday that she would have such a thing to confess, she would have thought them to be barmy.

Her mind started to race.

How could she expect Desmond to understand, after all, she could barely believe what she had done herself?

She needed to get away, leave before she made an even bigger fool of herself.

Without speaking, Kelly stood up and starting walking towards the gate at the far end of the park.

With her head bowed and her arms folded she began to sob again, although this time she made a conscious effort not to make too much noise.

Before she had made it more than a couple of feet away, Desmond had run around in front of her, forcing her to stop.

Kelly tried to dodge around him, but Desmond moved sideways to block her.

He placed his hands on her elbows and gave them a gentle squeeze.

Their eyes met.

"I'm sorry," said Desmond, softly. "I didn't mean to upset you, it's just that you threw me a bit when you said that. It was the last thing I expected to come out of your mouth."

Kelly laughed, in spite of the fact that fresh tears were still spilling over her lids.

Desmond pulled her close and wrapped his arms around her.

Kelly put her arms around his waist and turned her face so that she could rest her cheek against his chest.

After a while, Desmond ventured. "I know that I'm only a man, and stupid an' all that, but why exactly were you so upset because you slept with a woman? Was it just because you regretted it?"

Still keeping her arms around him, Kelly pulled back slightly so that she could see his face. His eyes conveyed a combination of concern and empathy. There was absolutely nothing judgmental in his gaze.

Kelly wiped her eyes with the back of her hand, before she replied.

"That's the problem," she began, "I didn't regret it at all."

Desmond nodded. "Oh, OK, I see."

Kelly could tell from his voice that Desmond was feeling dejected.

She was starting to feel more confident that he did in fact have feelings for her, and she wanted to make sure that she came clean and put him in the picture.

The problem was, the picture was as hazy to her as it doubtless would be to him.

Kelly tenderly rubbed his chin with her thumb.

Desmond still had his arms around her, and she purposely

did not do anything to make him think that she wanted him to let go.

She liked the feeling of being in his embrace, and she wanted this moment to last as long as possible.

"I know that it's confusing," she began, earnestly, "believe me; no one is more confused right now than me." She managed a slight smile. "I know now that marrying Jack was a huge mistake, but the fact is that I took my marriage vows very seriously, we were married in the eyes of god, even though it wasn't in a church, I still felt his presence."

Desmond nodded his understanding. He had always known how religious Kelly was and how important her belief was to her.

"And now I've been unfaithful," Kelly continued, "and the worse bit is, deep down, I don't feel guilty for it, and that's why Father Grace could not give me absolution." Kelly shrugged her shoulders as if to emphasise that fact that the situation she was in was completely out of her control.

Desmond waited until he was sure that Kelly was not ready to continue before he asked. "So, if you don't regret what you did, and I'm not saying that you should," he emphasised, "then why are you feeling so upset by it all?"

"Because I committed a sin, and I'm not willing to repent, and a catholic without absolution has no hope of making it past the pearly gates."

Although her words sounded as if they should be coming from someone far older than Kelly was, Desmond believed the sincerity behind them. He too had been raised a catholic, but he did not take his religion anywhere near as seriously as Kelly did.

He wondered if perhaps she had begun to take it too literally since her Mother's passing.

After another short pause, Desmond asked. "Did you enjoy it?"

Kelly blushed. "What a thing to ask!" she retorted, slapping him playfully on the arm.

"I'm only curious; I've never met a lesbian before."

This time Kelly did not hold back. She shrugged herself free from his clinch and began battering him jokingly with both fists as Desmond held up his hands to protect himself, feigning fear through his laughter.

"Alright, alright, I'm sorry," Desmond wailed, crouching down to allow Kelly to rein more blows upon him.

"Swine!" Kelly retorted, pretending to sound hurt.

Eventually, she ran out of steam and gave up on her onslaught.

She gave Desmond's crouching form a gentle kick for good measure before allowing him to stand up again.

The pair of them were laughing so hard that neither was able to start talking again right away.

Once his laughter had subsided, Desmond moved back in for another cuddle.

Kelly folded her arms as if she was still upset with him, but then she gave in immediately and snuggled up against him once more.

They kissed again and pulled each other in tight.

When they parted, Desmond asked. "So, what happens now?"

Kelly could hear the trepidation in his voice.

What she longed to say was that she wanted to be with him regardless of the consequences, but she knew, deep down, that that was not a viable option.

Their eyes locked.

Kelly knew that Desmond was waiting for her answer to his

question, even though she suspected that he already knew what that answer was likely to be.

Just at that moment, the first specks of rain started to fall on Kelly's face. She looked up at the sky and stared at the dark grey clouds which had started to build overhead.

Before she had a chance to look back at Desmond, they both heard the first peal of thunder in the distance, closely followed by the start of a downpour which started to soak through their clothes within seconds.

Instinctively, Desmond grabbed Kelly's hand and together they ran for cover to the nearest clump of trees.

They huddled for shelter as the rain beat down around them, the sparseness of the remaining leaves on the branches barely afforded them any proper protection, but it was just enough to shelter them from the brunt of the storm.

Once more Desmond wrapped a protective arm around Kelly, and in response she laid her head on his shoulder.

Together they watched the rain in silence, neither venturing to resurrect the conversation which had been left hanging in the air thanks to the intervention of the inclement weather.

After a while Kelly turned her head to look back at Desmond.

Without giving herself a chance to consider her options, she blurted out the words she had been longing to say for so long.

"You know I love you, don't you?"

Desmond did not hesitate to respond. As a huge smile crossed his lips, he replied. "And I love you too and have done for as long as I can remember."

Now that the words were out, Kelly felt her heart begin to lift.

The trauma of her confession and the confusion over her evening with Carol both began to fade away as she watched the torrential rain hammering down on the path.

She was truly in love for the first time in her life, and somehow, she was going to find a way to make it all work out.

CHAPTER TWENTY

Hardy and Russell pulled up outside Rob Drayton's house. It was a three-storey detached property in one of the more salubrious parts of town, with two main gates and a semi-circular driveway which allowed the occupants the luxury of not having to reverse their vehicle out once they had driven in.

The cloudburst which they had driven through had now petered out to a minimal splatter, so much so that for the last couple of hundred yards the windscreen wipers were no longer necessary.

Hardy suspected that Drayton would already be aware of their imminent arrival. When he and Russell had first tried to locate Drayton at his office, his personal assistant had been very insistent that her boss was at home and too ill for visitors.

After she had reluctantly handed over his home address, Hardy noticed her reaching for the phone as soon as they began to walk away, doubtless to warn her superior that the officers were on route.

They parked outside in the street and walked along the gravel drive towards the front door.

Russell nudged his superior officer when they were about twenty feet from the door, Hardy followed his gaze, and sure enough he could see one of the downstairs curtains twitching as someone behind them tried to casually have a look at the approaching officers.

The woman who opened the door was extremely tall and thin, with a sharp, pointy nose and gaunt features. Her jet-black hair was tied up in a bun on top of her head, which Hardy suspected caused her features to look even more severe, whether or not that was the desired effect.

The two of them introduced themselves and showed their identity cards before enquiring as to whether or not Drayton was at home.

Having studied the offered IDs intently, the woman looked back at the two men and stated. "I am his wife, why do you wish to speak to him?"

Hardy explained that if Drayton was at home it would be better if they came inside and explained.

Mrs. Drayton considered the prospect for a moment before stepping back just far enough to allow them entry.

Once they were inside the woman closed the front door and strode purposefully towards a room on the far side of the hallway, it was the same one Hardy noticed from which they had noticed the curtain moving.

The woman's heels *clacked* loudly on the Victorian tiled floor.

"This way," she barked back, curtly, not bothering to check if the two of them were in fact following.

When they entered the room, a man sitting in an armchair looked up from his newspaper in surprise, as if he was only just aware that they had visitors.

Before Hardy or Russell had a chance to introduce themselves, Mrs. Drayton did the honours.

"Robert," she announced, sternly, "these two police officers need to speak with you."

Rob Drayton folded his newspaper and placed it on a small table beside his chair, before he stood up and nervously approached the two men.

"Please sit down, gentlemen," he offered, politely. "May we offer you some refreshment—tea or coffee, perhaps?"

Both officers declined the offer of drinks, so Drayton invited them both to sit down, which they did, taking the sofa across from his chair.

From behind, they heard Mrs. Drayton close the living room door, before she moved over to where her husband had retaken his seat and stood beside him like a sentinel jealously guarding its charge.

Hardy and Russell exchanged a quick glance before the DI started to speak.

"Perhaps," he ventured, cautiously, "it might be better if we speak to Mr. Drayton alone."

He purposely did not look at the woman while he spoke. His message was most definitely aimed at the husband as a way of sparing him any matrimonial heartache, considering the subject matter.

But before Drayton had a chance to open his mouth or even consider the offer, his wife cut in.

"My husband and I have no secrets from each other officer; you may feel free to speak to him in my presence."

Hardy could tell by the expression on the man's face that he was not too enamoured by the idea, but he obviously knew better than to contradict his wife, so he stayed silent and merely offered a half-smile of reassurance.

"Very well then," began Hardy. "Last Saturday evening, were you in the company of a young lady named Gina Steele?"

"Yes, he most certainly was!" It was the man's wife who answered, again not giving him a chance to open his mouth.

Hardy looked up at the woman. Her facial features were cold and hard like stone, but her eyes conveyed a heat born of fury which she could not conceal.

"I am sorry, Mrs. Drayton, but I'm afraid that your husband needs to answer my questions for the sake of formality."

Hardy tried to offer her a smile of comfort, but the gesture was not well received, or appreciated.

He looked back at Drayton who had started to perspire heavily although the ambient temperature of the room was quite comfortably.

"Mr. Drayton?" Hardy continued with his questioning.

Drayton choked as he tried to speak, and then he cleared his throat before reattempting the action.

"Yes, officer, that's quite right, we were about to have dinner at the Crofton Hotel when...." The man trailed off as he half-turned to look up at his wife and then thought better of it.

"When what, sir?" Hardy pursued.

"When I caught the pair of them at it, is what I think my husband is trying to say, officer!"

Hardy switched his attention to the woman. "So, you were there too, Mrs. Drayton?" he asked, curiously.

"Yes indeed," the woman confirmed, not even attempting to keep the disgust out of her tone.

Hardy turned to ensure that Russell was taking notes before he continued.

"So just to be clear, you were both having dinner at the hotel with Miss Steele?"

Once more Drayton opened his mouth to answer, but his wife cut in front of him before the first word left his lips.

"Not at all!" the woman almost spat out her response which in turn made her husband jerk in his seat. She was clearly insulted at the intimation by Hardy that she was part of the soiree.

"I was supposed to be looking after my mother who is recovering from a very serious operation," she continued, satisfied by the fact that Hardy was now happy to let her speak. "I just happened to be passing on my way home because I needed to collect something which I had forgotten to take with me, when I noticed my husband's car parked outside the hotel."

The woman turned to stare down at her husband.

Whether Drayton realised that he was being stared down upon or not, he kept his focus straight ahead on the two officers.

The silence which hung in the air made all three of the men present feel uncomfortable. Although Hardy expected Drayton's wife to continue with her recollection of events from the evening, after a while he decided that it was best for him to continue, even if it was just to break the tension.

Hardy looked back at Drayton whose face was turning redder by the second.

"So, Mr. Drayton, you were already in the hotel with Miss Steele when your wife joined you?"

Drayton cleared his throat. He was not immediately sure if his wife was going to allow him to answer without taking over again.

"That's right, officer," he mumbled, "my wife joined us only a few minutes after we arrived."

Hardy nodded. "And what happened next?" he aimed the question at Drayton but was prepared for his wife to respond.

He was not disappointed.

"I'll tell you what happened next, shall I, officer?" Mrs. Drayton intervened, barely able to speak the words between her clenched teeth. "The minute my husband and that hussy saw me arrive she legged it out of the back and we never saw her again."

Hardy switched his focus back to Drayton. "Is that correct, sir?" he asked, hoping that the man would at least have a chance to answer for the record.

"That's quite correct, officer, my wife and I stayed at the hotel for dinner and then we came straight home at about 10.30 p.m."

"And neither of you have seen nor been in contact with Miss Steele since that evening?"

"We most certainly have not," it was the wife again who answered. "Nor do either of us ever intend to contact her again, do we, Robert?"

Drayton half-turned again, but he could not hold his wife's accusatory stare.

He looked back at Hardy, still blushing. "That's quite correct, Inspector, but may I ask why you are so interested in my movements for last Saturday, is there something wrong?"

Hardy shot Russell a quick glance before continuing.

At such an early stage in the investigation it was not always prudent to give out too much information, especially if on the face of it the Drayton's had no part in Gina Steele's disappearance.

Hardy glanced back over at the couple. Even though he was fairly convinced that neither of them knew anything, he still wanted to see their expressions when he made his next announcement.

"We received a call this morning from two of Miss Steele's flatmates. Apparently neither of them have seen anything of Miss Steele since she left for the hotel to meet you," he watched both of their faces, and although there was a glimmer of concern on Drayton's there was nothing to indicate that either of them was hiding anything.

"I see," offered Drayton, rubbing his forehead with the palm of his hand whilst he digested the information. "And they left it until now before saying anything?" he continued.

"Well," Hardy began, cautiously, not wanting to cause another eruption from Drayton's wife. "They were under the misapprehension that she might still be with you."

"And she probably would have been if I hadn't caught the pair of them red-handed!" Mrs. Drayton roared, slapping her husband hard across the shoulder from behind.

The man flinched at the blow but stayed seated and pretended as if nothing had happened.

Hardy and Russell used the incident as their cue to leave.

Both Drayton and his wife followed them to the front door.

As they were about to leave, Drayton said. "I hope Miss Steele is alright."

Hardy could tell that the man wanted to ask more questions, but with his wife standing behind him it was obviously not the right moment.

Hardy reached into his coat pocket and removed one of his business cards.

He handed it to Drayton. "That's just in case you happen to think of anything after we've gone."

Drayton accepted the card, gratefully, but before he had a chance to put it away his wife reached over and snatched it from his hand.

She studied the card for a moment as if she was expecting to read some sort of hidden code or message. Once she was satisfied that it was exactly what Hardy had stated, she clasped it tightly in her hand making no effort to conceal the fact that she had no intention of handing it over to her husband.

* * *

THE CREEPER GAZED LONGINGLY over the sleeping form of Natasha. He had used her to satisfy his lust several times since the keeper's last visit, until now he was completely spent.

The Creeper knew that his time left with her was growing short.

This was the longest he had ever kept one of his victims alive, and it knew that the keeper would not allow it to hold onto her past tonight.

It understood why!

Even so, if it had the choice it would definitely keep her for longer, even in this vegetated state she seemed to drift in and out of between prolonged bouts of sleep, she was still worth the effort.

There was something special about her, something which the Creeper had not experienced with one of its victims before.

It was a feeling!

A feeling it had never experienced before in its life, and although the Creeper did not know what it was or how to deal with it, it was still very real.

In the distance it heard the sound of a door opening. The familiar creaking of the rusty hinges followed by the scraping of metal on stone as the ancient door was forced open, announced the presence of the keeper's arrival.

Instinctively, the Creeper rearranged the tatters that remained of Natasha's once beautiful and hideously expensive outfit so that it covered what little of her modesty it was still capable of protecting.

The shadowy glow from the lantern cast an ever-increasing ring of light to announce the keeper's approach.

The Creeper knew that it had no say in the matter. The keeper had made it abundantly clear in the past that he alone had to decide when a victim had to be returned outside, regardless of what was left of it, which on occasion had been little more than bones and a smattering of flesh.

But at least Natasha was still whole!

The Creeper had considered gorging on her beautiful flesh once its other appetites had been satisfied and during its time alone with her the Creeper had taken the opportunity to explore her naked body, licking and nibbling at her soft, smooth flesh as its passion rose. On a couple of occasions, it even found itself opening its huge mouth and clamping its razor-sharp teeth down on her, but it found itself unable to even contemplate making the first full bite.

The Creeper whimpered pitifully as the keeper came around the final bend which led to its lair.

The keeper smiled warmly as he lay down the platter of assorted meat cuts and bones which he had brought to placate his charge.

The Creeper shuffled backwards on the cold stone floor, holding out its massive arms as if to protect Natasha from some intended harm.

The keeper placed his lantern on the floor a few feet in front of the huddled pair and knelt down on one knee so as to be closer to the Creeper's level.

"Now then, Eric," the keeper began, his voice gentle and comforting, "you know that I have to take her away tonight, you do understand, don't you?"

The Creeper puffed out its enormous chest as it began to breathe with ever increasing palpitations, its eyes fixed firmly on the keeper trying desperately to convey its sadness and despair at his words.

The Creeper turned and gently began to brush down what was left of Natasha's clothes, like a parent checking their child's clothing before letting them run into school. It used its claw-like talons to comb through her hair, gently tugging at the knots caused by her fitful tossing and turning during sleep while she had been its captive.

The keeper could hear the low whining which escaped his charge's lips as it worked. He had never seen it behave in this manner before, and he was immediately touched by the human compassion the Creeper was demonstrating at the thought of losing its prize.

But the keeper knew that there could be no alternative to the usual ritual, save for the fact that this time he was not merely removing scattered remains, but a live victim, although he suspected that her mind might never recover from what she had been through since her arrival.

When the Creeper turned back to face him, the keeper was sure that he could actually see the beginnings of tears at the corners of its eyes. Even in the dim light cast by the lamp he could not be mistaken.

The keeper felt a lump rise in his throat, this scenario was one which he had not anticipated, and for a moment he was almost convinced to allow his charge to keep his treasure for as long as it wanted.

But then the enormity of the situation took hold of his compassion and brought him back to the realisation of the potential consequences of allowing such an action.

The keeper edged forward and placed a reassuring hand on the Creeper's arm.

"I'm so sorry, Eric," he offered in a gentle whisper, "if there was any other way you know that I would happily concede, but you have always known how things are, we have to be so careful."

There was no mistaking now the flood of tears that started to stream from the Creeper's eyes. Unable to communicate its frustration and sadness in any other way, it turned away from the keeper and folded its mighty arms around its knees, staring at the blank wall ahead.

The keeper rose to his feet and placed the platter of meat he had brought with him within reach of his charge.

Without looking back, the Creeper pushed the food away, scraping the platter across the stone floor.

The keeper nodded to himself and bent down to collect his lantern.

As he turned to leave, he stopped for a moment and once more considered his options.

But in the end, he just shook his head.

"I'm so sorry, Eric," he said, apologetically. "I will be back for her later tonight."

With that, he turned and left.

On his way back to the exit, he could hear the guttural sobs of the Creeper.

The sound almost broke his heart!

CHAPTER TWENTY-ONE

Acting DCI Pamela Holmsley pulled her Mini Clubman into an unmarked space in the police station car park and switched off the engine. Before exiting the car, she tilted the rear-view mirror to check her hair and make-up. First impressions were essential in her book and as usual, she intended to make a very professional first one today.

At just twenty-four she had already risen through the fast-stream ranks to the height of Detective Inspector, which in itself was a remarkable feat. But she was not at all content to stay in her present grade for one minute longer than was absolutely necessary.

She was determined to become the youngest female Commissioner ever appointed, and to that end she ensured that wherever she was working, her superiors were aware that she would be happy to take on any role which had even the merest scent of a possible promotion attached to it, regardless of where in the country it was.

The two large suitcases in her car's boot were evidence of her willingness to put her career before everything else. Her entire life was contained in those two bags for the time being, save for some of her more treasured items which she still had back at her parents' house, hidden away in their loft.

For the most part, Pamela had spent the last two years living in cheap hotels and boarding houses while she chased the next elusive promotion. Always ready to pack up and leave at a moment's notice, she ensured that she did not allow herself to grow too fond of any one place or any person in particular, thus allowing her the luxury of not having to deal with any conflict of interest should the call for the next move come along.

Once she was satisfied that her hair and make-up were just right, she leaned down and removed the pumps she wore for driving and slipped her feet into her patent black leather heels.

She opened her driver's door and swivelled on her seat so that she could place both feet firmly on the floor to boost herself out of her car. She retrieved her briefcase from the back seat and after slamming the door shut, she walked towards the main building, locking her car as she walked via the remote on her key fob.

Once inside the main building, Pamela gazed around at the set-up of the foyer. After two years and many dozen station entrances, they all began to blend into each other as far as she was concerned. But she always liked to take a moment to familiarise herself with the layout of what would presumably be her new place of business for the next couple of months or so.

When she noticed the uniformed officer behind the desk looking at her, Pamela strode over purposefully, and presented her identification.

"Acting DCI Holmsley reporting to see Superintendent Carlisle," she announced, not giving the officer time to study her ID in any depth.

"Yes ma'am," replied the officer smartly. He reached under

the desk and pressed the door release which *buzzed* audibly to indicate that Pamela could enter.

Before giving her directions, the officer handed her a visitor's badge to save her being stopped around the station by any keen-eyed uniforms who might be passing.

"Just go through the door and turn right, and it's the last door at the end of the corridor."

Pamela thanked him and made her way through the door, holding it open with her elbow as she pinned her badge to her suit.

She walked briskly towards the superintendent's door, sneaking a glance at the offices she passed along the way which had their doors open.

Due to her diminutive size she did not cut an imposing figure, and with her fresh-faced complexion it had been suggested at one of her previous stations that she could pass as an undercover schoolgirl should the need ever arise, which, although she took it as a backhand compliment, meant that Pamela always made a point of carrying herself in a way which conveyed, to those looking on, an air of authority.

She had worked hard to cultivate this persona so that now it was almost second nature to her.

Pamela had found her guise to be especially useful when dealing with subordinate officers who were far older than her and sometimes did not feel it necessary to treat her with the deference her rank commanded.

Once she reached Carlisle's door, she took a deep breath before knocking hard twice on the wooden panel.

Having already been informed by the front desk of her arrival, Carlisle opened the door almost immediately. He welcomed Pamela in, and she took the seat opposite his, but refused the coffee offered because she did not want to risk spilling any down her suit, especially with a press conference called for the afternoon.

Carlisle spent the next half hour bringing the acting DCI up to speed on the case. From inside her briefcase Pamela produced a pad and pen and began making copious notes as the senior officer spoke.

Pamela acted with great patience and did not interrupt her superior while he was speaking. This was something which instantly warmed Carlisle to his latest charge, so he ensured that he gave her ample opportunity once he was finished to ask any pertinent questions.

"So, let's just see if I've got this straight," began Pamela, hastily looking over her notes. "As yet, we don't have a formal identification for the latest two victims found this morning."

"That's correct," replied Carlisle, leaning forward on his desk, and linking his fingers together in one of his favourite poses. "DI Hardy is chasing those up as we speak, and we've asked our forensic team to try and pull the stops out in light of this afternoon's press conference.

Pamela nodded, and then went back to studying her pad. "But judging from the condition of the remains, it would seem likely that we are looking for the same perpetrator as the killer of our first victim?"

Carlisle pulled a face. "Well to be honest, at the moment that is more speculation than anything else. Certainly, the way in which all three victims were attacked lends itself to the possibility of it being the same assailant, but we need to tread carefully at this," he made a gesture with his hands in the air as if he was struggling to find the right words. "Shall we say embryonic stage?"

Pamela nodded.

She knew full well why the superintendent was not overly keen to accept that all three killings were committed by the same individual; because that would mean that they had a serial killer in his quaint little town.

Either way, she knew the benefit of presenting a united front to the press, so hopefully once the DI returned, he would have some more up to date information which would clarify the situation one way or the other.

Pamela had already decided to go for a *softly softy* approach with her new DI. As always, she had done her homework, and from what she had gleaned he was a good, hard-working copper who would doubtless have been a DCI himself in London by now had he stuck it out.

She knew from past experience that she needed her second in command to be on her side to gain maximum prestige whilst working on the case, because doubtless his team would follow his lead regarding how they treated their new superior officer.

When the time was right, she intended to have a little heart to heart with Hardy, away from the hustle and bustle of the investigation. Such discussions she believed could have a miraculous effect on their future working relationship.

HARDY HEARD his mobile go off in his right-hand pocket. As usual he had forgotten to place it in the hands-free holder on his dashboard before starting to drive.

Whilst holding the wheel with one hand he groped in his pocket with the other and eventually presented the handset to Russell.

Russell glanced at the screen before answering, it was the station.

"Russell," he answered. Hardy could hear some garbled murmurs on the other end before Russell said, "OK, will do." As he reached over to place the handset in the holder, he informed Hardy that Superintendent Carlisle wanted to see him the moment he returned to the station so that he could meet the new acting DCI.

"Can't wait," replied Hardy, unenthusiastically.

They arrived at the station ten minutes later and were reminded upon their entry by the desk sergeant that Carlisle was waiting for them.

Before heading for the superintendent's office, Hardy branched off back to his own to see if there was any update that might be worth repeating to Carlisle.

As he entered the room, several of the detective team looked up from their desks and acknowledged him.

At the far end of the room by the incident board, Hardy saw PC Grant on the telephone. He approached her from the side and leaned against the nearest desk while she finished her conversation.

When she replaced the handset back into its cradle, she smiled a greeting to Hardy and Russell before she began to speak. "That was the Pathologist sir," she appeared to Hardy to be a little flushed, and her voice quivered as if she was nervous about what she was about to say. "I managed to have Ben Green's dental records sent over to them as you asked, and they confirm that the male victim is in fact him."

Hardy looked back at Russell and the two of them exchanged a knowing glance.

"What about the woman?" Hardy enquired, turning back to face the young constable. "Any luck identifying her?"

"There was actually," she began, "her fingerprints were on the database; seems she was involved in fracas outside a pub in the town centre last year."

"So, who was she?" Russell butted in, anxious to find out if their hunch was right.

"Gina Steele," replied PC Grant, "the ME says there's no doubt."

Just at that moment, Hardy saw the looming figure of his superintendent entering the office. For a brief second, he did not notice the waif-like female in the business suit walking beside him, but when he did, he immediately put two-and-two together.

"I think we're about to be introduced to our new DCI," he whispered to Russell under his breath, making sure that he had his back turned slightly to one side so that neither Carlisle nor the woman would realise that he was speaking about either of them.

Carlisle made a beeline for Hardy the moment he saw him.

Hardy could tell by the frown on his superior's face that he was not happy about something.

Hardy managed to fake an impressive smile as Carlisle approached, although in truth it was more for the benefit of the lady trying to keep up with the tall man's lengthy stride.

"Good afternoon, Superintendent," Hardy offered, ensuring that he got in first to try and set the tone.

Carlisle stopped in front of the three officers and let out a pent-up sigh. He was not fooled for one moment by Hardy's affability, but at the same time he did not want to create the impression that there was any dissention amongst the ranks.

"Inspector Hardy," Carlisle began, evidently biting his tongue, "allow me to introduce you to acting DCI Pamela Holmsley."

Hardy extended his hand and Pamela smiled as she shook it.

"May I introduce DS Russell and PC Grant?" replied Hardy, turning to introduce the two officers behind him.

Russell took the offered hand and the young PC followed suit.

Hardy could tell from the look of surprise and shock on her face that Grant was not expecting to be included in the introductions. After all, she was not actually a member of his team, but Hardy felt bad for the fact that she was still here after he almost bullied her into working for him when her shift finished that morning.

So, a little recognition for her efforts was more than overdue in his opinion.

Hardy turned back to face Carlisle. "PC Grant here has been helping us with our inquiries," he indicated with his thumb to the young officer behind him. "She was just bringing us up to date on the identification of the two bodies we recovered this morning."

"Oh, really," Carlisle butted in, with genuine excitement in his tone. "Please carry on, Constable."

PC Grant blushed as all eyes turned in her direction.

She hated herself for feeling and acting so unprofessional, but she could not staunch the fact that at that moment she felt like a schoolgirl being picked at morning assembly to make a presentation to the class.

Taking a deep breath, the young woman relayed the details of the ME's findings to Carlisle and the DCI. She knew full well that having already told them, either Hardy or Russell could have done the honours, and for a moment she was not entirely sure why Hardy had thrust her forward into the limelight.

She sincerely hoped that it was not a case of him making fun at her expense.

She thought better of him than that!

"Good work, Constable," Carlisle stated, forthrightly, making it almost sound as if he was barking out an order rather than offering praise.

"How long have you been attached to DI Hardy's team?" asked Pamela, curiously.

The young PC felt herself blush again. "Oh, I'm not part of the team as such," she offered, hesitantly, suddenly feeling as if she had been caught out for playing in the big league without the proper authorisation.

"PC Grant very kindly offered to help out in her spare time," Hardy cut in, "she's been off duty since this morning having finished a night shift on the front desk."

"Is that so," stated Pamela, glancing quickly at Carlisle before turning her attention back to the constable. "Well you sound like you're made of the right stuff, how do you fancy being seconded to my team during the course of this investigation?"

Hardy noticed Carlisle open his mouth to speak, and then immediately think better of it.

It was the first time that Hardy had ever seen his superior stuck for words and he had to make an effort to hide his smile.

It was obvious to the others gathered that the young PC had been completely taken aback by Pamela's offer. But before the pause in the conversation grew too long and became embarrassing, she managed to clear her throat and answer.

"Thank you, ma'am, that would be wonderful."

Pamela's smile broadened. "Good, well that's settled then." She turned to face Carlisle with a winning smile. "Can I leave you to sort out the details for me?"

Carlisle nodded. "Yes, of course," he muttered, still not quite convinced that Pamela had not just made a decision over his head.

"Excellent," she continued, "and let's start by making sure that you are paid the appropriate overtime rate for your hours since you officially came off shift."

Pamela aimed the comment in the superintendent's direction, which left Carlisle with little alternative other than to smile weakly, and nod again.

Just then, a middle-aged uniformed officer entered the room and made his way towards the group.

Russell recognised the man and acknowledged him as he approached.

"Hello, Jim, what's up mate?" he asked, pleasantly.

"Sorry to bother you, Sarge," he quickly glanced at the others, "Sir, ma'am," and then turned his attention back to Russell's familiar face. "The press is starting to gather downstairs."

Carlisle immediately looked at his wristwatch. "Yes, good heavens," he blustered, "is that the time already?" He inadvertently straightened his tie and did up his jacket buttons. "We'd better head down for the press conference."

Hardy left Grant and Russell and followed Pamela and the superintendent down to the conference room.

He was beginning to think that he might not actually have to say anything himself at the conference after all, what with his new DCI taking over the reins. That would certainly be a blessing he could live with.

CHAPTER TWENTY-TWO

The small conference room was full fit to bursting when the three officers walked in. At the door, Carlisle stood back and signalled Pamela to go in first, then he followed her leaving Hardy to bring up the rear.

As they walked towards the front of the room, Hardy glanced around the assembled crowd and noticed some all-too-familiar faces in the audience.

He had already experienced run-ins with some of them in the past, and he knew full well what a pain in the backside they could be.

As he expected, right in the middle of the front row sat Cyril Carney, head reporter at the local Chronicle who was not above littering his articles with hearsay and rumour just to grab a headline.

Hardy had been warned off Carney when he first arrived at the station, and sure enough on the DI's second day in the job he was accosted by Carney in the car park, bombarding him with questions about on-going investigations and his departure from London, while offering to buy him a pint so that they could discuss the matter at a more leisurely pace.

Forewarned was forearmed, and Hardy made short work of warning the reporter off. The following morning there was a story on page four of the Chronicle detailing some very inaccurate particulars concerning Hardy's reasons for leaving the big city in favour of country life.

The article itself seemed to bother Carlisle more than it did Hardy. His superintendent seemed to be petrified of any bad press related to his station, and with Hardy barely over the threshold it somehow made the situation, in his eyes at least, even worse.

Carlisle insisted that Hardy invite the reporter in for an interview to clear the air and hopefully encourage him to retract some of his more outlandish statements.

But Hardy refused point blank!

He had come across several maggots cut from the same cloth as Carney back in London, and he was not about to start pandering to one of them now.

When Carlisle realised that he was not going to win the argument, he took it upon himself to invite the reporter in to try and calm the waters.

The story around the station suggested that Carlisle in an effort to ingratiate himself with the reporter as a means of preventing further misunderstandings, unearthed the bottle of single malt he kept in his bottom drawer for special occasions and visits from senior dignitaries.

The only problem was that Carney was an old soak and thus managed to drink Carlisle under the table, leaving the superintendent passed out in his office, though not before he had managed to take a couple of very incriminating pictures which found their way onto the front page the following morning, along with an article penned by Carney illustrating his concerns at the state of modern policing.

Everyone knew that Carlisle had received a severe dressing down by the ACC, and he was not able to hold his head up at the station for weeks afterwards.

As the three officers passed the front row, Carney smiled and nodded in their direction, the gesture was largely ignored.

When they reached the dais, Hardy noticed that five chairs had been set out behind the desk. Carlisle directed Pamela to take the middle seat and Hardy to take the one on her far right. The superintendent sat between them, leaving the two seats to the DCI's left empty.

Just then a door at the far end of the hall opened and a uniformed officer led Natasha's parents down the outside of the congregation and up towards the platform where the others were already seated.

As the reporters realised who the new arrivals were, they all stood up as one and began firing off questions, each trying to make themselves heard above their colleagues.

Cameras and mobiles started clicking from all directions and instinctively, the Spencer's held up their hands to shield their eyes from the onslaught.

Eventually, Carlisle stood up and held out his arms as he called for everyone to sit back down and wait patiently for the press conference to begin. But his words fell on deaf ears and some of the reporters even tried to surge forward for a better chance to be heard. This in turn resulted in the sound of chair legs scraping across the floor being added to the overall melee.

Out of nowhere, a sharp whistle caused everyone to halt in their tracks.

Hardy turned just in time to see Pamela standing behind the table, removing her fingers from her mouth.

She waited a moment to ensure that she had everyone's attention, before she lifted the microphone to her mouth to speak. "Now then, ladies and gentlemen," she began, calmly, "if you would all like to take your seats this conference can begin."

The stunned silence from those in the audience was something to behold, and Hardy was extremely impressed with the way his new DCI had handled the situation.

There was a shuffling of chairs as the attendees complied with Pamela's request, while Carlisle rose to welcome the Spencer's to their seats.

Carlisle looked incredibly pleased with himself as he addressed the gathering now that his voice could actually be heard.

Hardy wondered if in his mind Carlisle was taking credit for Pamela's actions.

Either way, the crowd stayed quiet long enough to hear the superintendent's introduction, and then he passed the chair over to the new DCI.

Pamela made a brief appeal to the reporters to show consideration for Natasha's parents who were both obviously distraught due to the fact that their daughter's whereabouts were still unknown.

She reiterated what aspects of the case she felt it appropriate to divulge, whilst apologising and asking for understanding concerning pertinent facts she could not release at this stage.

When Pamela offered the attendees the chance to ask some questions of their own, Carney was on his feet before the others had a chance.

"Is it true that we have a serial killer roaming the streets of Moreton?" he bellowed out, keeping a watchful eye on Natasha's parents for a reaction.

The rest of the room murmured their combined agreement with Carney's question.

Pamela was not at all flustered by it. She had half expected such a response, so she took it in her stride.

"With the information we have presently it is far too early to speculate on whether or not we have a single assailant."

Before she had a chance to continue, Carney jumped in again.

"But surely after the discovery of the two bodies this morning, you now have at least three victims so far?"

Pamela aimed her response directly at the reporter. "As I said earlier, the pathology lab is still working on the evidence, so until we have definitive proof it is not appropriate for us to speculate."

"Do you have any suspects yet?"

The question came from a young reporter towards the back.

"We are presently looking into several lines of investigation and we trust an arrest will be imminent."

Hardy raised his eyebrows at Pamela's answer. Surely Carlisle would have briefed her properly in his office. He casually looked across at his superintendent, he could tell that Carlisle himself was none too pleased with the DCI's answer, but it was too late to retract it now.

More than anything else, the first rule in press conferences is to show a united front, regardless of the circumstances.

"Is it true that the killer has mutilated all of his victims, so that identification has had to be concluded using dental records only?" This time it was a female journalist sitting two rows behind Carney.

Pamela turned her attention towards the lady in question. "As I say, it is too early to be talking about a single perpetrator, but yes, I'm afraid that the fatal wounds inflicted were of a particular grievous nature."

"Does he eat parts of his victims?" this was Carney again.

Before Pamela had a chance to consider her answer, Hilary Spencer pushed her chair back and placing her hand over her mouth to muffle a scream, climbed down from the dais and ran towards the far door from which she and her husband had entered. Several of the audience surged forward to try and capture a picture of the distraught woman as she left, but in her haste, Hilary barged her way through them, knocking a couple off their feet and sending them tumbling back into their colleagues.

By this point Gerald Spencer was also on his feet, urged on by his wife's obvious distress. He too was about to leap off the podium and race to his wife's aid when Pamela shot her arm out and placed a firm hand on his wrist.

"She'll be fine, we'll look after her," she said, reassuringly, as one of the uniformed constables who had been standing at the back of the room followed the near-hysterical woman out into the corridor.

Gerald Spencer could feel his blood boiling, but Pamela's words and the sight of the uniformed officer following his wife had the desired effect of helping to keep him calm.

Once again Pamela called for order and like obedient children the journalists turned back to retake their seats.

When order had been restored, Pamela continued. "As many of you would have seen on the television last night, Mr. Spencer here made an emotional appeal for the safe return of his daughter Natasha, who has been missing since Sunday evening." Pamela turned and smiled comfortingly at Spencer, who appeared to be back in control after his wife's outburst.

He looked back at Pamela and nodded his head.

Pamela sat down and handed her microphone over to him.

As a Queen's Counsel, Gerald Harper was used to making long speeches in front of total strangers, but it was still evident from his mannerisms that he was not at all comfortable in the present circumstance.

"I would like to appeal to all your readers," he began, clearing his throat after the first few words to clear away the croak in his voice, "to come forward with any information they may have concerning the disappearance of my daughter Natasha. Regardless of how small or insignificant they think it might be, please contact the officers in charge of her case and let them decide how pertinent it might be."

He glanced over towards Carlisle who gave him a nod of affirmation.

Turning back to the audience, Spencer continued. "As I stated last night, I will be happy to pay a substantial reward for any information which proves pertinent to my daughter's safe return. Both my wife and I are available twenty-four hours a day if for some reason your readers which to contact us directly," he indicated towards the back of the room. "There are posters at the back with our daughter's picture and all our contact information, please publish them all and encourage someone to come forward."

Hardy rubbed his forehead with the palm of his hand.

In his experience, nothing brought the maggots out of the woodwork than an open invitation to speak directly to the parents of a missing child, even if, as in this case, she was a grown woman.

Spencer paused for a moment to think of what else he might like to say.

Carney grabbed the opportunity. "Do you honestly believe that your daughter is still alive, even with the discovery of those two bodies this morning?"

Spencer looked up. His brow furrowed and his eyes

became slits as he focused all his attention of the reporter. "What a stupid bloody question," he almost spat the words out through clenched teeth, "of course I believe that my daughter is still alive, how dare you ask such an impertinent and offensive question!"

Carney opened his mouth to retaliate, but before he had a chance Pamela took the microphone from Spencer and called the conference to an end.

There was a general cacophony of objections and several questions were randomly fired off at the panel. But the officers ignored them, and Carlisle signalled to the officers at the back to escort the reporters from the building, while he and Hardy assisted Pamela in helping Spencer down from the dais and back down the aisle towards the door they had entered by.

Even as they were being herded out, some of the journalists, including Carney, still tried to provoke Spencer into responding to their questions, but the man kept his head down and his mouth shut as he allowed himself to be led away.

THE CREEPER WAS STIRRED from its fitful slumber by the familiar sound of *squeaking* from the approaching wheelchair.

It lifted its head from Natasha's warm and comforting breasts, knowing that it would be for the last time.

As the light cast from the keeper's torch penetrated the darkness, the Creeper shifted position as if it was trying to protect Natasha from the approaching light. In truth it knew that this was the end, and although it had already resigned itself to the situation after the keeper's last visit, there was still a part of it that was struggling with the concept of losing Natasha forever.

As the wheelchair emerged into view, the Creeper immediately shot up and stood erect, pushing out its mighty chest and spreading its arms out at its sides to enhance the fierceness of its overall bearing.

The confrontational posture was not lost on the keeper as he turned the corner and came face to face with his charge.

To anyone else, the Creeper's stance would have caused instant panic and the predisposition to turn and run away as fast as possible. But the keeper fully understood the reason behind the Creeper's anxious state, and in many ways, he sympathised with its plight.

The keeper placed his torch on the table beside him and walked around the wheelchair so that he could stand face-to-face with his charge.

Regardless of the stance the Creeper had adopted, there was no indication of evil or malevolence in its eyes, merely sadness tinged with resignation.

As the keeper approached, the Creeper relaxed its challenging pose and dropped its arms down by its sides. As its head began to slump forward and its shoulders drooped, the keeper placed a comforting hand on its shoulder and offered what few words of comfort he could.

"You know that this is for the best, Eric," he began, looking up into the Creeper's face to try and engage its eyes. "This has to happen; it has already been too long." The keeper thought for a moment, and then hesitantly added. "Unless of course, you decide to devour her, then I can remove her remains in a couple of days!"

At his words, the Creeper grew agitated and began to move from side to side, whimpering softly.

The keeper patted it on the shoulder. "I understand, of course you don't want to hurt her." There was genuine sympathy in the keeper's tone. "Well come on then, you know that I need your help to do this?"

With reluctant obedience the Creeper bent down and swept the docile form of Natasha up into its arms and carried her over to the wheelchair, before gently placing her in the bucket seat.

The Creeper made a point of painstakingly rearranging what was left of her tattered clothing, so that at least some of her modesty could be protected.

Once she was in situ, the Creeper took his place behind the wheelchair and began to propel the slumped Natasha towards the exit at the far end of its lair.

From behind, the keeper retrieved his torch and followed.

CHAPTER TWENTY-THREE

Once the commotion had died down and the majority of the journalists had left the area in front of the station to write their articles, Superintendent Carlisle arranged for a car to take the Spencer's home, exiting through one of the secure side entrances to the station.

He thanked Hardy and Pamela for all their help and made his way out to the car park.

He could still see a few of the diehard's clustered around the exit barrier, but thankfully the two uniformed officers in charge were ensuring that they all kept far enough back so as not to interfere with the incoming and outgoing traffic.

Carlisle raised his hand in acknowledgement as they lifted the metal breaker to allow him to exit. He ignored the shouts from the reporters as he passed, especially Carney who he almost knocked over as he tried to launch himself in front of the superintendent's vehicle as he rounded the corner.

Once he was away from the station, Carlisle finally felt the stresses of the day starting to lift.

He was already feeling the benefit of having a senior officer like Pamela in charge and he hoped that her presence would allow him to take a step back and concentrate on the over-whelming number of e-mails he had stockpiling on his computer.

He only hoped that Pamela was as good as the ACC had said she was, although he had to admit that judging by her performance this afternoon at the press conference, she did appear to be a safe pair of hands in which to leave matters.

Back at the station Hardy showed Pamela the incident board and explained what directions the investigation had taken them in thus far.

Overall, Pamela seemed relatively impressed with the way Hardy was running the show, and although she offered a few alternative theories she made a point of not turning them into criticisms.

When they were finished, Hardy showed Pamela where his desk was situated at one corner of the office and asked her where she would like to position herself within the open-plan setting.

Pamela pointed to a small room separate from the main floor and asked Hardy what the probability was of having that turned into her office.

Hardy nodded. "It'll need to be cleared out a bit, we sort of use that for storing old files and spare chairs, but I'll see to that if you'd like," he offered.

"Thank you, Inspector," replied Pamela, "I just think that it is better for me to have an enclosed office in case I need to discuss something in private with one of the team."

Hardy felt as if his new DCI was trying to justify her request for her own office, when in fact he knew that the rest of the team would probably feel more comfortable without her breathing over their shoulders all the time.

Hardy grabbed the pad on his desk in order to write himself

a memo to ask maintenance to clear the room out in the morning. As he went to flip over the first page, he noticed a message from Russell, informing him that he and PC Grant had gone to inform Ben Green's father that they had received confirmation that one of the bodies found that morning was in fact his.

As he read further, squinting to decipher some of Russell's scribble, he saw that Gina Steele's flatmates had been contacted again and had given Russell the contact details for Gina's parents. As they lived in Surrey, Russell had arranged for a visit from a senior member of their detective division to break the terrible news.

Hardy relayed the pertinent facts of the note to Pamela.

"That's good work," she stated, approvingly.

"Russell is a good man to have as your backup," Hardy agreed.

"And that young PC seemed very promising."

Hardy nodded. "Yes, and thank you for giving her a chance to join in the investigation, that was a nice offer."

Pamela pulled a face. "I wasn't being nice, Inspector, she impressed me almost immediately, but if she doesn't carry her weight she's back on the front desk, quick-smart!"

Hardy was somewhat taken aback by the DCI's manner, but he nodded his agreement just the same. The last thing he needed was to cross swords with her this early on in their relationship.

"And speaking of having someone's back," continued Pamela, "I'm relying on you to have mine; I hope that isn't just a presumption on my behalf?"

Hardy frowned. "How do you mean?"

Pamela took a step forward so that she did not have to speak above a whisper to be heard by the DI. "I mean that I am relying on you to work with me on this investigation, and not to go behind my back to the super if we disagree on something!"

Hardy felt slightly awkward with the DCI standing so close to him, but he made an effort not to take a step back in case it was incorrectly misinterpreted.

"Understood, ma'am" replied Hardy, keeping his voice level, and showing no indication of how insulted he was by Pamela's suggestion.

He surmised that in her position his new superior may well have come across a couple of disgruntled subordinates who thought that a quick way of getting rid of her was to run and tell tales to the top brass. But that was not Hardy's way and never had been, so hopefully in time the DCI would come to realise that.

Pamela smiled and nodded her understanding, although Hardy was convinced that her smile never reached her eyes, so was probably just reactionary rather than sincere. But he still accepted it with good grace.

"Right then," continued Pamela, taking back a step to show that she was at ease with the DI. "Now if you'll afford me one more favour, we can call it a night."

Hardy shrugged. "Anything I can do," he exclaimed, helpfully.

"Would you mind showing me the way to my hotel?" Pamela asked. "I haven't had a chance to book in yet."

Hardy wondered for a moment why she did not just type the details into her sat-nav, but he supposed that it made sense for her to ask him as those contraptions often took you a longer way round than was necessary.

Hardy led the way in his car. When they reached the high street, the road had been closed off by uniform as there had been a collision between a bus and someone on a motorbike.

Everything appeared to be under control and there was already an ambulance attending, so Hardy veered off and made sure that Pamela was directly behind him as he cruised through some of the back-doubles to make his way to her hotel.

Once they reached the main entrance, Hardy pulled over on the road, leaving Pamela amble room to manoeuvre around him to the entrance of the hotel's car park.

She pulled up alongside his car and rolled down her window.

Hardy took the hint and did the same.

"One more favour, then you're a free man," Pamela yelled out from across her passenger seat.

"What do you need ma'am?" Hardy called back, curiously.

"A drink and someone to have it with, my treat."

Once Pamela had booked in, she left Hardy to find them a table in the bar area while she followed the porter up to her room.

Once she was alone, Pamela quickly unpacked some of her things, laying out the clothes she wanted to wear the next day as well as her night things.

She took her wash bag into the bathroom and set down what she needed before bed on the bath stand.

She quickly rechecked her reflection in the mirror before returning to the bedroom and unpacking the clothes she had which would fit neatly in the drawers provided.

At the bottom of her suitcase she located her vibrator and checked the battery to make sure that it was still working on full power.

Satisfied that it was, she placed in one of the drawers discreetly beneath some clothes, not that she suspected that someone would come along and riffle through them, but it was something she always did, especially when in a strange environment.

Pamela joined Hardy in the bar. He had found them a

quiet table off to one side of the lounge so that they could talk without the risk of being overheard.

As instructed, he had ordered them a bottle of Bordeaux, and when he noticed Pamela arriving, he began to pour them both a glass.

They *clinked* their glasses.

"To your health, ma'am," Hardy offered.

"I think that as we're off-duty, Inspector, we can dispense with the formalities," the DCI replied, "it's Pamela, and how do you wish to be addressed after we've clocked off?"

"Oh, I'll answer to anything," Hardy joked, "but Mal will be fine."

The wine was full-bodied and although a little dryer than Pamela's usual tipple, it went down extremely well after the sort of day that she'd had.

They talked shop while they drank, and Hardy filled his DCI in on his thoughts regarding the investigation.

After a while, a waiter appeared and asked them if they wished to order some food. Pamela ordered a toasted cheese and ham, but Hardy declined the offer.

By the time her sandwich arrived, Pamela had already finished her second glass of wine, whilst Hardy was still on his first.

She reached out to top him off, but Hardy held his hand up. "Better not," he said, "I've still got to drive home."

Pamela shrugged and did not bother to argue, finishing the bottle would not be a problem for her.

Although she had read a background file on Hardy, Pamela asked him for a "nutshell" version of his career to date. She listened intently as she blew on her sandwich before taking a bite.

Hardy's brief of his career was certainly short and seemingly without incident.

It left Pamela with the impression that Hardy was content to remain at his present rank until his retirement, unlike her.

In return she gave him some of her own background information but kept it within professional peripheries without disguising her ambitions.

"I make no apologies, Inspector," she stated, placing her hand over her mouth so as not to let any of her half-chewed sandwich spill out. "I entered the service as a graduate trainee because I recognised the opportunities for rapid promotion through the ranks."

She swallowed what was in her mouth and washed it down with another sip of wine. "And believe me when I say," she continued, replacing her glass on the table, "I don't care whose toes I have to dig my stiletto's into to make my way up the ladder."

Hardy inadvertently moved his feet back from under the table.

Pamela laughed out loud. "I don't mean you, Inspector, I'm sure that I can rely upon your support and cooperation in this matter. A speedy resolution to this investigation will be in both our interests, don't you agree?"

Hardy lifted his glass and finished his wine before answering. "I just want to stop whoever is doing this before they find another victim." He thought for a moment, and then added, "And preferably before Natasha Spencer meets a grizzly end."

Pamela nodded in agreement. "Me too," she offered, "and the faster we catch the perpetrator the better for all of us."

Hardy nodded, although he could not dismiss the feeling that his new DCI seemed, to him, to be more focused on her career than on the saving of a few innocent lives.

He hoped that he was wrong!

* * *

Kevin Johnson was seriously hacked off!

This night had not ended the way he had anticipated and the consolation of the six cans of lager he had at home waiting for him in the fridge, would not suffice in washing away the bad taste left in his mouth.

Of all the stupid, dumb luck!

He could almost hear his mates laughing at him behind his back.

After all, they must have known, surely?

But if so, then why did one of them not tell him?

Some mates they turned out to be!

The worst part was, it was his idea to go clubbing in the first place, and when his mates asked why, he joked that he felt lucky tonight and that he was sure that he was going to pull.

Kevin could still see himself returning from the toilet and seeing Julie sitting with the rest of his crowd. The others were all laughing and joking with her and as she had taken the empty chair next to where Kevin had been sitting it made it easy for him to slide in and take over the conversation.

When she readily agreed to dance with him and did not object when he started to feel her up on the dimly lit dance floor, Kevin knew that he was on a promise, but even then, he was taken aback when she whispered in his ear that she wanted him to go back to her place.

Kevin called them a taxi and they snogged and groped each other all the way back to Julie's flat.

Once inside, Julie left Kevin to get undressed while she went to the bathroom, and when she reappeared in the bedroom doorway she was dressed in a beautiful red teddy with fishnets and all the trimmings.

Julie worked on him for ages and Kevin was happy to just lay back and let it happen.

When it was his turn to repay the compliment, Kevin

climbed on top of her and slowly peeled down her knickers to reveal one of the biggest cocks he had ever seen.

It took a moment for the message to get through his drunken haze and reach his brain. When it finally did, Kevin slid off the bed and stood naked in the corner, retching.

Through his coughing and spluttering he could hear Julie- or whatever her/his name was-demanding to know what was wrong.

Evidently, she/he had been under the misapprehension that Kevin had been fully aware that Julie was a transvestite, or a transsexual, Kevin did not know, or care about the difference. All he did know right then and there was that he had to get away before he lost the three pints of lager he had consumed before leaving the club.

Once Kevin had leapt out of the lift on the ground floor of the block, he spewed forth his guts on the pavement.

He could faintly hear the sound of voices as a couple of girls passed by, commenting on how disgusting men were in general, and he was, specifically.

As much as he wanted to argue in his defence, Kevin could not form any words that made any sense at that moment, so he just watched through bleary eyes as the two girls wandered off into the night.

By the time he was able to stand again, Kevin felt as if his abdomen had been turned inside out.

He considered hiring a cab, but he could not trust himself not to throw up on the back seat, so he decided to let the night air help to settle his stomach and walk home.

As bad as the cramps in his belly were, Kevin still could not stop himself from vomiting once more as he turned into the park. He stopped by the entrance and slumped against the railings to let it all come out.

After he had finished, he staggered on through the night, trying desperately not to revisit his ordeal in his mind.

Suddenly, in the distance he could see a shadow moving behind a clump of high bushes.

Kevin was in no fit state for any trouble and at first, he considered turning around and going home the long way.

He stopped in his tracks and waited for a moment to see whether or not he could ascertain who or what was ahead.

He strained his eyes to penetrate the gloom and focus on the area where he had first seen the movement.

After a while he began to think that it was just his imagination, or possibly a trick of the darkness, as the only movement he could detect now was the branches on the trees swaying in the breeze.

Convinced that it had all been in his mind, Kevin went to move forward, but just as he did, he saw it again!

There was definitely a figure moving in the distance, and although it was masked by the foliage between them, he could definitely see a pair of legs moving back and forth as if the owner was undecided upon which way to go.

Kevin decided that it must be a drunk, unable to stand still due to overindulgence, but by the same token, not ready to fall down asleep just yet.

Once he was convinced that there was only one person behind the bushes, he decided to take his chances and continue walking along the path, past the spot where whoever it was, was staggering. If they tried anything, as awful as he was feeling, his temper was at the stage where he would lash out first and ask questions later.

Kevin sucked in a lungful of night air and stuck out his chest. As he approached the bushes, he balled his hands into fists in anticipation of a possible confrontation.

He initially intended to keep his focus straight ahead and

try not to even acknowledge whoever was behind the bush, but the closer he grew to it the more he resigned himself to the fact that his curiosity was inevitably going to get the better of him.

At the turning, Kevin glanced to his right, and what he saw made him stop dead in his tracks.

Behind the bush was the bedraggled form of Natasha. The torn remnants of her dress barely covered her bruised and scratched skin, and Kevin could not help but notice that one of her naked breasts was fully on display.

Even in her present state, Natasha was still a stunning young woman, and Kevin wondered if perhaps she was one of the Toms from the truck stop over at the far end of town, touting for trade.

He could feel himself grow hard at the prospect.

Perhaps she had been in a fight with one of the other tarts or even her pimp. That would explain the torn dress and her dishevelled appearance.

Ordinarily, Kevin would not consider paying for it, but after the experience he had just suffered he reasoned that the feel of a real woman rubbing her soft hands all over him might be just what the doctor ordered.

He took a tentative step towards Natasha. "Hello, darling'" his voice came out higher than usual, so he cleared his throat and tried again. "Are you looking for company?" he asked, more confidently this time.

In truth, as he had never approached a prostitute before, Kevin had no idea how the transaction phase should be conducted, but he knew that he only had about thirty quid left in his wallet after paying for the taxi earlier, so if she wanted to charge anymore, the deal was off!

At first, Natasha did not appear to hear his offer.

At this point she turned so that she now had her back to

him, and she seemed to be slowly dancing on the spot as if to some music which only she could hear.

Kevin looked around. There was no sign of anyone else in the area, so he moved in closer until he was directly behind Natasha.

From this distance he could hear that she was quietly humming a tune to herself, and for a moment he wondered if perhaps she had a pair of earphones on under her hair.

That would certainly explain why she seemed unaware of his presence.

Kevin listened to Natasha's tune for a little while longer before frustration took hold and he moved forward and placed his hand on her shoulder.

The moment he touched her, Natasha turned around to face him and started screaming.

Kevin panicked.

At first, he tried to reassure her that he had not meant to scare her, but she seemed oblivious to his words and just continued to shriek and screech louder and louder until Kevin felt sure that someone nearby would call the police.

Kevin looked around him, hoping that perhaps someone else might be close enough to be a witness that he had not harmed the girl before she started to scream, but there was no one in sight.

In desperation he tried holding out his hands to calm Natasha down, but the second he stepped closer to her she began to cry out even louder and more hysterically.

From this proximity, Kevin could see Natasha's eyes quite clearly.

At first, he presumed that she was just staring at him because he had frightened her. But then he noticed that she was not actually looking at him, but more like through him.

Her frozen stare appeared to be focussed directly in front

of her and for a moment Kevin felt as if someone was creeping up from behind, so he quickly spun around, but there was still no one there.

He turned back to face Natasha wishing to god that he had walked the long way around after all.

He considered running, but if he was seen, or worse still caught just as the police arrived, he knew that it would be that much harder for him to explain away his predicament.

Taking a couple of steps back, Kevin decided that the best way to exonerate him was to make the call himself, so he fumbled in his jeans and took out his mobile.

When the emergency operator answered, Kevin had to put a finger in his ear to try and hear her above Natasha's shrieking cries.

Eventually, he managed to blurt out their location and what was happening, and the operator assured him that the police were on their way and should be with him within minutes.

Sure enough, just as he cut off the call, he heard the sound of sirens in the distance.

CHAPTER TWENTY-FOUR

Ten seconds after Hardy had switched his alarm clock off, his mobile buzzed into life. He swung his legs out of bed and sat up before answering.

"Hardy," he said, mid-yawn.

"Sorry guv, I thought you would be awake by now." It was Russell on the other end.

"I was, just," replied Hardy, sleepily. "What's going on?"

"Well," began Russell, "the good news is that we've found Natasha Spencer alive."

Hardy stood up too quickly and he felt the room starting to spin, so he slumped back down on his bed. "She's alive!" he exclaimed, in shock and surprise. Even though he had not let on to anyone, he was already convinced that when they found Natasha—if they ever did—she would almost certainly be dead.

Before Hardy had a chance to say anything else, Russell continued.

"That's the good news guv; the bad news is that she hasn't been able to say a word since we found her."

"How do you mean?" Hardy's mind cleared and he began

to regain his composure.

"She was picked up in the park in the early hours, not far from where she disappeared," Hardy could hear Russell turning pages in his notebook as he relayed the full details. "She was found wandering alone and half naked by a Kevin Johnson, on his way back from a night out. By the time our lads got there, she was apparently screaming the place down."

"What did this Johnson character have to say for himself?" asked Hardy, inquisitively.

There was more turning of pages in the background.

"Not much, he insisted that he saw her wandering around half-dressed, asked if she was alright, and then she just started screaming and didn't stop, that's why he called us."

"And do we believe him?" asked Hardy, suspiciously.

"Well, they let him go after he gave his statement; we've got his contact details in case we need to interview him again should we...."

"Hang on," Hardy interrupted, "what time did all this take place?"

"Earlier this morning," replied Russell, feeling a little sheepish now for not having contacted Hardy when he was first called out.

"So why wasn't I contacted?" demanded Hardy, annoyed that he appeared to have been left out of the loop.

Russell sighed, deeply. "That's my fault, guv. They called me immediately, so I decided to get the full story before contacting you, sorry if that was wrong!"

Hardy relaxed. The fact that Russell had taken it upon himself to evaluate the situation and act accordingly showed good initiative, and Hardy always encouraged that in his team.

"Not to worry," Hardy responded, "I needed the beauty sleep anyway."

He heard Russell let out a nervous laugh of relief.

"So where are we now?" he continued.

"I sent a car round to pick up Natasha's parents and take them straight to the hospital; they've been with her since she was brought in."

"And she hasn't managed to give us anything we can use?"

"Not one single word," Russell stated, emphatically. "The doctors have examined her as best they could, but they had to sedate her because she kept on screaming."

"What have they said so far?" asked Hardy, hopeful that there might be something tangible that they could use to assist them in their investigation.

"Not much," admitted Russell, dejectedly. "They've confirmed that she's been the victim of an assault, but to be honest I could tell that just by looking at the state of her dress, it was torn to shreds and her skin was all scratched and grazed. It looked like the poor girl had been through a bacon slicer."

"Was there any sign of sexual interference?" enquired Hardy, tentatively, afraid that he already knew the answer.

"Oh yes," replied Russell, emphatically. "The docs said the poor girl looked as if she had been raped repeatedly and with such ferocity, the wall of her vagina was completely lacerated. As yet they have no idea what he used, but they are sure that it wasn't just his dick."

"Christ almighty," breathed Hardy, "the poor kid."

"They have managed to collect some swab samples, so they are hoping to be able to identify the attacker's DNA. Then maybe we can catch this bastard sooner rather than later"

"Well, that will be something at least," agreed Hardy. He glanced at his wristwatch, it was almost 6.15 a.m. "Have you told Carlisle or our new DCI yet?" he enquired.

"No, guv," Russell replied, "I thought I'd bring you up to speed first."

"Well, it's late enough now so I'll call the DCI, and I'll give you the pleasure of letting the super know, how's that?"

"Wonderful," Russell responded, with just the merest hint of sarcasm in his tone.

Hardy waited until after he had showered and dressed before calling Pamela. From the sound of her voice his call had woken her up, so he apologised before explaining the latest series of events.

Pamela listened without interrupting him, but Hardy could hear her yawning down the receiver.

Once he was finished, he informed her that he was on his way to the hospital.

"OK, good idea," Pamela agreed, "give me the directions from my hotel and I'll meet you there as soon as I've sorted myself out."

KELLY HANDED Jack his lunchbox containing the cheese and ham sandwiches she had made him for lunch.

He pulled her close for a goodbye kiss and Kelly reluctantly complied, even though the mere touch of her husband repulsed her, now.

She knew in her heart that she could not carry on with her sham of a marriage much longer, but she knew that the guilt she was already feeling having made her decision would increase ten-fold by the time she finally called it a day.

Kelly wondered if Desmond had not reappeared on the scene, would she have had the strength of character to make such a decision.

Certainly, after her night with Carol, she already felt more empowered than she had done for as long as she could remember, and Carol's offer to let her stay with her if she needed a roof over her head was an invitation she found most welcoming.

But now that Desmond had declared his feelings for her, Kelly realised that she could not afford to waste another minute of her life with Jack.

The one and only consideration that was still holding her back, was Father Grace's reproach yesterday at her confession.

First and foremast Kelly knew that she was a catholic before anything else, and regardless of her circumstance she needed reassurance that she would not be disregarding her faith and moral upbringing at the cost of her own happiness.

But what could she say or do that would possibly make Father Grace give her his blessing?

Whenever Kelly had felt in herself in turmoil the church had always been there for her, and she needed to know that she would still be welcomed there if she left her husband and made a new life with Desmond.

She checked the time on the kitchen clock. It was still early, and she wondered if Carol had left for work yet.

Pulling off her pyjamas and slippers and leaving them in a pile on the floor, Kelly grabbed a sweater and a pair of track pants and hopped on one leg at a time as she pulled on her trainers, before leaving the flat.

As soon as she knocked, she could see a shadow moving behind the frosted glass.

Carol answered the door wearing the same dressing gown she had worn after their night of passion.

"Hello, kiddo," Carol said cheerfully when she saw her visitor. "I was about to get into the shower, wanna join me?" she offered with a wink.

Kelly felt her cheeks blush. "No," she barked, then immediately realised how rude she sounded, "I'm sorry, I didn't mean that to sound so defensive, you took me by surprise."

Carol laughed. "That's how I always get them. You coming

in?" she asked, standing back, and holding the door a little wider.

Kelly made her way into the kitchen while Carol closed the door before joining her.

"So, to what do I owe the pleasure?" she asked, pleasantly.

Kelly bit her bottom lip.

She had not anticipated how awkward she would feel standing in front of her most recent lover and asking for advice about her new love interest.

Carol sensed Kelly's hesitation was probably as a direct result of their night together, so she tried to break the ice. "If you've come around here to tell me the other evening was a mistake and that it has to be a one-off, then that's not a problem, kiddo," she offered, comfortingly.

Kelly threw her arms around her friend and gave her a big hug.

Carol reciprocated, and the two of them stayed together for a moment locked in each other's embrace.

When they pulled apart, Kelly took a deep breath before she started her unrehearsed speech.

"Carol," she started, nervously, "I don't know how to say this but, I think I've fallen in love with someone."

Carol looked stunned, almost as if she had just received a slap across her face.

"Please tell me you don't mean with me?" she asked, cautiously.

Kelly almost burst out laughing. Carol had a way of delivering statements which always managed to make Kelly want to chuckle.

"No, silly," she replied, hoping that Carol would not be offended by her tone. "I'm talking about a boy that I've fancied for ages who I just met up with yesterday."

"Oh, right, I see." Carol definitely sounded relieved to

Kelly, which was a good thing because Kelly did not want to do or say anything which might ruin their friendship.

"In that case," Carol continued, "I think that I can afford to be a little late for work, let's put the kettle on and you can tell me all about him."

They stayed in the kitchen while Kelly filled her friend in on the details of what happened to her the previous day. She told her about her guilt at their union and her visit to see Father Grace, and how upset she was by what he said and then about her meeting up with Des in the park, and how he managed to turn everything around for her.

Once she had finished relaying her story, Kelly waited for Carol to offer her some advice on what she should do.

After a moment to digest the full details, Carol began. "Well if you want my opinion, kiddo, I say first thing you need to do is dump that useless excuse for a human being you call a husband, and if he refuses to go, get the council to evict him. After all, he's only in that flat because he married you, it was your home long before he arrived on the scene."

Kelly could feel her heart lift.

What her friend was saying was exactly what she wanted to hear.

But it was more than just that!

The sound of hearing someone else saying out loud what she had been thinking ever since meeting Desmond in the park, made it appear all the more achievable.

Carol's words gave Kelly the courage she needed to start putting the wheels in motion.

But there was still the problem of winning around the priest.

Kelly's faith was extremely important to her and she could not simply dismiss it out of hand, even for the man she loved.

Carol could tell by the way her friend's brow was furrowed

that Kelly still had reservations.

Carol put her arm around Kelly's shoulders and planted a kiss on the side of her head. "So, what's the trouble?" she asked, patiently. "Are you worried about Jack kicking off, because if you are, I know some lads who will take care of him and get him off your back."

Kelly nudged her friend playfully in the ribs. "No! Nothing like that," she sighed, "It's just that I know how the church feels about divorce, and after speaking to the priest yesterday I have the distinct feeling that there won't be much sympathy or understanding coming my way."

Carol thought for a moment. "Look, kiddo," she offered, sympathetically, "I know how religious you are, and I respect that, it's not my thing but each to their own, as my old dad used to say. However, I cannot believe that god or Jesus or any of the saints would want you to spend the rest of your life in misery just because of one stupid mistake, and if your priest doesn't understand that, well then perhaps he needs to take a refresher course on how to deal with his parishioners with a little more compassion and a little less zeal."

With every word her friend uttered, Kelly could feel her resolve growing stronger.

Now her mind was firmly made up!

Tonight, she would speak to Jack and regardless of his response, she would begin divorce proceedings first thing in the morning.

Infused with her new steadfastness, Kelly decided that she was going to return to work that morning. She had initially thought to take at least one more day off to allow her bruised face the chance to heal completely but having made up her mind about Jack she felt strong enough to take on the world.

She gave Carol a parting hug and thanked her for all her help, before heading home to shower and get ready.

CHAPTER TWENTY-FIVE

Moreton Ripper claims third victim:
Fourth potential victim still unaccounted for.

C arlisle began reading the article as he stirred his morning coffee. He knew straightaway whose name would be on the by-line and sure enough, when he checked, it was Cyril Carney.

The superintendent was not altogether surprised by the report; Carney always went for the sensationalism angle regardless of how pertinent the facts may be.

As Carlisle read on, he could feel his frustration rising. Carney had likened their situation to Yorkshire during the reign of the Yorkshire Ripper, and Whitechapel

at the height of the Jack the Ripper investigation.

According to Carney the local police were completely out of their depth which was why they had drafted in a senior officer from outside the district to take charge of the investigation.

Naturally, there was no mention whatsoever that the decision to bring in Pamela Holmsley was Carlisle's, and Carney's article made it seem as if the decision was made above Carlisle's head as a result of him being incapable of running the show himself.

Before he finished, Carlisle had read the entire article twice without pausing and by the time he lifted his cup to his mouth to drink his coffee it had turned tepid.

He pulled a face as he sloshed the lukewarm liquid around his mouth and, for a moment, he was tempted to spit it back into his cup, but he decided it was not worth the risk of him splashing his shirt and tie in the process, so he closed his eyes and swallowed, grimacing as he did so.

The one saving grace which he had to hold onto was that Natasha Spencer had been found alive. That at least was one nightmare he would not have to face the backlash of. Naturally, he hoped that in time she would make a full recovery, but for now he was just relieved that they had found her before it was too late.

The fact that her discovery was more as a result of luck rather than judgement was neither here nor there. She was alive and that was what counted.

Carlisle could imagine the ACC giving himself a pat on the back for recommending Pamela for the transfer. After all, she had barely been on the job a day and already they had found Natasha who they all suspected would end up being the fourth victim of this maniac.

His main wish now was that she would be able to identify her kidnapper before he had the chance to find another potential victim.

Without bothering to read anything else the Chronicle

might have to offer, Carlisle scrunched up the newspaper and threw it into the waste paper bin under his desk.

Hitting the call button next to his phone he requested a fresh cup of coffee.

His day had not started well!

* * *

HARDY AND PAMELA sat in an anteroom adjacent to Natasha's private suite in the hospital. Through the glass partition, Hardy could see the girl's parents talking animatedly with the doctor on duty. The mumbled sound of raised voices occasionally penetrated the glass pane between the rooms, and Hardy could tell by the gesturing and overall body language of the Spencer's that they were not at all satisfied with whatever the consultant was relaying to them.

Hardy looked over to the bed which dominated the room. In it lay the motionless form of Natasha, her arms on top of the covers each with several tubes protruding from her tanned skin which, along with numerous wires taped to her exposed flesh, lead up to the machines standing on either side of her bed.

Her eyes were closed and from the slight movement of her chest, Hardy could tell that she was breathing steadily.

As much as he hated to admit it to himself, he had reached the stage where he thought that they would not find the girl alive, so the mere fact that she was still in one piece was a blessing, although they were yet to ascertain the true extent of any internal or psychological damage her time in captivity might have caused.

When he had first arrived at the hospital to take over from Russell, Hardy had hoped that Natasha may have been compos mentis enough to be able to at least give them a description of her attacker, or possibly even some idea of where she had been held. But he soon realised that Russell had not exaggerated the extent of her condition, and so for now he and Pamela were just waiting to see if the doctor could give them some idea as to when they might be able to speak to her.

Hardy had been in similar situations to this before, so he had learned to be patient. Pamela on the other hand seemed to be growing more frustrated with each passing minute.

Unlike Hardy who was slumped in a chair awaiting the consultant, Pamela was pacing up and down the room like a wild animal trapped in a cage. Every so often she would stop and gaze out of the window at the car park below, but whatever she saw down there obviously did not hold her interest sufficiently, and after a moment she would continue with her strutting, sighing deeply to herself as she did so.

As she walked the floor, Pamela's legs would occasionally rub against each other, causing her stockings to make a *rasping* sound which Hardy soon realised was causing him to become aroused.

Before Pamela had a chance to notice, the DI grabbed a magazine from the pile on the waiting room table and placed it over his lap as he flicked through the pages pretending to read it.

Now that his embarrassment was concealed, Hardy found himself gazing up whenever Pamela had her back to him, just so that he could catch another glimpse of her legs. She was wearing a skirt cut slightly above her knees, and as she moved the split at the side allowed him an occasional glimpse at her suspenders.

"How are they getting on with the search of the area?" Pamela's sudden intrusion shattered through Hardy's thoughts, catching him off guard. It almost felt to him as if Pamela had somehow known what he was thinking and wanted to prove it by catching him unawares, just so that she could revel in his obvious discomfort.

Hardy instinctively sat up in his chair. In doing so, he managed to let the magazine slide off his lap onto the floor.

He reached down to grab it.

By the time he was back up he could feel his cheeks glowing.

At first, he felt too embarrassed to meet Pamela's gaze. It took him back to an incident in secondary school when his science teacher Miss Danker caught him staring at her legs in class. Even after she had asked him out loud in front of everyone else what he was doing, he was so engrossed in her beautiful long legs, encased as they were in gorgeous black nylon, that he was blissfully unaware that she was even addressing him.

That was until she started striding towards his desk.

By the time Hardy realised what was going on, it was too late!

Much to the amusement of his classmates, Hardy was marched out of the room and ushered to the Headmistress's office where he received a thousand lines and a stern warning that if he ever displayed such unacceptable behaviour again, his parents would be contacted formally and asked to come to school for a meeting with the Head.

The memory of his childhood antics made Hardy blush an even darker shade of red.

When he finally managed to return his senior officer's gaze, he could tell immediately from the puzzled expression on her face that she was wondering why he was finding it so difficult to answer a straightforward question.

Hardy cleared his throat as if he was about to speak.

He opened his mouth, but then for a split second his mind went blank.

"Well!" Pamela demanded, impatiently.

The abruptness of her tone suddenly snapped Hardy out of his stupor.

"Ah, well," he began, trying not to stumble over his own words, "they cordoned off the area until first light, and then the search of the area began in earnest. Sergeant Russell will be there by now to take charge and oversee the operation."

Pamela nodded. "He seems like a competent officer," she observed, "I take it he will report back to you as soon as he finds anything?"

"Yes indeed," Hardy assured her, "he knows that I'm with you, so he'll let us know as soon as anything turns up."

Pamela thought for a moment, before adding. "When we get back to the station, I want to see a map of the area we're talking about. Can you sort that out for me?"

Hardy nodded. "No problem ma'am."

"What sort of conditions are we talking about, is it a large area?"

"Well the park itself is quite vast as it stretches clear across town, but worse still is that where the park ends it leads into the woods, and they're enormous."

Pamela strode back over to the window once more. "Is that the same wood where we found the two bodies yesterday?" she asked, not turning around to face Hardy.

"That's right," replied Hardy, "but we are talking several miles of park and woodland between the two sites."

The DCI turned back to face her junior officer. "Then I think that we should concentrate on the house-to-house once the park has been checked."

Hardy nodded.

Just then there was a knock at the door.

Before either of them had a chance to call out, the handle

turned and the doctor who had been talking to Natasha's parents in the next room appeared.

He was a tall man with a swarthy complexion and very tired-looking eyes.

He closed the door behind him before he started to speak.

"Good morning, officers," he announced, "I am Doctor Rah."

Hardy found his tone of address somewhat formal considering it was just the two of them, but he surmised that the doctor was probably so used to making formal announcements to grieving parents and relatives that he probably switched to his professional mode without thinking.

"Good morning, doctor," Pamela answered for both of them, and walked over to shake the medic's hand.

Hardy rose to his feet and smiled at the consultant, but as Pamela was now standing between them, he did not think that it was worth the effort to reposition himself in order to offer his hand.

The three of them stood together in an informal huddle.

"I have explained to Miss Spencer's parents," the doctor began, "that under the circumstances my colleagues and I do not think it wise to try and rouse their daughter, for the moment."

Hardy glanced across at the window between the two rooms.

Gerald Spencer was standing over by the window talking animatedly on his mobile phone, while his wife sat by their daughter's bedside, resting the palm of one hand on the motionless girl's arm whilst using the other to dab her moist eyes with a tissue.

"Is she in a coma?" The suddenness of Pamela's question refocused Hardy's attention to those in the room with him.

The doctor thought for a second before answering. "Not as

such," he explained. "It's true that several of her symptoms are the same but judging by her condition when she was first brought in my colleagues and I believe that her mind is in extreme catatonic collapse. We have no need to induce a coma, indeed the medication we have given her was intended purely to calm her down before she did herself more harm."

"My sergeant informed me that when they found her, she was screaming and close to being hysterical," Hardy ventured.

The doctor nodded. "Very much so, the paramedics gave her something milder in the ambulance on the way over here, but even then, they had to keep her strapped down on the gurney to prevent her from thrashing around."

"Do you suspect that she might have been given something prior to being found which caused her to act in such a manner?" Pamela ventured.

The doctor sighed. "Well we did suspect something of that nature at first, but we ran a toxicology test and that came back negative, so we're more inclined to the notion that it is her mental state which was causing her to act in such a manner."

"Have you managed to collect any samples of DNA for analysis yet doctor?" Pamela persisted, unable to mask the anticipation in her voice. "I presume that you have been made aware of the circumstances under which Miss Spencer was discovered?"

"Yes indeed," the medic nodded, "I believe that one of my colleagues has despatched a few samples to your Pathologist's office, hopefully they will be of some probative use."

"That's wonderful," Pamela responded, "now is there any way you can give me some sort of time frame as to when I might be able to interview Miss Spencer?"

For the first time since entering the room the doctor almost cracked a smile, but Hardy figured that it was probably just an involuntary reaction to the DCI's question.

The doctor quickly restored his professional exterior before answering.

He looked Pamela directly in the eyes. "Officer, at this moment in time we are naturally hopeful that Miss Spencer will make a full recovery," he kept his voice calm but firm, almost as if he was dishing out instructions rather than just offering an explanation. "However, you must understand that for the moment her mind is fighting with itself and there is no way of ascertaining precisely how long that conflict will continue, or what the definitive outcome will be."

"Yes, I understand," Pamela confirmed, barely able to keep the terseness out of her voice. "But surely you have some way of bringing her round just long enough so that she can answer a few simple questions, I cannot over emphasise how incredibly important this is to our investigation."

The doctor took a step back. He was evidently shocked and alarmed by Pamela's statement and he needed time to process it before answering.

After a few seconds he took in a deep breath, before stating his case as firmly and as succinctly as he knew how.

"Officer, let me assure you that I fully appreciate the urgency of your investigation, but you must understand that Miss Spencer is my patient and her health and wellbeing are my sole concerns, and to that end I will not do anything which I believe, in my professional capacity, might cause her any further distress, alarm, or might indeed actually endanger her chances of making a full recovery."

The doctor kept his eyes fixed on Pamela as if baiting her to make another statement along the lines of her earlier one.

Hardy could feel the tension in the air rising, but he felt helpless to intervene in case the DCI suddenly turned on him.

After all, he was a copper first and last and it had been his investigation before Pamela was brought in so no one wanted to see the perpetrator brought in more than him, but by the same token he could see what the doctor was saying made perfect sense and that there was no point in pushing the issue.

The silence was becoming too uncomfortable to bear.

Eventually, Hardy decided that he needed to intervene regardless of the consequences.

"Doctor," he offered, ensuring that he kept his voice low and his tone pleasant, "you will let us know the minute anything changes in Miss Spencer's condition?"

The doctor slowly turned away from Pamela and focused on Hardy.

"Of course, officer, your colleague gave us your contact details earlier, rest assured as soon as we have something to report we will let you know."

The doctor excused himself, giving both the officers a slight nod of his head before he made his way back out into the corridor.

"Fuck it!" Pamela hissed through gritted teeth. She did not appear too concerned that the door the doctor had just exited by was still partially ajar when she let forth her expletive.

Hardy had to restrain himself from laughing. Pamela was so petite and refined; although he imagined that her cut-glass accent was falser than she would care to admit. Even so, it did sound odd when someone like her swore, especially when it was so unexpected.

Pamela stared at the carpeted floor for a moment with her bottom lip clenched between her teeth.

Hardy decided it was best not to distract her from her train of thought, so he waited, patiently.

After a moment, Pamela yanked open the door and walked out into the corridor. "Come on, let's go," she called back, not bothering to check if Hardy was following her or not.

CHAPTER TWENTY-SIX

Father Grace sat at his kitchen table with his head in his hands. The cup of tea he had made just before he received the phone call lay cold and untouched in front of him.

Deep down, the priest had always known that this day might come, but it was still a shock now that it had finally arrived.

Part of him felt as if he was being nudged towards retirement, but the thought of living out the rest of his days in one of the many retirement homes designated for priests, with no flock to preach to and having to spend each day listening to the bitter resentment spewed out by his fellow alumni who had also been dumped in the same position before they felt that they had served out their time, was not a predicament he felt he wanted to embrace.

The alternative which had been presented to him was by far the lesser of two evils.

Even so, the thought of having to effectively start again at a new parish at his age, did not exactly fill his heart with delight at the 'new challenges'—as the Bishop's representative had put it—which lay ahead.

The spokesperson from the Bishop's office who had been tasked with making the call was obviously very uncomfortable with the duty, judging by the way her voice was shaking on the other end of the line, along with the numerous times she apologised for something which, when all was said and done, she had no control over.

The priest knew that he had the option of appealing the decision to the Bishop directly. But what would be the point!

In all his years in office he had never heard of one single successful appeal. The ordination of priests set out the rules and conditions under which you were expected to practice quite clearly, and it was an unwritten rule that whatever the Bishop's decision was, you were expected to accept it with good grace. Indeed, it was frowned on wholeheartedly by everyone else in the diocese if you so much as registered a concern regarding your next placement.

Ever since her confession yesterday, Father Grace had been wrestling with his conscience concerning Kelly Soames. He had known her long enough to appreciate what turmoil she must be in after he refused to give her absolution.

As much as it went against catholic doctrine, the priest had decided that he was going to absolve Kelly after all. He could not live with himself knowing what the poor child must be going through; much less deny her god's mercy for her one and only indiscretion.

Now, doubtless as a result of the pride he had allowed himself to feel as a result of his decision, god had given him something far worse to deal with, something which he could not just smile and brush off with just a few kind words.

This present predicament he had been landed in would take a considerable amount of thought and careful planning, and for the moment Father Grace did not even have a starting position.

As with every obstacle the priest had encountered during his life his first thought was to turn to god, but in the present instance he knew that that was not a viable option.

God would have no part in his plan!

Father Grace lifted his head and exhaled a long breath.

He knew that he needed to clear his head so that he could concentrate on the problem at hand in order to determine an effective course of action.

As if from out of nowhere, a sudden wave of compassion swept over him.

Father Grace pushed back his chair as he stood up from the table, the bare wooden legs scraped across the stone floor as he rose.

He walked over to the large welsh dresser which dominated one side of his kitchen and opened one of the drawers to retrieve a sturdy metal key.

He placed the key carefully in the pocket of his cassock, just below the cincture, and patted it through the thick cloth to ensure that it was securely in place. The last thing he needed was to draw any unwanted attention by dropping the key on the parquet flooring on his way to the far end of the church. It had happened once before, and the echo which emanated as a result of the accident caused all those at silent prayer within the church to stop and look up.

Not ideal under the circumstances.

Father Grace made his way out into the vestibule and peered through the glass partition of the nearest door to see if anyone was at worship.

Morning confession was only fifteen minutes away and already he could see a lone figure sitting in the pew, waiting patiently.

He recognised the narrow-shouldered form immediately.

Anita Price was one of the more ardent and devout members of his congregation, and the priest was not in the least bit surprised to see her waiting in line for confession.

Apart from Anita there were only a handful of parishioners scattered amongst the other pews, each lost in their own private prayers.

Father Grace made his way through the door, cringing inside when it squeaked on a rusty hinge, and walked slowly down the nearest aisle to the far end of the church.

He genuflected as he approached the main altar before turning to his left and disappearing from view behind an ornate purple and gold drape which hung down from one of the stone supports almost to the floor.

Once he had ensured that the heavy material had folded back into place shielding him from any inquisitive eyes.

In the pitch-black behind the drape, the priest fumbled on the high ledge to his right where he had left his torch. When his fingers felt the familiar handle, he clasped it firmly and lifted the torch down.

Checking once more that he could not be seen from behind, Father Grace pressed the button and the short corridor before him was instantly illuminated. He shone the beam down to the floor to help him navigate the uneven surface of the old stone floor until he reached the door at the far end.

Using the key from his cassock, the priest unlocked the oak-panelled arched door, and once he felt the lock slide in its barrel, he placed his shoulder against the wood and heaved it open.

Securing it behind him, Father Grace made his way cautiously down the spiral of stone steps, ensuring that he kept the penetrating beam from his torch aimed at the floor so as not to risk missing his step and tumbling down to the bottom.

Once he reached the bottom, he made his way along the familiar winding labyrinthine path towards the makeshift accommodation which he had set up in one corner.

As he turned the last corner his torch beam illuminated the arch built into the solid rock under which the Creeper lay curled up in a foetal position, fast asleep.

Father Grace veered the torch beam to one side so that the light did not shine directly at the Creeper's eyes. He did not want to risk waking the slumbering figure, and besides, he enjoyed watching his charge at peace.

The old priest stood there for a while and gazed down at the sleeping form like any loving parent guarding over their new-born in the crib. As the Creeper's chest rose and fell with each lungful of air, the priest suddenly became aware of a trickle of tears sliding down his wrinkled cheeks. He raised his hand and absentmindedly wiped them away.

After a while he could feel his sorrow turn to anger. But as much as he felt justified in blaming the Bishop for his present predicament Father Grace knew full well that his charge was his responsibility and that he should have made plans for the inevitable day he had always known would eventually come.

Now that that day was fast approaching, the old priest knew that he needed to work on a plan of action, and his options were sorely limited.

Glancing at his watch Father Grace realised that he was running late for morning confession. With a heavy heart he stole one more glance at the sleeping form of the Creeper before turning away to make his way back out through the surrounding tunnels.

Having locked the heavy door behind him, Father Grace emerged from behind the drapery and looked over towards the confessional bench.

Anita Price was still the only member of his flock waiting.

He had hoped that perhaps Kelly might have stopped by again. After yesterday he needed to alleviate the remorse he was feeling at having turned her away so abruptly. He had to admit to himself that the way he was feeling at the moment with the pressure being put on him by the Bishop, he needed to deal with Kelly's issues, not just so that he could be there for her but also because it would help him to clear his mind so that he could concentrate on his other pressing business.

But she was obviously still too ashamed or angry with him to come in yet, and who could blame her?

He knew that he would definitely see her at Sunday mass, but right now that seemed to him a long way off.

Father Grace could feel the weight of his guilt lying on his chest as surely as if it were a millstone pressing down on him. But in his mind, he decided that he deserved to carry that guilt as a punishment for his unforgivable behaviour, so he had no option but to wait for the moment that Kelly decided to forgive him by returning to his church.

He turned and crossed over towards the altar, genuflecting once more as he passed on his way to the vestry.

Once inside he pulled his white surplice over his cassock and chose the purple stole he always wore when taking confession and placed it around his neck.

Just then, a thought struck him!

He stopped in his tracks to give the idea a moment to take root in his mind.

His mind began to race, could the answer be staring him virtually in the face? The priest opened the door of the vestry a couple of inches and stared back out towards where a pensive Anita Price sat with her head bowed in silent prayer.

As he watched her from afar, Father Grace pondered over the thought that was spinning in his mind.

Did he dare risk it?

Right now, what other options did he have available to him!

Out of habit more than anything else the old priest looked up to the statue of Jesus nailed to the cross above the altar for inspiration, but then realising what he was considering, he looked back down immediately and felt his shame deepen.

Both his head and his heart were in turmoil.

Did he dare put his plan into action?

Releasing a huge sigh, the priest made his way back out of the vestry and proceeded to walk down the nearest aisle towards the confessional.

Anita Price looked up from her reverie of silent prayer as she heard the approaching footsteps of her confessor.

She immediately felt her skin starting to heat up from embarrassment.

She averted her eyes before Father Grace drew close enough to acknowledge her and looked over her shoulder to ensure that there was no one else waiting in line.

Even when—as usual—she was the first one in line for confession, Anita preferred to let everyone else waiting go before her regardless of how late they arrived. As desperate as she always was to have her burden of shame lifted, she could never escape the feeling that those waiting outside could somehow hear the sins she was confessing through the stout wooden frame.

On occasion, she had actually been standing in front of the confessional with her fingers wrapped around the handle of the door when she had heard a late arrival enter the church, and at that point she had still felt obliged to usher them in in her place and wait a while longer, just so that she could be the last one.

Although she was still only in her mid-twenties Anita looked far older than her tender years, due mainly to the fact that unlike her peers she very rarely smiled and did not seem to care about enhancing her appearance with fashionable clothes or make-up, on a day to day basis.

Her long brown hair was usually wrapped up into a bun on top of her head, which again added weight to her overall appearance of being older than her years.

By most people's standards, Anita had had a very tough upbringing, and it was doubtless as a result of this that she tended to look and act the way she did.

The first seven years of Anita's young life had been as happy and joyful as any child could wish for. Her parents doted on her and her younger brother whom she also absolutely adored. The sibling's days were filled with love and sunshine hours.

That was until one fateful Sunday afternoon when their car was hit head-on by a drunk driver racing to beat the traffic light.

Anita's father did not have did not have time to swerve out of the way before they were hit, sending their vehicle tumbling over across the dual carriageway and down the embankment.

Her mother and baby brother were both pronounced dead at the scene. Her mother managed to hang on for a few hours more, but she too died later that same day in the hospital.

Anita, still oblivious to what was happening to her world, miraculously managed to escape death although she remained in a coma for over a week.

As both sets of her grandparents were already deceased the only blood relatives the authorities could find were Anita's two maiden aunts. They were in fact her mother's elder siblings, but due to the age gap between them and Anita's mother they were not close and at the time of the accident Anita had not met either of them.

Although Anita was too young to understand at the time, the only reason her aunts stepped forward and agreed to take the youngster in was because by doing so they both benefitted from the sizeable insurance payout awarded by the Criminal Compensation Board as a result of the accident.

Neither of the spinsters had any maternal instincts to speak about and if the truth had been known, they each regarded children as nothing more than a nuisance and an inconvenience full of mischief and with natural tendencies to misbehave.

In short, they considered Anita an irritation. But neither was willing to lose the chance of the sizeable pay-out that the child would bring with her, so for the benefit of the authorities they played the part of loving and caring aunties who wanted nothing more than to ensure that their orphaned niece received all the love and care that she deserved, now that her parents were both gone.

Once they had the little girl in their clutches their true nature revealed itself.

The spinsters had always lived a life of solitude and frugality. They were not poor by any means, both having worked throughout their lives and never wasting a penny on fancy clothes, restaurants, holidays, or any of the usual trappings enjoyed by the majority of their fellow human beings.

The sizeable house which they had purchased together many years before, was bleak and sparsely furnished, and the inside had not seen a can of paint or a roll of wallpaper since they day they moved in.

Neither had ever considered the prospect of starting a family, and although they had both dabbled in relationships in their youth, when it came to it, they both shied away from human contact and any form of physical love.

However, they both shared one driving passion, their religion. As far as they were concerned anyone who did not embrace the catholic faith was damned, and they only had themselves to blame for it.

Life, to them, was all about repentance, solitude, and economy.

Traits which they expected their new charge to adopt without question.

Having come from such a loving warm environment it took poor little Anita quite a while to adapt to her new lifestyle. Discipline was an integral part of her education and on more than one occasion the little girl was sent to bed without any supper for some perceived indiscretion.

As she grew older, her aunts made a point of tutoring her in the wicked ways of the world and how indulging in such atrocities would eventually lead to her damnation.

Once she reached puberty the rules changed dramatically.

Men were the enemy and were all only after one thing, and that was to bring shame and disgrace on young girls like Anita.

As a result, Anita had to endure the embarrassment of being escorted by one or, on some occasions, both of her guardians to and from school, just in case she was tempted to partake in any pleasures of the flesh with the young hoodlums from the boy's school at the other end of town.

By this point, young Anita was already considered by her fellow classmates as a little odd, due mainly to the fact that unlike them she did not go out at weekends or indulge in schoolgirl fantasies about the latest boy bands or film stars. The fact that Anita's aunts refused to buy a television or go to the cinema excluded their niece from being able to pander to such distractions.

But the fact that she was still being brought and collected from school as if she were still in kindergarten, merely added to her misery and her isolation from the rest of her peers.

As much as Anita tried to adhere to all the rules and regulations her aunts laid down for her, she was forever being accused by them of wicked indiscretions and immoral thoughts, regardless of the fact that there was never an evidence to verify their misconceptions.

The end result for Anita was that her punishments grew in severity and frequency. Having to miss supper was no longer in itself considered by her aunts to be sufficient penance for her behaviour.

On one fateful journey home from school, Anita was unfortunate enough to be whistled at by some local boys in front of her aunts. For her part, the young girl did not even acknowledge, let alone respond to the act. But that was not what mattered as far as her guardians were concerned.

As soon as they closed the front door behind them the two spinsters began to berate their niece for her disgraceful behaviour. Anita's protests at her innocence were futile. She was marched into the living room and forced to strip naked before being ordered to stand against the wall with her nose and toes touching the cold stone, while her aunts prayed out loud for guidance as well as for her wayward soul.

After two solid hours Anita could feel her whole body becoming numb. Although it was the middle of winter the heating was not set to come on for several hours and the poor girl could feel her skin turning blue from the cold.

Once the two spinsters had exhausted their repertoire of prayers and incantations, they were both convinced that more sterner methods of punishment needed to be implemented in order to cast out the demon of lust which had somehow managed to infiltrate their niece, regardless of their teachings.

Anita was ordered to bend over the arm of the sofa with her feet barely able to meet the floor. Once she was in position, one of her aunts took hold of her wrists and held them tightly to ensure that she could not move or struggle free. Her other aunt went out to the garden shed and returned with one of the long thin bamboo sticks which they had bought for use in the garden.

Ten strokes were administered directly on Anita's bare bottom.

Her screams and cries were ignored by both spinsters, and the aunt holding her wrists squeezed them so tightly that Anita could feel her blood supply being severely restricted as a result of the pressure.

After the last stroke was delivered there was moments pause while the two women decided between them if the punishment was sufficient.

Anita pleaded and begged for mercy, promising faithfully that she would not allow such wicked thoughts to enter her mind again. She was only repeating what she now knew her aunts wanted to hear; when in reality such thoughts had never been in her head in the first place.

Fortunately for her, on this occasion, the two women decided that Anita had received adequate chastisement, and she was allowed to stand up and get dressed. But she was warned that if such an occurrence should repeat itself that future beatings would be more severe and would continue to increase in severity until she learned to keep her thoughts and actions pure.

From that day forward, the beatings became a regular part of home life for Anita. On each occasion the *lapse* in the purity of her thoughts or deeds were merely perceived in the minds of her guardians, never as the result of any actual wrongdoing by the young girl.

As promised, the beatings grew in severity as well as frequency. As time passed, the spinsters began to take it in turns as to which one of them would administer the required strokes.

Anita always knew that any form of protest would only

increase the number she received, so she learned to take what was coming without protest, save for the occasional yelp or scream that might escape her lips during her ordeal.

Anita endured this torment throughout her teens and into her twenties. By now she had left school and managed to secure a position at one of the local building societies. She had always been good with figures at school and as such she found her new position well within her capabilities.

Although she was now an adult with a respectable position and was contributing to society by paying her taxes, Anita's aunts treated her in many respects as if she were still a child.

The spinsters still chose their niece's clothes for her to make sure that she did not wear anything too revealing which might give men the wrong idea. She was still not permitted to wear any make-up, and her hair had to be kept in such a fashion so as not to entice male attention.

Her working day ended at 5:30 p.m. and the walk back from her place of business took exactly twenty minutes. Therefore, if Anita arrived home later than 5:50 p.m. she needed to have a very good reason for her tardiness.

Her aunts took all her wages and gave her just enough to purchase her lunch.

The beatings continued as always and there were even occasions where Anita had to sit on a cushion at work as her buttocks were too sore for the hard seats supplied.

Anita had long since resigned herself to the fact that her life would never change, and she would spend her days under the strict control of her domineering aunts. Until one afternoon when she was summoned to her manager's office, and there she was met by a plain clothes police officer who informed he that there had been a burglary at her home and that both her aunts had been killed by the intruders.

While the officer spoke, Anita's mind was unable to focus

on his words. All that she could think of was that finally she was alone in the world, and thus no longer under the strict regime imposed by her aunts.

As Anita was their next of kin, she inherited their house and all their money, a large part of which was made up of her wages since she had started working, along with what was left from the insurance pay-out from her parents' accident.

Anita arranged for the simple funeral service and subsequent cremation of her aunt's bodies. She was the only attendee at the service beside the priest and a scattering of parishioners who just happened to be in attendance.

She certainly did not invite anybody!

On her way home from the service Anita stopped off and bought herself two bottles of wine. She had never tasted alcohol before, so she was unsure which ones to choose, so she just went with the prettiest labels.

She drank them both that night in celebration of her freedom.

When the burglars were caught, as she was not a witness to the actual killings, Anita was not obliged to attend court, although both the police and the press expected her to. Instead she just took some extended leave from work and stayed at home.

As the months rolled on, Anita's way of life changed dramatically. Although she still remained the same quiet and reserved employee at the office, outside of work she underwent a strange metamorphosis which took many forms, each one as bizarre as the next.

Often, she would return home from work, draw the curtains and strip naked, and then proceed to walk around the house drinking wine in the nude.

She bought herself some of the modern conveniences which had previously been forbidden, starting with a large television with a built-in DVD and a CD player with eight speakers, which she had fitted throughout the house so that she could hear her music from every room.

Anita treated herself to her first mobile phone and a top of the range laptop. She set up several accounts on-line so that she could order clothes, wine, shoes, CDs and DVDs to her heart's content.

But she still craved something more!

At twenty-five she was still a virgin, and although she tried to keep her work colleagues at arm's length, some had started to notice the transition in her since she lost her controlling guardians, and a couple of the lads at work had even asked her out on a date.

But Anita was not ready for the closeness or committal of such a relationship. In truth, she often wondered if she would ever be able to embrace the kind of romantic interludes her peers took for granted.

Instead, Anita decided to opt for a more impersonal type of relationship. One where she felt in total control with the option of backing out if the mood took her.

She set up a profile on several dating apps which were designed specifically for people looking for one-night stands.

Anita arranged to meet these men at locations far away from where she lived for fear of being recognised. She even created her own alter ego and called herself Sherry, changing her appearance with the application of make-up and sometimes even a wig.

The first time she had sex in a strange motel, five miles outside of town; she immediately went into the bathroom afterwards and threw up. But over time she began to relish her little encounters but stuck to her golden rule of never contacting the same man twice.

The one thing she had not taken into account when making

her plans, was the enormous feeling of guilt she suffered with each interaction.

She knew, deep down, that it had to be something to do with her upbringing, and even though she was determined to shake it off she found herself unable to function as a person without finding some way of unburdening herself.

The more she thought about it the less sense it made. Why should she feel any guilt or remorse, after all, she was not hurting anyone else?

Finally, unable to free herself of the shame eating away at her, Anita found herself sitting in line waiting to take confession.

After the funeral, she decided that she would never enter the church again, having been forced to attend mass several times a week by her aunts to pray for her soul and cleanse her of sin she had never committed.

This time however, she knew that her sins were real, and she only had herself to answer for them. Therefore, she had become one of Father Grace's regulars at confession. It was a vicious circle which she could not break.

Anita looked up from her silent prayer and saw the priest walking towards her down the aisle.

She quickly looked back down as if in shame that he had seen her waiting, as always.

She listened to the sound of his approaching footsteps on the cold wooden floor, fully aware that he was making a beeline directly for her.

Anita shifted nervously and looked behind, but there was no one else waiting for the priest to hear their confession, only her.

Instead of going straight to the confessional box, Father Grace stopped just in front of Anita's pew and waited.

Anita kept her head down, unwilling to gaze up and look

into her confessor's eyes for fear that her shame would encompass her completely. But the old priest did not move, and eventually Anita felt compelled to lift her head and acknowledge him.

He welcomed her with his usual warm and friendly smile, but Anita still felt the weight of her conscience bearing down on her. She offered a weak smile in return.

Father Grace checked that there was no one else within earshot before he spoke. "Anita, my child," he whispered, "would you come with me, I have a favour to ask?"

CHAPTER TWENTY-SEVEN

Upon arrival back at the station Pamela went straight in to see Carlisle to update him on Natasha's condition. Hardy made his way into the main office to check on the update from the search of the area where Natasha had been found.

He was hoping that Sergeant Russell might have returned by now, but he was nowhere to be seen.

Hardy checked in with a couple of the plain clothes officers who were busy chasing up leads—slim as they were—as a result of the initial house-to-house enquiries.

As Hardy looked up a ruddy-faced Constable Grant entered the room. Hardy signalled to her to come over before he turned away and walked towards his desk.

When Grant stood before him, she appeared to Hardy as if she had been running. Her face was flushed, and her cheeks especially were a bright pink hue, plus she was obviously trying to control her heavy breathing.

"What have you been up to?" asked Hardy, bemused by Grant's attempts to catch her breath.

Grant put her hand to her mouth and coughed before trying to reply. "We've just finished the search of the area where Natasha Spencer was found," she had to take in another breath before continuing. "We found a mobile phone case which Sergeant Russell believed might belong to our victim, so he asked me to take it straight round to the forensic lab to check for DNA."

"And did you run all the way?" Hardy could not keep the smirk from his lips, not that he was trying particularly hard to conceal it.

The young PC took in another deep breath through her mouth. "I went to the scene with some uniforms but they were still needed for the house-to-house so I thought it best just to get the evidence in as soon as I could."

Hardy left the girl to catch her breath properly before speaking again.

He was impressed by her keenness and commitment to the case, but he still could not help but smile when he considered how many uniforms had passed by his way during his career, and how sad it was to see that initial enthusiasm wane, as Grant's doubtless would at some point.

When she looked as if she finally had her breathing under control, Hardy asked her what she planned to do next.

"Well, I just thought I would pop in here, sir, to see if there was anything I could do before I made my way back to help with the knocking on doors."

"Good idea," agreed Hardy, "but first you have something far more vital to carry out."

"Yes, sir?" asked the young PC, her eyes wide in anticipation of the task she was about to be bestowed on her by her superior.

"Yes, you can make me a coffee, and a real one, not one from the machine."

PC Grant could not hide the crestfallen look on her face when she heard her task. Having worked on the front desk for so long she was used to spending a proportion of her time fetching and carrying for her superiors, but somehow having been given the chance to join this major investigation she believed that her position would be elevated above what she was used to.

It appeared not to be the case.

"Yes, sir," she replied, forcing a willing smile.

As she turned to commence her duty, Hardy called her back.

"Yes, sir?" she asked, presuming that Hardy had some further order to make before she went.

"Black, two sugars, and hold the spit, I can always tell."

The constable burst out laughing, she could not help herself. The other officers in the room looked up from their phone calls and paperwork at the sound of their colleague's laughter.

This time PC Grant's red face was as a result of embarrassment rather than exertion.

Hardy smiled to himself as she turned away to fetch his coffee.

Looking back over his shoulder he noticed that the maintenance team had managed to clear the small back office as he had requested for his new DCI.

He stood up from his desk and walked over to inspect it. They had cleared it out as requested, and now all that remained was a desk with a lamp and a telephone on it, a chair and a couple of filing cabinets. They had even prepared a makeshift sign for the door which Hardy presumed would please Pamela.

As he finished inspecting the room, Pamela entered the main office.

Hardy smiled at her and held out his hand as if to introduce her to her new working environment. He could tell immediately by the look on her face that her conversation with Carlisle had not gone well.

Pamela walked straight past Hardy into her new office and sat down behind her desk, planting the files she had with her face up.

"Is this OK?" asked Hardy, deciding not to wait until she was ready to break the silence.

Pamela spun back and forth in her new chair a few times. "It'll have to do I suppose," she announced, tersely.

Just then, PC Grant reappeared with Hardy's coffee.

Before she had a chance to hand it over, Pamela snapped, "What's that?"

Slightly taken aback by the DCI's mood, the young officer quickly glanced up at Hardy as if for moral support, before turning her attention back to their superior.

"It's coffee, black with two sugars, ma'am," she answered, timidly.

By this time, Pamela had opened the first file and was pouring over the contents. "Well, dump some milk in it and bring it back," she replied, not bothering to look up from her work to acknowledge the young constable.

This time Hardy caught the PC Grant's eye and raised his eyebrows as a warning to her not to react. If she intended to make a career in the force she needed to know how to deal with the arrogance of some senior officers, and to realise that they could change their attitude whenever the wind changed direction.

Before PC Grant had a chance to respond, Pamela called out. "And make sure it's the good stuff, not that semi-skimmed nonsense."

"Yes, ma'am."

Hardy watched his junior officer stride back over towards where the tea and coffee making facilities were kept.

His initial instinct was to slam the door shut and demand to know why the DCI was being so rude to the young officer, but he quickly realised that this was not the time nor the place for such a conversation, so let the matter slide.

Instead he asked. "I take it Superintendent Carlisle is not cock-a-hoop with our progress at the moment then?"

Pamela glanced up in his direction with a disdainful expression on her face. She removed a copy of the newspaper with Carney's cover story and slammed it on the desk facing Hardy. "Well, this didn't help!" she barked.

Hardy opened out the paper on the desk and skim-read the article.

After a moment he answered. "Well. Carney is nothing to get excited about; the super should have known to expect this kind of thing from him."

Pamela sighed, loudly. I think that it's more the fact that we cannot get any information out of Natasha Spencer that's bugging him. Apparently, her father has already been on the blower shouting the odds and threatening to sue the force for not finding his precious daughter sooner."

"You'd think," ventured Hardy, "that he'd be happy that she was at least found alive."

Pamela sat back in her chair and began to massage her brow. "I know, but our problem is that we're no closer to finding her kidnapper because we're not being allowed to speak to her!"

Hardy looked surprised. "Did you explain to Carlisle that the doctors had to sedate her in order to get her to calm down? It's not as if they are playing hardball with us, they need to put her welfare first."

Pamela sat back up and slammed her palm down on her

desk. "You're missing the point, Inspector, I was brought into this investigation to make things happen, and the first real lead we get, and my hands are being tied by medical protocol!"

Hardy was taken back by the callousness of her remark. She appeared to be totally oblivious to the fact that the poor girl had just been through a horrendous ordeal from which, judging by her present condition, she might never fully recover.

At that moment PC Grant returned holding two cups of coffee. She placed the one with milk in front of Pamela and handed the black one to Hardy.

Pamela muttered a thank you under her breath, while Hardy made a point of saying it clearly and directly to the young PC.

"Are you heading back to help with the door-to-door enquiries?" asked Hardy, blowing on the hot liquid.

"Yes, sir, I promised Sergeant Russell I'd get back there as soon as possible." replied the officer with a slight smile.

"Before you go," Pamela called out over her coffee, "can you find me a map of the area where the victims have been located?"

"Yes, ma'am," PC Grant responded cheerfully, before turning and setting off on her task.

Hardy felt a slight twinge of guilt as he remembered that Pamela had asked him to arrange the map for her earlier. But he knew that it was not exactly an arduous task, so he managed to rein in his guilt.

* * *

DESMOND FELT his mobile buzzing in his pocket. His heart jumped when he noticed that it was Kelly calling him. Even so, he hesitated before answering. He remembered Kelly telling him that Jack sometimes grabbed her phone and called random numbers from her call log just to see who answered.

He decided to answer as if he did not know who was calling him.

"Hello," he replied, nonchalantly, purposely not giving anything away with his tone.

"Des, it's Kelly."

"Hi, babe, I wasn't sure if Jack had got hold of your phone, how are you?"

"I'm fine," Kelly answered, a little unconvincingly. "Missing you though."

Desmond smiled broadly. Kelly's words felt like sunshine on his skin, warming him all over and making him feel good about life.

"I'm missing you too, babe," he responded, holding his handset closer to his cheek as if the act might make Kelly seem closer. "Can I see you tonight?" he asked, enthusiastically.

Kelly let out a long breath on the other end. "That's what I wanted to talk to you about."

Desmond held his breath, instinctively. From the tone in her voice, he was afraid that Kelly was about to tell him something he would rather not have to hear. Since they shared their romantic kiss in the park the day before, Desmond had not been able to think of anything else other than the prospect of being with Kelly.

He knew that not asking her out years ago was something which he would regret forever. But at least if they could make a fresh start now, they would still have the rest of their lives to look forward to.

Their one complication was Kelly's possessive husband, Jack!

She had opened her heart to Desmond while they were together yesterday afternoon, and all he could think of throughout the conversation was how to get her away from Jack and keep her safe.

The more she spoke, the more he felt the need to protect her.

Desmond knew that Kelly was not just looking for sympathy; she clearly believed that she had made her own choices, but now she knew that they were the wrong ones and she was willing to address whatever it took in order to change the status quo.

"Are you still there?" Kelly's voice brought Desmond back from his reverie.

"Yes, babe, I'm here, what was it you wanted to tell me?"

It was only a few seconds before Kelly answered, but to Desmond it seemed like a lifetime. Part of him did not want to hear what she was about to say, and then part of him knew that he had to, whatever it turned out to be.

"I've decided I'm leaving Jack!"

It took a moment for Kelly's words to sink in, but once they had, Desmond was ready to start turning cartwheels. But as elated as he was by her announcement, he quickly realised that Kelly must be going through turmoil inside. He knew full well that divorce was forbidden by the catholic religion, and Kelly took her faith very seriously.

Desmond did his best to keep the excitement out of his voice.

He knew that whatever his reaction was, it might have a crucial impact on their future together.

Finally, he said. "Kelly, I know that this isn't easy for you, babe, and it has obviously taken a lot of thought on your behalf to come to this decision, but you know that it is the right thing to do. That bloke does not love you, whatever he might say, he treats you like dirt, and they say actions speak louder than words."

Desmond waited with bated breath, hoping that he had said the right thing.

Finally, Kelly put him out of his misery. "I know what you're saying is true" she replied. "My friend Carol has been telling me to do this for ages, and to be honest, deep down, I've always known that Jack was a bad sort."

Desmond heaved a sigh of relief. "Can I come and see you?" he asked, hopefully.

Kelly laughed. "I'm at work, silly, some of us have to earn a living you know."

The sudden levity in Kelly's voice made Desmond laugh, too. "Oi, not so much of it if you don't mind," he replied, cheekily. "Now that I've finished my studies, I'm going to have to join you working stiffs too you know."

They both giggled at each other's remarks.

After a moment, Desmond asked. "Seriously though, when are you going to tell him?"

"Tonight," Kelly sighed, "I don't want to drag it out now that I've made up my mind. In fact, I wish I could tell him right now, the sooner the better."

"Do you want me to be with you when you do?" asked Desmond, feeling overwhelmingly protective towards Kelly, especially as he could almost sense her vulnerability coming through the phone.

"Thanks, but to be honest the sight of you would probably just antagonise him. I really want this to go as smoothly as possible."

Desmond decided to go for broke. He was not at all comfortable with Kelly being alone with Jack considering what she was going to tell him.

After all, the man was capable of anything, and Desmond had read enough stories in the paper about men killing their partners rather than allowing them to walk out on them.

He could feel his pulse starting to quicken. "I really don't like the idea of you telling him on your own, hon. What if he turns violent, the man's a thug and we both know it!"

Desmond bit his tongue. His statement had sounded rather more aggressive than he had intended it to. He did not want to end up sounding like one of those controlling boyfriends; Kelly had certainly had enough of that in her life. But he needed her to know that he was there for her now and ready to support her in every way possible.

That and the fact that he really felt he ought to be with her in case Jack lashed out. Desmond was quite prepared to take the brunt of the beating if needs be, he just did not want Kelly on the receiving end.

"It's OK," Kelly reassured him, "Carol is going to be with me, and Jack knows better than to start anything with her around."

Desmond definitely felt better knowing that Kelly was not going to be on her own, but in truth he would still much rather have been the one there to protect her.

Even so, he had to respect her decision, so he decided to back off.

"Will you let me know how it goes?" he asked, tentatively.

What he really wanted was reassurance that she was safe and sound after the act, but he did not want to lay it on too thickly.

"Of course, I will," Kelly assured him. "Tell you what; I might be spending the night at Carol's tonight depending on how things go. I'd like you to meet her so perhaps you can meet me at hers for a drink?"

"I'd love that, yes, please." Desmond replied, eagerly. Seeing that Kelly was still in one piece tonight would definitely set his mind at rest, so this seemed like the perfect solution.

"Alright, darling, I'll give you a call tonight," Kelly promised. "I'd better go now, my break's up."

"I love you." The words rolled out of Desmond's mouth before he had a chance to stop them. As much as he meant them, he did not think that this was the right moment to confess his undying love.

He was afraid that Kelly was going to react badly, probably from shock more than anything else. Or worse still, she could just put down the phone without answering and he would not be sure whether she had just not heard him speak or had chosen to ignore his comment because she did not want to hear it yet.

"I love you too. See you tonight."

Desmond's heart flipped again in his chest.

The world suddenly seemed a much warmer and more wonderful place to be.

CHAPTER TWENTY-EIGHT

J ack Soames staggered out of the Nag's Head public
house, tripping on the main step as he left and almost
losing his balance completely and falling headfirst onto
the gravel driveway.

Once he had regained his balance, Jack stood still for a
moment to allow the night air to waft in through his nostrils.
This in turn caused the car park to spin around him until he
shut his eyes and shook the apparition clear.

In truth, he had only intended stopping in for a couple of
pints, but there was a new barmaid on duty tonight and Jack
thought that he would try his luck before one of the other regulars had the idea.

As it was, she seemed interested enough and Jack was sure
that she was giving him the 'come-on', but when he finally got
around to asking her out, she told him that she was happily
married and wanted to remain that way.

Jack offered a token argument because of the fact that she
was not wearing a wedding ring, but the girl put him firmly

back in his place and made it clear that ring or not, there was no way that she would ever consider going out with him.

He knew better than to push it, he had already almost been barred from the pub a couple of months earlier, so Jack held up his hands in defeat and finished his sixth pint without making another sound.

As he reached the end of the car park, Jack felt a sudden need to urinate. He turned and looked back towards the pub, but somehow the distance which he had covered in a matter of minutes now seemed like a bridge too far.

Instead, he staggered over towards a clump of trees off to his left and unzipped his jeans in order to unburden himself.

The night air was cold and sharp as it whistled past him, and it rustled the branches of the tree against which he was leaning.

For a second Jack felt sure that someone was watching him from the shadows. He craned his neck around as far as he could for a better look, but there was no one in sight.

He concentrated, trying to listen for the sound of any movement other than that cause by the wind, but there was still no indication of anyone being nearby.

Finishing off, Jack tucked himself away carefully before pulling up his zip. He could feel the familiar dampness on his fingers caused by a few drops of urine leaking through as he shook himself off, so he brushed his hand vigorously against the leg of his jeans and shuffled off back towards the exit.

As he turned into the lane Jack noticed a solitary figure a couple of hundred yards away, staying in the shadows.

Jack's immediate thought was that someone was lurking around hoping to find an easy target to mug. Well, whoever they were they were in for a big surprise if they decided to tackle Jack Soames. He could dish it out with the best of them, even in his present condition, so he was happy for them to try their luck with him.

He strode on purposefully, hoping to convey to whoever was ahead that he was not a man to be trifled with.

As he drew a little closer, it suddenly dawned on Jack that the person ahead might be part of a gang, and that the rest of them were waiting within shouting distance to pounce on him once their fellow assailant had weighed in.

The thought made him take stock for a moment.

Jack slowed down his pace and shifted his gaze back and forth for any signs that he was right.

The streetlight just ahead near where the individual was standing was not working, which created a darkened tunnel of shadows leading up to the next lamp along the road. That was doubtless why the person had chosen to stand where they were, less chance of being recognised, he surmised.

Still moving forward Jack squinted through the darkness to try and attain a better view of what lay ahead.

Suddenly, the figure moved towards him. Just a couple of steps, but it was enough to make Jack stop dead in his tracks.

As the figure approached and came into the light cast by the working lamppost behind him, Jack realised that his potential assailant was a woman.

Not realising that he had been holding his breath, Jack let out his pent-up air in a large gust of carbon dioxide which drifted away and disappeared into the night.

The closer the woman drew towards Jack the more the light behind him revealed. She had lovely long legs which appeared to be dressed in black nylon stockings with a pair of black patent leather boots which came up to her knees.

Her leather skirt was extremely short and barely covered the tops of her thighs, and even though the weather was still very chilly she seemed to be wearing a tube-style top which left her midriff bare.

As she finally came close enough for Jack to see her face, he was completely stunned to see how beautiful she was.

The woman stopped when she was only a couple of feet away from him.

Jack could not help but let his eyes wander up and down her slender figure.

A sudden thought struck him. Could she possibly be one of the working girls who normally hung out by the truck depot on the other side of town?

He had never heard of one of them plying their trade this far into the suburbs, but perhaps she was new and did not know the rules.

The thought excited him.

He instinctively fumbled in his pocket until he could feel his wallet. He was sure that he still had at least twenty quid in there, and even if the going rate was higher, these tarts were all the same and the sight of his money was bound to be enough to persuade her to let him have a quickie.

They stared at each other for what seemed to Jack like an eternity, but he was so engrossed in her gorgeous figure that he did not care. He could feel his lips were starting to go very dry, probably as a result of the amount he had had to drink. Unconcerned with how repulsive he must look, Jack stuck his tongue out and slowly traced a circle around his mouth to moisten it, while he continued to letch over the young girl's fit body.

Jack turned around to make sure that no one else was within earshot before he spoke. "Hello there, darlin'" he drooled, "are you lookin' for some company?"

Anita Price stayed put as if she were considering his offer.

She stared at the shambling, drunken form of Jack before her to make sure in her mind that he was the same man Father

Grace had pointed out to her earlier from the entrance to the pub.

Once she was convinced that it was indeed him, she relaxed slightly, no longer afraid that she might be picking up the wrong man, which would doubtless have led to some embarrassing questions being answered later.

When Anita did not answer, Jack pulled out his wallet and waved it in front of him. "I've got the dosh if you're up fer it," he grinned, wiping his chin with the back of his hand when he felt a faint trickle of spittle meandering its way through his stubble.

Anita pursed her lips and then a smile slowly crept across her face.

She signalled Jack to follow her as she made her way across the road towards the park entrance.

Jack followed, eagerly anticipating the pleasure waiting for him beneath that tight mini-skirt.

Anita walked ahead at a quick pace, so much so that Jack was finding it hard to keep up with her.

"'ang on darlin' what's yer 'urry?" Jack called, somewhat breathlessly.

Anita turned around and began to walk backwards, enticing Jack to keep up with her by giving him the 'come-on' signal with her index finger.

Jack knew that he had let himself go over the years, but considering the girl was wearing high heels her pace was extremely impressive. Although his breathing was already strained, Jack tried to pick up his pace until he was almost trotting.

As they approached a dense clump of woodland Anita finally stopped.

She was still facing Jack and her abrupt halt made him trip over his feet as he attempted not to crash into her.

Jack yelled as he put his hands out in front of him to break his fall on the concrete path. The thud from his landing sent a shaft of pain up both his arms and into his shoulder joints.

Jack rolled onto his back, grabbing his elbows with both hands, and hugging himself tightly.

From above him he could hear the girl laughing softly.

Evidently his comic fall had amused her.

Right, Jack thought to himself, let's see who is laughing once I get inside you!

Anita carried on giggling as Jack slowly made his way back up to his knees. He looked up at her, still in pain but trying to put a brave face on as he continued to rub his aching joints.

Eventually, Jack managed to force his way back up to a standing position.

He was half expecting the girl to turn on her heels and run away having teased him with the expectation of things to come. Jack surmised that perhaps she was not on the game after all but a cheeky little bitch who just like to make a fool out of some bloke who'd had a skinful.

But to his surprise, Anita stopped laughing and stayed where she was. She held out her hand to him.

Jack leaned forward tentatively, still half expecting her to move away when he drew too close, but once she was within reaching distance Jack lurched forward and grabbed her fingers tightly, almost crushing them in his far larger palm.

Anita squealed instinctively and tried to pull away, but now that Jack had her he was not about to risk giving up his prize.

Walking behind the largest bush, Jack yanked the helpless girl after him. Her protests at the way she was being manhandled met with stern silence and the occasional grunt.

Once they were under cover, Jack swung Anita around

almost twisting her arm out of its socket and sent her crashing down onto the grass verge.

Anita lay there for a moment in stunned shock. Her rump hurt from where she had hit the ground and she was instantly grateful that at least her fall was on a softer surface than his had been.

Through her tousled hair which now lay in a criss-cross pattern across her face, Anita looked up and saw that Jack was busy fumbling with the belt on his jeans.

Before she had a chance to change position, Jack fell down on top of her with his full weight, knocking the wind out of her.

While she was still gasping for breath, Jack lowered himself so that his face was just in front of hers. Anita could not help but smell his putrid body odour and disgusting beer-breath as he started to speak to her through gritted teeth.

"You fuckin' 'hores are all the same," he spat out the words, not seeming to notice or care that saliva dripped from his mouth as he spoke, splashing Anita's face, and forcing her to gag.

"Please...don't hurt me," she managed to splutter, her breathing still recovering from Jack's initial impact.

Jack laughed, scornfully. "'urt yer? I'll do more than just' 'urt yer, yer fuckin' tart!" With that, Jack lifted his hand and slapped Anita hard across the face.

Anita could feel the hot sting of tears brimming over the lids of her eyes.

She gazed up at her assailant through the watery haze and watched as Jack struggled to pull down his jeans.

At that moment, a shadow cast down over the pair of them and Jack was yanked off Anita and hoisted into the air.

It all happened so fast that Jack was completely unaware of how he suddenly came to be looking up at the night sky.

Before he had a chance to scream or call out, the Creeper

slammed him down onto its bended knee, snapping Jack's spine like a toothpick.

The awful sound of Jack's backbone breaking made Anita shudder inside.

The Creeper threw Jack's lifeless torso to one side on the grass and stood over the dishevelled form of Anita, as she lay on the ground staring up at her saviour.

For a moment, Anita was suddenly afraid that she too was about to become a victim. Although Father Grace had introduced them to each other earlier that day, Anita was not wholeheartedly convinced that the Creeper fully understood the instructions the old priest had given it.

She knew that if the Creeper decided for whatever reason to turn on her, she would be completely powerless to defend herself, and because of the chosen location, there was no one else within earshot to come to her rescue.

Not that anyone would have stood a chance against the Creeper, regardless.

Anita shied away as the Creeper leaned down over her. But when she noticed that it was in fact offering her its hand to help her up, she took it gratefully.

Once she was back up on her feet, Anita dusted herself off and straightened her clothing. She rubbed her hand across her cheek where Jack had slapped her, and she could feel the heat being generated from the area as a result. Doubtless she would have a bruise there by tomorrow.

Even so, she smiled up at the Creeper to convey her gratitude.

The Creeper stood there watching her for a moment longer before it finally turned away and slipped back into the night.

CHAPTER TWENTY-NINE

Hardy was in Pamela's office going over the lack of information they had collated after the house-to-house enquiries which had taken place that day, when the message reached them that another dead body had been discovered near the site where Natasha was found.

They raced to the scene, grabbing Sergeant Russell, PC Grant, and whoever was still in the main office and was part of the investigation team on route.

By the time they arrived at the park the uniformed officers had cordoned off the area, and Hardy could tell by the van parked outside that the forensic team were already in attendance.

Hardy barely had time to engage the handbrake before Pamela shot out of the passenger seat of his car and began to make her way towards the park entrance.

Hardy waited for Russell to join him before he followed their DCI inside.

A large group of people had gathered around the cordon, eagerly trying to see what was going on inside the park.

As Pamela reached the entrance, she flashed her identity card at the two uniforms on the gate and barked at them to move the crowd back so that they did not contaminate the scene.

By the time Hardy and the rest of the team caught up with Pamela she was standing just outside the canvas tent the forensics team had set up to protect Jack's body in case it rained.

The first member of the forensic unit to exit the tent was pounced on by Pamela. "What can you tell me about the cause of death?" she demanded. Then, without giving the young man a chance to answer, she continued firing questions in his direction, "Do the injuries look the same as those inflicted on our earlier victims? Is there any chance of a decent DNA sample this time? How accurate can you be about the time of death?"

The young man pulled down his mask and looked from Pamela to Hardy and back to the DCI. Hardy could tell that he was already regretting being the first one to leave the tent, and the chances were that he was only coming out to collect something for his superior, and then he had walked straight into Pamela's machinegun-style of questioning.

To his credit, the young forensic operator did his best to respond to Pamela's demands, but it was obvious that it was too soon for him to be able to give her any concrete answers, and even though he assured her that she would receive a full report once the post mortem was complete, Pamela was not in the least bit impressed.

Without trying to hide her frustration, Pamela spun around to look at Hardy and the others. "Who called this in?" she yelled, not directing the command at anyone in particular.

Russell stood forward. "There was an anonymous tip-off from a young girl apparently made from a telephone box around the corner," he informed her. "She did not give her name, and when pressed she just hung up."

"Bugger!" Pamela exclaimed, unable to mask her growing agitation. "Who was the first officer on the scene?" she continued, her voice still raised.

"That'll be me, ma'am," answered a middle-aged constable, stepping forward from the group of uniforms milling around the scene.

Pamela spun around and looked at the officer through narrowed eyes.

"What can you tell me about what you saw when you came upon the scene?"

The officer cleared his throat. "Well, ma'am, I received the call about two men fighting whilst I was on my rounds, so I made my way here. At first, there was no indication of any trouble, but I decided it was best to survey the surrounding area, which was when I came across that poor chap," he indicated towards the tent which covered Jack.

"Was there any sign of the perpetrator?" Pamela snapped.

The officer shook his head. "No, ma'am, of course once I found the body, I didn't leave the spot until help arrived, but there was certainly no sign of anyone else in the vicinity."

Pamela ignored the officer's remarks and turned around as if she were surveying the scene for herself.

After a moment she turned back to Hardy. "Right then, Inspector, I want that lot questioned and statements taken," she pointed over to the crowd which had gathered outside. "Anything they can tell us, I don't care how small or insignificant it might be, I want taken down. Names, addresses, the lot. Also, I want a thorough search of this area made as soon as possible, organise some lights, I want every blade of grass turned over just in case laddo left us a clue, can you sort that out for me?"

Hardy nodded, nonchalantly. "I'll call the station for some more help."

"Good." Pamela turned back to face the tent just as one of the side flaps opened and another forensic officer appeared.

He pulled down his mask and walked straight over to Pamela.

Hardy presumed that the man had heard his senior officer ranting at his subordinate earlier, so he knew who to aim for. He produced an old leather wallet which he held out for the DCI. "Thought you might like this, ma'am," he offered, "should hopefully contain some form of identification for the victim."

Pamela took the wallet and muttered a thank you under her breath.

Hardy turned to the rest of his team. "Come on then," he muttered, "you all heard the DCI, we've got work to do."

Pamela looked up briefly to see the officers moving away, and then she returned her attention to the wallet she had been given.

She opened the first zip and found Jack's driving license.

At least she had a name and address to start from.

She considered the fact that this killing might be totally unconnected with the previous ones, and that this might be just the result of a random fight as was first reported.

She had not had a chance to inspect the body yet, so as the forensic officer turned to leave, she called out to him. "Excuse me."

He turned back but did not attempt to move any closer to her.

"What can you tell me about the mutilations on this body?" she asked, indifferently, rather as if she were ordering a coffee as opposed to enquiring as to how another human being met their fate.

The forensic officer thought for a moment before he answered. "What mutilations exactly were you interested in?" he asked, somewhat perplexed.

Pamela stared at him as if she were about to admonish a child. "The mutilations," she repeated, emphasising the words. "All the other victims were slashed to pieces!"

The officer shook his head. "Well from what I've seen so far there are no such abrasions of the type you've mentioned. Of course, I'll know more when we get the fellow on the table."

"Then how did he die?" Pamela asked, holding her arms out to her side as if she were unable to fathom what she was hearing.

"Well from a preliminary examination, I'd say he has a broken back."

"Caused by?" Pamela pressed.

The man shrugged. "Can't tell you that until the PM I'm afraid."

He could tell that Pamela was clearly not impressed, but this time she held her tongue, realising perhaps that there was no way that she was going to get anywhere by trying to harass the officer.

The man did not wait for a thank you, instead he turned and re-entered the tent.

Pamela mulled over her next move. She was seriously disappointed that they did not appear to have more to go on from the scene, but perhaps the search she had ordered would turn something useful up.

It concerned her that this latest victim did not seem to have the same level of injuries inflicted on him as the others. But then she remembered that Natasha too showed very few signs of exterior harm, so perhaps that was no indication after all.

This had to be the same assailant!

It was bad enough that they did not seem to have any concrete leads as it was, the last thing she wanted was to find out that she was hunting more than one perpetrator, especially if their crimes were unrelated.

Pamela turned on her heel to walk back towards the main gate. As she lifted her foot, she left her shoe behind trapped in the soft mud. Cursing, she managed to balance herself on one leg as she carefully manoeuvred her foot back into her shoe.

Once she was confident that she had a solid hold she bent down and grabbed her shoe, prising the heel out of the ground.

Pamela walked on the balls of her feet until she was back on the solid concrete path. She strode purposefully towards where Hardy was instructing his team and the gathered uniforms concerning the interviewing of the crowd and the search of the area.

Pamela waited until he was finished before she signalled to him to follow her.

Once they were out of earshot Pamela showed Hardy Jack's driving license. He studied the small card as well as he could in the dim light. There was

something about the address on it which seemed familiar to him, but he could not make the connection for now.

While he read, Pamela cut into his thoughts. "We'd better go and see if Mr. Soames has any nearest and dearest we need to inform," she stated. "I hate this part so I might let you do all the talking and I'll look for any unusual reactions."

"Thank you, ma'am," Hardy managed to keep the sarcasm out of his tone.

As they reached Hardy's car a voice called out from behind.

They both turned to see Cyril Carney rushing out from the crowd with his pad and pen in one hand and a small Dictaphone in the other.

"DCI Holmsley," he called, cheerfully, "Can you give me any information regarding this latest victim? This is another victim of the Ripper I take it?"

Pamela ignored the man's questions and climbed into the

passenger seat of Hardy's car. The DI took his lead from his superior and he too ignored the reporter's questions before slipping behind the wheel.

Carney, relentless as always, knocked on the window on Hardy's side, still firing off questions.

Hardy shot the reporter a stern glance and signalled with his hand for the man to back away.

Through the glass both Hardy and Pamela could hear Carney starting to plead now, as he realised that his chance of an interview was about to disappear.

Hardy put the car in gear and pulled away, leaving the reporter to stroll back towards the crowd to try his luck there instead.

The traffic was fairly light, and they arrived at Jack's estate in about ten minutes.

As they pulled into the area Hardy immediately remembered why the address had seemed so familiar. Hardy had visited the next estate along to see Ben Green's father when he was first reported missing.

He mentioned the coincidence to Pamela.

"Do you think there might be some connection?" she asked, eagerly.

Hardy sighed. "How do you mean?"

"Well if Ben Green and this bloke Jack Soames are somehow connected, maybe by a mutual friend or drinking buddy, don't you think that might give us an angle to work from?"

Hardy could tell that Pamela was clearly enamoured by the possibility, so he decided that it was best to play along until they had a chance to ascertain if that was in fact the case.

As far as he was concerned, it was just as likely to be a coincidence that the two of them lived near each other and his DCI was desperately grabbing at straws.

They took the stairs leading up to the address on Jack's driving licence.

Hardy rang the bell, but when there was no immediate answer he rapped on the door with his fist, twice.

They heard the sound of another door opening further down the corridor and before they had a chance to see who was there, Kelly called out to them.

"May I help you?" she asked, timidly, staying half inside the entrance to Carol's flat rather than coming all the way out into the corridor.

Hardy walked towards Kelly, leaving Pamela behind.

Pulling out his warrant card Hardy flashed it at Kelly. "Do you know the occupants of number forty-five, please, miss?" he asked, in his most professional tone.

Kelly stared briefly at the ID, and then back at Hardy.

The immediate look of concern on her face was not an unusual response in Hardy's experience to being approached by a senior detective.

"Yes, it's me," Kelly stuttered in response.

Just then, Carol appeared from behind her clutching a glass of wine.

Hardy acknowledged the new arrival with a slight nod of his head.

"Do you know a Jack Soames?" he asked, directing his attention back towards Kelly.

At the sound of his name, Kelly instinctively moved backwards until she felt the comforting warmth of her friend standing behind her.

"Yes," she spluttered, "he's my husband, why?"

Hardy ignored her question for the moment. He turned back and signalled to Pamela to join him.

At the sound of Pamela's heels clicking on the concrete

floor to signal her approach, Hardy looked back at the two women standing in the doorway.

"Do you think that we might come inside and have a quick word, please?"

Kelly turned to her friend as if for confirmation. After all, it was her flat they were coming into.

Carol shrugged and moved backwards so that she could usher the two new arrivals inside.

They all moved to the living room and Carol offered the officers some drinks, but they politely refused.

Once they were seated, Hardy began. "May I ask when it was that you last saw or spoke to your husband?"

Kelly was already finding it a difficult task to keep her hands from shaking. She knew instinctively that something was not right, the police were not in the habit of calling on people to pass the time, but for the moment she could not envisage what the trouble might be.

She slipped her hands under her thighs so as not to make her shaking a focus of attention.

She cleared her throat. "That would be this morning when he left for work."

"And you've had no contact with him since then?" Hardy pressed.

Kelly shook her head. "No, why, what's the matter, can you please tell me?"

Hardy glanced over at Pamela who was sitting beside him.

She nodded her response.

"I am sorry to have to tell you Mrs. Soames, but this evening a body was discovered near Monk's wood, which we believe to be that of your husband Jack."

Kelly's hands shot up from under her and she covered her mouth as if trying to prevent a scream from leaving it.

Carol moved forward and put a comforting arm around her friend.

Taking careful note of their initial reaction, Hardy pulled out Jack's wallet and driving licence and held the picture card towards Kelly.

"This was found in the victim's possession; do you recognise it?"

Before she could control herself, Kelly felt a flood of hot tears brimming over her eyelids. Through her distorted vision she could still make out the smug look on her husband's face.

She nodded. "Yes, that's him."

Kelly turned in her seat and buried her face in Carol's chest as she began to sob.

Hardy and Pamela waited for a couple of minutes until Kelly's tears started to subside.

Finally, Kelly lifted her head. "What happened?" she asked, tearfully.

Hardy let out a deep breath. "Well it appears that he might have been the victim of an attack, we are still trying to piece together the full picture."

Carol reached towards the table in front of them and pulled a couple of tissues free from their box, handing them to Kelly who took them gratefully. She wiped her eyes and then blew her nose.

Hardy took this as his cue. "Do you have any idea why he might have been in the park this evening?" he asked, keeping his voice as calm and soothing as possible.

The girl was evidently upset by the news that they had brought.

Either that or she was a very good actress.

On instinct, Hardy decided to go with the former on this occasion.

Kelly held the tissue at her nose as she shook her head

slowly.

"What time were you expecting him home?" Hardy continued.

"With him it could be anytime, right up to closing time," Carol decided to chime in on behalf of her friend.

"I take it that you knew him too?" asked Hardy, switching his attention to the flat owner.

Carol glugged back the contents of her glass before answering. "Yep, you could say that, but it's Kelly who's my friend, Jack just sort of came along as part of the deal."

Hardy nodded. "So, can you think of any reason why he might have gone to the park after work?"

Carol squeezed her friend a little tighter. "To be honest, I would have said that the pub was the only place Jack would have gone."

Hardy looked back over towards his DCI, but her expression was not giving anything away at the moment, so he decided to just run with the ball.

"We will need to make a formal identification," he looked at Kelly who gazed up at him through her tear-streaked eyes. "Perhaps if you're feeling up to it, we could make an appointment for you to come down to the morgue tomorrow?"

"How do you mean a formal identification?" it was Carol who made the comment on Kelly's behalf. "Was it Jack or not?" she demanded.

Hardy looked at her without letting his overall countenance give anything away. "Well, as I said, we found this on him," he held up the wallet and driving licence together in one hand, "and the picture which you've stated is that of your husband matches the victim, but to be absolutely sure we do require someone who actually knew him to confirm it."

Carol visibly calmed down at Hardy's words.

Kelly wiped her eyes. "Yes, OK then, I'll come down tomorrow, or do you want me to do it now?"

And get it over with! she thought to herself.

"To be honest," Pamela piped up, "our forensics experts will probably need a couple of hours to check for any evidence his assailant might have left behind, so tomorrow is probably a better idea all round."

Kelly nodded, keeping her head down as she dried her eyes once more with the corner of the tissue.

Hardy took out his notebook and scribbled a note to himself to arrange the morgue visit for the following day.

"You said earlier that as far as you are aware your husband was in the pub. Any pub in particular?" Pamela aimed the question at Kelly, even though it had been Carol who mentioned the pub.

Even so, Kelly answered by shrugging her shoulders. "He may have been in the Nag's," she offered, "but he didn't specify anyone in particular."

Hardy made a note. "The Nag's?" he asked, just to confirm that he had heard it right.

"The Nag's Head," Carol confirmed, "funny enough, the car park leads out across from the park, depending on which part you found him in."

Hardy nodded as he changed the details.

"I wonder," Pamela leaned in a little closer towards Kelly as she spoke. "Did your husband ever mention knowing a Ben Green, by any chance?"

Kelly thought for a moment. The name certainly did not ring any bells, but then she did not know half the people her husband associated with.

She lifted her eyes to meet Pamela's gaze. "No, I'm sorry; he never mentioned that name to me."

Pamela nodded and sat back. "That's OK," she said, reassuringly, "it's not important."

CHAPTER THIRTY

Once the two officers left the flat, Kelly broke down once again, only this time she cried for a full twenty minutes without let-up. Carol, for her part, judged that this was not the right moment to try and persuade her friend that her husband was no great loss and if anything, she should be celebrating finally being free of him.

Instead, she decided to just be there for Kelly. She wrapped her arms around her friend and sat there with her until Kelly's sobs finally subsided.

Eventually, Kelly ceased her sobbing and grabbed some fresh tissues to dry her cheeks.

Carol poured them both a fresh glass of wine and handed one to Kelly.

Kelly grabbed hers, almost spilling the contents in the process. She clinked against Carol's and downed the warming liquid in one gulp.

Carol almost choked on her first sip as she watched Kelly empty her glass with such fervour. "Steady on, kiddo," she warned, "there's plenty more where that came from."

Kelly did not wait for a second invitation. She leaned forward and grabbed the bottle off the table and refilled her glass. Without speaking she clinked with Carol again, but this time Kelly only took a moderate swig.

Carol ruffled Kelly's hair, playfully. "Go on, kiddo, you have as much as you want, tomorrow is another day."

For a while, Kelly just sat there staring into space.

Carol stayed there with her, purposely waiting for her friend to start the conversation as she was the one who needed to process everything that was going on in her life right now.

When Kelly finally spoke up, her voice was low and croaky from all the crying. "I really cannot believe this," she said, rhetorically. "There I was, just about to give Jack his marching orders, and the next minute, he's dead!"

Carol took another sip of her wine before she joined in. "Listen, kiddo, I know what you're like," she began, ensuring that she kept her voice calm and soothing. "Just because you finally decided to give your old man the big push has nothing whatsoever to do with the fact that he's been killed. What's more, you can't go feeling guilty for something over which you had no control."

Carol waited a moment, hoping that her words would sink in and make sense to Kelly.

Kelly took in a deep breath and seemed as if she was about to answer, but then she exhaled and just took another drink from her glass.

Carol decided that it was time to dish out some tough love to her friend although she was still mindful of the fact that Kelly had been on edge before they had received the news about Jack, but that was for a different reason which now was no longer an option they needed to consider.

"Listen to me, kiddo," Carol began, "you cannot waste your time moping about a man who treated you like dirt and was never going to change. No one wished him dead, least of all you, regardless of what he did to you, so the only one to blame is the person who killed him."

Carol watched Kelly very carefully as she spoke to see what kind of reaction her words might have.

For the moment, Kelly just kept staring straight ahead, taking small sips of wine every couple of seconds.

Carol decided to plough on. "If this is just your catholic guilt kicking in, then you know only too well that you let it rule your life and it's not healthy. Fate has given you a chance to start again with a new man who from what you've told me, has always loved and respected you."

Kelly suddenly turned to face her friend. "What if it was Des?"

Carol looked puzzled. "What if what was Des?"

Fresh tears streaked down Kelly's cheeks. "What if it was Des who killed Jack? Maybe he bumped into him outside the pub and they started arguing, then one thing led to another and Des ended up killing Jack."

Carol was dumbfounded by her friend's suggestion.

Part of her was relieved that Kelly was not focussing directly on the fact that Jack was dead, but on who might be responsible, and although her argument did make some sense, Carol did not believe that fate could be that cruel to her friend, especially when she was feeling so vulnerable.

But if her worst fear was true, Carol was afraid that it might send her friend over the edge, possibly for good!

Carol put down her glass and placed her hands firmly on Kelly's shoulders.

She held Kelly's gaze. "Now listen to me," she began, again keeping her tone soft but now with added firmness to get her point across. "I understand what you're saying, but this is not some plot from the television so let's keep things real, you need to phone Des right now and put your mind at rest."

Kelly shrank back in her seat as if she were suddenly trying to move away from Carol. But Carol held her firmly, refusing to let her go.

Carol rubbed her friend's shoulders, soothingly. "Come on," she insisted, "you won't be able to sleep tonight until you know for sure and there's only one way that you can be definite, and that's to call Des."

Kelly shuddered. "I don't know if I can. What if it was him? I'll just die!"

Carol hugged Kelly tightly once more.

With Kelly still in her embrace, she said. "Come on, kiddo, you need to do this."

When they parted Kelly nodded her response. She dried her eyes and blew her nose once more before reaching for her phone.

Carol left her friend alone while she went out into the kitchen to fetch some more wine.

There was only a partition wall between the two rooms so Carol could not help but hear her friend's side of the conversation, and as much as she did not want to pry it was virtually impossible to block out the sound.

Carol waited until she heard Kelly ring off before re-entering the room.

Before Carol had a chance to set the fresh bottle down, Kelly sprang up from the sofa and gave her friend an enormous hug.

Carol could hear that her friend was still crying, but at least now they sounded like tears of joy.

After a while, she asked, "So I take it that Des knew nothing about it?"

Kelly pulled back, smiling though her tears and nodding her head.

"Well that at least is good news," Carol smiled.

"He couldn't believe it when I told him; he's been in all afternoon helping a couple of his friends with job applications."

"Good," agreed Carol, "that means he also has witnesses who can testify to where he was, should it ever come to that."

"I know," Kelly beamed, "I hope you don't mind, but I've asked him to come around to meet you."

Carol laughed. It was so good to see Kelly happy again. "That's fine, kiddo; in fact, if you don't fancy going back to yours just now the pair of you can stay here tonight, I can make do on the sofa, you know where the bedroom is." She winked.

Kelly burst out laughing and threw her arms around her friend yet again.

For the first time, in a long time, Kelly was starting to feel as if her life was truly worth living.

* * *

WHEN PAMELA and Hardy arrived back at the scene, they were met by Russell.

Pamela slipped out of the car first. "Any news?" she asked, hopefully.

Russell hastily looked through his notebook, turning the pages with such speed that he ended up ripping some of them off the spiral.

Finally, he found the page he wanted. "Well we've questioned all the onlookers; as usual no one saw anything. We've managed to ascertain that he had been drinking in the pub behind us," Russell indicated by pointing his pen over his shoulder, "but from what we can gather he left alone about twenty minutes before the phone call came in."

"Any word on the girl who made the call?" Pamela enquired, her tone giving away the fact that she was not hopeful of a positive answer.

Russell looked up from his notes. His eyes automatically looked at Hardy first before he switched his gaze to Pamela.

She did not miss the gesture. "I'm over here, Sergeant!" Pamela called out, sharply, satisfied when she noticed Russell's cheeks starting to glow.

"Yes ma'am," Russell responded, feeling like an admonished schoolboy. "We've managed to locate the phone box she used, and we've lifted all the prints we could find, although as you can imagine, there were quite a lot."

"I thought everybody used mobiles these days," Hardy offered.

"It's a good way of having a private conversation without worrying about your partner checking your mobile," Pamela explained. "Let's get those prints to forensics as fast as possible, you never know, she might be in the system."

"They're already on their way ma'am," Russell assured her.

"How's the search of the area coming along?" asked Hardy, gazing over towards the gate leading into the park.

"It's almost done," replied Russell, "they've taken the body away, so we've been able to search right from where he was found, spreading outwards, but so far nothing conclusive."

Pamela leaned against the open door of Hardy's car and surveyed the surrounding area. Now that Jack's body had been removed and most of the gathering crowd had been spoken to, there was only a smattering of people wandering about, and most of them appeared to be heading off home.

After a while, Hardy asked. "Something on your mind, ma'am?"

Pamela sighed. "I find it increasingly hard to believe that in such a relatively small town like this, that a crazed maniac seems able to strike at will without anyone ever seeing him!"

The two men thought for a while before Hardy offered a thought. "It might not be so much that he's never been seen, just not seen by someone willing to come forward. Wouldn't be the first-time certain members of a community band together to protect one of their own."

Pamela turned on him. "Even someone who commits atrocities such as we've seen?" she asked, not attempting to conceal her exasperation. "Seriously, Inspector, what kind of a monster would protect a lunatic like this, and allow him to carry on butchering innocent people?"

Hardy shrugged. "Well I grant you it's not so commonplace around here, but when I was back in London some of the vilest criminals I ever met often slipped the net several times because they were given a decent alibi by their nearest and dearest."

Pamela thought for a moment.

She knew that what Hardy was saying made perfect sense. She herself had witnessed several examples of the scenario he was putting forward, and it often made it hard to believe that anyone was telling the truth when they were making a statement.

"I suppose you're right, Inspector," she mumbled, offering the closest thing Hardy was going to receive as an apology for jumping on him.

At that moment, the rest of the officers who had been searching the park began to emerge from the main gate. They started milling together around the numerous squad cars which were parked haphazardly outside the park and across the road.

Hardy noticed PC Grant emerge surrounded by a bunch of uniformed officers. She seemed to be enjoying a joke with some of her colleagues. Even at this distance Hardy could tell that she had one of those infectious laughs which made everyone else want to join in.

He watched while she and some of the others made their way to the caravan which had been set up to supply them with tea and coffee. He tried to catch her eye to signal for her to bring one his way, but she seemed oblivious to the fact that he was there.

From out of nowhere Hardy suddenly noticed the looming figure of Cyril Carney making his way towards them.

"Ma'am," Hardy called to get Pamela's attention. When she looked over and saw the reporter approaching, Pamela groaned.

Hardy looked at Russell and gave him a nod.

Russell walked over to intercept the reporter and prevent him from annoying his superiors.

"Oi, you can't do this!" screamed Carney as Russell blocked his way. "The people 'ave a right to know if their hard-earned taxes are being wisely spent; have you never 'eard of freedom of the press?"

Although Carney's gripe was with Russell for holding him back, he was actually aiming his protestations towards Pamela and Hardy who were both trying their best not to look in the reporter's direction.

As Carney grew louder, Russell signalled for some of the uniforms to come and take care of him. Once they had the reporter under control, Russell went back to join his superiors.

"I suppose this is going to mean another press conference?" offered Pamela.

Hardy laughed. "Sounds like you've already got our superintendent sussed ma'am."

Pamela checked her watch.

It was 11:15 p.m.

"Come on, Inspector," she called over to Hardy whilst she

climbed back into the passenger seat of his car. "You can drop me off at the station."

Hardy looked over to Russell. "If you've got everything, wind this lot down and I'll see you in the morning."

Russell nodded and bent down to wave a goodbye to the DCI, but she was too busy studying the face of her phone to notice the gesture.

* * *

ONCE PAMELA HAD DRIVEN herself back to her hotel, she drew a hot bubble bath and poured herself a large gin and tonic from the mini-bar and finished it in two gulps.

The sudden rush from the alcohol mellowed her out somewhat and she considered having another but decided to wait until after her bath.

As she languished in the sudsy water, she could feel her stress levels starting to fall. She was sorely disappointed with the lack of any kind of a tangible result tonight.

Once they had found Natasha, Pamela felt confident that the end of the investigation was imminent, but with the girl being unable to communicate in any effective manner, that ship was well and truly blown out of the water.

From that point Pamela had set her sights on finding the culprit the next time he struck. Although she had not envisioned the next killing being so soon, when they received the call, she had been confident that tonight would be the night.

After all, she had been drafted in in order to make things happen, and so far, they were no closer to catching the perpetrator than they were before she arrived.

Carlisle would doubtless have something to moan about in the morning!

Not that Pamela cared so much about what her superintendent thought. She was not out to impress him so much as she was to just get the job done and move onto the next high-profile case.

She had heard through the grapevine that Carlisle was likely to remain in his present position until he retired, so he was obviously not interested in impressing his superiors and was probably just pleased to keep them off his back.

Whereas Pamela had no intention of stopping her meteoric rise any time soon.

Tomorrow, she decided, she was going to make things happen!

At this moment in time she was not sure exactly what she was going to do to motivate the rest of the team into achieving results, but whatever it was, woe betide anyone who tried to stand in her way, including her alleged superior officer.

Felling a little happier with the situation now that she had made her decision, Pamela slid further down the bath until the soapy water covered her right up to her chin.

The heat penetrated her entire body and she could feel her pent-up tension starting to evaporate.

The combination of the alcohol and the hot water was starting to make her feel sleepy.

She would need a good night's rest for the day ahead.

She knew that there was one definite way for her to fall asleep as soon as her head hit the pillow. It was something which she had come to rely upon since first discovering how conducive the act was to a good night's slumber.

Pamela considered it for a moment.

She knew that she wanted to, and that once she had thought about it her mind was already made up.

She cursed herself for not bringing her vibrator into the bath with her.

She considered using her fingers instead. She slipped one

hand towards her lips and began to gently stroke herself under the water.

She shuddered from the sensation, but as skilled and as practised as her fingers were, they were no substitute for her *whopper!*

Pamela had even paid the extra for the waterproof model because she knew that the bath was the perfect place for her to use it.

Her mind made up, she hoisted herself from the bath, feeling the loss of the soothing warmth immediately.

Pamela's bare feet slapped across the tiled bathroom floor as she made her way back into the bedroom to recover her toy.

Once she had it firmly in her grasp, she made her way back into the bathroom, almost slipping and losing her balance on the wet floor.

Once she was back under the water, Pamela relaxed and allowed the heat to seep back into her body.

Once she felt completely relaxed again, she switched on her vibrator and gently slid it under the water to guide it towards her eager opening.

CHAPTER THIRTY-ONE

Kelly's viewing of Jack's dead body at the mortuary made a bigger impact on her than she had anticipated.

Up until the moment that she was led by Hardy into the room and the sheet was pulled back, Kelly was of the opinion that she could take the event in her stride.

But the moment she looked down at Jack's lifeless corpse, all the guilt which she had initially felt the previous evening when Hardy and Pamela had broken the news to her, came flooding back.

Once Kelly had nodded her confirmation that the corpse was indeed that of her late husband, Hardy led her back out to the antechamber where Carol was waiting to comfort her friend.

Kelly fell into Carol's arms, sobbing, while Hardy pulled back the curtain across the rectangular window so that she could not see them wheeling her dead husband away.

Hardy moved a couple of chairs to where the women were standing, being careful not to let the legs scrape against the cold stone floor.

He helped Carol manoeuvre Kelly onto one of the chairs, and she took the other one, gratefully.

Hardy's offer of tea or coffee was declined by both of them, so the officer decided to just stay put and wait until Kelly was in a fit state to leave.

The previous evening, Kelly and Des had declined Carol's kind offer to stay at her place. Instead, Kelly decided that she needed to face the demon of her own flat as soon as possible, because in her mind that flat was still her home and she was not about to allow the memory of her vile husband to keep her from it.

Kelly was very happy that Des and Carol had finally managed to meet.

They all shared a drink and a laugh together, and Kelly was comforted at being with the two most important people in her life.

When she and Des arrived back at her flat, Kelly suddenly felt the urge to start clearing out all of Jack's stuff as a therapeutic exercise to banish the last stigma of his hold over her.

Des managed to convince her that there would be plenty of time for the clearance later, and together they changed the sheets on the bed and curled up in each other's arms to go to sleep.

Neither of them made a move to be intimate.

Instead the pair of them were just happy to finally be together.

But sometime during the night they both found themselves awake and staring into each other's eyes.

They started to kiss, and before long, their pent-up passion for each other gave way, and they made love.

The following morning when Kelly received the call from Hardy to view Jack's body, Des offered to accompany her to the mortuary. But Kelly was afraid that the sight of her with

Des might raise questions which she did not want to face right now.

So instead she hurried to catch Carol before she left for work, and her friend immediately agreed to go with her.

The pair of them had been quite jovial on their way down, considering the fact that such a trip was usually quite a sombre affair.

Carol at first had held back on her usual sense of humour out of respect for Kelly, but once she realised that her friend was not allowing the occasion to bring her down, she too joined in.

Now with Kelly sobbing in her arms, Carol realised that Kelly's attitude had probably sprung from a combination of relief, tinged with guilt and massive helping of bravado.

As nasty and a spiteful as Jack had been to her, it was obvious that Kelly would be carrying around the burden of remorse for some time to come.

Carol only hoped that her feelings did not mar her chances of a fresh start with Des. It was obvious from seeing them together the previous evening that they were both very much in love, and as far as Carol was concerned, that was the best medicine her friend could do with, right now.

When Kelly had eventually managed to stop her tears, Carol took her out for a coffee and a large piece of chocolate cake to cheer her up.

Carol's recipe for lifting the spirits usually centred around wine and a takeaway, but as it was still only morning, chocolate was the order of the day.

It came as no great shock to Carol when Kelly only picked at her cake with her fork. She also allowed her first cappuccino to go cold, and even though she protested, Carol insisted on buying her another one, this time making sure that Kelly did not leave it for too long before drinking it.

Carol did her best to keep the conversation flowing, but she could tell whenever Kelly started to drift off into her own world, that her mind was still on other things.

Just when Carol was about to give up trying to force a conversation out of her friend, Kelly turned to Carol and grabbed her hand across the table.

Carol, shocked by the suddenness of her friend's action, looked her in the eye and placed her own hand on top of her friend's. "What's up, kiddo?" she asked, keeping her voice low and her tone soothing.

Kelly blinked away her tears. "I want you to know that I really appreciate you coming with me this morning."

Carol patted her hand, gently. "Don't be silly, you don't have to thank me for that, I was happy to help."

Kelly wiped her eyes.

Carol could tell that she was about to make a statement, and she obviously felt uncomfortable about whatever it was.

"Listen," Carol prompted her, "whatever is on your mind just blurt it out, you're starting to worry me, kiddo."

Kelly tried a half smile to reassure her friend and gave her hand a slight squeeze. "I just don't want to seem ungrateful but, I really need to do something, and I need to do it alone, that's all."

Carol pulled back, smiling. "Is that all," she said, sounding relieved. "I thought that you were about to divulge something deep and dark to me, like you killed off Jack or paid the mafia to do it or something."

This time Kelly smiled for real. "No, nothing so sinister, I just feel that I need to go and see my priest, but I hate just walking off and leaving you after all you've done for me."

"Don't be silly," Carol assured her. "Listen, kiddo, you go and do whatever you need to, don't worry about me, this is a perfect excuse for me to indulge in some retail therapy, not that I usually need an excuse. Just call me if you need me, OK?"

They both walked out of the coffee shop together.

Before they went their separate ways, Kelly gave her friend another massive hug, and thanked her once more for all her help and support.

When Kelly arrived at St Luke's, she dipped her fingers in the holy water font and made the sign of the cross. Instantly she could feel the tension starting to build inside her at the thought of facing Father Grace once again.

When she turned and looked through the glass partition, she could see the old priest down at the front of the church talking to an elderly couple who were seated in the first pew.

Kelly held back in the vestibule, not wanting to disturb him until he was finished with his parishioners, although in truth, whether she admitted it to herself or not, it was just another excuse to put off the inevitable.

Father Grace had made his position, and that of the church, very clear to her in the confessional. The fact that Jack was dead now, did nothing to alter the fact that she had been unfaithful and was not willing to show remorse for her actions.

At this point, Kelly did not even know what she was going to say to him.

She just knew that she needed the comfort and reassurance that only her faith could give her.

As if by some divine form of telepathy, Father Grace suddenly looked up from his conversation and stared down the aisle directly at Kelly.

She could feel herself subconsciously shrinking back into the shadows, but she knew full well that the priest had seen her and there was no turning back now.

Kelly waited for Father Grace to finish his conversation

before she opened the door from the vestibule and met him halfway down the aisle.

She feared that the priest would still be angry with her from their last meeting, but instead he appeared to be overjoyed to see her, and he held out his arms to welcome her, placing them gently on her shoulders.

"Kelly, how marvellous it is to see you, my child," he whispered, obviously conscious of not allowing his voice to carry and disturb the smattering of worshippers quietly lost in prayer.

"Hello, Father," Kelly stuttered, "I hope you don't mind, but I really need to speak to you."

The priest beamed, and his entire face seemed to light up at her words.

"Mind," he answered, "of course I don't mind, I can't tell you how overjoyed I am that you came back."

Kelly instantly felt her entire body relax.

This was certainly not the reaction she had expected, and she immediately felt at ease at the sound of the priest's voice.

"Come with me," Father Grace ushered Kelly towards his private quarters, "and we can sit down and have a nice cup of tea and a chat."

Kelly sat at the large wooden table in the priest's kitchen.

She had never been invited back here before and she secretly wondered if Father Grace had somehow found out about Jack, and that was why he was being so kind to her. Not that he had ever been anything but charming and polite in the past, but Kelly could not get past the fact that, in her mind, she had let him down in the confessional.

"Tea alright with you?" asked the priest, filling the kettle from the tap.

"Lovely, thank you, Father," Kelly replied. As she gazed around the large room, she could not help but admire all the matching sets of crockery which were laid out military style along the oak dressers.

In fact, the entire kitchen was immaculately presented. The tiles on the floor had been scrubbed so clean that you could almost see your reflection in them.

She surmised that Father Grace probably had a house-keeper, or an army of willing volunteers amongst his congregation who made sure that he was well looked after.

The old priest set down a large silver serving plate in front of Kelly, and when he lifted the ornate cover, he revealed a beautifully decorated chocolate gateau underneath.

"A gift from one of my parishioners," he winked. "You'll have some with me?"

Kelly nodded.

In truth, she felt guilty for the fact that she had hardly touched the one that Carol had bought her only an hour ago. But at the time her stomach had been in knots as a result of the tension she was suffering from in anticipation of seeing Father Grace.

However, since arriving at the church, the priest had set her mind at rest with his amiable manner and kind words.

She was certainly feeling a great deal more human now than she had been earlier.

Father Grace cut Kelly a huge slice of the cake, ignoring her protestations that she only wanted a sliver.

He placed it on a china plate in front of her and went back to the counter to make their tea.

While they ate, they talked amicably on general topics such as the weather and the rising cost of living.

Kelly was desperate to tell the priest about her husband, but she wanted to wait for the right moment, and they were having such a pleasant chat that she was afraid of spoiling the mood.

Eventually, Father Grace saved her the trouble.

"Did you hear that there was another one of those awful murders last night?"

Kelly immediately put down her fork.

She knew that this was the right moment, and she did not want to let it pass.

"Yes, Father, I did, in fact that was what I wanted to talk to you about,"

The priest replaced his fork in his plate and looked at Kelly with a curious expression on his face.

"You see, Father," Kelly continued, "that was my husband Jack who was killed last night, the police came around, and told me straight after."

Father Grace looked truly horrified at her words. "Your husband!" he exclaimed, unable to hide his shock. "Are you sure? I mean, they sometimes make mistakes when identifying victims, I've read about several cases in the newspaper."

Kelly shook her head. "There's no mistake, Father, I had to go and identify him this morning."

The priest held his hands up to his mouth in disbelief.

Once he had taken it all in, he pushed away his chair and came around the table to give Kelly a fatherly hug.

The material of his cassock was coarse and felt rough against her skin, but Kelly did not mind. From her seated position she wrapped her arms around the priest and buried her face amongst the folds of material.

After a while, the priest let go and moved back to his chair.

He rested his elbows on the table and made a steeple of his fingers. Resting his chin on top, he gazed at Kelly across the table for a moment, before he spoke again.

"You poor child, I can only imagine what is going through your mind right now, especially considering what you confessed to me the other day."

Kelly flushed, immediately.

Father Grace leaned across the table and placed a comforting hand on top of hers. "You must not reproach yourself, my child," he assured her. "I have been wrestling with my own conscience since we last met and I know now that I should have offered you absolution, without question."

Kelly met his gaze. "But, Father, I refused to repent, you had no choice."

The priest smiled at her. "We always have a choice Kelly. How can I believe in a god who is just and forgiving if I, as one of his representatives here on earth, am not prepared to offer his forgiveness to one of his own children when they are most in need of it?"

Kelly allowed herself a half smile.

After a moment, she asked. "Father, do you think that god took Jack to punish me for breaking our marriage vows, so that I now have to carry the burden of that guilt around with me forever?"

Father Grace smiled and shook his head. "No, my child, absolutely not." The priest assured her. "God takes us when he sees fit, and it is not for us to question his motives, but by the same token our god is not a vengeful god, so he would have no reason to punish you. He can see into our hearts, and he knows full well the guilt and shame you were feeling as a result of your actions."

The old priest closed his eyes and still holding onto Kelly's hands he began to recite the words of the prayer of absolution.

Kelly had heard it often enough to recognise what it was, so she too closed her eyes in silent prayer and waited for Father Grace to finish.

At the end, the priest said "Amen," and Kelly responded accordingly.

As she exited the main entrance of the church and started

to descend the stone steps which led to the park, Kelly could feel a great weight being lifted from her shoulders.

The guilt of her husband's death was still there, and would be for some time to come, she supposed, but somehow, she felt happier and more confident than she had done in a very long time.

As she reached the bottom step, she took out her phone and called Des.

CHAPTER THIRTY-TWO

After leaving Kelly and Carol, Hardy picked up the results from the Post Mortem on Jack and took them back to the station with him to show to Pamela and the rest of the team.

When he arrived, he found Pamela in the middle of a briefing, Hardy could hear the sound of her voice from halfway down the corridor and it was obvious from the tone of her voice as well as the volume, that she was not best pleased with the progress of the investigation to date.

For a second, Hardy considered turning around before he was seen and going down to the café on the corner for some breakfast. That way he could casually return when all the screaming and shouting was over.

But, deep down, he felt obliged to at least be on hand to deflect some of the DCI's wrath and take one for the team, so instead he kept on going and made his way into the incident room.

As he expected, Pamela was holding court at the front of the room with their incident board listing all their victims and any information they had received which was deemed pertinent to the inquiry, behind her.

The rest of the squad were all assembled in front of her, some standing, others sitting, and the rest squatting on the edge of desks or leaning up against the walls.

To Hardy's surprise, Carlisle was also in attendance, and by the expression on his face he was very impressed with the tongue-lashing which Pamela was dishing out.

As Pamela saw Hardy arrive, she signalled for him to come to the front and stand beside her, doubtless, Hardy reflected, to make it seem as if the senior ranks were all together in support of the DCI's admonishing of the team.

Reluctantly, Hardy made his way to the front and stood shoulder to shoulder with Pamela and the superintendent.

"Now today," Pamela continued, "I want you all to go back over every statement we've taken so far."

There was a chorus of groans from amongst those in attendance which from the sound of it, Pamela had been expecting.

"Yes, I know, I know," she continued, holding up her hand to call for quiet. "But with all the people we've interviewed someone must know or have seen something, no matter how slight, perhaps they themselves don't realise the significance of what they know, so we have to sift through what we've got and see if we can find that proverbial needle."

Pamela turned to Hardy and indicated to the file he had tucked under his shoulder. "Is that the PM results from the latest victim?" she asked, hopefully.

"Yes ma'am," replied Hardy, offering her the file.

Instead of taking it from him, Pamela stood back and announced. "DI Hardy will now fill us in on the details of last night's victim's Post Mortem examination."

Hardy cleared his throat and opened the file to check the details.

"We have just had confirmation from the widow of the deceased that the victim is indeed her husband, Jack Soames," he began, looking up from the file as he spoke and surveying the tired faces of his colleagues around him.

"The pathologist has confirmed that Mr. Soames died from a broken back, which upon investigation was definitely not as a result of a fall, but more likely caused by external pressure being applied until it just snapped."

There was a combination of murmurs to match the shocked looks on the faces of those gathered.

Hardy waited a moment for the details to take hold before he continued.

He quickly glanced over at Carlisle. His expression demonstrated genuine concern, which to Hardy was a positive sign because it meant that he was becoming a team player and not just the aloof superior trying to distance himself from the men and women on the ground.

"There was a small quantity of DNA which the lab managed to lift from the body, and they have confirmed that it matches that found on some of the earlier victims."

"Have they managed to identify the killer?" Pamela burst in, excitedly.

Hardy looked at her and shook his head. "No, I'm afraid not ma'am, in fact they still cannot conclusively say what species the DNA came from. As with the other samples, they say that it is part human, part animal." He turned back to look at his team. "But which animal, they cannot pinpoint."

The worried looks on the faces of the team were perfectly justified in Hardy's opinion. They were dealing with something here, the likes of which even the medical officers could not specify.

So far it seemed as if the only people who could possibly identify the perpetrator were the victims, and they were all dead, with the exception of Natasha who was still so heavily sedated that she was incapable of answering any such questions at this moment in time.

Pamela shot a glance over at Carlisle.

They held each other's stare for a few seconds before Carlisle gave a slight nod of head, which no one else noticed save for the DCI.

Pamela turned back to the group.

She did not wait for the mumblings of concern and worry to die down before she began to speak.

"Superintendent Carlisle and I have decided that tonight we are going to hold a stake out around the area where Natasha Spencer was found, and our latest victim was attacked."

She waited a few seconds for the message to get through.

"This will naturally be an undercover operation in order to try and lull the perpetrator into a false sense of security which might cause him to show himself unwittingly."

The mumblings grew in volume, so Pamela raised her voice even higher to slam the point home.

"This is not a request, I am not asking for volunteers, I will need all of you in attendance, so any plans you had for tonight, cancel them!"

A couple of the objections from the team started to grow in intensity as both male and female officers began to complain to each other about the short notice, but Pamela had clearly anticipated such a reaction and she was only too pleased to demonstrate in front of her superior that she knew what it meant to be in charge.

"Whatever it is, I've heard it all before and I'm not interested!" she called out over the heads of those assembled. "This is what we're doing, so get used to the idea!"

The protestations died down to barely a whisper. It was obvious that no one wanted to risk being pulled up and ridiculed in front of their colleagues for trying to push their private agenda.

After a moment, Pamela continued. "So, let's all start going through those statements, and I'll let you all know the details of tonight's operation as the day unfolds. Thank you."

As the group started to disperse, Pamela caught PC Grant's eye, and signalled her to come to the front.

The young PC made her way forward as instructed.

Once there was only her, Pamela, the superintendent and Hardy within earshot, Pamela began to speak.

"PC Grant," she started, pleasantly, "for tonight's little party I am going to need a decoy, how do you fancy applying for the role?"

The young girl looked puzzled. "Decoy, ma'am?" she asked, evidently unsure of what would be expected of her.

"That's right," confirmed Pamela. "I need someone, preferably suited to out killer's taste to stand out from the crowd to try and draw him in." She looked the girl directly in the eye. "Can I count on you?"

Hardy could see the awkwardness of the position Pamela was putting the young PC in, so he decided to speak up on her behalf, figuring it was better that he was lambasted rather than her.

"Hang on just a minute ma'am, we don't even know what we are dealing with yet." He began, focusing his attention towards the DCI and the superintendent who had taken up a commanding position directly beside his junior officer, doubtless to give the impression of his support and commitment to her scenario.

Hardy turned towards PC Grant who was looking very uncomfortable.

Hardy started to feel guilty in case he was making the young officer feel even more vulnerable because of his interference. But he still felt that he had to put his feelings across on the off chance she was just too shy and insecure to speak up for herself.

"Sir, ma'am," he continued, looking back at his superiors, "PC Grant may be a very able and committed member of the team, but as her superior I think that it is my duty to state that she is far too new and inexperienced to be such an integral part of this kind of operation. I'm sure that I can find one of the more mature female officers who will be willing to take on this role."

"He doesn't go for the more mature females though, does he, Inspector?" Pamela snapped.

"He went for a man last night," Hardy shot back, "and what about Ben Green, he wasn't a young girl."

Pamela took a step forward, it was an obvious ploy to try and intimidate Hardy, but he was too long in the tooth for it to work on him and he even had to stop himself from saying so, at the risk of the whole incident being blown out of proportion.

"Jack Soames was not torn to shreds, so clearly he must have just got in the way of whatever this maniac planned to do to his intended victim, probably the girl who called in the incident," Pamela stated, keeping her eyes locked on Hardy's.

Hardy took in a deep breath and bit his tongue.

"Furthermore," continued Pamela, "Ben Green was obviously just in the way when the attacker grabbed Natasha Spencer, which was why he ended up being killed."

Hardy could feel his temper rising.

But he hated to admit that Pamela was making sense.

"Caroline Seymour and Gina Steele on the other hand, just like Natasha, were attractive, young girls; just like PC Grant here, so it stands to reason that she is the obvious choice for such an operation, doesn't it, Inspector?"

Hardy let his pent-up breath out through his nostrils.

What he refused to admit to himself was that it was more the fact that PC Grant herself was being chosen, rather than just some random female officer that bothered him.

He was indirectly to blame for her being on the investigation in the first place, so if anything happened to her he knew that he would never be able to forgive himself.

As he was about to launch in with another protest Hardy felt a hand rest on his arm.

He looked down and saw that it belonged to PC Grant and whether it was as a result of shock, surprise, or a combination of both, the gesture left him stuck for words.

"It'll be fine ma'am," the young PC was looked directly at Pamela while she gave Hardy's forearm a comforting squeeze, and then almost immediately she let go.

Hardy still had his mouth half-open as if about to speak, although now he realised that any further assertions were futile. The officer had made up her mind for better or worse, and Hardy did not wish to come over like some overbearing Victorian patriarch trying to tell the young PC what was best for her.

Pamela, on the other hand, obviously wished to labour the point to cause Hardy the maximum embarrassment.

"Any further objections, Inspector?" she asked him, making a point of keeping her voice as light and sweet now as it had been bombastic and argumentative seconds before.

Hardy shot PC Grant a quick side glance, but she was purposely keeping her eyes straight ahead of her.

"No ma'am, I guess not," replied Hardy, reluctantly.

"Good," Pamela continued, "right then, I'll go and finalise the details," she turned to Carlisle who Hardy could not help but notice had a very smug expression on his face. Hardy wondered if Carlisle had anticipated his objection and tipped Pamela the wink beforehand.

Either way, it was all over now, and if Hardy had made a fool of himself, he did not really care.

He had meant every word that he said, but wrong or right, he knew that he had to respect PC Grant's decision even if he did not agree with it.

* * *

PAMELA GATHERED the plain clothed officers together for a briefing at 7pm that evening.

As everyone mingled around the front of the office, the sound of wolf-whistles and cat-calls started to echo from behind.

Hardy turned to see PC Grant entering the main office.

She was dressed in a short leather bomber jacket over a roll-neck jumper, a black mini-skirt, black stockings and on her feet, she wore a pair of patent leather Dr. Martin lace up boots.

Her blonde hair, which she usually kept tied back, was left free to cascade down over she shoulders. She was wearing make-up, which she never seemed to on duty, and the overall effect of which enhanced her cheekbones and made her lips seem fuller and more voluptuous. She had also applied her eyes shadow quite liberally which made her eyes look as if they were about to pop out of her head.

For a moment, the sight of the young officer made Hardy forget the unprofessional behaviour of some of his colleagues around him.

He reprimanded himself for staring, but at least he was doing it discreetly.

PC Grant for her part appeared to take it in good heart and she began twisting and turning as if she were posing on the catwalk.

All of a sudden, Hardy realised that the young PC had

noticed him looking at her. A saucy smile started to spread across her lips and Hardy quickly put his hands up to his face and rubbed it as if he were trying to wake himself up.

He hoped that the action looked convincing.

"That will do thank you, gentleman," Pamela's bark brought everyone's attention back to the front of the room. "Unless any of you fancy ending up on a charge of sexual impropriety whilst on duty, I suggest you remember why we are all here!"

Pamela waited for silence before she continued.

The map which Hardy had arranged at her request was now pinned up on the incident board, and various coloured pins had been attached to show the sites where victims had either disappeared or been found.

As the map was quite high on the board to allow everyone a decent view, Pamela used a pointer for emphasis as she spoke. "Now I want you all to spread out over this area," she stated, using the pointer in an arced movement across the map. "I realise that it is quite a large circumference, but we will all be in radio contact with each other and I don't want our suspect to slip past us because we have not anticipated the path he might take."

From the murmurs in the room, Pamela could tell that everyone agreed with her assertion that the area chosen was far too large for the officers to cover sufficiently, but she also knew that she could not face the embarrassment of demanding such a big operation if the perpetrator still managed to strike and evade capture.

Naturally, she and all those in attendance knew that there was no guarantee that he would show himself tonight. But Pamela also knew that unless she could demonstrate that she was doing everything possible to make things happen, she might well find herself taken off the investigation.

The truth was, she had more to lose than the others, although she had no intention of letting them know her feelings for fear that they might take it as a sign of weakness, and that was something she would never allow.

"Now," she continued, "because of the lack of viable information we've received as a result of the witness statements you've all gathered thus far, we have no way of knowing from which direction this manic might appear, so I need all of you to keep your eyes and ears open, and report anything, no matter how small it may seem, back over the air, and then I will decide what action is appropriate, understand?"

There were several nods and agreements mumbled from those gathered.

"DI Hardy and I will be positioned just outside the park and Sergeant Russell will act as coordinator. PC Grant here," she nodded towards the young PC, "will be making a round of the entire park, leading up to the woods and back again, so Sergeant Russell," the officer looked up to show his DCI that she had his full attention, "please be sure that you spread the team out evenly so that there is always someone in close proximity should PC Grant need assistance."

Hardy looked around the room, surveying all those gathered.

They were a good bunch, all in all, and he had worked with most of them before, so he was fairly confident that they were all willing to pull their own weight.

But he also knew the vastness of the area they were supposed to be covering, and in his opinion, they would need at least another ten to fifteen bodies to ensure that there was sufficient coverage.

He considered sharing his observation with his DCI but immediately thought better of it.

After the pleasure she obviously derived from his earlier

challenge, Hardy decided he was not going to give her another opportunity to belittle him in front of his team.

Hardy turned and stole another glance at PC Grant.

He wondered if she were the only reason he was concerned about the ratio of officers compared to the area that they had to cover.

There were other female officers spread around the room who were also part of the evening's festivities, and he knew several of them, but they were all experienced detectives who had been in the job long enough to take care of themselves.

That and the fact that the other female officers-like the men-were all dressed in jeans and casual jackets, whereas the young PC seemed to have gone out of her way to dress provocatively to try and attract this maniac, made Hardy suspicious that Pamela had requested it specifically, and PC Grant would hardly feel in a position to refuse.

Hardy turned back to face the front before anyone noticed him staring.

He was only half paying attention to what Pamela was saying.

His mind was too busy fretting about the event ahead. He understood the DCI's thinking behind using PC Grant as bait, regardless of his outburst when it was first suggested. But he was just not comfortable with it.

He decided that regardless of whatever else went down, he was going to make sure that PC Grant came out of it in one piece.

CHAPTER THIRTY-THREE

A little over half an hour later Hardy and Pamela were parked up opposite the main entrance to the park.

Pamela busied herself by barking orders into her radio handset every couple of seconds, while Hardy kept mainly silent.

It was obvious to anyone looking in from outside that he was not happy with the situation, but Pamela seemed—or at least acted—oblivious to the situation.

Hardy had watched as PC Grant and the rest of the stake-out team made their way into the park and disappeared behind the first clump of bushes.

As coordinator, Russell was the one answering all of Pamela's demands. As a highly trained and experienced officer who had led multiple stake-outs in the past, Russell was already acutely aware of what needed to be done, but to his credit he answered the DCI in such a way so as to make her feel as if she was coming up with all the sound ideas.

Hardy had to admire his junior colleague.

The way he was on edge at the moment he was sure that he would have lost his temper by now and switched off his radio.

Hardy had dropped a subtle hint on the drive over that there was no point in both of them staying behind, and that he at least should go and join the officers in the park. But as he expected, Pamela shot him down and informed him that at his rank, he needed to keep a certain distance from the rest of the team during such operations.

This galled Hardy. As a team player he preferred to be on the front line leading the troops, rather than staying behind the lines and cowering away from the real action.

But he was all too aware of the modern thinking concerning the practicalities of leadership in the police force, and those of Pamela's breed had been tutored to believe that more time spent in the classroom and less on the streets made for the best leaders.

It was at times like this that Hardy looked long and hard at his career path and wondered if he was cut out for the job after all.

His main problem was that after so long in the force, what else could he do?

Whilst he was still lost in thought, Russell appeared from the park and walked towards Hardy's car, veering off at the last minute to ensure that he ended up outside Pamela's side of the vehicle.

Pamela opened her window and the sergeant handed her an A4 sheet of paper.

"There you are, ma'am," he began, pointing towards the paper while she studied its contents. "I've put a cross where each member of the team has been stationed, and PC Grant has already begun to walk around the perimeter of the area."

"How are the radio's working?" asked Hardy, leaning in closer towards Pamela to ensure that he could be heard.

"They're a little crackly to be honest guv, and I think we've managed to find a few areas where the interference is so bad that reception is virtually nil, but on the whole we're running at about seventy five percent efficiency."

Hardy turned to Pamela who appeared to be so engrossed in the layout of the troops that she was oblivious to the conversation going on around her.

Finally, Hardy gave up waiting for her to speak.

"What do you think, ma'am?" he asked, respectively.

Pamela looked up. "About what?" she answered, clearly uninterested.

"About what Sergeant Russell has just told us about the lack of communication between the officers?"

Hardy struggled to keep the anguish out of his tone.

"Oh, that," Pamela fired back, matter-of-factly, "that's not unusual considering the terrain we are dealing with, they'll be fine so long as they move about enough to find a good spot."

Hardy looked over at Russell who could tell how hard his boss was finding it to keep his cool.

"Well, that is a problem, ma'am," Russell ventured, making sure that he got in first, before Hardy. "The team are trying to lie low so as not to spook the perpetrator should he show himself."

Pamela raised her head and sighed, not trying to disguise her exasperation.

"Well, so long as some of them are in touch with PC Grant when she passes near their area, that's all we really need."

This time Hardy was not prepared to bite his tongue.

"No, Chief Inspector, that is not all we need!" Hardy emphasised his words as if he were trying to explain something to a kindergartener. "Have you forgotten that we do not even know what kind of a man we are dealing with here? If indeed it is even a man!"

His manner was not lost on Pamela, which was exactly what Hardy wanted.

He needed to drive home the fact that he was in no way satisfied with the ramshackle operation she had thrown together, especially, the lack of concern she appeared to have over the possibility that the person she had chosen to use as bait might end up alone and out of range of her colleagues when the killer struck.

But Pamela was having none of it!

She slammed down the paper she had been holding and turned to look directly at Hardy so that their faces were only a couple of inches apart.

"Detective Inspector, if you are in any way dissatisfied with the way I am running this operation then I suggest that you speak to Superintendent Carlisle about it when we get back to the station. In the meantime, I would remind you that I am your superior officer and I expect nothing short of complete loyalty from you, do I make myself clear?"

Hardy was seething, but he knew well enough how close he was to a disciplinary if he pushed things too far.

There was no way that Carlisle would support him against the DCI, and he knew that Pamela was fully aware of that fact also.

She was holding all the cards right now, and it made him feel completely inadequate that he was expected to sit out here with her instead of being in the field with his team.

Hardy swung open his door and slid out of his seat.

"Crystal clear, Chief Inspector!" he called back before he slammed his door shut and started walking towards the main entrance to the park.

From behind he heard Pamela's voice. "Where the hell do you think you're going?" she demanded, evidently unconcerned if her shouting should draw any unwanted attention.

"I need a piss," Hardy called back over his shoulder, purposely not bothering to turn around and give his superior the courtesy of a face-to-face answer.

"Come straight back when you're finished." Pamela called after him, sounding like an angry parent shouting at her offspring.

Hardy did not bother acknowledging his DCI this time and carried on walking as if he had not heard her shouting after him.

Once he was out of sight of the car, he waited patiently for his sergeant to re-enter the park.

After a couple of minutes Russell appeared.

Hardy called out to him in a hushed voice so as not to attract any attention.

When Russell came close Hardy could tell by the look on his face that he was not pleased with something.

"What's up?" Hardy asked, keeping his voice low.

The sergeant signalled over his shoulder. "She just sent me in to find you; she wants you back there with her."

"Why, what's she afraid of, someone coming up to her and asking if she's looking for a good time?"

Russell held his hand to his mouth to stifle his laughter.

"Come on," said Hardy, "I'm joining the party." With that, Hardy started to walk towards the main path.

"What about ma'am?" Russell called after him, conscious of the fact that he needed to keep his voice down.

Hardy looked back. "If she asks, you couldn't find me."

"But what are you going to say to her when she wants to know why you didn't go back to the car?" asked the sergeant, clearly worried for his colleague.

Hardy shrugged. "I'll think of something."

* * *

PC GRANT WAS HALFWAY through her second round of the park, and so far, she had encountered nothing out of the ordinary.

As she approached the area which led into the wood she automatically slowed down. This was her least favourite part of her round, but she knew that if the perpetrator were in hiding that this would be the perfect place for him to jump out at her.

She adjusted her earpiece and rechecked that the volume control of the radio attached to her inside jacket pocket was up to the maximum.

For most of her journey she could hear reports from her colleagues stating that they could see her approaching, although she herself could not see any of them as they were hidden well back behind the trees and bushes which surrounded the area.

But for some reason this stretch seemed to be a dead zone. Either that or no one was speaking because all she could hear was the faint hum of static buzzing in her ear.

As instructed, she stopped walking when she reached the edge of the wood.

She pretended to be searching for something in her pockets, all the while listening intently for any sound that might signal someone approaching. But with the static in one ear and the sound of the wind rustling the branches of the trees surrounding her, it was hard for her to make out anything else.

Casually, the young PC turned and gazed over her shoulders in as nonchalant a manner as she could manage.

The local council could really do with putting in some better lighting around here, she thought to herself.

The path leading into the woods had no direct lighting until after the first bend, therefore the area that the young officer was looking at was mostly cast in shadow, making it almost impossible for her to ascertain where the trees and bushes ended, and the path began.

Just then, she heard something coming through her earpiece.

The voice was extremely muffled and there was still an awful lot of static interference.

She placed a finger in her free ear to help cut out the sound of the wind so that she could concentrate on what was being said.

Suddenly, from behind a large hand clamped across her mouth and pulled her backwards, almost knocking her off her feet!

PC Grant kicked and struggled in the vice-like grip of her assailant, but it was all to no avail.

His other arm reached around her and clamped her arms to her side, making it impossible for her to even try and fight back.

She was hauled backward towards the woods, her heels dragging on the floor leaving deep channels in the mud as she desperately tried to gain purchase. Each time she felt as if she were about to manage it, her attacked yanked her back even harder forcing her to lose her traction once more.

The young PC was terrified.

All that she had gleaned from her training, preparation, groundwork, and practical exercises had disappeared in an instant.

Now she was just another defenceless victim at the mercy of her attacker.

Once they were behind the first clump of trees her assailant stopped pulling at her and just kept the young officer held tightly in his vice-like grip.

The hand covering her mouth had slipped upwards during their struggle and now it was also blocking her nostrils, making it almost impossible for her to breathe.

The hand over her face stank of bad body odour, stale sweat, and urine.

Officer Grant could feel herself starting to gag, and she was afraid that if she did vomit, she would choke on her own bile.

She could feel her attacker starting to fondle her breasts through her jumper, his huge rough hands squeezed and tweaked her nipples almost as if he were trying to flick a light switch.

The young PC could feel the man growing hard against her back, and she was in doubt what his intentions were.

She was at last able to stand firmly on the ground.

She felt the man's tongue start to slobber drool down her neck as he attempted to nibble her ear.

Raising her right foot high in the air, PC Grant brought the heel of her boot crashing down on the man's instep.

He yelled out in pain and released his grip on her just enough to allow the constable to release the telescopic baton she had secreted up her jacket sleeve.

Her survival instinct took over as she timed the drop perfectly and caught the handle of the baton just at the right moment, allowing it to fully extend.

Her assailant was hopping on one leg as a result of her stamping on his toe.

PC Grant aimed her baton down and slammed it against the man's bent knee.

This time he actually fell to the ground behind her, releasing her completely from his hold.

In an instant she spun around to face her foe.

His head was bowed so she still could not see his face, but it did not matter. Without warning the PC smacked him hard across the side of his head with her

baton. The metal rod made a sickening squelch as if made

contact with her aggressor's ear, causing him to cry out once more as he slumped to the ground,

face-first.

In the distance the officer could hear the sound of approaching voices.

Not wanting to take any chances, she straddled the prone figure's back and pulled his arms behind him so that she could handcuff him.

Once he was secure, the young PC rolled off of him and crawled a few feet to one side before she threw-up the sandwich she had eaten earlier in the evening.

She wiped her mouth and made it back up to her feet just as the rest of the team ran up to her. Most of them, including Hardy, sweating profusely, and heaving from the exertion.

Russell was the first to catch his breath sufficiently to enable him to speak.

"Why didn't...you call for...backup?" he heaved, his chest lifting and falling in rapid succession.

PC Grant looked down at her moaning assailant. "He didn't give me much of a chance," she answered, shrugging her shoulders.

As the other officers moved in and yanked the attacker to his feet, Hardy moved in and placed a comforting hand on the young P C's shoulder.

Are you really OK?" he asked, with genuine concern in his voice.

Constable Grant nodded and smiled. "I could do with some water though," she pointed behind her, "I kind of lost my lunch back there and it's left a nasty taste in my mouth."

One of her colleagues who overheard her conversation handed her a bottle of water which she accepted gratefully.

Hardy waited behind whilst she gargled away from the

immediate vicinity, whilst the rest of the team bundled the perpetrator back across the park towards the main gate.

Once PC Grant was ready, she walked over to Join the DI.

"Where's everyone go?" she asked, surprised that they appeared to have been abandoned.

"They're taking your new friend back to the station. Come on," he said, smiling, "you'll want to be there when he's charged, it was your collar."

As they began to move off, Hardy suddenly stopped in his tracks and looked back in the direction he had originally come from.

"What's up?" his companion asked, squinting into the darkness to see if she could ascertain exactly what he was looking at.

After a moment, Hardy replied. "It's nothing, I just dropped my radio when I was running over here, never mind," he turned back to the PC, "just more bloody paperwork."

The constable smiled and grabbed him by the arm. "Come on," she ushered him towards the area he had indicated. "I've got a torch; I'll bet we find it in no time."

Hardy was about to object, but before he had a chance to, he was pulled along by his enthusiastic junior.

They made their way back across the park. PC Grant took out her pencil torch from her inside jacket pocket and began to scan the ground in an arc in front of where they were walking.

They could both hear static and the occasional word or two coming from PC Grant's handset. At one point, Hardy was positive that he could make out Pamela's voice, but he chose to ignore it and continue with their search instead.

The wind started to pick up pace as they trudged through the vast expanse of trees and bushes which enclosed the park. On a couple of occasions, they both saw what they thought might be Hardy's hand-set, but in both cases, it turned out to be nothing more than a loose branch poking up through the greenery.

Eventually, Hardy had had enough. "Come on," he said, trying not to sound ungrateful, "this is a waste of time, let's go back."

"Quitter," chided his young colleague, "I'll bet if we stick at it, we'll find it in the next five minutes."

Hardy sighed, resignedly. "OK, five more minutes, then it's back to the station to a mountain of paperwork and a bollocking from you-know-who."

PC Grant chuckled, and they continued to scan the ground.

Neither of them were aware of the Creeper lurking in the bushes until they were virtually upon it.

At the sound of it closing in on them, PC Grant raised the beam of her torch and shone it directly in the Creeper's face.

The Creeper held up its hands to shield its eyes from the light.

For a moment Hardy was stunned into shock at the sight before them. But then the sound of his junior officer screaming brought him out of his reverie.

As the Creeper advanced on them, Hardy shoved the young PC out of the way.

"Run!" he screamed at her, just as the Creeper reached him and grabbed him by the lapels of his jacket.

Hardy felt himself being hoisted into the air, but before he had a chance to retaliate the Creeper threw him into the bushes off to one side.

Constable Grant stood frozen to the spot.

Her senior officer's command to run had come too late as she found herself unable to move.

She stared up at the hideous visage of the approaching Creeper.

In the beam from her torch the young PC could see it's gaping maw with its razor-sharp pointed teeth, and slobbering tongue lolling out over its bottom lip.

Its eyes were large and menacing and the constable could see that its stare directed straight at her.

Without realising it, she lifted her handset to her mouth and depressed the button on the side.

A few mumbled words beseeching her colleagues for help spilled out before the Creeper reached out its hand and clamped it around the officer's neck.

As the Creeper's talon-like claws began to tighten its grip the young PC could feel her windpipe starting to close.

Within second she could no longer take in a breath, and she could feel her entire body going limp and unresponsive.

Instinctively she reached up and grabbed hold of the Creeper's wrist with both hands and tried to prise it away from her, but her attempts seemed futile as the strength ebbed from her body and she felt her senses starting to close down.

From out of nowhere, Hardy flew at the Creeper hitting it at waist height with a rugby tackle putting his full weight behind it.

Although Hardy's effort did not manage to bring the Creeper down, the impact from the charge at least caused it to release its hold on the young constable, leaving her limp body to fall to the ground in a crumpled heap.

Hardy felt a sharp pain emanate from his shoulder where he had crashed into the Creeper. The throbbing immediately swept its way down his spine causing his legs to buckle underneath him.

Before Hardy's body had hit the floor, the Creeper bent down and caught him, and then it scooped him up off the ground. This time it held him above its head with its massive arms at full stretch.

The Creeper kept Hardy at arm's length for what seemed to him an eternity, before it finally hurled him through the air and sent him crashing into a tree, which was some twenty feet in front of them.

Hardy hit the tree with such force that just before he passed out, he was sure that he felt his spine snap.

CHAPTER THIRTY-FOUR

When Hardy awoke, he found himself in a hospital bed. There was a middle-aged black nurse checking charts at the foot of his bed, and when she realised that he had opened his eyes she smiled at him showing off a perfect set of pure white teeth.

"Welcome back, darlin'" she announced, cheerfully, "we was gettin' worried about you."

Hardy tried to sit up, but as soon as he placed his weight on the bed to lift himself his back went into a spasm and he slumped back down.

"No, no, you mustn't try that me darlin'" the nurse ran around the bed and stood beside him. "Doctor says that you might 'ave some spinal bruisin', she's given you something for the pain and they're going to send you for an MRI in the mornin'"

The nurse pulled his bed sheet up around Hardy's upper torso, leaving his arms out on top of it. There was also a light blanket which had been folded back so that it only covered the bottom of his bed, and even though he was only wearing a hospital gown which did not feel to him as if it had been fastened properly at the back, he was still very warm.

The nurse busied herself checking the machines monitoring Hardy's pulse and heartbeat while singing merrily to herself as she worked.

When she was satisfied that he had not dislodged any of the wires in his haste to move, she placed her meaty fists on her hips and looked down at him.

"Now then," she said with a sly wink, "your young lady has been waiting outside ever since you came in."

The nurse was obviously not concerned by the way Hardy's brow furrowed at her announcement. With a broad grin still on her face she went and opened the door which led out into the corridor and Hardy could hear her telling someone that they could come in now.

Hardy turned his head to face the door and he was both shocked and happily surprised when PC Grant entered the room.

She was still dressed in the same clothes she had worn for the stake-out, except that she had removed her bomber jacket and jumper and was now only wearing a black cap-sleeved T-shirt. She had tied her hair back in a ponytail and Hardy could tell from her smudged mascara that she had obviously been crying.

She had managed to wipe some of it away, but in doing so she had spread it around her eyes.

It made her look a bit like a Goth-girl, which just seemed to enhance her overall attractiveness.

The young PC walked up to Hardy's bedside and grabbed his hand.

"How're you feeling?" she asked, with genuine concern in her voice.

Hardy tried to sit up, then immediately thought better of it.

"Sore," he answered, "what happened, it's all a bit hazy?"

Before the PC had a chance to answer, the nurse slid a chair over to where the female officer was standing to allow her to get more comfortable. PC Grant accepted it, gratefully.

"Now I've got some more of my rounds to make," the nurse announced to both of them, "so I'll be back a little later to see to your blanket bath."

She nodded towards the bowl of water and the flannel that were sitting on the table at the far end of the room.

"Unless you want to save me the bother," she nudged the young PC with her elbow and smiled at her.

Hardy could feel his face flush, but PC Grant merely burst out laughing.

She did have an incredibly infectious laugh, Hardy thought to himself.

Once the nurse had left the room PC Grant squeezed Hardy's hand and lifted it to her lips to kiss his finger.

"You saved my life, that's what happened." She answered his earlier question with a smile.

Hardy looked perplexed. "I remember us walking through the park," he ventured, "and then did someone attack us?"

PC Grant nodded. "Someone, or something! Don't you remember what it looked like?" she was obviously astounded that Hardy could not remember the Creeper leaping out at them from the shadows.

The DI thought for a moment. "I remember that it was big, very big now I think of it."

"And the rest," the young constable added for him. "It was gigantic, with huge great arms and vicious-looking eyes, it tried to kill me!"

The vagueness of his recollection began to clear and suddenly Hardy could see the monstrous form of the Creeper looming before him.

"That's right!" he announced, feeling as if had had a breakthrough. "It was holding you up, trying to strangle you."

"Succeeding," the PC corrected him, "and then my hero charged forward and saved me."

Hardy blushed again but pretended that he had not realised.

He was very conscious of the fact that his junior officer was still holding his hand with her tender fingers.

"So, what happened next?" he asked, "it's all a blank after that."

"Well I was still half out of it myself while I was on the ground, but just as the thing threw you against that tree, I could hear shouting as the rest of the team came running."

Hardy nodded. "So, what happened to the thing that attacked us?"

The young PC shrugged. "As soon as it heard the commotion and saw the torches approaching it ran off, they're probably still looking for it now. I left them all there and rode with you in the ambulance."

Forgetting his condition, Hardy tried once more to rise, but the pain kicked in straightaway, so he relaxed his posture.

"Take it easy," PC Grant advised, "you heard what the nurse said."

Hardy knew not to argue.

Then another thought came to him. "What about that other bloke who attacked you earlier, the one you cuffed?"

"Oh, yes I almost forgot, turns out he was just some creep who had been recently released from a seven year stretch for rape."

"Well, I hope he liked the food in there because he's going straight back," offered Hardy.

They both laughed together, although Hardy winced with the effort.

The young PC stood up and let go of Hardy's hand.

"Right then," she announced, matter-of-factly, "let's get you bathed and then you can try and have a good night's sleep."

The shock of her statement hit Hardy like a blast of cold water straight in the face.

"What!" he exclaimed, still unable to comprehend what she had said.

"Constable Grant, I take it you're joking?"

He tried to sound stern and authoritative, but it did not work.

Hardy watched as the young PC strolled over to the table and came back carrying the basin of water with the flannel draped over her wrist.

The pair of them looked at each other as if each were waiting for the other to speak first.

The PC placed the basin on top of her chair and started to soak the flannel in the warm water.

"Police Constable Grant," Hardy squeaked, and then cleared his throat before continuing. "You will cease this operation immediately."

The PC ignored his words as if she knew that she had total control over him, and he could do nothing whatsoever about it.

"It's Patience, by the way," she answered, holding the dripping wet flannel above the basin, and squeezing it to let the excess water splash back down into it.

"What is?" Hardy asked, staring at the wet flannel in her hand as if it were a sharp knife which he was afraid she was going to use on him.

"My name is Patience, but most of my friends call me Patti."

With that, Patti pulled back Hardy's top sheet and fondled with his gown until she managed to slide the wet flannel under it.

Hardy took in an involuntary gasp of air as the soft moist fabric touched his skin.

Before he could object any further, Patti began to glide the soothing fabric over his skin, working it in small circles to catch any dribbles which might escape.

Once she had finished with his upper torso, she dipped the flannel back in the water and squeezed it off.

This time she grabbed hold of Hardy's gown and lifted it back to allow her access to his lower belly area.

"Whoa there!" Hardy called out in surprise, but Patti ignored his protest and continued with her task.

As she reached lower with the cloth, Hardy could feel himself starting to grow hard. Although Patti pretended to ignore it, he knew that she could see the bulge in his gown rising and he needed her to stop before she went too far.

But he had to admit, at least to himself, that part of him did not want her to stop!

As Patti swept the flannel along the underside of Hardy's belly button, her hand brushed against the swollen tip of his penis.

Hardy gasped, and he could see a sly smile starting to creep across Patti's face. Even though she continued to concentrate on what she was doing rather than

look at him, Hardy knew that she was touching him there on purpose, and he felt himself about to pass the point of no return.

He watched, tentatively, as Patti placed the flannel back in the water for a third time and begin to wring it out.

The inspector knew full well that if he allowed her to continue that there was only one place that she intended cleaning next.

As she turned to face him once again with the flannel in her hand, Hardy knew that he had to speak up. "PC Grant," he began.

Patti looked down at him.

A frown now replaced her smile. "What's my name?" she demanded, sternly.

Hardy felt himself about to lose the argument.

"Patti," he whispered.

Patti smiled. "Good, that's better," she replied, and immediate returned to the job at hand.

Biting her bottom lip, Patti slipped her hand, draped in the wet flannel, down between Hardy's legs and gently began to massage his testicles.

A wicked grin replaced her frown as Hardy began to whimper as she rubbed him gently, up and down. She could feel him trying to part his legs as she continued with her massage, but it was obvious to her that the discomfort that the movement caused him made it virtually impossible for him to comply.

After a moment Patti slipped her hand up along the underside of Hardy's erection, and she gently but firmly began to stroke him.

Hardy moaned even louder this time, unable to keep his voice under control.

Patti stared down at him and winked. "I think this bad boy wants to come out and play, what do you think, Inspector?" she purred, seductively.

Hardy had lost all feeling in his body by this point, and all he could concentrate on was Patti bringing him up to orgasm.

Patti kept the rhythm going at a steady pace.

She could tell from Hardy's facial expression that he was about to come, so she bent down and pressed her lips against his. Hardy responded immediately, and together their tongues entwined for the final few seconds before Hardy exploded into the wet flannel in Patti's hand.

Hardy sucked in a huge lungful of air which he allowed to escape slowly as Patti continued to work him more slowly this time, ensuring that he was full spent.

Afterwards, she removed the flannel and scrubbed it with both hands vigorously in the water, before using it once more, this time to clean away any remnants of Hardy's ejaculation which might have escaped the cloth.

When she was satisfied that Hardy was completely clean, Patti dumped the flannel back in the basin and dried her hands on the towel the nurse had left on the little table.

She bent down and the two of them shared a passionate kiss, neither one of them holding back.

When they parted, Hardy looked up at Patti with a broad smile on his face.

"You know," he said, "you really need to learn to take orders from your superior officer."

They held each other's gaze for a few seconds and then they both started to laugh.

CHAPTER THIRTY-FIVE

Pamela sat at her desk with her head in her hands.

The evening's operation had not gone the way that she had hoped it would, and as far as she was concerned her team had let her down.

Especially Hardy and PC Grant!

When Pamela had first received the message that they had caught the killer, she contacted the superintendent to give him the good news.

He in turn passed the details on up the command chain, with all the praise and kudos for the operation going to Pamela.

She was on such a high as she watched the team bundle the suspect into the back of the van that she was even willing at that point to ignore Hardy's disobedience and let the incident pass.

Then came the call form the PC Grant that she and Hardy were under attack.

It soon became very clear to those in attendance that the real killer they had been hoping to arrest was in fact the second attacker, not the first who was now safely on his way to the station.

Naturally, they did not manage to arrest the real culprit, which would have been too much to ask for.

So, then Pamela had the embarrassing task of calling Carlisle back to apologise for her earlier premature haste in contacting him before being fully aware of the facts.

Carlisle, for his part, made sure that Pamela was under no illusion that any backlash he would subsequently receive now that he had to re-contact those above him with the unfortunate news, would rebound back on her ten-fold.

In the space of that conversation Pamela could feel her promotion prospects ebbing away.

The thing that made it even worse was that because of Hardy's condition she could not even chew him out for the blunder.

But that would come!

Oh yes, Pamela consoled herself that she would make sure that Hardy received the full weight of a senior officer's reprimand for insubordination before she was finished with him.

Added to that, as far as she was concerned PC Grant had also had her part to play in Pamela's disgrace, and she was going to find herself back on traffic duty by the morning.

Pamela glared down at the file belonging to Colin Brent, the toerag who had attacked PC Grant in the park. Granted, it was still a good collar, but if only he had not been there tonight, they might have managed to apprehend the real killer.

Wasters like Brent always reoffended sooner or later so it would only have been a matter of time before he was caught.

But he was not the prize that Pamela had wanted.

Of all the rotten luck.

Pamela shoved his file across the desk and pushed back her chair as she stood up. She wandered out into the deserted incident room. After spending over an hour searching the park and surrounding area for the real killer, Pamela called off the hunt.

It was almost as if the perpetrator had disappeared into the night without a trace.

After that, she sent everyone else home. She needed some alone time, plus she was not about to continue paying the overtime bill for an operation that had already failed.

Pamela noticed a newspaper poking out from under a pile of papers on one of the desks. As she had not had time that day to read it, she prised it out, being careful not to topple the pile.

Typically, it was the local paper, and there on the front cover was a story by Cyril Carney covering the discovery of Jack Soames' body the previous night. Or at least, it was his made-up version of events.

Pamela leaned against the desk and began to read the story, but after a while the inaccuracy of the details just started to make her feel even more frustrated.

Carney had not spared her either, claiming that her superiors were considering replacing her because she had not proved to be the hotshot detective they had hoped for.

Well that may not have been true or accurate this morning when the paper was printed, but now it might well be a different story.

In anger Pamela scrunched up the paper and threw it at the nearest bin. It missed its target, hit the corner edge of the metal receptacle, and bounced onto the floor.

She left it there for the cleaners to retrieve in the morning.

Pamela turned to go back into her office when the map on the incident board caught her attention.

The multicoloured pins showing all the pertinent points of interest thus far during the investigation stared back at her as if challenging her to discover their hidden clues.

She walked over to the board and stared at each of them in

turn, checking the key chart at the side of the board listing what each pin stood for.

There was no distinct pattern to observe, no obvious blueprint which sang out to her as she surveyed the board.

At the police training college Pamela took a couple of seminars from a professor of criminology from some prestigious university in America, and she always remembered his assertion that with any series of attacks there was always a pattern which, if you could find it, would lead you to the culprit.

She wished that he was here with her now so that she could ram his know-it-all face into the board and demand that he showed her the pattern that was eluding her, right now.

The more she gazed at the pins, the more sporadic and random they appeared.

Suddenly, something caught her eye on the map.

She moved in for a closer look as the image was barely perceptible to the naked eye because of where the map had been folded when in storage.

Pamela squinted at the spot, which looked to all intents and purposes like a brown smudge on the paper as if someone had been careless with a piece of chocolate when setting it up on the wall.

It took her a moment to focus on the words beneath the distorted blotch.

St Luke's Church.

Pamela did not remember seeing the church when she visited the area, and to the best of her memory she could not recall anyone mentioning it to her either.

She wondered if perhaps it was derelict or abandoned, which would explain why no one had seen fit to bring it up in conversation.

She headed over to the desk which presently housed all the witness statements taken since the investigation began.

She thumbed through each one taking note of the address of the witness on the top left-hand corner.

Pamela flicked through the pile twice, just to make sure.

There was definitely no witness statement taken from anyone at the church.

Puzzled, she walked back over to the map for another look.

To be fair, the church was not exactly in the middle of the attacks and locations where the victims had been found, but in her mind, it was close enough in proximity to warrant a visit.

Pamela bit her bottom lip in frustration.

The chances were that it would lead to nothing, just like the rest of their investigation to date, but she was peeved by the fact that no one had bothered to check it out before now.

At least then when she made her report tomorrow, she could emphatically state that all leads had been followed through.

Pamela looked at her wristwatch; it was a little after 10 p.m.

Too late now to go waking up some member of the clergy who would probably repay the interruption to their sleep by making a formal complaint in the morning.

Even so, the situation at least justified a drive past on her way back to her hotel.

As Pamela exited the station the officer on duty was busy dealing with an excitable couple who were carrying on about being ripped off at a local club, so she did not bother to acknowledge him as she left.

Pamela did not fancy walking through the park at this hour to try and find the church, so instead she drove around the back of the park and found a dirt road through the woods which led to the back entrance to St Luke's.

The old church was mainly cast in shadow due to the fact

that the majority of uplighters surrounding it were either fused or broken.

Pamela stayed in her car and gazed out of the window, still hoping for some sign of life from inside, but there was none.

She could not understand why it was that none of the officers on her team had covered this location as part of the investigation. But she was going to demand some answers the following morning that was for sure.

Just as she was about to leave, she saw a sliver of light coming from behind the first set of railings off to one side.

Pamela held her hand over her eyes to try and get a better view, but it was too dark and cloudy to make out anything specific.

Thinking that this might be too good an opportunity to miss, Pamela leapt out of her car and walked over to where the light was emanating from.

Her high heels on the soft mud made her advance slow and awkward, but she managed to reach the gate which led to the small garden behind the church before the light was extinguished.

Through the bars Pamela could see the form of an old priest as he placed a large black plastic bag outside the door.

"Hello," she called, waving frantically in the hope that he would at least see her even if he could not hear her from this distance.

The priest looked up and squinted in the dim light towards where Pamela was standing.

"May I help you?" he asked, in a kind, sincere voice.

Pamela pulled out her warrant card and held it up, even though she knew that there was no way the old man could see her details from such a distance.

"Sorry to bother you," she announced, "I am DCI Holmsley, county police, I realise that it is late, but I was wondering if you could spare me a few minutes."

Father Grace made his way carefully down the stone steps which led to the garden. As he approached the gate, he took out a large metal key from the pocket in his cassock.

Pamela kept holding her ID up, trying to manoeuvre it into the light for the priest to see. But by now he seemed unconcerned with her identification, and he did not even look up as he concentrated on making the key work in the lock.

The old iron gate creaked open on rusty hinges.

Father Grace stood back. "Would you care to come in?" he asked, smiling, "it's much warmer inside, and brighter."

Pamela accepted his hospitality and walked past him towards the door from which he had emerged.

She waited at the bottom of the steps for the old priest to lead the way in and followed him through the arched wooden door which he locked behind them.

Once inside, Father Grace took Pamela into the kitchen.

He was right about it being a good deal warmer inside, although the overhead bulbs were obviously of low wattage, which gave the room an eerie glow which initially made Pamela shiver, involuntarily.

"Please sit down and make yourself comfortable," the priest offered, signalling to the large oak table with several sturdy-looking wooden chairs placed around it, in the middle of the room.

Pamela smiled her thanks and took her seat.

"I was just about to make some tea," announced the old priest, "could I tempt you to a cup?"

"Oh, no, thank you," replied Pamela, "I don't want to put you to any trouble."

Father Grace smiled broadly. "It's no trouble I can assure you, in fact, I would be grateful for the company."

"In that case, thank you, I will."

The priest busied himself filling the kettle and placing it on the hob.

As he worked, he hummed a tune which made Pamela feel as if she did not want to disturb him with questions until he was ready to come and sit down.

She gazed around the room, taking in the abeyance.

When Father Grace returned to the table he was carrying a large dish which he placed in front of her. He whipped off the cover to display a half-eaten chocolate gateau which made Pamela's mouth water.

She had missed dinner due to the stake-out, so she had not eaten since midday. Not that food had been the first thing on her mind. But having been presented with such a delicious-looking cake suddenly made her ravenous.

"You will have a slice, won't you?" asked the priest, almost pleadingly. "Even if it is just to stop me feeling guilty."

Pamela grinned. "Go on then, you've talked me into it."

Father Grace produced a couple of plates from a large Welsh dresser at the far end of the room and brought them over along with some forks and napkins.

He cut a huge slice for Pamela, ignoring her somewhat mediocre protest.

When the kettle started whistling, he went back to the stove to retrieve it.

While he prepared their tea, he turned slightly so as not to give offence and asked. "So how may I help you, officer?"

Pamela had just shoved a large wedge of cake into her mouth, so she held a hand up to it while she tried to answer.

"I presume...that you've heard of these...attacks that have taken place recently...around this area?" she caught a few crumbs as they shot out of her mouth and placed them back on her plate.

"Oh yes, some of my parishioners were discussing them the other day, terrible business." The priest began to take out cups and saucers, and he took down a large colourful tin from the top shelf.

"Well," continued Pamela, "I was wondering if you had seen or heard anything unusual at all. It appears that we have neglected to come and speak to you sooner, when in fact you are situated almost slap bang in the middle of everything."

Father Grace spooned some of the contents from the tin into a teapot, then closed the lid and replaced it back on its shelf.

"No, I'm afraid I haven't," he responded, keeping his back to his visitor as he continued preparing the tea.

Pamela looked around her. "This must be a very old church?" she observed, casually. "When was it built?"

Father Grace carried over the teapot and accompanying accoutrements on a large wooden tray with knurled handles and placed them on the table. "Well," he began, "our original records date right back to the 7th century," he announced, proudly as he began to pour the tea through a silver strainer.

"Really!" exclaimed Pamela, genuinely surprised, "I had no idea it went back that far."

She accepted her cup of tea gratefully, adding milk and sugar from the containers on the tray.

As she stirred the brew, she asked, "I suspect that during the reformation many priests would have hidden out here to avoid the king's men?"

"Oh yes," agreed the priest, "I believe that over the years we were used as quite the bolthole."

Pamela blew gently on the surface of her tea and then drank it all in one go.

"My, you certainly needed that," remarked the priest.

Pamela replaced her cup in its saucer and wiped her mouth

with the back of her hand. "Yes," she agreed, "I didn't realise how parched I was."

Father Grace blew on his tea and then took a few swallows before putting his cup down.

"You'll have another cup?" he asked, expectantly.

"Yes, please," replied Pamela, "that was absolutely lovely."

Father Grace stood up and lifted the teapot from the table. "This only holds a few cups," he indicated to the pot by lifting it slightly, "I'll make a fresh one."

"Oh no, please, not on my account," Pamela protested, but the priest just smiled and continued with his task.

As the fresh water boiled, Pamela enquired. "What you were saying earlier about your church being used to hide priests all those years ago, I suppose that means that there must be some kind of cavern or crypt underground?"

Father Grace dropped the lid of the teapot on the counter.

He grabbed it up, immediately. "Oh, how clumsy of me," he stammered, "Yes, yes, indeed I believe that there is some kind of a tunnel formation below the main floor. I was warned when I first arrived here not to attempt to access it as the ground is very uneven and there is no lighting down there."

From where she sat, Pamela could not see that the priest's hands were shaking as he spoke.

"I see," replied Pamela, "well I was wondering if you'd mind if we searched them, just to be on the safe side."

Father Grace turned around. "Search them, I don't understand, for what plausible reason?" He barely succeeded in keeping the tremor out of his voice.

Pamela paused with her fork just in front of her mouth.

"Oh, it's just for the sake of formality, Father. We must show that we have exhausted every avenue, and if this killer somehow managed to find a secret entrance to your crypt, he might be hiding out in there without your knowledge."

As the kettle began to whistle once more, the old priest turned back to his task.

"I see," he replied, nervously, "and do you want to search it now, only I'm not sure that I have a working torch to hand?"

Pamela laughed, almost spraying more cake crumbs from her mouth.

"No, Father, not tonight," she assured him, "I'll have to arrange a proper search in the morning and bring in some uniformed constables for the task."

"Oh, I see," the priest muttered, nervously, "and there was me thinking you had a team waiting outside in a van."

Pamela swallowed her mouthful of cake. "Nothing so organised, Father, in fact, I was on my way home when I suddenly thought of driving by here, to be honest I didn't think you'd still be up."

"Yes, I am a bit of a night owl I suppose." Father Grace muttered, under his breath.

With his back to her, Pamela did not see the priest reach down under the counter and bring out a small silver jar with a screw-top lid.

He opened the jar and spooned out some of the contents into the teapot before pouring the boiling water.

He stirred it vigorously, making sure that the contents of the silver jar mixed in with the tea leaves already in the pot to form an overall uniform brown colour.

Once he was satisfied, the priest carried over the teapot and poured Pamela a fresh cup.

She thanked him, and as she started to add her own milk and sugar, Father Grace announced. "I'm so sorry, please excuse me for a moment but I think I might have left the main door unlocked. I shan't be long."

As the priest shuffled out of the kitchen, Pamela finished the last two mouthfuls of her gateaux. It was definitely one of the tastiest cakes she had ever eaten, and although she was tempted to ask if she could have another small slice, she decided to resist the temptation and just enjoy her tea.

She stirred the contents of her cup once more, and then blew on it before taking her first sip.

Her tea tasted slightly bitter this time, but she put that down to the fact that she had just eaten the cake.

Pamela added another half spoon of sugar, just to make sure.

When Father Grace returned a few minutes later, he sat down and started to drink his tea.

"That must be cold by now, Father," Pamela observed, "would you like a fresh one from the pot?" With that, she lifted the teapot as if she were about to refill his cup.

"No, no," the priest replied, hastily, "it's fine, thank you, I like it like this, can't take hot drinks like I used to." He smiled over his cup as he poured the tepid liquid down his throat.

Pamela took another sip of hers.

It definitely had a bitter aftertaste, even with the added sugar.

Either way, she decided not to make a fuss over it and appear ungrateful, so she took another couple of gulps, leaving just a trickle in the bottom of the cup.

Bitter or not, it was certainly warming her insides, she thought to herself.

She would certainly sleep well tonight.

The mere thought of her warm, comfortable bed back at the hotel made her yawn, involuntarily.

Pamela put her hand to her mouth. "Oh, pardon me," she said, apologetically.

"It looks like you need your bed, Chief Inspector," the priest observed.

Pamela nodded in agreement. "Yes, I think you're right,"

she managed to stifle another yawn. "But before I go, could we fix a time for me to come back tomorrow with my team?"

Father Grace smiled and nodded. "Of course, morning service is usually over by nine, so shall we say nine thirty, just to be on the safe side?"

Pamela lifted her arms to stretch out her sudden fatigue.

She found the movement awkward and uncomfortable.

In the distance she thought that she could hear a heavy door creak open, but she felt too disorientated to be sure. She needed her bed.

"These killings must be awful for the victim's families," the priest offered, sympathetically. "I can't imagine anything worse than losing one's own child, I couldn't bear the thought of losing mine."

Although Pamela had not been concentrating fully on the priest's words, she felt sure that she had misheard him.

"I'm sorry, Father, I'm afraid I might have drifted off for a moment, I thought that you said you'd hate to lose your child," she almost laughed at her own misinterpretation, but her jaw was starting to feel heavy.

"That's quite right," Father Grace confirmed, "I did say my child."

Pamela looked up at him in astonishment.

She was no expert on the Catholic Church, but she felt sure that priests were supposed to be celibate.

She half-opened her mouth to ask a question, but the effort appeared too much for her to manage at the moment.

Once again, Pamela was sure that she could hear something happening outside the kitchen in the main building.

It sounded a bit like heavy furniture being dragged across the floor.

Or was she imagining it, as she felt she was imagining this surreal conversation?

The old priest smiled warmly and reached across the table to pat her hand.

"It's quite all right," he assured her, "I appreciate that it is a little hard to take in at first." He sat back in his chair and toyed with his empty cup.

Outside there came another noise, much like the last one, only this time it definitely sounded to Pamela as if it were growing louder.

She needed to say something!

Whether it was to draw the priest's attention to the noise, or just ask him exactly what he meant about him having a child.

But the more her mind raced, thinking up questions, the more her body resisted the effort to ask them.

Without prompting, the priest continued. "I was on missionary work in Africa when I was a novice. There were a group of us, young future priests and nuns, keen and eager to spread the good word and to do god's holy work. Of course, the local tribal doctors did not take kindly to us administering western medicines, they felt as if we were interfering in their tribal practices."

He leaned back in his chair. "Some of them actually put a curse on us, but we had god to protect us, so we were not afraid."

For a moment he gazed straight into space as if he had forgotten that he had an audience in front of him.

"One night, a young nun and I travelled to a nearby village to see about the possibility of setting up a church in the vicinity. What we didn't know was that the tribal doctors had arranged to have something slipped into our water bottles, and by the time we arrived both of us had been affected by their potion."

Father Grace stood up, letting his wooden chair scrape against the cold stone floor.

He walked over to the kitchen window and reshuffled the

curtains, ensuring that they were completely closed. He over-lapped the heavy drapes in the middle just to be sure.

"To be honest," he continued, "neither the novice nun nor I were fully aware of what happened next. The potion we had been given was a very powerful aphrodisiac, which also had the side effects of lowering our inhibitions as well as blocking our capacity to remember what happened whilst we were under its influence."

The old priest moved slowly back to his chair.

By now, Pamela could not feel any sensation whatsoever in her limbs.

It was as if she were completely paralysed.

She strained, trying to make even the smallest of gestures but her body refused to respond to her mind.

Even her eyes remained wide open, unable to blink.

Just then, she heard another noise, this one sounded as if it came from directly outside the kitchen door, but she found it impossible to turn her head to see what the cause might be.

Father Grace slumped back down in his seat.

The expression on his face conveyed to Pamela that he was carrying a heavy burden, one which he appeared unable to share.

"When we awoke the next morning," he continued, "we were both horrified to find ourselves naked and in each other's arms."

Tears began to trickle down the priest's craggy features as his eyes stared off once more into the vast yonder.

"We both prayed for forgiveness, naturally," he wiped his eyes with the back of his hand, smearing his tears across his cheeks. "But soon after it became apparent that she was preg-nant, and we both knew that we had broken one of god's most fervent laws and as a result we were no longer worthy of his protection and comfort."

Father Grace removed a handkerchief from his cassock pocket and blew his nose, hard. "Before the young nun started to show through her habit, we took ourselves away where the others could not find us. We travelled to another remote location under the guise of searching for more souls to save, and that was where she finally gave birth."

He folded the hanky and replaced it in his pocket.

His glazed eyes stared directly into Pamela's.

"The baby emerged sideways from his poor mother," he continued, forcing his voice to remain steady and not succumb to another flood of tears.

"The local doctors attempted a caesarean, but the baby would not wait. He literally clawed his way out of her womb, killing her in the process due to the enormous amount of blood she lost." He stood up, abruptly. "Blood which he then started to lick at and drink, but it wasn't his fault you understand, he had been brought into this world as a result of a mortal sin and so he was our punishment for what we had done."

The priest moved slowly towards Pamela until he was standing by her side.

"I managed to smuggle him home on a cargo ship in a crate marked as religious artefacts," he laughed to himself. "Things were so much easier in those days; no one ever questioned a member of the church. Now everyone is so suspicious."

He patted Pamela gently on the shoulder, although she was unaware of the action due to her present lack of sensation.

Father Grace cleared his throat, obviously still choking back the tears.

"At first," he continued, "I took him to live with my sister; she has a remote farmhouse where the nearest neighbour is miles away. But after a while, as he grew older, his appetites grew more, shall we say, unsavoury? So, in the end I had to bring him back here with me. After all, he was my punishment to bear, not here."

The old priest cleared his throat once more, evidently determined not to allow himself to become choked-up again.

"But what child is a punishment for its parents?" he asked, rhetorically. "All children are a blessing, regardless of how they came to be."

Pamela was acutely aware that something had entered the kitchen from the door behind her. Although she was unable to turn her head to see, she could sense that there was a presence hovering directly at her back.

"Have you heard what they've been calling him in the newspapers?" asked the priest, aware that Pamela was unable to answer. "The Mutilator, I ask you, how utterly disgusting. He's nothing of the sort, he's just my son."

From her position, Pamela was suddenly conscious of a shadow moving around from her left side, past the old priest, eventually entering her limited field of vision.

As she beheld the sight of the Creeper towering over her, with its massive frame, talon-like claws, and razor-sharp teeth, she tried desperately to force out the scream which was lodged in her throat.

But no sound would come!

"Chief Inspector," announced the priest, with a certain amount of undisguised pride. "I would like you to meet my son, Eric."

EPILOGUE

Hardy pulled his car onto the driveway and climbed out of the air-conditioned vehicle into the scorching summer sun. The forecast for July had promised one of the hottest on record and by the look of things, they were not kidding.

He could immediately feel perspiration starting to trickle down the inside of his shirt as he made his way to the front door.

A drink and a shower in that order were the order of the evening, he decided.

It had been almost nine months since the disappearance of DCI Holmsley, and still they were no closer to discovering what had happened to her than they were on the first day of the investigation.

Her car had been found abandoned on the outskirts of Monk's Wood with her mobile phone and shoes on the driver's seat.

With the team already stretched to breaking point with the ongoing investigation, Superintendent Carlisle had drafted in backup from Serious Crimes, but after three months with no new leads they had to be reassigned.

The one and only spark of good news was that the killings seemed to have stopped after Jack Soames' body was found.

Although they knew that the killer was still at large, there was an unspoken wish amongst the team that he—or whatever it was that had attacked him and Patti that night—had moved out of the area and become someone else's problem now.

As he opened the front door, he heard the welcoming sound of Patti calling to him from upstairs. "Hi, darling, can you come upstairs and help me for a moment."

Oh terrific, thought Hardy. The hottest day of the year and she decides to spend her day off doing DIY.

As he climbed the stairs, Hardy envisioned Patti in those overalls she insisted on wearing whenever she decided to embark on another household project.

He certainly had to admire her enthusiasm, personally he detested any form of decorating, and as for self-assembly furniture—forget it!

If there were three words in the English language which never failed to cause a shiver to run up his spine, they were 'Easy Home Assembly'.

Hardy slung his jacket over the banister and began to remove his tie as he entered the bedroom.

To his surprise, Patti was lying on top of the bed wearing a stunning navy-blue negligee and a huge grin.

"Whaddya think?" she asked, winking at him, seductively.

Hardy let out a long whistle through his teeth. "I think," he replied, smiling, "that I wish I wasn't so sweaty and horrible, I really need a shower," he admitted.

Patti rolled over and crawled towards the end of the bed towards him.

He pointed her index finger and signalled for him to come to her.

Hardy complied, without objection.

Once he was near enough, Patti grabbed hold of the waist-band of his trousers and pulled him right up to her.

"What's the point of a shower when you're only going to get all sweaty and messy straight after?"

Hardy allowed himself to be pulled onto the bed.

Anita Price sat patiently at the far end of the bar, sipping her mineral water, and surveying the crowd inside the wine bar.

She had never been to this one before and she was relieved that the closed-circuit cameras covered the front door only.

She stared at her reflection in the mirror behind the counter.

In her short blond spiky-haired wig and tinted glasses she did not recognise herself.

Anita looked over as the door to the bar opened, she recog-nised the man who entered from the profile pictures he had sent her. She purposely did not wave or even acknowledge him as she was wary of drawing unwanted attention.

Instead, she just looked over in his direction as he scanned the mass throng until his gaze finally alighted on her.

As the man made his way over to her, Anita moved over to one of the pillars planted around the outskirts of the large room, to ensure privacy. She propped her glass on the adjacent stand and waited for the man to join her.

The man was dressed in a very expensive suit, the fabric of which appeared to Anita to be far too heavy for the stifling weather.

He was in his mid-fifties, or so he had elected to state in his profile and was a little taller than Anita had expected. He was grossly overweight, and Anita could tell that he tried to comb his hair in such a way as to hide his receding hairline.

The man stopped short just in front of Anita and held out his hand.

"Hello," he said, cheerfully, "I'm Basil Thornton, lovely to meet you."

Anita touched his hand lightly in place of a full shake and smiled sweetly.

"Janice Connors," she lied. "Do you have a car nearby?"

Basil Thornton looked shocked and a little disappointed at her request. Obviously, he knew the true reason behind their meeting, but he had hoped to at least have a glass of something refreshing before they set off.

"Ah, yes," he replied, sombrely, "it's parked in the street at the side of this place." he indicated the direction with his hands. "It's a red Mercedes."

Anita leaned in a little closer to his ear. "Well, you go outside and wait in it for me, I'm just going to the ladies, I'll be out in a minute, OK?"

Basil nodded.

He admired the departing figure of Anita as she made her way to the toilet.

She certainly had not exaggerated about her stunning figure in her profile, she was absolutely gorgeous.

Basil could feel the excitement rising in his stomach.

He wondered if he still had time for a quick drink before they left. The lady was obviously keen to get things started, and he did not want to annoy or upset her by not following her instructions. She had made it quite clear in her text that if he wanted to end up with her, he had to do whatever she told him, without question.

Basil decided that it was not worth the risk after all.

He hurried out to his car and climbed in behind the wheel to wait for his date.

Anita waited until the bathroom was empty before she readjusted her wig in the mirror. It was not the most comfortable of accessories in this heat, but a necessity nonetheless.

She checked in her bag for the can of pepper spray, and once she had located it, she removed it and put it in her left-hand jacket pocket, just in case she needed to grab it in a hurry.

She slipped out of the bar, purposely not making eye contact with any of the patrons or staff.

Once in Basil's car, Anita directed him to her house, instructing him to park up around the back.

Although her property was nestled back away from the rest of the street and surrounded by a high hedge, she still did not want to take the chance that one of her neighbours might see them entering.

Once safely inside her house, Anita offered Basil a drink and while she was pouring it, she asked, "Now you remember what I said in my text, you know what I'm into and what I expect?"

"Oh yes, certainly," Basil agreed, enthusiastically. He took out a pocket handkerchief and wiped a stream of perspiration off his forehead. "You're a lady after my own heart."

Anita nodded. "Good, you'd better follow me then."

She led him down the stairs to the basement. Once at the bottom, Anita walked to the door at the far end of the corridor and using a key she retrieved from a hook on the wall, she opened it and switched on the light before ushering Basil inside.

The overhead lights all had red bulbs which flooded the room with a pink hue which did not quite reach every corner.

In the middle of the room was a double bed completely

covered in dark red rubber sheets, with leather cuffs chained at the four corners.

Once Basil's eyes focused in the gloom a broad smile stretched across his face.

He turned to Anita and without thinking, almost leaned in close enough to kiss her. But Anita's reaction was far quicker than he had anticipated. She held up her hand to his chest and pushed him away, almost making Basil lose his balance.

"I'm not going to have any trouble from you, am I?" she demanded, pointing directly at his face with her outstretched hand.

"No, no, not at all," Basil apologised, racing to get the words out before she changed her mind. "I am so sorry, I don't know what came over me, it's probably the heat." He grovelled.

Anita remained silent for a moment, watching him from behind her tinted frames.

After a while, Basil broke the silence. "I really am most awfully sorry, please don't be cross with me," he beseeched her.

"But I am," replied Anita, in a stern tone. "Very cross, and you will have to pay for that, now strip off and get on the bed!" she demanded, planting both hands firmly on her hips.

Basil eagerly complied.

In his haste to free himself of his clothing he almost lost his balance and fell but managed to right himself in the nick of time.

Once he was completely bare, Basil slipped onto the bed.

The coolness of the rubber sheets was a blessing against his hot skin.

"Lie down and spread out your arms and legs!" Anita instructed, while she bent down and started to collect his discarded attire from the floor.

Anita placed Basil's clothes on a chair at the far end of the room, and then walked back over to the bed and began to fasten the leather cuffs around her willing victim's ankles and wrists.

She could not help but observe his excitement as she worked, but she pretended not to notice.

Anita removed a ball gag from a small pedestal beside the bed and placed the rubber ball into Basil's mouth before fastening the tight strap behind his head.

Next, she took a black scarf from the same drawer and used it to blindfold her guest, before she rechecked the straps on the leather cuffs.

Once she was satisfied that he could not move or break free, Anita walked back over to the chair and picked up Basil's clothes.

"Now stay there!" she demanded. "I will be back shortly."

Basil mumbled a compliant reply from behind the gag.

Anita exited the room leaving the door ajar. She walked to the other end of the short corridor and knocked three times on the door which led to the adjoining room.

She did not wait for an answer for the occupant inside, instead, she climbed the stairs back up to the hallway and shut the door behind her to muffle the noise.

Anita waited until it was dark before she drove Basil's car to a remote spot, ten miles outside the town.

Once there, she left Basil's clothes strewn across the back seat, along with his wallet, mobile, and car keys.

She removed the chip from the pay-as-you-go mobile which she had purchased for this operation and crunched it beneath the heel of her boot before discarding it in the undergrowth.

She then smashed the mobile against a jagged rock and threw it into the lake on the other side of the bank.

Anita walked across the field to where she had parked her own car the previous day and drove home.

Once back inside, she fixed herself a large tumbler of whiskey and downed it in one, before going to bed.

Several hours later, Anita was woken by the sound of someone making their way up the stairs. She listened to the heavy footfalls as they lurched along the landing towards her bedroom.

As the door to her room slowly swung open, in the shadowy darkness cast by the moonlight shafting in through the landing window, Anita beheld the monstrous form of the Creeper looming in her doorway.

They stared at each other for a moment, without speaking, but Anita could still hear the low guttural breathing of her night guest echoing down the corridor.

She threw back the covers revealing her nakedness.

Holding out her hand towards her visitor Anita coaxed the Creeper into entering her room, as she had done so many times before.

As the Creeper drew closer to her, Anita could see its enormous member jutting out, and she deftly used her fingers to ready herself for its invasion.

She clasped the Creeper gently with her extended hand and guided him towards her, arching her back and sucking in a deep lungful of air as she finally felt him enter her.

THE NURSE BUSIED herself taking the readings from the various monitors around Natasha Spencer's hospital bed.

The private room was beautifully decked out with bunches of fresh flowers, bowls of fruit and fluffy stuffed toys placed around it.

Natasha Spencer lay strapped to her bed. The restraints on her wrists and ankles allowed her minimum movement, but they had been placed there several months earlier at the insistence of the medical staff after Natasha's latest assault on one of their number.

Natasha's parents, especially her mother, had voiced their displeasure with such an extreme measure being imposed on their daughter, but once the chief of Psychiatry at the facility had made it clear that it was either that or they remove their daughter from his care, they backed down, albeit reluctantly.

Natasha's eyes were open and staring directly above her at the ceiling.

She was conscious, but heavily drugged to keep her from screaming and thrashing about against her restraints.

The nurse pulled back the covers and lifted Natasha's hospital gown to reveal the patient's swollen belly.

Natasha was due to give birth any day now and all the indications were that the baby had a strong heartbeat and was fully developed inside the womb.

When they first discovered that their daughter was pregnant, Gerald Spencer had demanded an immediate termination. But his wife overruled him.

Although she appreciated her husband's concern that the father of the child could well be their daughter's attacker, Hilary Spencer argued that it would still be their grandchild, regardless.

Furthermore, she had every confidence that Natasha would eventually overcome the trauma of her ordeal and return to them, and when she did, they could present her with her beautiful baby and more importantly, a positive reason to carry on.

The nurse looked up from her work as the door to the room opened.

She smiled when she saw Hilary Spencer enter the room carrying a big bunch of multi-coloured chrysanthemums.

Hilary ignored the nurse's greeting and merely handed her the flowers as she walked around her daughter's bed.

"Have these put in some water will you," she snapped, not bothering to wait for an answer.

The nurse dutifully took the flowers outside as requested.

Hilary placed her coat over the back of one of the chairs near the window and carried another one over to Natasha's bedside.

She sat down and held her daughter's hand as she looked for any signs of recognition or acknowledgment, but there were none.

Hilary leaned in a little closer. "Natasha, Natasha, darling, it's mummy."

But still Natasha's glassy stare remained fixed on the ceiling.

Hilary placed a hand on her daughter's belly, hoping to feel some movement from her imminent grandchild.

She immediately felt a kick, and then another straight after.

She smiled. "Your son's feeling very frisky today, darling," she stated, proudly. "It won't be long now."

Suddenly, Natasha's belly expanded as if it were being pumped with air.

Hilary Spencer instinctively snatched her hand away.

She watched in horror as her daughter's stomach continued to grow, until it appeared almost twice the size it had been when she first arrived.

Hilary shot up, knocking her chair over, and looked around frantically for a call button to summon the nurse back.

Unable to locate one, she ran out of the door and into the corridor, screaming wildly at the top of her lungs for someone to come and help her daughter.

Several doors along the corridor began to open as members of the medical staff cautiously responded to her cries.

Hilary was suddenly grabbed from behind at the elbows, by a pair of strong hands. She turned and found herself staring into the face of one of the facility's security staff.

"Now what's all the trouble about?" he asked, keeping his voice calm but authoritative, as per his training.

Half out of her mind with panic; Hilary wrenched herself free from the man's grasp and started to gesture behind him towards her daughter's room, shouting hysterically "My daughter...where's the doctor?"

Just then, a gut-wrenching scream filled the corridor.

For a split second, everyone was frozen to the spot.

Then just as quickly, the spell was broken, and Hilary was almost barged out of the way as several men and women in white attire ran past her towards Natasha's room.

Hilary immediately joined the throng, and when she reached her daughter's door, she elbowed her way through the mass of white coats, demanding to be given access to Natasha.

As she reached the side of the bed, the first thing Hilary noticed was that her daughter's belly was no longer swollen.

In fact, it was virtually as flat as it had been prior to being pregnant.

Hilary looked at her daughter's face, hoping that the scream they had all heard would at least indicate that she had finally woken from her drug-induced stupor, and was at last ready to rejoin the human race.

But to her dismay, Natasha's gaze was still fixed, unblinking, at the ceiling.

As she looked along the bed, Hilary saw that the sheets had been saturated with blood.

She held her hands up to her mouth to impede the scream that threatened to escape her lips.

Everyone seemed to be standing around without actually doing anything to assist her daughter.

Then came a voice from the other side of the bed.

"Oh my god, look?" It was the nurse who had been attending to Natasha when Hilary first entered the room.

The nurse suddenly pointed towards the end of the bed.

Everyone, including Hilary, followed the direction in which she was indicating.

They all saw the covers around Natasha's groin area starting to move.

There was something underneath the bedclothes!

One of the doctors in attendance leaned in and slowly peeled back the blood-soaked sheets from Natasha's body.

When Hilary saw her grandchild revealed, her scream mingled with those of some of the others present in the room.

Then, she mercifully passed out.

The End.

ABOUT THE AUTHOR

I have always loved horror stories, whether in literary form, on film, or being recited by a good storyteller. When I was little, I did not realise that books had been written that so closely resembled the kind of films I loved watching. My grandparents —who brought me up—were extremely religious and believed that if I was to read such literature, I would doubtless end up practising sorcery, devil-worship, cannibalism or even worse, becoming a serial killer.

In those days, horror films which had been deemed to be too scary for young minds, were shown far too late for me to stay up and watch, and of course the video recorder had not been invented, so if you missed a live showing the film may not come back on for another year, or even longer. Therefore, it was mainly thanks to my older cousin Maria that I was ever allowed to see such creations as Dracula, Frankenstein, the Wolfman, and the Creature from the Black lagoon. Whenever Maria stayed over, she would charm my grandmother into letting me stay up with her, with the promise that if the film became too scary, she would put me to bed—which bless her, she never did.

My real love of horror fiction started with the old Pan books of horror, a regular anthology series which ran for many years during my formative years. From there I graduated to full-size novels and became an ardent fan of authors such as: James Herbert, Guy N. Smith, Shaun Hutson, and later, Stephen King and Richard Laymon. I found it so easy to immerse myself in their world of monsters, demons, gigantic creatures, and things that went bump in the night.

For years, a good horror novel was my constant companion. Even whilst I was at university, a good horror book or film was the perfect way of unwinding after the hard slog of hitting the text books and trudging through some of the more turgid dryness of ancient law.

Although it is true to say that over the years my reading tastes have diversified into many other genres, I still find myself automatically drawn back to a good horror yarn.

Over the years, I have written many short horror stories for friends and colleagues, and I attempted my first novel almost twenty years ago, back in the days when you had to physically send in typed sheets to a prospective publisher, which were usually returned—in my case—unread, with extremely crumpled and torn pages due to the poor handling by the sorting office.

Due to family life, work, etc, my writing dreams were put on hold until last year when I finally decided to set myself a goal of completing a full novel within a year. Writing mainly in the evenings and at weekends (and rewriting many times over), I finally achieved my goal. Even then, I never imagined that one day I would become a published author and be given the opportunity to share my imaginings with readers all over the world.

I am very much looking forward to embarking on my journey with Creativia and hope that it will prove to be a long and successful one, allowing me the opportunity to expand my readership and connect with like-minded people who, like me, still love a good scare.

Made in the USA
Monee, IL
15 April 2022

94834100R00236